PENGUIN TWENTIE...

P9-CQZ-773

THE WOMAN WHO RODE AWAY
AND OTHER STORIES

David Herbert Lawrence was born at Eastwood, Nottinghamshire, in 1885, fourth of the five children of a miner and his middle-class wife. He attended Nottingham High School and Nottingham University College. His first novel, *The White Peacock*, was published in 1911, just a few weeks after the death of his mother to whom he had been abnormally close. At this time he finally ended his relationship with Jessie Chambers (the Miriam of *Sons and Lovers*) and became engaged to Louie Burrows. His career as a schoolteacher was ended in 1911 by the illness which was ultimately diagnosed as tuberculosis.

In 1912 Lawrence eloped to Germany with Frieda Weekley, the German wife of his former modern languages tutor. They were married on their return to England in 1914. Lawrence was now living, precariously, by his writing. His greatest novels, *The Rainbow* and *Women in Love*, were completed in 1915 and 1916. The former was suppressed, and he could not find a publisher for the latter.

After the war Lawrence began his 'savage pilgrimage' in search of a more fulfilling mode of life than industrial Western civilization could offer. This took him to Sicily, Ceylon, Australia and, finally, New Mexico. The Lawrences returned to Europe in 1925. Lawrence's last novel, *Lady Chatterley's Lover*, was banned in 1928, and his paintings confiscated in 1929. He died in Vence in 1930 at the age of 44.

Lawrence spent most of his short life living. Nevertheless he produced an amazing quantity of work – novels, stories, poems, plays, essays, travel books, translations and letters ... After his death Frieda wrote: 'What he had seen and felt and known he gave in his writing to his fellow men, the splendour of living, the hope of more and more life ... a heroic and immeasurable gift.'

D. H. LAWRENCE

The Woman Who Rode Away

AND OTHER STORIES

PENGUIN BOOKS

PENGUIN BOOKS

Published by the Penguin Group
Penguin Books Ltd, 27 Wrights Lane, London W8 5TZ, England
Penguin Books USA Inc., 375 Hudson Street, New York, New York 10014, USA
Penguin Books Australia Ltd, Ringwood, Victoria, Australia
Penguin Books Canada Ltd, 10 Alcorn Avenue, Toronto, Ontario, Canada M4V 3B2
Penguin Books (NZ) Ltd, 182–190 Wairau Road, Auckland 10, New Zealand

Penguin Books Ltd, Registered Offices: Harmondsworth, Middlesex, England

First published by Martin Secker 1928
Published, with the addition of 'A Modern Lover', 'Strike-Pay' and
a new introduction in Penguin Books 1950
19 20 18

Introduction copyright 1950 by Richard Aldington
All rights reserved

Printed in England by Clays Ltd, St Ives plc
Set in Linotype Granjon

Contents

Gratis

103140

Introduction

BY RICHARD ALDINGTON

THE two earliest stories in this book are *Strike-Pay* and *A Modern Lover*, which were found among Lawrence's papers after his death. As a matter of fact, *Strike-Pay* had appeared in the *Westminster Gazette* for 13 September 1913, under the title of *Ephraim's Half-Sovereign*. It belongs to Lawrence's studies of the Midland coal-miners, such as *The Miner at Home* (in *Phoenix*) and *Her Turn*, which was rejected by the *Daily News* in March 1912. That was clearly the date of *Strike-Pay*, for a letter to Edward Garnett, dated early March 1912, has a passage which prefigures the story:

'Here, in this ugly hell, the men are most happy. They sing, they drink, they rejoice in the land ... Every blessed place was full of men in the larkiest of spirits. I went in the Golden Crown and a couple of other places. They were betting like steam on skittles – the "seconds" had capfuls of money.'

Strike-Pay was not issued in book form until 1934, in *A Modern Lover*. The story which gave its name to that volume is a first attempt at treating the theme of the jilting lover returning to his girl – only to find her engaged to another man. This story reappears as *The Shades of Spring* in *The Prussian Officer*. Curiously enough *A Modern Lover* is simpler, more sincere and fuller of heart-break than the later and more sophisticated story, and just as poetically vivid. Cyril is the name Lawrence gave himself in *The White Peacock*, and the girl Muriel is the Emily of that novel and the Miriam of *Sons and Lovers*, to whom Lawrence in real life actually gave the nickname of Muriel. *A Modern Lover* has a touch of bitter tragedy, in that it shows us that demon of perversity in Lawrence which led him so often to do senseless battle with those he loved most and to estrange them. What is so rare in a writer is that he sees himself as he really is, and ruthlessly puts down the truth, showing himself a prig and in the wrong.

The American edition of this, the third collection of Lawrence's short stories, contained *The Man Who Loved Islands*, which was withheld in England until after the author's death, since it was supposed to satirize a living person, as indeed many of these stories do. A group of four, *Smile*, *The Border Line*; *Jimmy and the Desperate Woman*; and *The Last Laugh*, can confidently be placed as written early in 1924. All of them are personal satires, and three of them have the originality of combining virulent satire with the occult and the uncanny.

The experiences which went to the making of these stories are complicated, but show how Lawrence utilized his life for his art. In December 1923 he yielded very unwillingly to the persuasions of his wife and his English friends and returned from Mexico to London. It was a disaster. He fell ill, was angry with his friends, and went off to Shropshire to visit Frederick Carter, an artist versed in occultism. Lawrence then visited his wife's relatives in Baden-Baden, stayed a short time in Paris and London, and returned to New Mexico in March 1924. The reader will see for himself how all these elements turn up in the four stories named.

Jimmy and the Desperate Woman is a masterpiece of ruthless satire. The squirming Oxford-and-London intellectual, with his queer dishonesty and self-deception and silliness, was a type Lawrence detested, and here contrasts so effectively with the hard, downright, unlovable people of the Midlands he knew so well. It seems *a priori* most improbable that a London editor would want to run off with the wife of a coal-miner merely on the strength of a few letters and poems, but quite possible with an impulsive, unstable neurotic like Jimmy. And it is thoroughly in character that when Jimmy had persuaded the woman to come he was appalled at what he had done, yet hadn't the courage to tell her so directly. The story was first published in *The Criterion* for October 1924.

A similar type of character is satirized in the three 'uncanny' stories, all of which are gruesome. *Smile* may have been remotely suggested by a story of Maupassant, but it is much more deadly. The awful hysteria of the ineffective husband which makes him smile when he sees the face of his dead wife, the unintentionally mocking expression of the nuns, and finally the subtle change in the dead mouth to an ironic smile, make a grisly impression. Still more grisly is *The Border Line* where the woman's dead husband returns as a materialized spirit to take her back from the other man she has married. The feeling is intensified by the evocation of Strasbourg in winter under the sinister brooding cathedral. *The Last Laugh* is perhaps more macabre and preposterous, for Lawrence brings himself into the opening page and it is obvious that he imagined himself somehow exercising the occult powers he describes so vividly. That he would have used such powers to strike his natural enemy, a policeman, with club-foot, and to slay a friend he disliked, does not make the story any the less gruesome. *The Last Laugh* was first published in Volume Four of *The New Decameron*, Oxford, 1925; *The Border Line* appeared in *Hutchinson's Magazine* for September 1924; and *Smile* in *The Nation and Athenaeum* for 19 June 1926. A letter of Lawrence's implies that the story appeared also in *The New Masses* ('funny sort of home things find for themselves'), but I cannot confirm this.

The Woman Who Rode Away gives us Lawrence at one of his most inspired moments. The opening was suggested by his wanderings through remote parts of Mexico in the autumn of 1923. How he used his experiences in the story may be seen from his letter of 5 October from Navajoa:

'There is a blazing sun, a vast hot sky, big lonely inhuman green hills and mountains . . . and the door of life shut on it all, only the sun burning the clouds of birds passing, the zopilotes like flies, the lost lonely palm-trees. There seems a sentence of extinction written over it all. In the middle of the little covered market at Alamos, between the meat and the vegetables, a dead dog lay stretched as if asleep.'

All this, transfigured by imagination, reappears in the story, with the weird terrific scenery into which the woman rides. Mabel Luhan believes that the cave is one near Taos, and the story was suggested to Lawrence by her account of her psychic experiences. However this may be, he seems to have intended her as the woman, while the rites and sacrifice of the Indians are partly from the two Mexicos and partly imaginary. It is a grim though magnificently written tale, but Lawrence was at once horror-stricken and fascinated by the old Mexican belief that power could be acquired by cutting out the heart from a living victim to hold up, still palpitating, to the blood-red sun. The story appeared in *The Dial* for July–August 1925, in *The New Criterion*, January 1926, and in an American collection, *The Best British Stories of 1926*.

The other stories in this book were written after Lawrence's permanent return to Europe in September 1925. In *Sun* Lawrence once more returned to the theme of sun-worship. But his return to Europe seemed to obliterate entirely all that Indian savagery of sacrifice, and under the civilized influence of the Mediterranean (he was living at Spotorno on the Italian Riviera) he imagined the Sun-god, not as Destroyer but as Healer. True, he blends in a little of his 'solar plexus' theosophy, but not enough to injure the essential truth of the city-blanched woman and child growing into health and life under the Sicilian sun. Why Sicilian, when a New York business man would naturally send his wife and child to California or Florida for the sun cure? Lawrence was remembering, rather wistfully, his own life on the slopes of Etna, and re-describes his place there even down to the snake which figures in one of his *Birds, Beasts, and Flowers* poems. The story first appeared in England in an edition limited to a hundred copies in September 1926, and an expanded version came out with the Black Sun Press in Paris in October 1928. Lawrence's letters show that it was written before December 1925, and that he received thirty guineas for the Paris edition, which he modestly thought too much.

Glad Ghosts is another of Lawrence's supernatural stories said to have been intended for Lady Cynthia Asquith's *Ghost Book*, for which she eventually chose *The Rocking-Horse Winner*. If the identification of the main characters is correct, the finale of the story was a piece of reckless impudence. It is another of these situations where he imagines himself wielding supernatural powers, but this time beneficently. His ghosts involve him in a dilemma which he serenely ignores, for how could spirits partake of that 'life in the flesh' which he evokes with such passionate eloquence? You cannot be disembodied and embodied at the same time. But how easily this can be forgotten under the spell of his writing, even though the dialogue shows his fault of running to prolix triviality at times. How much he made himself the measure of all things! Morier, who is Lawrence, complains that all the guests at dinner mutter inaudibly, whereas the plain fact is that he was going deaf. This also was written at Spotorno. A letter of 29 December 1925 speaks of it as 'much too long', and on 10 January 1926, he was 'still struggling' with it. *The Dial* published it serially in July–August 1926, and it appeared as a booklet in England in November 1926.

The remaining three stories are slighter, and unkind rather than satirical, though there is clearly personal vindictiveness in *Two Blue Birds*, which was written at the Villa Mirenda, near Florence, in the spring of 1926.

It seems to have been preferred to some of his finer work, since it was published in *The Dial* for April 1927, in *Pall Mall* for June 1928, and in an American compilation called *Great Stories of All Nations*. In *Love* probably was written a little later since *The Dial* used it in November 1927, and the rather squalidly cruel *None of That* was never published serially. Lawrence was quite aware that as a writer of short stories he was completely out of touch with the popular and high-paying magazines of the 1920s. Instead of trying to conform, he preferred to write newspaper articles for bread and butter, and to write his stories in his own way.

Two Blue Birds

THERE was a woman who loved her husband, but she could not live with him. The husband, on his side, was sincerely attached to his wife, yet he could not live with her. They were both under forty, both handsome and both attractive. They had the most sincere regard for one another, and felt, in some odd way, eternally married to one another. They knew each other more intimately than they knew anybody else, they felt more known to one another than to any other person.

Yet they could not live together. Usually, they kept a thousand miles apart, geographically. But when he sat in the greyness of England, at the back of his mind, with a certain grim fidelity, he was aware of his wife, her strange yearning to be loyal and faithful, having her gallant affairs away in the sun, in the south. And she, as she drank her cocktail on the terrace over the sea, and turned her grey, sardonic eyes on the heavy dark face of her admirer, whom she really liked quite a lot, she was actually preoccupied with the clear-cut features of her handsome young husband, thinking of how he would be asking his secretary to do something for him, asking in that good-natured, confident voice of a man who knows that his request will be only too gladly fulfilled.

The secretary, of course, adored him. She was *very* competent, quite young, and good-looking. She adored him. But then all his servants always did, particularly his women-servants. His men-servants were likely to swindle him.

When a man has an adoring secretary, and you are the man's wife, what are you to do? Not that there was anything 'wrong' – if you know what I mean! – between them. Nothing you could call adultery, to come down to brass tacks. No, no! They were just the young master and his secretary. He dictated to her, she slaved for him and adored him, and the whole thing went on wheels.

He didn't 'adore' her. A man doesn't need to adore his secretary. But he depended on her. 'I simply rely on Miss Wrexall.' Whereas he could never rely on his wife. The one thing he knew finally about *her* was that she didn't intend to be relied on.

So they remained friends, in the awful unspoken intimacy of the once-married. Usually each year they went away together for a holiday, and, if they had not been man and wife, they would have found a great deal of fun and stimulation in one another. The fact that they were married, had been married for the last dozen years, and couldn't live together for the last three or four, spoilt them for one another. Each had a private feeling of bitterness about the other.

However, they were awfully kind. He was the soul of generosity, and held her in real tender esteem, no matter how many gallant affairs she had. Her gallant affairs were part of her modern necessity. 'After all, I've got to *live*. I can't turn into a pillar of salt in five minutes, just because you and I can't live together! It takes years for a woman like me to turn into a pillar of salt. At least I hope so!'

'Quite!' he replied. 'Quite! By all means put them in pickle, make pickled cucumbers of them, before you crystallize out. That's my advice.'

He was like that: so awfully clever and enigmatic. She could more or less fathom the idea of pickled cucumbers, but the 'crystallizing out' – what did that signify?

And did he mean to suggest that he himself had been well pickled, and that further immersion was for him unnecessary, would spoil his flavour? Was that what he meant? And herself, was she the brine and the vale of tears?

You never knew how catty a man was being, when he was really clever and enigmatic, withal a bit whimsical. He was adorably whimsical, with a twist of his flexible, vain mouth, that had a long upper lip, so fraught with vanity! But then a handsome, clear-cut, histrionic young man like that, how could he help being vain? The women made him so.

Ah, the women! How nice men would be if there were no other women!

And how nice the women would be if there were no other men! That's the best of a secretary. She may have a husband but a husband is the mere shred of a man, compared to a boss, a chief, a man who dictates to you and whose words you faithfully write down and then transcribe. Imagine a wife writing down anything her husband said to her! But a secretary! Every *and* and *but* of his she preserves for ever. What are candied violets in comparison!

Now it is all very well having gallant affairs under the southern sun, when you know there is a husband whom you adore dictating to a secretary whom you are too scornful to hate yet whom you rather despise, though you allow she has her good points, away north in the place you ought to regard as home. A gallant affair isn't much good when you've got a bit of grit in your eye. Or something at the back of your mind.

What's to be done? The husband, of course, did not send his wife away.

'You've got your secretary and your work,' she said. 'There's no room for me.'

'There's a bedroom and a sitting-room exclusively for you,' he replied. 'And a garden and half a motor-car. But please yourself entirely. Do what gives you most pleasure.'

'In that case,' she said, 'I'll just go south for the winter.'

'Yes, do!' he said. 'You always enjoy it.'

'I always do,' she replied.

They parted with a certain relentlessness that had a touch of wistful sentiment behind it. Off she went to her gallant affairs, that were like the curate's egg, palatable in parts. And he settled down to work. He said he hated working, but he never did anything else. Ten or eleven hours a day. That's what it is to be your own master!

So the winter wore away, and it was spring, when the swallows homeward fly, or northward, in this case. This winter, one of a series similar, had been rather hard to get through. The bit of grit in the gallant lady's eye had worked deeper in the more she blinked. Dark faces might be dark, and icy cocktails might lend a glow; she blinked her hardest to blink that bit of grit away, without success. Under the spicy balls of the mimosa she thought of that husband of hers in his library, and of that neat, competent but *common* little secretary of his, for ever taking down what he said!

'How a man can *stand* it! How *she* can stand it, common little thing as she is, I don't know!' the wife cried to herself.

She meant this dictating business, this ten hours a day inter-course, *à deux,* with nothing but a pencil between them, and a flow of words.

What was to be done? Matters, instead of improving, had grown worse. The little secretary had brought her mother and sister into the establishment. The mother was a sort of cook-housekeeper, the sister was a sort of upper maid – she did the fine laundry, and looked after 'his' clothes, and valeted him beautifully. It was really an excellent arrangement. The old mother was a splendid plain cook, the sister was all that could be desired as a *valet-de-chambre,* a fine laundress, an upper parlour-maid, and a table-waiter. And all economical to a degree. They knew his affairs by heart. His secretary flew to town when a creditor became dangerous, and she *always* smoothed over the financial crisis.

'He', of course, had debts, and he was working to pay them off. And if he had been a fairy prince who could call the ants to help him, he would not have been more wonderful than in securing this secretary and her family. They took hardly any wages. And they seemed to perform the miracle of loaves and fishes daily.

'She', of course, was the wife who loved her husband, but helped him into debt, and she still was an expensive item. Yet when she appeared at her 'home', the secretarial family received her with most elaborate attentions and deference. The knight returning from the Crusades didn't create a greater stir. She felt like Queen Elizabeth at Kenilworth, a sovereign paying a visit to her faithful subjects. But perhaps there lurked always this hair in her soup : Won't they be glad to be rid of me again !

But they protested No! No! They had been waiting and hoping and praying she would come. They had been pining for her to be there, in charge : the mistress, 'his' wife. Ah, 'his' wife !

'His' wife ! His halo was like a bucket over her head.

The cook-mother was 'of the people', so it was the upper-maid daughter who came for orders.

'What will you order for tomorrow's lunch and dinner, Mrs Gee?'

'Well, what do you usually have?'

'Oh, we want *you* to say.'

'No, what do you *usually* have?'

'We don't have anything fixed. Mother goes out and chooses the best she can find, that is nice and fresh. But she thought you would tell her now what to get.'

'Oh, I don't know! I'm not very good at that sort of thing. Ask her to go on just the same; I'm quite sure she knows best.'

'Perhaps you'd like to suggest a sweet?'

'No, I don't care for sweets – and you know Mr Gee doesn't. So don't make one for me.'

Could anything be more impossible! They had the house spotless and running like a dream; how could an incompetent and extravagant wife dare to interfere, when she saw their amazing and almost inspired economy! But they ran the place on simply nothing!

Simply marvellous people! And the way they strewed palm-branches under her feet!

But that only made her feel ridiculous.

'Don't you think the family manage very well?' he asked her tentatively.

'Awfully well! Almost romantically well!' she replied. 'But I suppose you're perfectly happy?'

'I'm perfectly comfortable,' he replied.

'I can see you are,' she replied. 'Amazingly so! I never knew such comfort! Are you sure it isn't bad for you?'

She eyed him stealthily. He looked very well, and extremely handsome, in his histrionic way. He was shockingly well-dressed and valeted. And he had that air of easy *aplomb* and good-humour which is so becoming to a man, and which he only acquires when he is cock of his own little walk, made much of by his own hens.

'No!' he said, taking his pipe from his mouth and smiling whimsically round at her. 'Do I look as if it were bad for me?'

'No, you don't,' she replied promptly : thinking, naturally, as a woman is supposed to think nowadays, of his health and comfort, the foundation, apparently, of all happiness.

Then, of course, away she went on the backwash.

'Perhaps for your work, though, it's not so good as it is for *you*,' she said in a rather small voice. She knew he couldn't bear it if she mocked at his work for one moment. And he knew that rather small voice of hers.

'In what way?' he said, bristles rising.

'Oh, I don't know,' she answered indifferently. 'Perhaps it's not good for a man's work if he is too comfortable.'

'I don't know about *that*!' he said, taking a dramatic turn round the library and drawing at his pipe. 'Considering I work, actually, by the clock, for twelve hours a day, and for ten hours when it's a short day, I don't think you can say I am deteriorating from easy comfort.'

'No, I suppose not,' she admitted.

Yet she did think it, nevertheless. His comfortableness didn't consist so much in good food and a soft bed, as in having nobody, absolutely nobody and nothing to contradict him. 'I do like to think he's got nothing to aggravate him,' the secretary had said to the wife.

'Nothing to aggravate him!' What a position for a man! Fostered by women who would let nothing 'aggravate' him. If anything would aggravate his wounded vanity, this would!

So thought the wife. But what was to be done about it? In the silence of midnight she heard his voice in the distance, dictating away, like the voice of God to Samuel, alone and monotonous, and she imagined the little figure of the secretary busily scribbling shorthand. Then in the sunny hours of morning, while he was still in bed – he never rose till noon – from another distance came that sharp insect-noise of the typewriter, like some immense grasshopper chirping and rattling. It was the secretary, poor thing, typing out his notes.

That girl – she was only twenty-eight - really slaved herself to skin and bone. She was small and neat, but she was actually worn out. She did far more work than he did, for she had not only to take down all those words he uttered, she had to type them out, make three copies, while he was still resting.

'What on earth she gets out of it,' thought the wife, 'I don't know. She's simply worn to the bone, for a very poor salary, and he's never kissed her, and never will, if I know anything about him.'

Whether his never kissing her – the secretary, that is – made it worse or better, the wife did not decide. He never kissed anybody. Whether she herself – the wife, that is – wanted to be kissed by him, even that she was not clear about. She rather thought she didn't.

What on earth did she want then? She was his wife. What on earth did she want of him?

She certainly didn't want to take him down in shorthand, and type out again all those words. And she didn't really want him to kiss her; she knew him too well. Yes, she knew him too well. If you know a man too well, you don't want him to kiss you.

What then? What did she want? Why had she such an extraordinary hang-over about him? Just because she was his wife? Why did she rather 'enjoy' other men – and she was relentless about enjoyment – without ever taking them seriously? And why must she take him so damn seriously, when she never really 'enjoyed' him?

Of course she *had* had good times with him, in the past, before – ah! before a thousand things, all amounting really to nothing. But she enjoyed him no more. She never even enjoyed being with him. There was a silent, ceaseless tension between them, that never broke, even when they were a thousand miles apart.

Awful! That's what you call being married! What's to be done about it? Ridiculous, to know it all and not do anything about it!

She came back once more, and there she was, in her own house, a sort of super-guest, even to him. And the secretarial family devoting their lives to him.

Devoting their lives to him! But actually! Three women pouring out their lives for him day and night! And what did they get in return? Not one kiss! Very little money, because they knew all about his debts, and had made it their life-business to get them paid off! No expectations! Twelve hours' work a day! Comparative isolation, for he saw nobody!

And beyond that? Nothing! Perhaps a sense of uplift and importance because they saw his name and photograph in the newspapers sometimes. But would anybody believe that it was good enough?

Yet they adored it! They seemed to get a deep satisfaction out of it, like people with a mission. Extraordinary!

Well, if they did, let them. They were, of course, rather

common, 'of the people'; there might be a sort of glamour in it for them.

But it was bad for him. No doubt about it. His work was getting diffuse and poor in quality – and what wonder! His whole tone was going down – becoming commoner. Of course it was bad for him.

Being his wife, she felt she ought to do something to save him. But how could she? That perfectly devoted, marvellous secretarial family, how could she make an attack on them? Yet she'd love to sweep them into oblivion. Of course, they were bad for him; ruining his work, ruining his reputation as a writer, ruining his life. Ruining him with their slavish service.

Of course she ought to make an onslaught on them! But how *could* she? Such devotion! And what had she herself to offer in their place? Certainly not slavish devotion to him, nor to his flow of words! Certainly not!

She imagined him stripped once more naked of secretary and secretarial family, and she shuddered. It was like throwing the naked body in the dust-bin. Couldn't do that!

Yet something must be done. She felt it. She was almost tempted to get into debt for another thousand pounds, and send in the bill, or have it sent in to him, as usual.

But no! Something more drastic!

Something more drastic, or perhaps more gentle. She wavered between the two. And wavering, she first did nothing, came to no decision, dragged vacantly on from day to day, waiting for sufficient energy to take her departure once more.

It was spring! What a fool she had been to come up in spring! And she was forty! What an idiot of a woman to go and be forty!

She went down the garden in the warm afternoon, when birds were whistling loudly from the cover, the sky being low and warm, and she had nothing to do. The garden was full of flowers: he loved them for their theatrical display. Lilac and snowball bushes, and laburnum and red may, tulips and anemones, and coloured daisies. Lots of flowers! Borders of forget-me-nots! Bachelor's buttons! What absurd names flowers had! She would have called them blue dots and yellow blobs and white frills. Not so much sentiment, after all!

There is a certain nonsense, something showy and stagey about spring, with its pushing leaves and chorus-girl flowers, unless you have something corresponding inside you. Which she hadn't.

Oh, heaven! Beyond the hedge she heard a voice, a steady, rather theatrical voice. Oh, heaven! – he was dictating to his secretary in the garden. Good God, was there nowhere to get away from it!

She looked around: there was indeed plenty of escapes. But what was the good of escaping? He would go on and on. She went quietly towards the hedge, and listened.

He was dictating a magazine article about the modern novel. 'What the modern novel lacks is architecture.' Good God! Architecture! He might just as well say: What the modern novel lacks is whalebone, or a teaspoon, or a tooth stopped.

Yet the secretary took it down, took it down, took it down! No, this could not go on! It was more than flesh and blood could bear.

She went quietly along the hedge, somewhat wolf-like in her prowl, a broad, strong woman in an expensive mustard-coloured silk jersey and cream-coloured pleated skirt. Her legs were long and shapely, and her shoes were expensive.

With a curious wolf-like stealth she turned the hedge and looked across at the small, shaded lawn where the daisies grew impertinently. 'He' was reclining in a coloured hammock under the pink-flowering horse-chestnut tree, dressed in white serge with a fine yellow-coloured linen shirt. His elegant hand dropped over the side of the hammock and beat a sort of vague rhythm to his words. At a little wicker table the little secretary, in a green knitted frock, bent her dark head over her notebook, and diligently made those awful shorthand marks. He was not difficult to take down, as he dictated slowly, and kept a sort of rhythm, beating time with his dangling hand.

'In every novel there must be one outstanding character with which we always sympathize – with *whom* we always sympathize – even though we recognize its – even when we are most aware of the human frailties.

Every man his own hero, thought the wife grimly, forgetting that every woman is intensely her own heroine.

But what did startle her was a blue bird dashing about near the feet of the absorbed, shorthand-scribbling little secretary. At least it was a blue-tit, blue with grey and some yellow. But to the wife it seemed blue, that juicy spring day, in the translucent afternoon. The blue bird, fluttering round the pretty but rather *common* little feet of the little secretary.

The blue bird! The blue bird of happiness! Well, I'm blest – thought the wife. Well, I'm blest!

And as she was being blest, appeared another blue bird – that is, another blue-tit – and began to wrestle with the first blue-tit. A couple of blue birds of happiness, having a fight over it! Well, I'm blest!

She was more or less out of sight of the human preoccupied pair. But 'he' was disturbed by the fighting blue birds, whose little feathers began to float loose.

'Get out!' he said to them mildly, waving a dark-yellow handkerchief at them. 'Fight your little fight, and settle your private affairs elsewhere, my dear little gentlemen.'

The little secretary looked up quickly, for she had already begun to write it down. He smiled at her his twisted whimsical smile.

'No, don't take that down,' he said affectionately. 'Did you see those two tits laying into one another?'

'No!' said the little secretary, gazing brightly round, her eyes half-blinded with work.

But she saw the queer, powerful, elegant, wolf-like figure of the wife, behind her, and terror came into her eyes.

'I did!' said the wife, stepping forward with those curious, shapely, she-wolf legs of hers, under the very short skirt.

'Aren't they extraordinary vicious little beasts?' said he.

'Extraordinary!' she re-echoed, stooping and picking up a little breast-feather. 'Extraordinary! See how the feathers fly!'

And she got the feather on the tip of her finger, and looked at it. Then she looked at the secretary, then she looked at him. She had a queer, were-wolf expression between her brows.

'I think,' he began, 'these are the loveliest afternoons, when there's no direct sun, but all the sounds and the colours and the scents are sort of dissolved, don't you know, in the air, and the whole thing is steeped, steeped in spring. It's like being on the inside; you know how I mean, like being inside the egg and just ready to chip the shell.'

'Quite like that!' she assented, without conviction.

There was a little pause. The secretary said nothing. They were waiting for the wife to depart again.

'I suppose,' said the latter, 'you're awfully busy as usual?'

'Just about the same,' he said, pursing his mouth deprecatingly. Again the blank pause, in which he waited for her to go away again.

'I know I'm interrupting you,' she said.

'As a matter of fact,' he said, 'I was just watching those two blue-tits.'

'Pair of little demons!' said the wife, blowing away the yellow feather from her finger-tip.

'Absolutely!' he said.

'Well, I'd better go, and let you get on with your work,' she said.

'No hurry!' he said, with benevolent nonchalance. 'As a matter of fact, I don't think it's a great success, working out of doors.'

'What made you try it?' said the wife. 'You know you never could do it.'

'Miss Wrexall suggested it might make a change. But I don't think it altogether helps, do you, Miss Wrexall?'

'I'm sorry,' said the little secretary.

'Why should *you* be sorry?' said the wife, looking down at her as a wolf might look down half benignly at a little black-and-tan mongrel. 'You only suggested it for his good, I'm sure!'

'I thought the air might be good for him,' the secretary admitted.

'Why do people like you never think about yourselves?' the wife asked.

The secretary looked her in the eye.

'I suppose we do, in a different way,' she said.

'A *very* different way!' said the wife ironically. 'Why don't you make *him* think about *you*?' she added, slowly, with a sort of drawl. 'On a soft spring afternoon like this, you ought to have him dictating poems to you, about the blue birds of happiness fluttering round your dainty little feet. I know *I* would, if I were his secretary.'

There was a dead pause. The wife stood immobile and statuesque, in an attitude characteristic of her, half turning back to the little secretary, half averted. She half turned her back on everything.

The secretary looked at him.

'As a matter of fact,' he said, 'I was doing an article on the Future of the Novel.'

'I know that,' said the wife. 'That's what's so awful! Why not something lively in the life of the novelist?'

There was a prolonged silence, in which he looked pained, and somewhat remote, statuesque. The little secretary hung her head. The wife sauntered slowly away.

'Just where were we, Miss Wrexall?' came the sound of his voice.

The little secretary started. She was feeling profoundly indignant. Their beautiful relationship, his and hers, to be so insulted!

But soon she was veering downstream on the flow of his words, too busy to have any feelings, except one of elation at being so busy.

Tea-time came; the sister brought out the tea-tray into the garden. And immediately, the wife appeared. She had changed, and was wearing a chicory-blue dress of fine cloth. The little secretary had gathered up her papers and was departing, on rather high heels.

'Don't go, Miss Wrexall,' said the wife.

The little secretary stoped short, then hesitated.

'Mother will be expecting me,' she said.

'Tell her you're not coming. And ask your sister to bring another cup. I want you to have tea with us.'

Miss Wrexall looked at the man, who was reared on one elbow in the hammock, and was looking enigmatical, Hamletish.

He glanced at her quickly, then pursed his mouth in a boyish negligence.

'Yes, stay and have tea with us for once,' he said. 'I see strawberries, and I know you're the bird for them.'

She glanced at him, smiled wanly, and hurried away to tell

her mother. She even stayed long enough to slip on a silk dress.

'Why, how smart you are!' said the wife, when the little secretary reappeared on the lawn, in chicory-blue silk.

'Oh, don't look at my dress, compared to yours!' said Miss Wrexall. They were of the same colour, indeed!

'At least you earned yours, which is more than I did mine,' said the wife, as she poured tea. 'You like it strong?'

She looked with her heavy eyes at the smallish, birdy, blue-clad, overworked young woman, and her eyes seemed to speak many inexplicable dark volumes.

'Oh, as it comes, thank you,' said Miss Wrexall, leaning forward.

'It's coming pretty black, if you want to ruin your digestion,' said the wife.

'Oh, I'll have some water in it, then.'

'Better, I should say.'

'How'd the work go – all right?' asked the wife, as they drank tea, and the two women looked at each other's blue dresses.

'Oh!' he said. 'As well as you can expect. It was a piece of pure flummery. But it's what they wanted. Awful rot, wasn't it, Miss Wrexall?'

Miss Wrexall moved uneasily on her chair.

'It interested me,' she said, 'though not so much as the novel.'

'The novel? Which novel?' said the wife. 'Is there another new one?'

Miss Wrexall looked at him. Not for worlds would she give away any of his literary activities.

'Oh, I was just sketching out an idea to Miss Wrexall,' he said.

'Tell us about it!' said the wife. 'Miss Wrexall, *you* tell us what it's about.'

She turned on her chair, and fixed the little secretary.

'I'm afraid' – Miss Wrexall squirmed – 'I haven't got it very clearly myself, yet.'

'Oh, go along! Tell us what you *have* got there!'

Miss Wrexall sat dumb and very vexed. She felt she was being baited. She looked at the blue pleatings of her skirt.

'I'm afraid I can't,' she said.

'Why are you afraid you can't? You're so *very* competent. I'm sure you've got it all at your finger-ends. I expect you write a good deal of Mr Gee's books for him, really. He gives you the hint, and you fill it all in. Isn't that how you do it?' She spoke ironically, and as if she were teasing a child. And then she glanced down at the fine pleatings of her own blue skirt, very fine and expensive.

'Of course, you're not speaking seriously?' said Miss Wrexall, rising on her mettle.

'Of course I am! I've suspected for a long time – at least, for some time – that you write a good deal of Mr Gee's books for him, from his hints.'

It was said in a tone of raillery, but it was cruel.

'I should be terribly flattered,' said Miss Wrexall, straightening herself, 'if I didn't know you were only trying to make me feel a fool.'

'Make you feel a fool? My dear child! – why, nothing could be farther from me! You're twice as clever, and a million times as competent as I am. Why, my dear child, I've the greatest admiration for you! I wouldn't do what you do, not for all the pearls in India. I *couldn't*, anyhow –'

Miss Wrexall closed up and was silent.

'Do you mean to say my books read as if –' he began, rearing up and speaking in a harrowed voice.

'I do!' said his wife. '*Just* as if Miss Wrexall had written them from your hints. I *honestly* thought she did – when you were too busy –'

'How very clever of you!' he said.

'Very!' she cried. 'Especially if I was wrong!'

'Which you were,' he said.

'How very extraordinary!' she cried. 'Well, I am once more mistaken!'

There was a complete pause.

It was broken by Miss Wrexall, who was nervously twisting her fingers.

'You want to spoil what there is between me and him, I can see that,' she said bitterly.

'My dear, but what *is* there between you and him?' asked the wife.

'I was *happy* working with him, working for him! I was

happy working for him!' cried Miss Wrexall, tears of indignant anger and chagrin in her eyes.

'My dear child!' cried the wife, with simulated excitement, 'go *on* being happy working with him, go on being happy while you can! If it makes you happy, why then, enjoy it! Of course! Do you think I'd be so cruel as to want to take it away from you? – working with him? *I* can't do shorthand and typewriting and double-entrance book-keeping, or whatever it's called. I tell you, I'm utterly incompetent. I never earn anything. I'm the parasite on the British oak, like the mistletoe. The blue bird doesn't flutter round my feet. Perhaps they're too big and trampling.'

She looked down at her expensive shoes.

'If I *did* have a word of criticism to offer,' she said, turning to her husband, 'it would be to you, Cameron, for taking so much from her and giving her nothing.'

'But he gives me everything, everything!' cried Miss Wrexall. 'He gives me everything!'

'What do you mean by everything?' said the wife, turning on her sternly.

Miss Wrexall pulled up short. There was a snap in the air, and a change of currents.

'I mean nothing that *you* need begrudge me,' said the little secretary rather haughtily. 'I've never made myself cheap.'

There was a blank pause.

'My God!' said the wife. 'You don't call that being cheap? Why, I should say you got nothing out of him at all, you only give! And if you don't call that making yourself cheap – my God!'

'You see, we see things different,' said the secretary.

'I should say we do! – *thank God*,' rejoined the wife.

'On whose behalf are you thanking God?' he asked sarcastically.

'Everybody's, I suppose! Yours, because you get everything for nothing, and Miss Wrexall's, because she seems to like it, and mine because I'm well out of it all.'

'You *needn't* be out of it all,' cried Miss Wrexall magnanimously, 'if you didn't *put* yourself out of it all.'

'Thank you, my dear, for your offer,' said the wife, rising.

'But I'm afraid no man can expect *two* blue birds of happiness
to flutter round his feet, tearing out their little feathers!'

With which she walked away.

After a tense and desperate interim, Miss Wrexall cried:

'And *really*, need any woman be jealous of *me*?'

'Quite!' he said.

And that was all he did say.

Sun

I

'TAKE her away, into the sun,' the doctor said.

She herself was sceptical of the sun, but she permitted herself to be carried away, with her child, and a nurse, and her mother, over the sea.

The ship sailed at midnight. And for two hours her husband stayed with her, while the child was put to bed, and the passengers came on board. It was a black night, the Hudson swayed with heavy blackness, shaken over with spilled dribbles of light. She leaned on the rail, and looking down thought : This is the sea; it is deeper than one imagines, and fuller of memories. At that moment the sea seemed to heave like the serpent of chaos that has lived for ever.

'These partings are no good, you know,' her husband was saying, at her side. 'They're no good. I don't like them.'

His tone was full of apprehension, misgiving, and there was a certain note of clinging to the last straw of hope.

'No, neither do I,' she responded in a flat voice.

She remembered how bitterly they had wanted to get away from one another, he and she. The emotion of parting gave a slight tug at her emotions, but only caused the iron that had gone into her soul to gore deeper.

So, they looked at their sleeping son, and the father's eyes were wet. But it is not the wetting of the eyes which counts, it is the deep iron rhythm of habit, the year-long, life-long habits; the deep-set stroke of power.

And in their two lives, the stroke of power was hostile, his and hers. Like two engines running at variance, they shattered one another.

'All ashore ! All ashore !'

'Maurice, you must go !'

And she thought to herself : For him it is *All ashore!* For me it is *Out to sea!*

Well, he waved his hanky on the midnight dreariness of the

pier, as the boat inched away; one among a crowd. One among a crowd! *C'est ça!*

The ferry-boats, like great dishes piled with rows of lights, were still slanting across the Hudson. That black mouth must be the Lackawanna Station.

The ship ebbed on, the Hudson seemed interminable. But at last they were round the bend, and there was the poor harvest of lights at the Battery. Liberty flung up her torch in a tantrum. There was the wash of the sea.

And though the Atlantic was grey as lava, she did come at last into the sun. Even she had a house above the bluest of seas, with a vast garden, or vineyard, all vines and olives dropping steeply, terrace after terrace, to the strip of coast-plain; and the garden full of secret places, deep groves of lemon far down in the cleft of earth, and hidden, pure green reservoirs of water; then a spring issuing out of a little cavern, where the old Sicules had drunk before the Greeks came; and a grey goat bleating, stabled in an ancient tomb, with all the niches empty. There was the scent of mimosa, and beyond, the snow of the volcano.

She saw it all, and in a measure it was soothing. But it was all external. She didn't really care about it. She was herself, just the same, with all her anger and frustration inside her, and her incapacity to feel anything real. The child irritated her, and preyed on her peace of mind. She felt so horribly, ghastly responsible for him : as if she must be responsible for every breath he drew. And that was torture to her, to the child, and to everybody else concerned.

'You know, Juliet, the doctor told you to lie in the sun, without your clothes. Why don't you?' said her mother.

'When I am fit to do so, I will. Do you want to kill me?' Juliet flew at her.

'To kill you, no! Only to do you good.'

'For God's sake, leave off wanting to do me good.'

The mother at last was so hurt and incensed, she departed.

The sea went white – and then invisible. Pouring rain fell. It was cold, in the house built for the sun.

Again a morning when the sun lifted himself naked and molten, sparkling over the sea's rim. The house faced south-west. Juliet lay in her bed and wached him rise. It was as if she had never seen the sun rise before. She had never seen the naked sun stand up pure upon the sea-line, shaking the night off himself.

So the desire sprang secretly in her, to go naked in the sun. She cherished her desire like a secret.

But she wanted to go away from the house – away from people. And it is not easy, in a country where every olive tree has eyes, and every slope is seen from afar, to go hidden.

But she found a place : a rocky bluff, shoved out to the sea and sun and overgrown with large cactus, the flat-leaved cactus called prickly bear. Out of this blue-grey knoll of cactus rose one cypress tree, with a pallid, thick trunk, and a tip that leaned over, flexible, up in the blue. It stood like a guardian looking to sea; or a low, silvery candle whose huge flame was darkness against light : earth sending up her proud tongue of gloom.

Juliet sat down by the cypress trees, and took off her clothes. The contorted cactus made a forest, hideous yet fascinating, about her. She sat and offered her bosom to the sun, sighing, even now, with a certain hard pain, against the cruelty of having to give herself.

But the sun marched in blue heaven and sent down his rays as he went. She felt the soft air of the sea on her breasts, that seemed as if they would never ripen. But she hardly felt the sun. Fruits that would wither and not mature, her breasts.

Soon, however, she felt the sun inside them, warmer than ever love had been, warmer than milk or the hands of her baby. At last, at last her breasts were like long white grapes in the hot sun.

She slid off all her clothes and lay naked in the sun, and as she lay she looked up through her fingers at the central sun, his blue pulsing roundness, whose outer edges streamed brilliance. Pulsing with marvellous blue, and alive, and streaming white fire from his edges, the sun ! He faced down to her with his look of blue fire, and enveloped her breasts and her face, her throat, her tired belly, her knees, her thighs and her feet.

She lay with shut eyes, the colour of rosy flame through her lids. It was too much. She reached and put leaves over her eyes.

Then she lay again, like a long white gourd in the sun, that must ripen to gold.

She could feel the sun penetrating even into her bones; nay, further, even into her emotions and her thoughts. The dark tensions of her emotion began to give way, the cold dark clots of her thoughts began to dissolve. She was beginning to feel warm right through. Turning over, she let her shoulders dissolve in the sun, her loins, the backs of her thighs, even her heels. And she lay half stunned with wonder at the thing that was happening to her. Her weary, chilled heart was melting, and, in melting, evaporating.

When she was dressed again she lay once more and looked up at the cypress tree, whose crest, a flexible filament, fell this way and that in the breeze. Meanwhile, she was conscious of the great sun roaming in heaven.

So, dazed, she went home, only half-seeing, sunblinded and sun-dazed. And her blindness was like a richness to her, and her dim, warm, heavy half-consciousness was like wealth.

'Mummy! Mummy!' her child came running towards her, calling in that peculiar bird-like little anguish of want, always wanting her. She was surprised that her drowsed heart for once felt none of the anxious love-anguish in return. She caught the child up in her arms, but she thought: He should not be such a lump! If he were in the sun, he would spring up.

She resented, rather, his little hands clutching at her, especially at her neck. She pulled her throat away. She did not want to be touched. She put the child gently down.

'Run!' she said. 'Run in the sun!'

And there and then she took off his clothes and set him naked on the warm terrace.

'Play in the sun!' she said.

He was frightened and wanted to cry. But she, in the warm indolence of her body, and the complete indifference of her heart, rolled him an orange across the red tiles, and with his soft, unformed little body he toddled after it. Then immediately he had it, he dropped it because it felt strange against his flesh. And he looked back at her, querulous, wrinkling his face to cry, frightened because he was stark.

'Bring me the orange,' she said, amazed at her own deep indifference to his trepidation. 'Bring Mummy the orange.'

'He shall not grow up like his father,' she said to herself. 'Like a worm that the sun has never seen.'

2

She had had the child so much on her mind, in a torment of responsibility, as if, having borne him, she had to answer for his whole existence. Even if his nose were running, it had been repulsive and a goad in her vitals, as if she must say to herself : Look at the thing you brought forth !

Now a change took place. She was no longer vitally interested in the child, she took the strain of her anxiety and her will from off him. And he thrived all the more for it.

She was thinking inside herself, of the sun in his splendour, and her mating with him. Her life was now a whole ritual. She lay always awake, before dawn, watching for the grey to colour to pale gold, to know if clouds lay on the sea's edge. Her joy was when he rose all molten in his nakedness, and threw off blue-white fire, into the tender heaven.

But sometimes he came ruddy, like a big, shy creature. And sometimes slow and crimson red, with a look of anger, slowly pushing and shouldering. Sometimes again she could not see him, only the level cloud threw down gold and scarlet from above, as he moved behind the wall.

She was fortunate. Weeks went by, and though the dawn was sometimes clouded, and afternoon was sometimes grey, never a day passed sunless, and most days, winter though it was, streamed radiant. The thin little wild crocuses came up mauve and striped, the wild narcissi hung their winter stars.

Every day she went down to the cypress tree, among the cactus grove on the knoll with yellowish cliffs at the foot. She was wiser and subtler now, wearing only a dove-grey wrapper, and sandals. So that in an instant, in any hidden niche, she was naked to the sun. And the moment she was covered again she was grey and invisible.

Every day, in the morning towards noon, she lay at the foot of the powerful, silver-pawed cypress tree, while the sun rode jovial in heaven. By now she knew the sun in every thread of her body, there was not a cold shadow left. And her heart, that anxious, straining heart, had disappeared altogether, like a flower that falls in the sun, and leaves only a ripe seed-case.

She knew that sun in heaven, blue-molten with his white fire edges, throwing off fire. And though he shone on all the world, when she lay unclothed he focused on her. It was one of the wonders of the sun, he could shine on a million people and still be the radiant, splendid, unique sun, focused on her alone.

With her knowledge of the sun, and her conviction that the sun *knew* her, in the cosmic carnal sense of the word, came over her a feeling of detachment from people, and a certain contempt for human beings altogether. They were so un-elemental, so un-sunned. They were so like graveyard worms.

Even the peasants passing up the rocky, ancient little road with their donkeys, sun-blackened as they were, were not sunned right through. There was a little soft white core of fear, like a snail in a shell, where the soul of the man cowered in fear of death, and in fear of the natural blaze of life. He dared not quite emerge : always innerly cowed. All men were like that.

Why admit men !

With her indifference to people, to men, she was not now so cautious about being unseen. She had told Marinina, who went shopping for her in the village, that the doctor had ordered sun-baths. Let that suffice.

Marinina was a woman over sixty, tall, thin, erect, with curling dark grey hair, and dark grey eyes that had the shrewdness of thousands of years in them, with the laugh that underlies all long experience. Tragedy is lack of experience.

'It must be beautiful to go unclothed in the sun,' said Marinina, with a shrewd laugh in her eyes, as she looked keenly at the other woman. Juliet's fair, bobbed hair curled in a little cloud at her temple. Marinina was a woman of Magna Graecia, and had far memories. She looked again at Juliet. 'But you have to be beautiful yourself, if you're not going to give offence to the sun? Isn't it so?' she added, with that queer, breathless little laugh of the women of the past.

'Who knows if I am beautiful !' said Juliet.

But beautiful or not, she felt that by the sun she was appreciated. Which is the same.

When, out of the sun at noon, sometimes she stole down over the rocks and past the cliff-edge, down to the deep gully where the lemons hung in cool eternal shadow, and in the silence slipped off her wrapper to wash herself quickly at one of the deep, clear green basins, she would notice, in the bare green twilight under the lemon leaves, that all her body was rosy, rosy and turning to gold. She was like another person. She was another person.

So she remembered that the Greeks had said, a white, unsunned body was fishy and unhealthy.

And she would rub a little olive oil in her skin, and wander a moment in the dark underworld of the lemons, balancing a lemon flower in her navel, laughing to herself. There was just a chance some peasant might see her. But if he did he would be more afraid of her than she of him. She knew the white core of fear in the clothed bodies of men.

She knew it even in her little son. How he mistrusted her, now that she laughed at him, with the sun in her face! She insisted on his toddling naked in the sunshine, every day. And now his little body was pink, too, his blond hair was pushed thick from his brow, his cheeks had a pomegranate scarlet, in the delicate gold of the sunny skin. He was bonny and healthy, and the servants, loving his red and gold and blue, called him an angel from heaven.

But he mistrusted his mother : she laughed at him. And she saw in his wide blue eyes, under the little frown, that centre of fear, misgiving, which she believed was at the centre of all male eyes, now. She called it fear of the sun.

'He fears the sun,' she would say to herself, looking down into the eyes of the child.

And as she watched him toddling, swaying, tumbling in the sunshine, making his little, bird-like noises, she saw that he held himself tight and hidden from the sun, inside himself. His spirit was like a snail in a shell, in a damp, cold crevice inside himself. It made her think of his father. She wished she could make him come forth, break out in a gesture of recklessness and salutation.

She determined to take him with her, down to the cypress tree among the cactus. She would have to watch him, because of the thorns. But surely in that place he would come forth from that little shell, deep inside him. That little civilized tension would disappear off his brow.

She spread a rug for him and sat him down. Then she slid off her wrapper and lay down herself, watching a hawk high in the blue, and the tip of the cypress hanging over.

The boy played with stones on the rug. When he got up to toddle away, she sat up too. He turned and looked at her. Almost, from his blue eyes, it was the challenging, warm look of the true male. And he was handsome, with the scarlet in the golden blond of his skin. He was not really white. His skin was gold-dusky.

'Mind the thorns, darling,' she said.

'Thorns!' re-echoed the child, in a birdy chirp, still looking at her over his shoulder, like some naked cherub in a picture, doubtful.

'Nasty prickly thorns.'

' 'Ickly thorns!'

He staggered in his little sandals over the stones, pulling at the dry wild mint. She was quick as a serpent, leaping to him, when he was going to fall against the prickles. It surprised even herself. 'What a wild cat I am, really!' she said to herself.

She brought him every day, when the sun shone, to the cypress tree.

'Come!' she said. 'Let us go to the cypress tree.'

And if there was a cloudy day, with the tramontana blowing, so that she could not go down, the child would chirp incessantly: 'Cypress tree! Cypress tree!'

He missed it as much as she did.

It was not just taking sunbaths. It was much more than that. Something deep inside her unfolded and relaxed, and she was given. By some mysterious power inside her, deeper than her known consciousness and will, she was put into connection with the sun, and the stream flowed of itself, from her womb. She herself, her conscious self, was secondary, a secondary person, almost an onlooker. The true Juliet was this dark flow from her deep body to the sun.

She had always been mistress of herself, aware of what she was doing, and held tense for her own power. Now she felt inside her quite another sort of power, something greater than herself, flowing by itself. Now she was vague, but she had a power beyond herself.

3

The end of February was suddenly very hot. Almond blossom was falling like pink snow, in the touch of the smallest breeze. The mauve, silky little anemones were out, the asphodels tall in bud; and the sea was cornflower blue.

Juliet had ceased to trouble about anything. Now, most of the day, she and the child were naked in the sun, and it was all she wanted. Sometimes she went down to the sea to bathe : often she wandered in the gullies where the sun shone in, and she was out of sight. Sometimes she saw a peasant with an ass, and he saw her. But she went so simply and quietly with her child; and the fame of the sun's healing power, for the soul as well as for the body, had already spread among the people; so that there was no excitement.

The child and she were now both tanned with a rosy-golden tan, all over. 'I am another being!' she said to herself, as she looked at her red-gold breasts and thighs.

The child, too, was another creature, with a peculiar quiet, sun-darkened absorption. Now he played by himself in silence, and she hardly need notice him. He seemed no longer to know when he was alone.

There was not a breeze, and the sea was ultramarine. She sat by the great silver paw of the cypress tree, drowsed in the sun, but her breasts alert, full of sap. She was becoming aware that an activity was rousing in her, an activity which would carry her into a new way of life. Still she did not want to be aware. She knew well enough the vast cold apparatus of civilization, so difficult to evade.

The child had gone a few yards down the rocky path, round the great sprawling of a cactus. She had seen him, a real gold-brown infant of the winds, with burnt gold hair and red cheeks, collecting the speckled pitcher-flowers and laying them in rows.

He could balance now, and was quick for his own emergencies, like an absorbed young animal playing silent.

Suddenly she heard him speaking : '*Look, Mummy! Mummy, look!*' A note in his bird-like voice made her lean forward sharply.

Her heart stood still. He was looking over his naked little shoulder at her, and pointing with a loose little hand at a snake which had reared itself up a yard away from him, and was opening its mouth so that its forked, soft tongue flickered black like a shadow, uttering a short hiss.

'Look, Mummy !'

'Yes, darling, it's a snake !' came the slow, deep voice.

He looked at her, his wide blue eyes uncertain whether to be afraid or not. Some stillness of the sun in her reassured him.

'Snake !' he chirped.

'Yes, darling ! Don't touch it, it can bite.'

The snake had sunk down, and was reaching away from the coils in which it had been basking asleep, and slowly was easing its long, gold-brown body into the rocks, with slow curves. The boy turned and watched it in silence. Then he said :

'Snake going !'

'Yes ! Let it go. It likes to be alone.'

He still watched the slow, easing length as the creature drew itself apathetic out of sight.

'Snake gone back,' he said.

'Yes, it's gone back. Come to Mummy a moment.'

He came and sat with his plump, naked little body on her naked lap, and she smoothed his burnt, bright hair. She said nothing, feeling that everything was passed. The curious soothing power of the sun filled her, filled the whole place like a charm, and the snake was part of the place, along with her and the child.

Another day, in the dry stone wall of one of the olive terraces, she saw a black snake horizontally creeping.

'Marinina,' she said, 'I saw a black snake. Are they harmful?'

'Ah, the black snakes, no! But the yellow ones, yes! If the yellow ones bite you, you die. But they frighten me, they frighten me, even the black ones, when I see one.'

Juliet still went to the cypress tree with the child. But she always looked carefully round before she sat down, examining everywhere where the child might go. Then she would lie and turn to the sun again, her tanned, pear-shaped breasts pointing up. She would take no thought for the morrow. She refused to think outside her garden, and she could not write letters. She would tell the nurse to write.

4

It was March, and the sun was growing very powerful. In the hot hours she would lie in the shade of the trees, or she would even go down to the depths of the cool lemon grove. The child ran in the distance, like a young animal absorbed in life.

One day she was sitting in the sun on the steep slope of the gully, having bathed in one of the great tanks. Below, under the lemons, the child was wading among the yellow oxalis flowers of the shadow, gathering fallen lemons, passing with his tanned little body into flecks of light, moving all dappled.

Suddenly, high over the land's edge, against the full-lit pale blue sky, Marinina appeared, a black cloth tied round her head, calling quietly: '*Signoral Signora Giuliettal*'

Juliet faced round, standing up. Marinina paused a moment, seeing the naked woman standing alert, her sun-faded fair hair in a little cloud. Then the swift old woman came on down the slant of the steep track.

She stood a few steps, erect, in front of the sun-coloured woman, and eyed her shrewdly.

'But how beautiful you are, you!' she said coolly, almost cynically. 'There is your husband.'

'My husband!' cried Juliet.

The old woman gave a shrewd bark of a little laugh, the mockery of the women of the past.

'Haven't you got one, a husband, you?' she taunted.

'But where is he?' cried Juliet.

The old woman glanced over her shoulder.

'He was following me,' she said. 'But he will not have found the path.' And she gave another little bark of a laugh.

The paths were all grown high with grass and flowers and nepitella, till they were like bird-trails in an eternally wild place.

Strange, the vivid wildness of the old places of civilization, a wildness that is not gaunt.

Juliet looked at her serving-woman with meditating eyes.

'Oh, very well!' she said at last. 'Let him come.'

'Let him come here? Now?' asked Marinina, her laughing, smoke-grey eyes looking with mockery into Juliet's. Then she gave a little jerk of her shoulders.

'All right, as you wish. But for him it is a rare one!'

She opened her mouth in a laugh of noiseless joy. Then she pointed down to the child, who was heaping lemons against his little chest. 'Look how beautiful the child is! That, certainly, will please him, poor thing. Then I'll bring him.'

'Bring him,' said Juliet.

The old woman scrambled rapidly up the track again. Maurice was standing grey-faced, in his grey felt hat and his dark grey suit, at a loss among the vine terraces. He looked pathetically out of place, in that resplendent sunshine and the grace of the old Greek world; like a blot of ink on the pale, sun-glowing slope.

'Come!' said Marinina to him. 'She is down here.'

And swiftly she led the way, striding with a rapid stride, making her way through the grasses. Suddenly she stopped on the brow of the slope. The tops of the lemon trees were dark, away below.

'You, you go down here,' she said to him, and he thanked her, looking up at her swiftly.

He was a man of forty, clean-shaven, grey-faced, very quiet and really shy. He managed his own business carefully, without startling success, but efficiently. And he confided in nobody. The old woman of Magna Graecia saw him at a glance: he is good, she said to herself, but not a man, poor thing.

'Down there is the Signora!' said Marinina, pointing like one of the Fates.

And again he said 'Thank you! Thank you!' without a twinkle, and stepped carefully into the track. Marinina lifted her chin with a joyful wickedness. Then she strode off towards the house.

Maurice was watching his step, through the tangle of Mediterranean herbage, so he did not catch sight of his wife till he came

round a little bend, quite near her. She was standing erect and
nude by the jutting rock, glistening with the sun and with warm
life. Her breasts seemed to be lifting up, alert, to listen, her
thighs looked brown and fleet. Her glance on him, as he came
like ink on blotting-paper, was swift and nervous.

Maurice, poor fellow, hesitated, and glanced away from her.
He turned his face aside.

'Hello, Julie!' he said, with a little nervous cough – 'Splendid!
Splendid!'

He advanced with his face averted, shooting further glances
at her, as she stood with the peculiar satiny gleam of the sun
on her tanned skin. Somehow she did not seem so terribly naked.
It was the golden-rose tan of the sun that clothed her.

'Hello, Maurice!' she said, hanging back from him. 'I wasn't
expecting you so soon.'

'No,' he said, 'No! I managed to slip away a little earlier.'
And again he coughed awkwardly.

They stood several yards away from one another, and there
was silence.

'Well!' he said, 'er – this is splendid, splendid! You are – er
– splendid! Where is the boy?'

'There he is,' she said, pointing down to where a naked
urchin in the deep shade was piling fallen lemons together.

The father gave an odd little laugh.

'Ah, yes! there he is! So there's the little man! Fine!' he said.
He really was thrilled in his suppressed, nervous soul. 'Hello,
Johnny!' he called, and it sounded rather feeble. 'Hello,
Johnny!'

The child looked up, spilling lemons from his chubby arms,
but did not respond.

'I guess we'll go down to him,' said Juliet, as she turned and
went striding down the path. Her husband followed, watching
the rosy, fleet-looking lifting and sinking of her quick hips, as
she swayed a little in the socket of her waist. He was dazed with
admiration, but also, at a deadly loss. What should he do with
himself? He was utterly out of the picture, in his dark grey
suit and pale grey hat, and his grey monastic face of a shy
business man.

'He looks all right, doesn't he,' said Juliet, as they came

through the deep sea of yellow-flowering oxalis, under the
lemon trees.

'Ah! – yes! yes! Splendid! Splendid! – Hello, Johnny! Do
you know Daddy? Do you know Daddy, Johnny?'

He crouched down and held out his hands.

'Lemons!' said the child, birdily chirping. 'Two lemons!'

'Two lemons!' replied the father. 'Lots of lemons.'

The infant came and put a lemon in each of his father's open
hands. Then he stood back to look.

'Two lemons!' repeated the father. 'Come, Johnny! Come
and say "Hello" to Daddy.'

'Daddy going back?' said the child.

'Going back? Well – well – not today.'

And he gathered his son in his arms.

'Take a coat off! Daddy take a coat off!' said the boy, squirming debonair away from the cloth.

'All right, son! Daddy take a coat off.'

He took off his coat and laid it carefully aside, then again
took his son in his arms. The naked woman looked down at
the naked infant in the arms of the man in his shirt sleeves. The
boy had pulled off the father's hat, and Juliet looked at the
sleek, black-and-grey hair of her husband, not a hair out of place.
And utterly, utterly indoors. She was silent for a long time,
while the father talked to the child, who was fond of his Daddy.

'What are you going to do about it, Maurice?' she said,
suddenly.

He looked at her swiftly, sideways.

'Er – about what, Julie?'

'Oh, everything! About this! I can't go back into East Forty-
Seventh.'

'Er –' he hesitated, 'no, I suppose not – not just now at least.'

'Never,' she said, and there was a silence.

'Well – er – I don't know,' he said.

'Do you think you can come out here?' she said.

'Yes! – I can stay for a month. I think I can manage a month,'
he hesitated. Then he ventured a complicated, shy peep at her,
and hid his face again.

She looked down at him, her alert breasts lifted with a sigh,
as if a breeze of impatience shook them.

'I can't go back,' she said slowly. 'I can't go back on this sun. If you can't come here –'

She ended on an open note. He glanced at her again and again, furtively, but with growing admiration and lessening confusion.

'No!' he said. 'This kind of thing suits you. You are splendid! No, I don't think you can go back.'

He was thinking of her in the New York flat, pale, silent, oppressing him terribly. He was the soul of gentle timidity, in his human relations, and her silent, awful hostility after the baby was born, had frightened him deeply. Because he had realized she couldn't help it. Women were like that. Their feelings took a reverse direction, even against their own selves, and it was awful – awful! Awful, awful to live in the house with a woman like that, whose feelings were reversed even against herself! He had felt himself ground down under the millstone of her helpless enmity. She had ground even herself down to the quick, and the child as well. No, anything rather than that.

'But what about *you* ?' she asked.

'I? Oh, I! – I can carry on the business, and – er – come over here for the holidays – as long as you like to stay. You stay as long as you wish.' He looked a long time down at the earth, then glanced up at her with a touch of supplication in his uneasy eyes.

'Even for ever?'

'Well – er – yes, if you like. For ever is a long time. One can't set a date.'

'And I can do anything I like?' She looked him straight in the eyes, challenging. And he was powerless against her rosy, wind-hardened nakedness.

'Er – yes! – I suppose so! So long as you don't make yourself unhappy – or the boy.'

Again he looked up at her with a complicated, uneasy appeal – thinking of the child, but hoping for himself.

'I won't,' she said quickly.

'No!' he said. 'No! I don't think you will.'

There was a pause. The bells of the village were hastily clanging midday. That meant lunch.

She slipped into her grey crepe kimono, and fastened a broad green sash round her waist. Then she slipped a little blue shirt over the boy's head, and they went up to the house.

At table she watched her husband, his grey city face, his fixed, black-grey hair, his very precise table manners, and his extreme moderation in eating and drinking. Sometimes he glanced at her, furtively, from under his black lashes. He had the gold-grey eyes of an animal that has been caught young, and reared completely in captivity.

They went on to the balcony for coffee. Below, beyond, on the next podere across the steep little gully, a peasant and his wife were sitting under an almond tree, near the green wheat, eating their midday meal from a little white cloth spread on the ground. There was a huge piece of bread, and glasses with dark wine.

Juliet put her husband with his back to this picture; she sat facing. Because, the moment she and Maurice had come out on the balcony, the peasant had glanced up.

5

She knew him, in the distance, perfectly. He was a rather fat, very broad fellow of about thirty-five, and he chewed large mouthfuls of bread. His wife was stiff and dark-faced, handsome, sombre. They had no children. So much Juliet had learned.

The peasant worked a great deal alone, on the opposite podere. His clothes were always very clean and cared-for, white trousers and a coloured shirt, and an old straw hat. Both he and his wife had that air of quiet superiority which belongs to individuals, not to a class.

His attraction was in his vitality, the peculiar quick energy which gave a charm to his movements, stout and broad as he was. In the early days before she took to the sun, Juliet had met him suddenly, among the rocks, when she had scrambled over to the next podere. He had been aware of her before she saw him, so that when she did look up, he took off his hat, gazing at her with shyness and pride, from his big blue eyes. His face was broad, sunburnt, he had a cropped brown moustache, and thick brown eyebrows, nearly as thick as his moustache, meeting under his low, wide brow.

'Oh!' she said. 'Can I walk here?'

'Surely!' he replied, with that peculiar hot haste which characterized his movement. 'My padrone would wish you to walk wherever you like on his land.'

And he pressed back his head in the quick, vivid, shy generosity of his nature. She had gone on quickly. But instantly she had recognized the violent generosity of his blood, and the equally violent *farouche* shyness.

Since then she had seen him in the distance every day, and she came to realize that he was one who lived a good deal to himself, like a quick animal, and that his wife loved him intensely, with a jealousy that was almost hate; because, probably, he wanted to give himself still, still further, beyond where she could take him.

One day, when a group of peasants sat under a tree, she had seen him dancing quick and gay with a child – his wife watching darkly.

Gradually Juliet and he had become intimate, across the distance. They were aware of one another. She knew, in the morning, the moment he arrived with his ass. And the moment she went out on the balcony he turned to look. But they never saluted. Yet she missed him when he did not come to work on the podere.

Once, in the hot morning when she had been walking naked, deep in the gully between the two estates, she had come upon him, as he was bending down, with his powerful shoulders, picking up wood to pile on his motionless, waiting donkey. He saw her as he lifted his flushed face, and she was backing away. A flame went over his eyes, and a flame flew over her body, melting her bones. But she backed away behind the bushes, silently, and retreated whence she had come. And she wondered a little resentfully over the silence in which he could work, hidden in the bushy places. He had that wild animal faculty.

Since then there had been a definite pain of consciousness in the body of each of them, though neither would admit it, and they gave no sign of recognition. But the man's wife was instinctively aware.

And Juliet had thought: Why shouldn't I meet this man for an hour, and bear his child? Why should I have to identify my life with a man's life? Why not meet him for an hour, as long as the desire lasts, and no more? There is already the spark between us.

But she had never made any sign. And now she saw him looking up, from where he sat by the white cloth, opposite his black-clad wife, looking up at Maurice. The wife turned and looked, too, saturnine.

And Juliet felt a grudge come over her. She would have to bear Maurice's child again. She had seen it in her husband's eyes. And she knew it from his answer, when she spoke to him.

'Will you walk about in the sun, too, without your clothes?' she asked him.

'Why – er – yes! Yes, I should like to, while I'm here – I suppose it's quite private?'

There was a gleam in his eyes, a desperate kind of courage of his desire, and a glance at the alert lifting of her breasts in her wrapper. In this way, he was a man, too, he faced the world and was not entirely quenched in his male courage. He would dare to walk in the sun, even ridiculously.

But he smelled of the world, and all its fetters and its mongrel cowering. He was branded with the brand that is not a hall-mark.

Ripe now, and brown-rosy all over with the sun, and with a heart like a fallen rose, she had wanted to go down to the hot, shy peasant and bear his child. Her sentiments had fallen like petals. She had seen the flushed blood in the burnt face, and the flame in the southern blue eyes, and the answer in her had been a gush of fire. He would have been a procreative sunbath to her, and she wanted it.

Nevertheless, her next child would be Maurice's. The fatal chain of continuity would cause it.

The Woman Who Rode Away

I

SHE had thought that this marriage, of all marriages, would be an adventure. Not that the man himself was exactly magical to her. A little, wiry, twisted fellow, twenty years older than herself, with brown eyes and greying hair, who had come to America a scrap of a wastrel, from Holland, years ago, as a tiny boy, and from the gold-mines of the west had been kicked south into Mexico, and now was more or less rich, owning silver-mines in the wilds of the Sierra Madre: it was obvious that the adventure lay in his circumstances, rather than his person. But he was still a little dynamo of energy, in spite of accidents survived, and what he had accomplished he had accomplished alone. One of those human oddments there is no accounting for.

When she actually *saw* what he had accomplished, her heart quailed. Great green-covered, unbroken mountain-hills, and in the midst of the lifeless isolation, the sharp pinkish mounds of the dried mud from the silver-works. Under the nakedness of the works, the walled-in, one-storey adobe house, with its garden inside, and its deep inner verandah with tropical climbers on the sides. And when you looked up from this shut-in flowered patio, you saw the huge pink cone of the silver-mud refuse, and the machinery of the extracting plant against heaven above. No more.

To be sure, the great wooden doors were often open. And then she could stand outside, in the vast open world. And see great, void, tree-clad hills piling behind one another, from nowhere into nowhere. They were green in autumn time. For the rest, pinkish, stark dry, and abstract.

And in his battered Ford car her husband would take her into the dead, thrice-dead little Spanish town forgotten among the mountains. The great, sun-dried dead church, the dead portales, the hopeless covered market-place, where, the first time she went, she saw a dead dog lying between the meat stalls and the vegetable array, stretched out as if for ever, nobody troubling to throw it away. Deadness within deadness.

Everybody feebly talking silver, and showing bits of ore. But silver was at a standstill. The great war came and went. Silver was a dead market. Her husband's mines were closed down. But she and he lived on in the adobe house under the works, among the flowers that were never very flowery to her.

She had two children, a boy and a girl. And her eldest, the boy, was nearly ten years old before she aroused from her stupor of subjected amazement. She was now thirty-three, a large, blue-eyed, dazed woman, beginning to grow stout. Her little, wiry, tough, twisted, brown-eyed husband was fifty-three, a man as tough as wire, tenacious as wire, still full of energy, but dimmed by the lapse of silver from the market, and by some curious inaccessibility on his wife's part.

He was a man of principles, and a good husband. In a way, he doted on her. He never quite got over his dazzled admiration of her. But essentially, he was still a bachelor. He had been thrown out on the world, a little bachelor, at the age of ten. When he married he was over forty, and had enough money to marry on. But his capital was all a bachelor's. He was boss of his own works, and marriage was the last and most intimate bit of his own works.

He admired his wife to extinction, he admired her body, all her points. And she was to him always the rather dazzling Californian girl from Berkeley, whom he had first known. Like any sheik, he kept her guarded among those mountains of Chihuahua. He was jealous of her as he was of his silver-mine: and that is saying a lot.

At thirty-three she really was still the girl from Berkeley, in all but physique. Her conscious development had stopped mysteriously with her marriage, completely arrested. Her husband had never become real to her, neither mentally nor physically. In spite of his late sort of passion for her, he never meant anything to her, physically. Only morally he swayed her, downed her, kept her in an invincible slavery.

So the years went by, in the adobe house strung round the sunny patio, with the silver-works overhead. Her husband was never still. When the silver went dead, he ran a ranch lower

down, some twenty miles away, and raised pure-bred hogs,
splendid creatures. At the same time, he hated pigs. He was
a squeamish waif of an idealist, and really hated the physical
side of life. He loved work, work, work, and making
things. His marriage, his children, were something he was
making, part of his business, but with a sentimental income
this time.

Gradually her nerves began to go wrong: she must get out.
She must get out. So he took her to El Paso for three months.
And at least it was the United States.

But he kept his spell over her. The three months ended: back
she was, just the same, in her adobe house among those eternal
green or pinky-brown hills, void as only the undiscovered is void.
She taught her children, she supervised the Mexican boys who
were her servants. And sometimes her husband brought visitors,
Spaniards or Mexicans or occasionally white men.

He really loved to have white men staying on the place. Yet
he had not a moment's peace when they were there. It was as
if his wife were some peculiar secret vein of ore in his mines,
which no one must be aware of except himself. And she was
fascinated by the young gentlemen, mining engineers, who were
his guests at times. He, too, was fascinated by a real gentleman.
But he was an old-timer miner with a wife, and if a gentleman
looked at his wife, he felt as if his mine were being looted, the
secrets of it pryed out.

It was one of these young gentlemen who put the idea into her
mind. They were all standing outside the great wooden doors
of the patio, looking at the outer world. The eternal, motionless
hills were all green, it was September, after the rains. There
was no sign of anything, save the deserted mine, the deserted
works, and a bunch of half-deserted miners' dwellings.

'I wonder,' said the young man, 'what there is behind those
great blank hills.'

'More hills,' said Lederman. 'If you go that way, Sonora and
the coast. This way is the desert – you came from there. – And
the other way, hills and mountains.'

'Yes, but what *lives* in the hills and the mountains? *Surely*
there is something wonderful? It looks *so* like nowhere on earth:
like being on the moon.'

'There's plenty of game, if you want to shoot. And Indians, if you call *them* wonderful.'

'Wild ones?'

'Wild enough.'

'But friendly?'

'It depends. Some of them are quite wild, and they don't let anybody near. They kill a missionary at sight. And where a missionary can't get, nobody can.'

'But what does the government say?'

'They're so far from everywhere, the government leaves 'em alone. And they're wily; if they think there'll be trouble, they send a delegation to Chihuahua and make a formal submission. The government is glad to leave it at that.'

'And do they live quite wild, with their own savage customs and religion?'

'Oh, yes. They use nothing but bows and arrows. I've seen them in town, in the Plaza, with funny sort of hats with flowers round them, and a bow in one hand, quite naked except for a sort of shirt, even in cold weather – striding round with their savage's bare legs.'

'But don't you suppose it's wonderful, up there in their secret villages?'

'No. What would there be wonderful about it? Savages are savages, and all savages behave more or less alike : rather low-down and dirty, insanitary, with a few cunning tricks, and struggling to get enough to eat.'

'But surely they have old, old religions and mysteries – it *must* be wonderful, surely it must.'

'I don't know about mysteries – howling and heathen practices, more or less indecent. No, I see nothing wonderful in that kind of stuff. And I wonder that you should, when you have lived in London or Paris or New York –'

'Ah, *everybody* lives in London or Paris or New York' – said the young man, as if this were an argument.

And his peculiar vague enthusiasm for unknown Indians found a full echo in the woman's heart. She was overcome by a foolish romanticism more unreal than a girl's. She felt it was her destiny to wander into the secret haunts of these timeless, mysterious, marvellous Indians of the mountains.

She kept her secret. The young man was departing, her husband was going with him down to Torreon, on business : – would be away for some days. But before the departure, she made her husband talk about the Indians : about the wandering tribes, resembling the Navajo, who were still wandering free; and the Yaquis of Sonora : and the different groups in the different valleys of Chihuahua State.

There was supposed to be one tribe, the Chilchuis, living in a high valley to the south, who were the sacred tribe of all the Indians. The descendants of Montezuma and of the old Aztec or Totonac kings still lived among them, and the old priests still kept up the ancient religion, and offered human sacrifices – so it was said. Some scientists had been to the Chilchui country, and had come back gaunt and exhausted with hunger and bitter privation, bringing various curious, barbaric objects of worship, but having seen nothing extraordinary in the hungry, stark village of savages.

Though Lederman talked in this off-hand way, it was obvious he felt some of the vulgar excitement at the idea of ancient and mysterious savages.

'How far away are they?' she asked.

'Oh – three days on horseback – past Cuchitee and a little lake there is up there.'

Her husband and the young man departed. The woman made her crazy plans. Of late, to break the monotony of her life, she had harassed her husband into letting her go riding with him, occasionally, on horseback. She was never allowed to go out alone. The country truly was not safe, lawless and crude.

But she had her own horse, and she dreamed of being free as she had been as a girl, among the hills of California.

Her daughter, nine years old, was now in a tiny convent in the little half-deserted Spanish mining-town five miles away.

'Manuel,' said the woman to her house-servant, 'I'm going to ride to the convent to see Margarita, and take her a few things. Perhaps I shall stay the night in the convent. You look after Freddy and see everything is all right till I come back.'

'Shall I ride with you on the master's horse, or shall Juan?' asked the servant.

'Neither of you. I shall go alone.'

The young man looked her in the eyes, in protest. Absolutely impossible that the woman should ride alone!

'I shall go alone,' repeated the large, placid-seeming, fair-complexioned woman, with peculiar overbearing emphasis. And the man silently, unhappily yielded.

'Why are you going alone, mother?' asked her son, as she made up parcels of food.

'Am I *never* to be let alone? Not one moment of my life?' she cried, with sudden explosion of energy. And the child, like the servant, shrank into silence.

She set off without a qualm, riding astride on her strong roan horse, and wearing a riding suit of coarse linen, a riding skirt over her linen breeches, a scarlet neck-tie over her white blouse, and a black felt hat on her head. She had food in her saddle-bags, an army canteen with water, and a large, native blanket tied on behind the saddle. Peering into the distance, she set off from her home. Manuel and the little boy stood in the gateway to watch her go. She did not even turn to wave them farewell.

But when she had ridden about a mile, she left the wild road and took a small trail to the right, that led into another valley, over steep places and past great trees, and through another deserted mining-settlement. It was September, the water was running freely in the little stream that had fed the now-abandoned mine. She got down to drink, and let the horse drink too.

She saw natives coming through the trees, away up the slope. They had seen her, and were watching her closely. She watched in turn. The three people, two women and a youth, were making a wide detour, so as not to come too close to her. She did not care. Mounting, she trotted ahead up the silent valley, beyond the silver-works, beyond any trace of mining. There was still a rough trail, that led over rocks and loose stones into the valley beyond. This trail she had already ridden, with her husband. Beyond that she knew she must go south.

Curiously she was not afraid, although it was a frightening country, the silent, fatal-seeming mountain-slopes, the occasional distant, suspicious, elusive natives among the trees, the great carrion birds occasionally hovering, like great flies, in the distance, over some carrion or some ranch house or some group of huts.

As she climbed, the trees shrank and the trail ran through a thorny scrub, that was trailed over with blue convolvulus and an occasional pink creeper. Then these flowers lapsed. She was nearing the pine-trees.

She was over the crest, and before her another silent, void, green-clad valley. It was past midday. Her horse turned to a little runlet of water, so she got down to eat her midday meal. She sat in silence looking at the motionless unliving valley, and at the sharp-peaked hills, rising higher to rock and pine-trees, southwards. She rested two hours in the heat of the day, while the horse cropped around her.

Curious that she was neither afraid nor lonely. Indeed, the loneliness was like a drink of cold water to one who is very thirsty. And a strange elation sustained her from within.

She travelled on, and camped at night in a valley beside a stream, deep among the bushes. She had seen cattle and had crossed several trails. There must be a ranch not far off. She heard the strange wailing shriek of a mountain-lion, and the answer of dogs. But she sat by her small camp fire in a secret hollow place and was not really afraid. She was buoyed up always by the curious, bubbling elation within her.

It was very cold before dawn. She lay wrapped in her blanket looking at the stars, listening to her horse shivering, and feeling like a woman who has died and passed beyond. She was not sure that she had not heard, during the night, a great crash at the centre of herself, which was the crash of her own death. Or else it was a crash at the centre of the earth, and meant something big and mysterious.

With the first peep of light she got up, numb with cold, and made a fire. She ate hastily, gave her horse some pieces of oil-seed cake, and set off again. She avoided any meeting – and since she met nobody, it was evident that she in turn was avoided. She came at last in sight of the village of Cuchitee, with its black houses with their reddish roofs, a sombre, dreary little cluster below another silent, long-abandoned mine. And beyond, a long, great mountain-side, rising up green and light to the darker, shaggier green of pine-trees. And beyond the pine-trees stretches of naked rock against the sky, rock slashed already and brindled with white stripes of snow. High up, the new snow had already begun to fall.

And now, as she neared, more or less, her destination, she began to go vague and disheartened. She had passed the little lake among yellow aspen trees whose white trunks were round and suave like the white round arms of some woman. What a lovely place! In California she would have raved about it. But here she looked and saw that it was lovely, but she didn't care. She was weary and spent with her two nights in the open, and afraid of the coming night. She didn't know where she was going, or what she was going for. Her horse plodded dejectedly on, towards that immense and forbidding mountain-slope, following a stony little trail. And if she had had any will of her own left, she would have turned back, to the village, to be protected and sent home to her husband.

But she had no will of her own. Her horse splashed through a brook, and turned up a valley, under immense yellowing cotton-wood trees. She must have been near nine thousand feet above sea-level, and her head was light with the altitude and with weariness. Beyond the cotton-wood trees she could see, on each side, the steep sides of mountain-slopes hemming her in, sharp-plumaged with overlapping aspen, and, higher up, with sprouting, pointed spruce and pine tree. Her horse went on automatically. In this tight valley, on this slight trail, there was nowhere to go but ahead, climbing.

Suddenly her horse jumped, and three men in dark blankets were on the trail before her.

'*Adiós,*' came the greeting, in the full, restrained Indian voice.

'*Adiós!*' she replied, in her assured, American woman's voice.

'Where are you going?' came the quiet question, in Spanish.

The men in the dark sarapes had come closer, and were looking up at her.

'On ahead,' she replied coolly, in her hard, Saxon Spanish.

These were just natives to her: dark-faced, strongly-built men in dark sarapes and straw hats. They would have been the same as the men who worked for her husband, except, strangely, for the long black hair that fell over their shoulders. She noted this long black hair with a certain distaste. These must be the wild Indians she had come to see.

'Where do you come from?' the same man asked. It was always the one man who spoke. He was young, with quick, large, bright black eyes that glanced sideways at her. He had a soft black moustache on his dark face, and a sparse tuft of beard, loose hairs on his chin. His long black hair, full of life, hung unrestrained on his shoulders. Dark as he was, he did not look as if he had washed lately.

His two companions were the same, but older men, powerful and silent. One had a thin black line of moustache, but was beardless. The other had the smooth cheeks and the sparse dark hairs marking the lines of his chin with the beard characteristic of the Indians.

'I come from far away,' she replied, with half-jocular evasion. This was received in silence.

'But where do you live?' asked the young man, with that same quiet insistence.

'In the north,' she replied airily.

Again there was a moment's silence. The young man conversed quietly, in Indian, with his two companions.

'Where do you want to go, up this way?' he asked suddenly, with challenge and authority, pointing briefly up the trail.

'To the Chilchui Indians,' answered the woman laconically.

The young man looked at her. His eyes were quick and black, and inhuman. He saw, in the full evening light, the faint sub-smile of assurance on her rather large, calm, fresh-complexioned face; the weary, bluish lines under her large blue eyes; and in her eyes, as she looked down at him, a half-childish, half-arrogant confidence in her own female power. But in her eyes, also, a curious look of trance.

'*Usted es Señora?* You are a lady?' the Indian asked her.

'Yes, I am a lady,' she replied complacently.

'With a family?'

'With a husband and two children, boy and girl,' she said.

The Indian turned to his companions and translated, in the low, gurgling speech, like hidden water running. They were evidently at a loss.

'Where is your husband?' asked the young man.

'Who knows?' she replied airily. 'He has gone away on business for a week.'

The black eyes watched her shrewdly. She, for all her weariness, smiled faintly in the pride of her own adventure and the assurance of her own womanhood, and the spell of the madness that was on her.

'And what do *you* want to do?' the Indian asked her.

'I want to visit the Chilchui Indians – to see their houses and to know their gods,' she replied.

The young man turned and translated quickly, and there was a silence almost of consternation. The grave elder men were glancing at her sideways, with strange looks, from under their decorated hats. And they said something to the young man, in deep chest voices.

The latter still hesitated. Then he turned to the woman.

'Good!' he said. 'Let us go. But we cannot arrive until tomorrow. We shall have to make camp tonight.'

'Good!' she said. 'I can make a camp.'

Without more ado, they set off at a good speed up the stony trail. The young Indian ran alongside her horse's head, the other two ran behind. One of them had taken a thick stick, and occasionally he struck her horse a resounding blow on the haunch, to urge him forward. This made the horse jump, and threw her back in the saddle, which, tired as she was, made her angry.

'Don't do that!' she cried, looking round angrily at the fellow. She met his black, large, bright eyes, and for the first time her spirit really quailed. The man's eyes were not human to her, and they did not see her as a beautiful white woman. He looked at her with a black, bright inhuman look, and saw no woman in her at all. As if she were some strange, unaccountable *thing*, incomprehensible to him, but inimical. She sat in her saddle in wonder, feeling once more as if she had died. And again he struck her horse, and jerked her badly in the saddle.

All the passionate anger of the spoilt white woman rose in her. She pulled her horse to a standstill, and turned with blazing eyes to the man at her bridle.

'Tell that fellow not to touch my horse again,' she cried.

She met the eyes of the young man, and in their bright black inscrutability she saw a fine spark, as in a snake's eye, of derision. He spoke to his companion in the rear, in the low tones of the

Indian. The man with the stick listened without looking. Then, giving a strange low cry to the horse, he struck it again on the rear, so that it leaped forward spasmodically up the stony trial, scattering the stones, pitching the weary woman in her seat.

The anger flew like a madness into her eyes, she went white at the gills. Fiercely she reined in her horse. But before she could turn, the young Indian had caught the reins under the horse's throat, jerked them forward, and was trotting ahead rapidly, leading the horse.

The woman was powerless. And along with her supreme anger there came a slight thrill of exultation. She knew she was dead.

The sun was setting, a great yellow light flooded the last of the aspens, flared on the trunks of the pine-trees, the pine-needles bristled and stood out with dark lustre, the rocks glowed with unearthly glamour. And through this effulgence the Indian at her horse's head trotted unweariedly on, his dark blanket swinging, his bare legs glowing with a strange transfigured ruddiness in the powerful light, and his straw hat with its half-absurd decorations of flowers and feathers shining showily above his river of long black hair. At times he would utter a low call to the horse, and then the other Indian, behind, would fetch the beast a whack with the stick.

The wonder-light faded off the mountains, the world began to grow dark, a cold air breathed down. In the sky, half a moon was struggling against the glow in the west. Huge shadows came down from steep rocky slopes. Water was rushing. The woman was conscious only of her fatigue, her unspeakable fatigue, and the cold wind from the heights. She was not aware how moon-light replaced daylight. It happened while she travelled uncon-scious with weariness.

For some hours they travelled by moonlight. Then suddenly they came to a standstill. The men conversed in low tones for a moment.

'We camp here,' said the young man.

She waited for him to help her down. He merely stood holding the horse's bridle. She almost fell from the saddle, so fatigued.

They had chosen a place at the foot of rocks that still gave off a little warmth of the sun. One man cut pine-boughs, another erected little screens of pine-boughs against the rock for shelter, and put boughs of balsam pine for beds. The third made a small fire, to heat tortillas. They worked in silence.

The woman drank water. She did not want to eat – only to lie down.

'Where do I sleep?' she asked.

The young man pointed to one of the shelters. She crept in and lay inert. She did not care what happened to her, she was so weary, and so beyond everything. Through the twigs of spruce she could see the three men squatting round the fire on their hams, chewing the tortillas they picked from the ashes with their dark fingers, and drinking water from a gourd. They talked in low, muttering tones, with long intervals of silence. Her saddle and saddle-bags lay not far from the fire, unopened, untouched. The men were not interested in her or her belongings. There they squatted with their hats on their heads, eating, eating mechanically, like animals, the dark sarape with its fringe falling to the ground before and behind, the powerful dark legs naked and squatting like an animal's showing the dirty white shirt and the sort of loin-cloth which was the only other garment, underneath. And they showed no more sign of interest in her than if she had been a piece of venison they were bringing home from the hunt, and had hung inside a shelter.

After a while they carefully extinguished the fire, and went inside their own shelter. Watching through the screen of boughs, she had a moment's thrill of fear and anxiety, seeing the dark forms cross and pass silently in the moonlight. Would they attack her now?

But, no! They were as if oblivious of her. Her horse was hobbled; she could hear it hopping wearily. All was silent, mountain-silent, cold, deathly. She slept and woke and slept in a semi-conscious numbness of cold and fatigue. A long, long night, icy and eternal, and she aware that she had died.

2

Yet when there was a stirring, and a clink of flint and steel, and the form of a man crouching like a dog over a bone, at a red splutter of fire, and she knew it was morning coming, it seemed to her the night had passed too soon.

When the fire was going, she came out of her shelter with one real desire left : for coffee. The men were warming more tortillas.

'Can we make coffee?' she asked.

The young man looked at her, and she imagined the same faint spark of derision in his eyes. He shook his head.

'We don't take it,' he said. 'There is no time.'

And the elder men, squatting on their haunches, looked up at her in the terrible paling dawn, and there was not even derision in their eyes. Only that intense, yet remote, inhuman glitter which was terrible to her. They were inaccessible. They could not see her as a woman at all. As if she *were* not a woman. As if, perhaps, her whiteness took away all her womanhood, and left her as some giant, female white ant. That was all they could see in her.

Before the sun was up, she was in the saddle again, and they were climbing steeply, in the icy air. The sun came, and soon she was very hot, exposed to the glare in the bare places. It seemed to her they were climbing to the roof of the world. Beyond against heaven were slashes of snow.

During the course of the morning, they came to a place where the horse could not go farther. They rested for a time with a great slant of living rock in front of them, like the glossy breast of some earth-beast. Across this rock, along a wavering crack, they had to go. It seemed to her that for hours she went in torment, on her hands and knees, from crack to crevice, along the slanting face of this pure rock-mountain. An Indian in front and an Indian behind walked slowly erect, shod with sandals of braided leather. But she in her riding-boots dared not stand erect.

Yet what she wondered, all the time, was why she persisted in clinging and crawling along these mile-long sheets of rock. Why she did not hurl herself down, and have done? The world was below her.

When they emerged at last on a stony slope, she looked back, and saw the third Indian coming carrying her saddle and saddle-bags on his back, the whole hung from a band across his forehead. And he had his hat in his hand, as he stepped slowly, with the slow, soft, heavy tread of the Indian, unwavering in the chinks of rock, as if along a scratch in the mountain's iron shield.

The stony slope led downwards. The Indians seemed to grow excited. One ran ahead at a slow trot, disappearing round the curve of stones. And the track curved round and down, till at last in the full blaze of the mid-morning sun, they could see a valley below them, between walls of rock, as in a great wide chasm let in the mountains. A green valley, with a river, and trees, and clusters of low flat sparkling houses. It was all tiny and perfect, three thousand feet below. Even the flat bridge over the stream, and the square with the houses around it, the bigger buildings piled up at opposite ends of the square, the tall cotton-wood trees, the pastures and stretches of yellow-sere maize, the patches of brown sheep or goats in the distance, on the slopes, the railed enclosures by the stream-side. There it was, all small and perfect, looking magical, as any place will look magical, seen from the mountains above. The usual thing was that the low houses glittered white, whitewashed, looking like crystals of salt, or silver. This frightened her.

They began the long, winding descent at the head of the barranca, following the stream that rushed and fell. At first it was all rocks : then the pine-trees began, and soon, the silver-limbed aspens. The flowers of autumn, big pink daisy-like flowers, and white ones, and many yellow flowers, were in profusion. But she had to sit down and rest, she was so weary. And she saw the bright flowers shadowily, as pale shadows hovering, as one who is dead must see them.

At length came grass and pasture-slopes between mingled aspen and pine-trees. A shepherd, naked in the sun save for his hat and his cotton loin-cloth, was driving his brown sheep away. In a grove of trees they sat and waited, she and the young Indian. The one with the saddle had also gone forward.

They heard a sound of someone coming. It was three men, in fine sarapes of red and orange and yellow and black, and with brilliant feather head-dresses. The oldest had his grey hair braided with fur, and his red and orange-yellow sarape was covered with curious black markings, like a leopard-skin. The other two were not grey-haired, but they were elders too. Their blankets were in stripes, and their head-dresses not so elaborate.

The young Indian addressed the elders in a few quiet words. They listened without answering or looking at him or at the woman, keeping their faces averted and their eyes turned to the ground, only listening. And at length they turned and looked at the woman.

The old chief, or medicine-man, whatever he was, had a deeply wrinkled and lined face of dark bronze, with a few sparse grey hairs round the mouth. Two long braids of grey hair, braided with fur and coloured feathers, hung on his shoulders. And yet, it was only his eyes that mattered. They were black and of extraordinary piercing strength, without a qualm of misgiving in their demonish, dauntless power. He looked into the eyes of the white woman with a long, piercing look, seeking she knew not what. She summoned all her strength to meet his eyes and keep up her guard. But it was no good. He was not looking at her as one human being looks at another. He never even perceived her resistance or her challenge, but looked past them both, into she knew not what.

She could see it was hopeless to expect any human communication with this old being.

He turned and said a few words to the young Indian.

'He asks what do you seek here?' said the young man in Spanish.

'I? Nothing! I only came to see what it was like.'

This was again translated, and the old man turned his eyes on her once more. Then he spoke again, in his low muttering tone, to the young Indian.

'He says, why does she leave her house with the white men? Does she want to bring the white man's God to the Chilchui?'

'No,' she replied, foolhardy. 'I came away from the white man's God myself. I came to look for the God of the Chilchui.'

Profound silence followed, when this was translated. Then the old man spoke again, in a small voice almost of weariness.

'Does the white woman seek the gods of the Chilchui because she is weary of her own God?' came the question.

'Yes, she does. She is tired of the white man's God,' she

replied, thinking that was what they wanted her to say. She would like to serve the gods of the Chilchui.

She was aware of an extraordinary thrill of triumph and exultance passing through the Indians, in the tense silence that followed when this was translated. Then they all looked at her with piercing black eyes, in which a steely covetous intent glittered incomprehensible. She was the more puzzled, as there was nothing sensual or sexual in the look. It had a terrible glittering purity that was beyond her. She was afraid, she would have been paralysed with fear, had not something died within her, leaving her with a cold, watchful wonder only.

The elders talked a little while, then the two went away, leaving her with the young man and the oldest chief. The old man now looked at her with a certain solicitude.

'He says are you tired?' asked the young man.

'Very tired,' she said.

'The men will bring you a carriage,' said the young Indian.

The carriage, when it came, proved to be a litter consisting of a sort of hammock of dark woollen frieze, slung on to a pole which was borne on the shoulders of two long-haired Indians. The woollen hammock was spread on the ground, she sat down on it, and the two men raised the pole to their shoulders. Swinging rather as if she were a sack, she was carried out of the grove of trees, following the old chief, whose leopard-spotted blanket moved curiously in the sunlight.

They had emerged in the valley-head. Just in front were the maize fields, with ripe ears of maize. The corn was not very tall, in this high altitude. The well-worn path went between it, and all she could see was the erect form of the old chief, in the flame and black sarape, stepping soft and heavy and swift, his head forward, looking neither to right nor to left. Her bearers followed, stepping rhythmically, the long blue-black hair glistening like a river down the naked shoulders of the man in front.

They passed the maize, and came to a big wall or earth-work made of earth and adobe bricks. The wooden doors were open. Passing on, they were in a network of small gardens, full of flowers and herbs and fruit trees, each garden watered by a tiny ditch of running water. Among each cluster of trees and

flowers was a small, glittering white house, windowless, and
with closed door. The place was a network of little paths, small
streams, and little bridges among square, flowering gardens.

Following the broadest path – a soft narrow track between
leaves and grass, a path worn smooth by centuries of human
feet, no hoof of horse nor any wheel to disfigure it – they
came to the little river of swift bright water, and crossed on a
log bridge. Everything was silent – there was no human being
anywhere. The road went on under magnificent cotton-wood
trees. It emerged suddenly outside the central plaza or square
of the village.

This was a long oblong of low white houses with flat roofs,
and two bigger buildings, having as it were little square huts
piled on top of bigger long huts, stood at either end of the
oblong, facing each other rather askew. Every little house was a
dazzling white, save for the great round beam-ends which
projected under the flat eaves, and for the flat roofs. Round
each of the bigger buildings, on the outside of the square, was
a stockyard fence, inside which was garden with trees and
flowers, and various small houses.

Not a soul was in sight. They passed silently between the
houses into the central square. This was quite bare and arid,
the earth trodden smooth by endless generations of passing feet,
passing across from door to door. All the doors of the windowless houses gave on to this blank square, but all the doors were
closed. The firewood lay near the threshold, a clay oven was
still smoking, but there was no sign of moving life.

The old man walked straight across the square to the big
house at the end, where the two upper storeys, as in a house
of toy bricks, stood each one smaller than the lower one. A
stone staircase, outside, led up to the roof of the first storey.

At the foot of this staircase the litter-bearers stood still, and
lowered the woman to the ground.

'You will come up,' said the young Indian who spoke Spanish.

She mounted the stone stairs to the earthen roof of the first
house, which formed a platform round the wall of the second
storey. She followed around this platform to the back of the
big house. There they descended again, into the garden at the
rear.

So far they had seen no one. But now two men appeared, bareheaded, with long braided hair, and wearing a sort of white shirt gathered into a loin-cloth. These went along with the three newcomers, across the garden where red flowers and yellow flowers were blooming, to a long, low white house. There they entered without knocking.

It was dark inside. There was a low murmur of men's voices. Several men were present, their white shirts showing in the gloom, their dark faces invisible. They were sitting on a great log of smooth old wood, that lay along the far wall. And save for this log, the room seemed empty. But no, in the dark at one end was a couch, a sort of bed, and someone lying there, covered with furs.

The old Indian in the spotted sarape, who had accompanied the woman, now took off his hat and his blanket and his sandals. Laying them aside, he approached the couch, and spoke in a low voice. For some moments there was no answer. Then an old man, with the snow-white hair hanging round his darkly-visible face, roused himself like a vision, and leaned on one elbow, looking vaguely at the company, in tense silence.

The grey-haired Indian spoke again, and then the young Indian, taking the woman's hand, led her forward. In her linen riding habit, and black boots and hat, and her pathetic bit of red tie, she stood there beside the fur-covered bed of the old, old man, who sat reared up, leaning on one elbow, remote as a ghost, his white hair streaming in disorder, his face almost black, yet with a far-off intentness, not of this world, leaning forward to look at her.

His face was so old, it was like dark glass, and the few curling hairs that sprang white from his lips and chin were quite incredible. The long white locks fell unbraided and disorderly on either side of the glassy dark face. And under a faint powder of white eyebrows, the black eyes of the old chief looked at her as if from the far, far dead, seeing something that was never to be seen.

At last he spoke a few deep, hollow words, as if to the dark air.

'He says, do you bring your heart to the god of the Chilchui?' translated the young Indian.

'Tell him yes,' she said, automatically.

There was a pause. The old Indian spoke again, as if to the air. One of the men present went out. There was a silence as if of eternity, in the dim room that was lighted only through the open door.

The woman looked round. Four old men with grey hair sat on the log by the wall facing the door. Two other men, powerful and impassive, stood near the door. They all had long hair, and wore white shirts gathered into a loin-cloth. Their powerful legs were naked and dark. There was a silence like eternity.

At length the man returned, with white and dark clothing on his arm. The young Indian took them, and holding them in front of the woman, said :

'You must take off your clothes, and put these on.'

'If all you men will go out,' she said.

'No one will hurt you,' he said quietly.

'Not while you men are here,' she said.

He looked at the two men by the door. They came quickly forward, and suddenly gripped her arms as she stood, without hurting her, but with great power. Then two of the old men came, and with curious skill slit her boots down with keen knives, and drew them off, and slit her clothing so that it came away from her. In a few moments she stood there white and uncovered. The old man on the bed spoke, and they turned her round for him to see. He spoke again, and the young Indian deftly took the pins and comb from her fair hair, so that it fell over her shoulders in a bunchy tangle.

Then the old man spoke again. The Indian led her to the bedside. The white-haired, glassy-dark old man moistened his finger-tips at his mouth, and most delicately touched her on the breasts and on the body, then on the back. And she winced strangely each time, as the finger-tips drew along her skin, as if Death itself were touching her.

And she wondered, almost sadly, why she did not feel shamed in her nakedness. She only felt sad and lost. Because nobody felt ashamed. The elder men were all dark and tense with some other deep, gloomy, incomprehensible emotion, which suspended all her agitation while the young Indian had a strange look of ecstasy on his face. And she, she was only utterly strange and beyond herself, as if her body were not her own.

They gave her the new clothing: a long white cotton shift, that came to her knees: then a tunic of thick blue woollen stuff, embroidered with scarlet and green flowers. It was fastened over one shoulder only, and belted with a braid sash of scarlet and black wool.

When she was thus dressed, they took her away, barefoot, to a little house in the stockaded garden. The young Indian told her she might have what she wanted. She asked for water to wash herself. He brought it in a jar, together with a long wooden bowl. Then he fastened the gate-door of her house, and left her a prisoner. She could see through the bars of the great-door of her house, the red flowers of the garden, and a humming bird. Then from the roof of the big house she heard the long, heavy sound of a drum, unearthly to her in its summons, and an uplifting voice calling from the house-top in a strange language, with a far-away emotionless intonation, delivering some speech or message. And she listened as if from the dead.

But she was very tired. She lay down on a couch of skins, pulling over her the blanket of dark wool, and she slept, giving up everything.

When she woke it was late afternoon, and the young Indian was entering with a basket-tray containing food, tortillas and corn-mush with bits of meat, probably mutton, and a drink made of honey, and some fresh plums. He brought her also a long garland of red and yellow flowers with knots of blue buds at the end. He sprinkled the garland with water from a jar, then offered it to her, with a smile. He seemed very gentle and thoughtful, and on his face and in his dark eyes was a curious look of triumph and ecstasy, that frightened her a little. The glitter had gone from the black eyes, with their curving dark lashes, and he would look at her with this strange soft glow of ecstasy that was not quite human, and terribly impersonal, and which made her uneasy.

'Is there anything you want?' he said, in his low, slow, melodious voice, that always seemed withheld, as if he were speaking aside to somebody else, or as if he did not want to let the sound come out to her.

'Am I going to be kept a prisoner here?' she asked.

'No, you can walk in the garden tomorrow,' he said softly. Always this curious solicitude.

'Do you like that drink?' he said, offering her a little earthen-ware cup. 'It is very refreshing.'

She sipped the liquor curiously. It was made with herbs and sweetened with honey, and had a strange, lingering flavour. The young man watched her with gratification.

'It has a peculiar taste,' she said.

'It is very refreshing,' he replied, his black eyes resting on her always with that look of gratified ecstasy. Then he went away. And presently she began to be sick, and to vomit violently, as if she had no control over herself.

Afterwards she felt a great soothing languor steal over her, her limbs felt strong and loose and full of languor, and she lay on her couch listening to the sounds of the village, watching the yellowing sky, smelling the scent of burning cedar-wood, or pine-wood. So distinctly she heard the yapping of tiny dogs, the shuffle of far-off feet, the murmur of voices, so keenly she detected the smell of smoke, and flowers, and evening falling, so vividly she saw the one bright star infinitely remote, stirring above the sunset, that she felt as if all her senses were diffused on the air, that she could distinguish the sound of evening flowers unfolding, and the actual crystal sound of the heavens, as the vast belts of the world-atmosphere slid past one another, and as if the moisture ascending and the moisture descending in the air resounded like some harp in the cosmos.

She was a prisoner in her house and in the stockaded garden, but she scarcely minded. And it was days before she realized that she never saw another woman. Only the men, the elderly men of the big house, that she imagined must be some sort of temple, and the men priests of some sort. For they always had the same colours, red, orange, yellow, and black, and the same grave, abstracted demeanour.

Sometimes an old man would come and sit in her room with her, in absolute silence. None spoke any language but Indian, save the one younger man. The older men would smile at her, and sit with her for an hour at a time, sometimes smiling at her when she spoke in Spanish, but never answering save with this slow, benevolent-seeming smile. And they gave off a feeling of amost fatherly solicitude. Yet their dark eyes, brooding over her, had something away in their depths that was awesomely ferocious and relentless. They would cover it with a smile, at once, if they felt her looking. But she had seen it.

Always they treated her with this curious impersonal solicitude, this utterly impersonal gentleness, as an old man treats a child. But underneath it she felt there was something else, something terrible. When her old visitor had gone away, in his silent, insidious, fatherly fashion, a shock of fear would come over her; though of what she knew not.

The young Indian would sit and talk with her freely, as if with great candour. But with him, too, she felt that everything real was unsaid. Perhaps it was unspeakable. His big dark eyes would rest on her almost cherishingly, touched with ecstasy, and his beautiful, slow, languorous voice would trail out its simple, ungrammatical Spanish. He told her he was the grandson of the old, old man, son of the man in the spotted sarape: and they were caciques, kings from the old, old days, before even the Spaniards came. But he himself had been in Mexico City, and also in the United States. He had worked as a labourer, building the roads in Los Angeles. He had travelled as far as Chicago.

'Don't you speak English, then?' she asked.

His eyes rested on her with a curious look of duplicity and conflict, and he mutely shook his head.

'What did you do with your long hair, when you were in the United States?' she asked. 'Did you cut it off?'

Again, with the look of torment in his eyes, he shook his head.

'No,' he said, in a low, subdued voice, 'I wore a hat, and a handkerchief tied around my head.'

And he relapsed into silence, as if of tormented memories.

'Are you the only man of your people who has been to the United States?' she asked him.

'Yes. I am the only one who has been away from here for a long time. The others come back soon, in one week. They don't stay away. The old men don't let them.'

'And why did you go?'

'The old men want me to go – because I shall be the Cacique –'

He talked always with the same naïveté, an almost childish

candour. But she felt that this was perhaps just the effect of his Spanish. Or perhaps speech altogether was unreal to him. Anyhow, she felt that all the real things were kept back.

He came and sat with her a good deal – sometimes more than she wished – as if he wanted to be near her. She asked him if he was married. He said he was – with two children.

'I should like to see your children,' she said.

But he answered only with that smile, a sweet, almost ecstatic smile, above which the dark eyes hardly changed from their enigmatic abstraction.

It was curious, he would sit with her by the hour, without ever making her self-conscious, or sex-conscious. He seemed to have no sex, as he sat there so still and gentle and apparently submissive, with his head bent a little forward, and the river of glistening black hair streaming maidenly over his shoulders.

Yet when she looked again, she saw his shoulders broad and powerful, his eyebrows black and level, the short, curved, obstinate black lashes over his lowered eyes, the small, fur-like line of moustache above his blackish, heavy lips, and the strong chin, and she knew that in some other mysterious way he was darkly and powerfully male. And he, feeling her watching him, would glance up at her swiftly with a dark, lurking look in his eyes, which immediately he veiled with that half-sad smile.

The days and the weeks went by, in a vague kind of contentment. She was uneasy sometimes, feeling she had lost the power over herself. She was not in her own power, she was under the spell of some other control. And at times she had moments of terror and horror. But then these Indians would come and sit with her, casting their insidious spell over her by their very silent presence, their silent, sexless, powerful physical presence. As they sat they seemed to take her will away, leaving her will-less and victim of her own indifference. And the young man would bring her sweetened drink, often the same emetic drink, but sometimes other kinds. And after drinking, the languor filled her heavy limbs, her senses seemed to float in the air, listening, hearing. They had brought her a little female dog, which she called Flora. And once, in the trance of her senses, she felt she *heard* the little dog conceive, in her tiny womb, and begin to be complex, with young. And another day she could hear the vast sound of the earth going round, like some immense arrow-string booming.

But as the days grew shorter and colder, when she was cold, she would get a sudden revival of her will, and a desire to go out, to go away. And she insisted to the young man, she wanted to go out.

So one day, they let her climb to the topmost roof of the big house where she was, and look down the square. It was the day of the big dance, but not everybody was dancing. Women with babies in their arms stood in their doorways, watching. Opposite, at the other end of the square, there was a throng before the other big house, and a small, brilliant group on the terrace-roof of the first storey, in front of wide-open doors of the upper storey. Through these wide-open doors she could see fire glinting in darkness and priests in headdresses of black and yellow and scarlet feathers, wearing robe-like blankets of black and red and yellow, with long green fringe, were moving about. A big drum was beating slowly and regularly, in the dense, Indian silence. The crowd below waited –

Then a drum started on a high beat, and there came the deep, powerful burst of men singing a heavy, savage music, like a wind roaring in some timeless forest, many mature men singing in one breath, like the wind; and long lines of dancers walked out from under the big house. Men with naked, golden-bronze bodies and streaming black hair, tufts of red and yellow feathers on their arms, and kilts of white frieze with a bar of heavy red and black and green embroidery round their waists, bending slightly forward and stamping the earth in their absorbed, monotonous stamp of the dance, a fox-fur, hung by the nose from their belt behind, swaying with the sumptuous swaying of a beautiful fox-fur, the tip of the tail writhing above the dancer's heels. And after each man, a woman with a strange elaborate headdress of feathers and seashells, and wearing a short black tunic, moving erect, holding up tufts of feathers in each hand, swaying her wrists rhythmically and subtly beating the earth with her bare feet.

So, the long line of the dance unfurling from the big house opposite. And from the big house beneath her, strange scent of incense, strange tense silence, then the answering burts of in-human male singing, and the long line of the dance unfurling.

It went on all day, the insistence of the drum, the cavernous, roaring, storm-like sound of male singing, the incessant swinging of the fox-skins behind the powerful, gold-bronze stamping legs of the men, the autumn sun from a perfect blue heaven pouring on the rivers of black hair, men's and women's, the valley all still, the walls of rock beyond, the awful huge bulking of the mountain against the pure sky, its snow seething with sheer whiteness.

For hours and hours she watched, spell-bound, and as if drugged. And in all the terrible persistence of the drumming and the primeval, rushing deep singing, and the endless stamping of the dance of fox-tailed men, the tread of heavy, bird-erect women in their black tunics, she seemed at last to feel her own death; her own obliteration. As if she were to be obliterated from the field of life again. In the strange towering symbols on the heads of the changeless, absorbed women she seemed to read once more the *Mene Mene Tekel Upharsin*. Her kind of womanhood, intensely personal and individual, was to be obliterated again, and the great primeval symbols were to tower once more over the fallen individual independence of woman. The sharpness and the quivering nervous consciousness of the highly-bred white woman was to be destroyed again, woman-hood was to be cast once more into the great stream of impersonal sex and impersonal passion. Strangely, as if clair-voyant, she saw the immense sacrifice prepared. And she went back to her little house in a trance of agony.

After this, there was always a certain agony when she heard the drums at evening, and the strange uplifted savage sound of men singing round the drum, like wild creatures howling to the invisible gods of the moon and the vanished sun. Something of the chuckling, sobbing cry of the coyote, something of the exultant bark of the fox, the far-off wild melancholy exultance of the howling wolf, the torment of the puma's scream, and the insistence of the ancient fierce human male, with his lapses of tenderness and his abiding ferocity.

Sometimes she would climb the high roof after nightfall, and listen to the dim cluster of young men round the drum on the bridge just beyond the square, singing by the hour. Sometimes there would be a fire, and in the fire-glow, men in their white shirts or naked save for a loin-cloth, would be dancing and stamping like spectres, hour after hour in the dark cold air, within the fire-glow, for ever dancing and stamping like turkeys, or dropping squatting by the fire to rest throwing their blankets round them.

'Why do you all have the same colours?' she asked the young Indian. 'Why do you all have red and yellow and black, over your white shirts? And the women have black tunics?'

He looked into her eyes, curiously, and the faint, evasive smile came on to his face. Behind the smile lay a soft, strange malignancy.

'Because our men are the fire and the daytime, and our women are the spaces between the stars at night,' he said.

'Aren't the women even stars?' she said.

'No. We say they are the spaces between the stars, that keep the stars apart.'

He looked at her oddly, and again the touch of derision came into his eyes.

'White people,' he said, 'they know nothing. They are like children, always with toys. We know the sun, and we know the moon. And we say, when a white woman sacrifice herself to our gods, then our gods will begin to make the world again, and the white man's gods will fall to pieces.'

'How sacrifice herself?' she asked quickly.

And he, as quickly covered, covered himself with a subtle smile.

'She sacrifice her own gods and come to our gods, I mean that,' he said, soothingly.

But she was not reassured. An icy pang of fear and certainty was at her heart.

'The sun he is alive at one end of the sky,' he continued, 'and the moon lives at the other end. And the man all the time have to keep the sun happy in his side of the sky, and the woman have to keep the moon quiet at her side of the sky. All the time she have to work at this. And the sun can't ever go into the house of the moon, and the moon can't ever go into the house of the sun, in the sky. So woman, she asks the moon to come into her cave, inside her. And the man, he draws the sun down till he has the power of the sun. All the time he do this. Then when the man gets a woman, the sun goes into the cave of the moon, and that is how everything in the world starts.'

She listened, watching him closely, as one enemy watches another who is speaking with double meaning.

'Then,' she said, 'why aren't you Indians masters of the white men?'

'Because,' he said, 'the Indian got weak, and lost his power with the sun, so the white men stole the sun. But they can't keep him – they don't know how. They got him, but they don't know what to do with him, like a boy who catch a big grizzly bear, and can't kill him, and can't run away from him. The grizzly bear eats the boy that catch him, when he want to run away from him. White men don't know what they are doing with the sun, and white women don't know what they do with the moon. The moon she got angry with white women, like a puma when someone kills her little ones. The moon, she bites white women – here inside,' and he pressed his side. 'The moon, she is angry in a white woman's cave. The Indian can see it – and soon,' he added, 'the Indian women get the moon back and keep her quiet in their house. And the Indian men get the sun, and the power over all the world. White men don't know what the sun is. They never know.'

He subsided into a curious exultant silence.

'But,' she faltered, 'why do you hate us so? Why do you hate me?'

He looked up suddenly with a light on his face, and a startling flame of a smile.

'No, we don't hate,' he said softly, looking with a curious glitter into her face.

'You do,' she said, forlorn and hopeless.

And after a moment's silence, he rose and went away.

3

Winter had now come, in the high valley, with snow that melted in the day's sun, and nights that were bitter cold. She lived on, in a kind of daze, feeling her power ebbing more and more away from her, as if her will were leaving her. She felt always in the same relaxed, confused, victimized state, unless the sweetened herb drink would numb her mind altogether, and release her senses into a sort of heightened, mystic acuteness and a feeling as if she were diffusing out deliciously into the harmony of things. This at length became the only state of consciousness she really recognized : this exquisite sense of bleeding out into the higher beauty and harmony of things. Then she could actually hear the great stars in heaven, which she saw through her door, speaking from their motion and brightness, saying things perfectly to the cosmos, as they trod in perfect ripples, like bells on the floor of heaven, passing one another and grouping in the timeless dance, with the spaces of dark between. And she could hear the snow on a cold, cloudy day twittering and faintly whistling in the sky, like birds that flock and fly away in autumn, suddenly calling farewell to the invisible moon, and slipping out of the plains of the air, releasing peaceful warmth. She herself would call to the arrested snow to fall from the upper air. She would call to the unseen moon to cease to be angry, to make peace again with the unseen sun like a woman who ceases to be angry in her house. And she would smell the sweetness of the moon relaxing to the sun in the wintry heaven, when the snow fell in a faint, cold-perfumed relaxation, as the peace of the sun mingled again in a sort of unison with the peace of the moon.

She was aware, too, of the sort of shadow that was on the Indians of the valley, a deep, stoical disconsolation, almost religious in its depth.

'We have lost our power over the sun, and we are trying to get him back. But he is wild with us, and shy like a horse that has got away. We have to go through a lot.' So the young Indian said to her, looking into her eyes with a strained meaning. And she, as if bewitched, replied :

'I hope you will get him back.'

The smile of triumph flew over his face.

'Do you hope it?' he said.

'I do,' she answered fatally.

'Then all right,' he said. 'We shall get him.'

And he went away in exultance.

She felt she was drifting on some consummation, which she had no will to avoid, yet which seemed heavy and finally terrible to her.

It must have been almost December, for the days were short, when she was taken again before the aged man, and stripped of her clothing, and touched with the old finger tips.

The aged cacique looked her in the eyes, with his eyes of lonely, far-off, black intentness, and murmured something to her. 'He wants you to make the sign of peace,' the young man translated, showing her the gesture. 'Peace and farewell to him.'

She was fascinated by the black, glass-like, intent eyes of the old cacique, that watched her without blinking, like a basilisk's, overpowering her. In their depths also she saw a certain fatherly compassion, and pleading. She put her hand before her face, in the required manner, making the sign of peace and farewell. He made the sign of peace back again to her, then sank among his furs. She thought he was going to die, and that he knew it.

There followed a day of ceremonial, when she was brought out before all the people, in a blue blanket with white fringe, and holding blue feathers in her hands. Before an altar of one house, she was perfumed with incense and sprinkled with ash. Below the altar of the opposite house she was fumigated again with incense by the gorgeous, terrifying priests in yellow and scarlet and black, their faces painted with scarlet paint. And then they threw water on her. Meanwhile she was faintly aware of the fire on the altar, the heavy, heavy sound of a drum, the heavy sound of men beginning powerfully, deeply, savagely to sing, the swaying of the crowd of faces in the plaza below, and the formation for a sacred dance.

But at this time her commonplace consciousness was numb, she was aware of her immediate surroundings as shadows, almost immaterial. With refined and heightened senses she could hear the sound of the earth winging on its journey, like a shot arrow, the ripple-rustling of the air, and the boom of the great arrow-string. And it seemed to her there were two great influences in the upper air, one golden towards the sun, and one invisible silver; the first travelling like rain ascending to the gold presence sunwards, the second like rain silverily descending the ladders of space towards the hovering, lurking clouds over the snowy mountain-top. Then between them, another presence, waiting to shake himself free of moisture, of heavy white snow that had mysteriously collected about him. And in summer, like a scorched eagle, he would wait to shake himself clear of the weight of heavy sunbeams. And he was coloured like fire. And he was always shaking himself clear, of snow or of heavy heat, like an eagle rustling.

Then there was a still stranger presence, standing watching from the blue distance, always watching. Sometimes running in upon the wind, or shimmering in the heat-waves. The blue wind itself, rushing as it were out of the holes in the earth into the sky, rushing out of the sky down upon the earth. The blue wind, the go-between, the invisible ghost that belonged to two worlds, that played upon the ascending and the descending chords of the rains.

More and more her ordinary personal consciousness had left her, she had gone into that other state of passional cosmic consciousness, like one who is drugged. The Indians, with their heavily religious natures, had made her succumb to their vision.

Only one personal question she asked the young Indian:

'Why am I the only one that wears blue?'

'It is the colour of the wind. It is the colour of what goes away and is never coming back, but which is always here, waiting like death among us. It is the colour of the dead. And it is the colour that stands away off, looking at us from the distance, that cannot come near to us. When we go near, it goes farther. It can't be near. We are all brown and yellow and black hair, and white teeth and red blood. We are the ones that are here. You with blue eyes, you are the messengers from the far-away, you cannot stay, and now it is time for you to go back.'

'Where to?' she asked.

'To the way-off things like the sun and the blue mother of rain, and tell them that we are the people on the world again, and we can bring the sun to the moon again, like a red horse to a blue mare; we are the people. The white women have driven back the moon in the sky, won't let her come to the sun. So the sun is angry. And the Indian must give the moon to the sun.'

'How?' she said.

'The white woman got to die and go like a wind to the sun,

tell him the Indians will open the gate to him. And the Indian women will open the gate to the moon. The white women don't let the moon come down out of the blue corral. The moon used to come down among the Indian women, like a white goat among the flowers. And the sun want to come down to the Indian men, like an eagle to the pine-trees. The sun he is shut out behind the white man, and the moon she is shut out behind the white woman, and they can't get away. They are angry, everything in the world gets angrier. The Indian says, he will give the white woman to the sun, so the sun will leap over the white man and come to the Indian again. And the moon will be surprised, she will see the gate open, and she not know which way to go. But the Indian woman will call to the moon, *Come! Come! Come back into my grasslands. The wicked white woman can't harm you any more.* Then the sun will look over the heads of the white men, and see the moon in the pastures of our women, with the Red Men standing around like pine-trees. Then he will leap over the heads of the white men, and come running past to the Indians through the spruce trees. And we, who are red and black and yellow, we who stay, we shall have the sun on our right hand and the moon on our left. So we can bring the rain down out of the blue meadows, and up out of the black; and we can call the wind that tells the corn to grow, when we ask him, and we shall make the clouds to break, and the sheep to have twin lambs. And we shall be full of power, like a spring day. But the white people will be a hard winter, without snow –'

'But,' said the white woman, 'I don't shut out the moon – how can I?'

'Yes,' he said, 'you shut the gate, and then laugh, think you have it all your own way.'

She could never quite understand the way he looked at her. He was always so curiously gentle, and his smile was so soft. Yet there was such a glitter in his eyes, and an unrelenting sort of hate came out of his words, a strange, profound, impersonal hate. Personally he liked her, she was sure. He was gentle with her, attracted by her in some strange, soft, passionless way. But impersonally he hated her with a mystic hatred. He would smile at her, winningly. Yet if, the next moment, she glanced round at him unawares, she would catch that gleam of pure after-hate in his eyes.

'Have I got to die and be given to the sun?' she asked.

'Sometime,' he said, laughing evasively. 'Sometime we all die.'

They were gentle with her, and very considerate with her. Strange men, the old priests and the young cacique alike, they watched over her and cared for her like women. In their soft, insidious understanding, there was something womanly. Yet their eyes, with that strange glitter, and their dark, shut mouths that would open to the broad jaw, the small, strong, white teeth, had something very primitively male and cruel.

One wintry day, when snow was falling, they took her to a great dark chamber in the big house. The fire was burning in a corner on a high raised dais under a sort of hood or canopy of adobe-work. She saw in the fire-glow, the glowing bodies of the almost naked priests, and strange symbols on the roof and walls of the chamber. There was no door or window in the chamber, they had descended by a ladder from the roof. And the fire of pinewood danced continually, showing walls painted with strange devices, which she could not understand, and a ceiling of poles making a curious pattern of black and red and yellow, and alcoves or niches in which were curious objects she could not discern.

The older priests were going through some ceremony near the fire, in silence, intense Indian silence. She was seated on a low projection of the wall, opposite the fire, two men seated beside her. Presently they gave her a drink from a cup, which she took gladly, because of the semi-trance it would induce.

In the darkness and in the silence she was accurately aware of everything that happened to her: how they took off her clothes, and, standing before a great, weird device on the wall, coloured blue and white and black, washed her all over with water and the amole infusion; washed even her hair, softly, carefully, and dried it on white cloths, till it was soft and glistening. Then they laid her on a couch under another great indecipherable image of red and black and yellow, and now rubbed all her body with sweet-scented oil, and massaged all her limbs, and her back, and her sides, with a long, strange, hypnotic massage. Their dark hands were incredibly powerful, yet soft with a watery softness she could not understand. And the dark faces, leaning near her white body, she saw were darkened with red pigment, with lines of yellow round the cheeks. And the dark eyes glittered absorbed, as the hands worked upon the soft white body of the woman.

They were so impersonal, absorbed in something that was beyond her. They never saw her as a personal woman : she could tell that. She was some mystic object to them, some vehicle of passions too remote for her to grasp. Herself in a state of trance, she watched their faces bending over her, dark, strangely glistening with the transparent red paint, and lined with bars of yellow. And in this weird, luminous-dark mask of living face, the eyes were fixed with an unchanging steadfast gleam, and the purplish-pigmented lips were closed in a full, sinister, sad grimness. The immense fundamental sadness, the grimness of ultimate decision, the fixity of revenge, and the nascent exultance of those that are going to triumph – these things she could read in their faces, as she lay and was rubbed into a misty glow, by their uncanny dark hands. Her limbs, her flesh, her very bones at last seemed to be diffusing into a roseate sort of mist, in which her consciousness hovered like some sun-gleam in a flushed cloud.

She knew the gleam would fade, the cloud would go grey. But at present she did not believe it. She knew she was a victim; that all this elaborate work upon her was the work of victimizing her. But she did not mind. She wanted it.

Later, they put a short blue tunic on her and took her to the upper terrace, and presented her to the people. She saw the plaza below her full of dark faces and of glittering eyes. There was no pity : only the curious hard exultance. The people gave a subdued cry when they saw her, and she shuddered. But she hardly cared.

Next day was the last. She slept in a chamber of the big house. At dawn they put on her a big blue blanket with a fringe, and led her out into the plaza, among the throng of silent, dark-blanketed people. There was pure white snow on the ground, and the dark people in their dark-brown blankets looked like inhabitants of another world.

A large drum was slowly pounding, and an old priest was declaiming from a housetop. But it was not till noon that a litter came forth, and the people gave that low, animal cry which was so moving. In the sack-like litter sat the old, old cacique, his white hair braided with black braid and large turquoise stones. His face was like a piece of obsidian. He lifted his hand in token, and the litter stopped in front of her. Fixing her with his old eyes, he spoke to her for a few moments, in his hollow voice. No one translated.

Another litter came, and she was placed in it. Four priests moved ahead, in their scarlet and yellow and black, with plumed headdresses. Then came the litter of the old cacique. Then the light drums began, and two groups of singers burst simultaneously into song, male and wild. And the golden-red, almost naked men, adorned with ceremonial feathers and kilts, the rivers of black hair down their backs, formed into two files and began to tread the dance. So they threaded out of the snowy plaza, in two long, sumptuous lines of dark red-gold and black and fur, swaying with a faint tinkle of bits of shell and flint, winding over the snow between the two bee-clusters of men who sang around the drum.

Slowly they moved out, and her litter, with its attendance of feathered, lurid, dancing priests, moved after. Everybody danced the tread of the dance-step, even, subtly, the litter-bearers. And out of the plaza they went, past smoking ovens, on the trail to the great cotton-wood trees, that stood like grey-silver lace against the blue sky, bare and exquisite above the snow. The river, diminished, rushed among fangs of ice. The chequer-squares of gardens within fences were all snowy, and the white houses now looked yellowish.

The whole valley glittered intolerably with pure snow, away to the walls of the standing rock. And across the flat cradle of snow-bed wound the long thread of the dance, shaking slowly and sumptuously in its orange and black motion. The high drums thudded quickly, and on the crystalline frozen air the swell and roar of the chant of savages was like an obsession.

She sat looking out of her litter with big, transfixed blue eyes, under which were the wan markings of her drugged weariness. She knew she was going to die, among the glisten of this snow, at the hands of this savage, sumptuous people. And as she stared at the blaze of blue sky above the slashed and ponderous mountain, she thought: 'I am dead already. What difference does it make, the transition from the dead I am to the dead I shall be, very soon!' Yet her soul sickened and felt wan.

The strange procession trailed on, in perpetual dance, slowly across the plain of snow, and then entered the slopes between the pine-trees. She saw the copper-dark men dancing the dance-tread, onwards, between the copper-pale tree trunks. And at last she, too, in her swaying litter, entered the pine-trees.

They were travelling on and on, upwards, across the snow under the trees, past the superb shafts of pale, flaked copper, the rustle and shake and tread of the threading dance, penetrating into the forest, into the mountain. They were following a stream-bed: but the stream was dry, like summer, dried up by the frozenness of the head-waters. There were dark, red-bronze willow bushes with wattles like wild hair, and pallid aspen trees looking like cold flesh against the snow. Then jutting dark rocks.

At last she could tell that the dancers were moving forward no more. Nearer and nearer she came upon the drums, as to a lair of mysterious animals. Then through the bushes she emerged into a strange amphitheatre. Facing was a great wall of hollow rock, down the front of which hung a great, dripping, fang-like spoke of ice. The ice came pouring over the rock from the precipice above, and then stood arrested, dripping out of high heaven, almost down to the hollow stones where the stream-pool should be below. But the pool was dry.

On either side of the dry pool, the lines of dancers had formed, and the dance was continuing without intermission, against a background of bushes.

But what she felt was that fanged inverted pinnacle of ice, hanging from the lip of the dark precipice above. And behind the great rope of ice, she saw the leopard-like figures of priests climbing the hollow cliff face, to the cave that like a dark socket bored a cavity, an orifice, half-way up the crag.

Before she could realize, her little bearers were staggering in the footholds, climbing the rock. She, too, was behind the ice. There it hung, like a curtain that is not spread, but hangs like a great fang. And near above her was the orifice of the cave sinking dark into the rock. She watched it as she swayed upwards.

On the platform of the cave stood the priests, waiting in all their gorgeousness of feathers and fringed robes, watching her ascent. Two of them stooped to help her litter-bearers. And at length she was on the platform of the cave, far in behind the shaft of ice, above the hollow amphitheatre among the bushes below, where men were dancing, and the whole population of the village was clustered in silence.

The sun was sloping down the afternoon sky, on the left. She knew that this was the shortest day of the year, and the last day of her life. They stood her facing the iridescent column of ice, which fell down marvellously arrested, away in front of her.

Some signal was given, and the dance below stopped. There was now absolute silence. She was given a little to drink, then two priests took off her mantle and her tunic, and in her strange pallor she stood there, between the lurid robes of the priests, beyond the pillar of ice, beyond and above the dark-faced people. The throng below gave a low, wild cry. Then the priests turned her round, so she stood with her back to the open world, her long blonde hair to the people below. And they cried again.

She was facing the cave, inwards. A fire was burning and flickering in the depths. Four priests had taken off their robes, and were almost as naked as she was. They were powerful men in the prime of life, and they kept their dark, painted faces lowered.

From the fire came the old, old priest, with an incense-pan. He was naked and in a state of barbaric ecstasy. He fumigated his victim, reciting at the same time in a hollow voice. Behind him came another robeless priest, with two flint knives.

When she was fumigated, they laid her on a large flat stone, the four powerful men holding her by the outstretched arms and legs. Behind stood the aged man, like a skeleton covered with dark glass, holding a knife and transfixedly watching the sun; and behind him again was another naked priest, with a knife.

She felt little sensation, though she knew all that was happening. Turning to the sky, she looked at the yellow sun. It was sinking. The shaft of ice was like a shadow between her and it.

And she realized that the yellow rays were filling half the cave, though they had not reached the altar where the fire was, at the far end of the funnel-shaped cavity.

Yes, the rays were creeping round slowly. As they grew ruddier, they penetrated farther. When the red sun was about to sink, he would shine full through the shaft of ice deep into the hollow of the cave, to the innermost.

She understood now that this was what the men were waiting for. Even those that held her down were bent and twisted round, their black eyes watching the sun with a glittering eagerness, and awe, and craving. The black eyes of the aged cacique were fixed like black mirrors on the sun, as if sightless, yet containing some terrible answer to the reddening winter planet. And all the eyes of the priests were fixed and glittering on the sinking orb, in the reddening, icy silence of the winter afternoon.

They were anxious, terribly anxious, and fierce. Their ferocity wanted something, and they were waiting the moment. And their ferocity was ready to leap out into a mystic exultance, of triumph. But still they were anxious.

Only the eyes of that oldest man were not anxious. Black, and fixed, and as if sightless, they watched the sun, seeing beyond the sun. And in their black, empty concentration there was power, power intensely abstract and remote, but deep, deep to the heart of the earth, and the heart of the sun. In absolute motionlessness he watched till the red sun should send his ray through the column of ice. Then the old man would strike, and strike home, accomplish the sacrifice and achieve power.

The mastery that man must hold, and that passes from race to race.

Smile

HE had decided to sit up all night, as a kind of penance. The telegram had simply said: 'Ophelia's condition critical.' He felt, under the circumstances, that to go to bed in the *wagon-lit* would be frivolous. So he sat wearily in the first-class compartment as night fell over France.

He ought, of course, to be sitting by Ophelia's bedside. But Ophelia didn't want him. So he sat up in the train.

Deep inside him was a black and ponderous weight: like some tumour filled with sheer gloom, weighing down his vitals. He had always taken life seriously. Seriousness now overwhelmed him. His dark, handsome, clean-shaven face would have done for Christ on the Cross, with the thick black eyebrows tilted in the dazed agony.

The night in the train was like an inferno: nothing was real. Two elderly Englishwomen opposite him had died long ago, perhaps even before he had. Because, of course, he was dead himself.

Slow, grey dawn came in the mountains of the frontier, and he watched it with unseeing eyes. But his mind repeated:

> And when the dawn came, dim and sad
> And chill with early showers,
> Her quiet eyelids closed: she had
> Another morn than ours.

And his monk's changeless, tormented face showed no trace of the contempt he felt, even self-contempt, for this bathos, as his critical mind judged it.

He was in Italy: he looked at the country with faint aversion. Not capable of much feeling any more, he had only a tinge of aversion as he saw the olives and the sea. A sort of poetic swindle.

It was night again when he reached the home of the Blue Sisters, where Ophelia had chosen to retreat. He was ushered into the Mother Superior's room, in the palace. She rose and bowed to him in silence, looking at him along her nose. Then she said in French:

'It pains me to tell you. She died this afternoon.'

He stood stupefied, not feeling much, anyhow, but gazing at nothingness from his handsome, strong-featured monk's face.

The Mother Superior softly put her white, handsome hand on his arm and gazed up into his face, leaning to him.

'Courage!' she said softly. 'Courage, no?'

He stepped back. He was always scared when a woman leaned at him like that. In her voluminous skirts, the Mother Superior was very womanly.

'Quite!' he replied in English. 'Can I see her?'

The Mother Superior rang a bell, and a young sister appeared. She was rather pale, but there was something naïve and mischievous in her hazel eyes. The elder woman murmured an introduction, the young woman demurely made a slight reverence. But Matthew held out his hand, like a man reaching for the last straw. The young nun unfolded her white hands and shyly slid one into his, passive as a sleeping bird.

And out of the fathomless Hades of his gloom, he thought: What a nice hand!

They went along a handsome but cold corridor, and tapped at a door. Matthew, walking in far-off Hades, still was aware of the soft, fine voluminousness of the women's black skirts, moving with soft, fluttered haste in front of him.

He was terrified when the door opened, and he saw the candles burning round the white bed, in the lofty, noble room. A sister sat beside the candles, her face dark and primitive, in the white coif, as she looked up from her breviary. Then she rose, a sturdy woman, and made a little bow, and Matthew was aware of creamy-dusky hands twisting a black rosary, against the rich, blue silk on her bosom.

The three sisters flocked silent, yet fluttered and very feminine, in their volumes of silky black skirts, to the bedhead. The Mother Superior leaned, and with utmost delicacy lifted the veil of white lawn from the dead face.

Matthew saw the dead, beautiful composure of his wife's face, and instantly, something leaped like laughter in the depths of him, he gave a little grunt, and an extraordinary smile came over his face.

The three nuns, in the candle glow that quivered warm and quick like a Christmas tree, were looking at him with heavily compassionate eyes, from under their coif-bands. They were like a mirror. Six eyes suddenly started with a little fear, then changed, puzzled, into wonder. And over the three nuns' faces, helplessly facing him in the candle-glow, a strange, involuntary smile began to come. In the three faces, the same smile growing so differently, like three subtle flowers opening. In the pale young nun, it was almost pain, with a touch of mischievous ecstasy. But the dark Ligurian face of the watching sister, a mature, level-browed woman, curled with a pagan smile, slow, infinitely subtle in its archaic humour. It was the Etruscan smile, subtle and unabashed, and unanswerable.

The Mother Superior, who had a large-featured face something like Matthew's own, tried hard not to smile. But he kept his humorous, malevolent chin uplifted at her, and she lowered her face as the smile grew, grew, and grew over her face.

The young, pale sister suddenly covered her face with her sleeve, her body shaking. The Mother Superior put her arm over the girl's shoulder, murmuring with Italian emotion : 'Poor little thing! Weep, then, poor little thing!' But the chuckle was still there, under the emotion. The sturdy dark sister stood unchanging, clutching the black beads, but the noiseless smile immovable.

Matthew suddenly turned to the bed, to see if his dead wife had observed him. It was a movement of fear.

Ophelia lay so pretty and so touching, with her peaked, dead little nose sticking up, and her face of an obstinate child fixed in the final obstinacy. The smile went away from Matthew, and the look of super-martyrdom took its place. He did not weep : he just gazed without meaning. Only, on his face deepened the look : I knew this martyrdom was in store for me!

She was so pretty, so childlike, so clever, so obstinate, so worn – and so dead ! He felt so blank about it all.

They had been married ten years. He himself had not been perfect – no, no, not by any means ! But Ophelia had always wanted her own will. She had loved him, and grown obstinate, and left him, and grown wistful, or contemptuous, or angry, a dozen times, and a dozen times come back to him.

They had no children. And he, sentimentally, had always wanted children. He felt very largely sad.

Now she would never come back to him. This was the thirteenth time, and she was gone for ever.

But was she? Even as he thought it, he felt her nudging him somewhere in the ribs, to make him smile. He writhed a little, and an angry frown came on his brow. He was not *going* to smile! He set his square, naked jaw, and bared his big teeth, as he looked down at the infinitely provoking dead woman. 'At it again!' – he wanted to say to her, like the man in Dickens.

He himself had not been perfect. He was going to dwell on his own imperfections.

He turned suddenly to the three women, who had faded backwards beyond the candles, and now hovered, in the white frames of their coifs, between him and nowhere. His eyes glared, and he bared his teeth.

'*Mea culpa! Mea culpa!*' he snarled.

'*Macchè!*' exclaimed the daunted Mother Superior, and her two hands flew apart, then together again, in the density of the sleeves, like birds nesting in couples.

Matthew ducked his head and peered round, prepared to bolt. The Mother Superior, in the background, softly intoned a Pater Noster, and her beads dangled. The pale young sister faded farther back. But the black eyes of the sturdy, black-avised sister twinkled like eternally humorous stars upon him, and he felt the smile digging him in the ribs again.

'Look here!' he said to the women, in expostulation, 'I'm awfully upset. I'd better go.'

They hovered in fascinating bewilderment. He ducked for the door. But even as he went, the smile began to come on his face, caught by the tail of the sturdy sister's black eye, with its everlasting twink. And, he was secretly thinking, he wished he could hold both her creamy-dusky hands, that were folded like mating birds, voluptuously.

But he insisted on dwelling upon his own imperfections. *Mea culpa!* he howled at himself. And even as he howled it, he felt something nudge him in the ribs, saying to him: *Smile!*

The three women left behind in the lofty room looked at one another, and their hands flew up for a moment, like six birds flying suddenly out of the foliage, then settling again.

'Poor thing!' said the Mother Superior, compassionately.

'Yes! Yes! Poor thing!' cried the young sister, with naïve, shrill impulsiveness.

'*Già*' said the dark-avised sister.

The Mother Superior noiselessly moved to the bed, and leaned over the dead face.

'She seems to know, poor soul!' she murmured. 'Don't you think so?'

The three coifed heads leaned together. And for the first time they saw the faint ironical curl at the corners of Ophelia's mouth. They looked in fluttering wonder.

'She has seen him!' whispered the thrilling young sister.

The Mother Superior delicately laid the fine-worked veil over the cold face. Then they murmured a prayer for the anima, fingering their beads. Then the Mother Superior set two of the candles straight upon their spikes, clenching the thick candle with firm, soft grip, and pressing it down.

The dark-faced, sturdy sister sat down again with her little holy book. The other two rustled softly to the door, and out into the great white corridor. There, softly, noiselessly sailing in all their dark drapery, like dark swans down a river, they suddenly hesitated. Together they had seen a forlorn man's figure, in a melancholy overcoat, loitering in the cold distance at the corridor's end. The Mother Superior suddenly pressed her pace into an appearance of speed.

Matthew saw them bearing down on him, these voluminous figures with framed faces and lost hands. The young sister trailed a little behind.

'*Pardon, ma Mère!*' he said, as if in the street. 'I left my hat somewhere . . .'

He made a desperate, moving sweep with his arm, and never was man more utterly smileless.

The Border Line

KATHERINE FARQUHAR was a handsome woman of forty, no longer slim, but attractive in her soft, full feminine way. The French porters ran round her, getting a voluptuous pleasure from merely carrying her bags. And she gave them ridiculously high tips, because, in the first place, she had never really known the value of money, and secondly, she had a morbid fear of underpaying anyone, but particularly a man who was eager to serve her.

It was really a joke to her, how eagerly these Frenchmen – all sorts of Frenchmen – ran round her, and *Madamed* her. Their voluptuous obsequiousness. Because, after all, she was Boche. Fifteen years of marriage to an Englishman – or rather to two Englishmen – had not altered her racially. Daughter of a German Baron she was, and remained in her own mind and body, although England had become her life-home. And surely she looked German, with her fresh complexion and her strong, full figure. But, like most people in the world, she was a mixture, with Russian blood and French blood also in her veins. And she had lived in one country and another, till she was somewhat indifferent to her surroundings. So that perhaps the Parisian men might be excused for running round her so eagerly, and getting a voluptuous pleasure from calling a taxi for her, or giving up a place in the omnibus to her, or carrying her bags, or holding the menu card before her. Nevertheless, it amused her. And she had to confess she liked them, these Parisians. They had their own kind of manliness, even if it wasn't an English sort; and if a woman looked pleasant and soft-fleshed, and a wee bit helpless, they were ardent and generous. Katherine understood so well that Frenchmen were rude to the dry, hard-seeming, competent Englishwoman or American. She sympathized with the Frenchman's point of view; too much obvious capacity to help herself is a disagreeable trait in a woman.

At the Gare de l'Est, of course, everybody was expected to be Boche, and it was almost a convention, with the porters, to assume a certain small-boyish superciliousness. Nevertheless, there

was the same voluptuous scramble to escort Katherine Farquhar
to her seat in the first-class carriage. *Madame* was travelling
alone.

She was going to Germany via Strasburg, meeting her sister
in Baden-Baden. Philip, her husband, was in Germany, collecting some sort of evidence for his newspaper. Katherine felt a
little weary of newspapers, and of the sort of 'evidence' that is
extracted out of nowhere to feed them. However, Philip was
quite clever, he was a little somebody in the world.

Her world, she had realized, consisted almost entirely of little
somebodies. She was outside the sphere of the nobodies, always
had been. And the Somebodies with a capital 'S' were all safely
dead. She knew enough of the world today, to know that it is
not going to put up with any great Somebody; but many little
nobodies and a sufficient number of little somebodies. Which,
after all, is as it should be, she felt.

Sometimes she had vague misgivings.

Paris, for example, with its Louvre and it Luxembourg and
its cathedral, seemed intended for Somebody. In a ghostly way it
called for some supreme Somebody. But all its little men, nobodies
and somebodies, were as sparrows twittering for crumbs, and
dropping their little droppings on the palace cornices.

To Katherine, Paris brought back again her first husband,
Alan Anstruther, that red-haired fighting Celt, father of her
two grown-up children. Alan had had a weird innate conviction
that he was beyond ordinary judgement. Katherine could never
quite see where it came in. Son of a Scottish baronet, and cap-
tain in a Highland regiment did not seem to her stupendous. As
for Alan himself, he was handsome in uniform, with his kilt
swinging and his blue eye glaring. Even stark naked and without any trimmings, he had a bony, dauntless, overbearing manliness of his own. The one thing Katherine could *not quite*
appreciate was his silent, indomitable assumption that he was
actually first-born, a born lord. He was a clever man, too, ready
to assume that General This or Colonel That might really be
his superior. Until he actually came into contact with General
This or Colonel That. Whereupon his overweening blue eye
arched in his bony face, and a faint tinge of contempt infused
itself into his homage.

Lordly, or not, he wasn't much of a success in the worldly sense. Katherine had loved him, and he had loved her : that was indisputable. But when it came to innate conviction of lordliness, it was a question which of them was worse. For she, in her amiable, queen-bee self thought that ultimately hers was the right to the last homage.

Alan had been too unyielding and haughty to say much. But sometimes he would stand and look at her in silent rage, wonder and indignation. The wondering indignation had been *almost* too much for her. What did the man think he was?

He was one of the hard, clever Scotsmen, with a philosophic tendency, but without sentimentality. His contempt of Nietzsche, whom she adored, was intolerable. Alan just asserted himself like a pillar of rock, and expected the tides of the modern world to recede around him. They didn't.

So he concerned himself with astronomy, gazing through a telescope and watching the worlds beyond worlds. Which seemed to give him relief.

After ten years they had ceased to live together, passionate as they both were. They were too proud and unforgiving to yield to one another, and much too haughty to yield to any outsider.

Alan had a friend, Philip, also a Scotsman, and a university friend. Philip, trained for the bar, had gone into journalism, and had made himself a name. He was a little black Highlander of the insidious sort, clever, and *knowing*. This look of knowing in his dark eyes, and the feeling of secrecy that went with his dark little body, made him interesting to women. Another thing he could do was to give off a great sense of warmth and offering, like a dog when it loves you. He seemed to be able to do this at will. And Katherine, after feeling cool about him and rather despising him for years, at last fell under the spell of the dark, insidious fellow.

'You!' she said to Alan, whose overweening masterfulness drove her wild. 'You don't even know that a woman exists. And that's where Philip Farquhar is more than you are. He *does* know something of what a woman *is*.'

'Bah! the little –' said Alan, using an obscene word of contempt.

Nevertheless, the friendship endured, kept up by Philip, who had an almost uncanny love for Alan. Alan was mostly indifferent. But he was used to Philip, and habit meant a great deal to him.

'Alan really is an amazing man!' Philip would say to Katherine. 'He is the only real man, what I call a real man, that I have ever met.'

'But why is he the only real man?' she asked. 'Don't you call yourself a real man?'

'Oh, *I* – I'm different! My strength lies in giving in – and then recovering myself. I do let myself be swept away. But, so far, I've always managed to get myself back again. Alan –' and Philip even had a half-reverential, half-envious way of uttering the word – 'Alan *never* lets himself be swept away. And he's the only man I know who doesn't.'

'Yah!' she said. 'He is fooled by plenty of things. You can fool him through his vanity.'

'No,' said Philip. 'Never altogether. You *can't* deceive him right through. When a thing really touches Alan, it is tested once and for all. You know if it's false or not. He's the only man I ever met who *can't help* being real.'

'Ha! You overrate his reality,' said Katherine, rather scornfully.

And later, when Alan shrugged his shoulders with that mere indifferent tolerance, at the mention of Philip, she got angry.

'You are a poor friend,' she said.

'Friend!' he answered. 'I never was Farquhar's friend! If he asserts that he's mine, that's his side of the question. I never positively cared for the man. He's too much over the wrong side of the border for me.'

'Then,' she answered, 'you've no business to let him *consider* he is your friend. You've no right to let him think so much of you. You should tell him you don't like him.'

'I've told him a dozen times. He seems to enjoy it. It seems part of his game.'

And he went away to his astronomy.

Came the war, and the departure of Alan's regiment for France.

'There!' he said. 'Now you have to pay the penalty of having married a soldier. You find him fighting your own people. So it is.'

She was too much struck by this blow even to weep.

'Good-bye!' he said, kissing her gently, lingeringly. After all, he had been a husband to her.

And as he looked back at her, with the gentle, protective husband-knowledge in his blue eyes, and at the same time that other quiet realization of destiny, her consciousness fluttered into incoherence. She only wanted to alter everything, to alter the past, to alter all the flow of history – the terrible flow of history. Secretly somewhere inside herself she felt that with her queen-bee love, and queen-bee will, she *could* divert the whole flow of history – nay, even reverse it.

But in the remote, realizing look that lay at the back of his eyes, back of all his changeless husband-care, she saw that it could never be so. That the whole of her womanly, motherly concentration could never put back the great flow of human destiny. That, as he said, only the cold strength of a man, accepting the destiny of destruction, could see the human flow through the chaos and beyond to a new outlet. But the chaos first, and the long rage of destruction.

For an instant her will broke. Almost her soul seemed broken. And then he was gone. And as soon as he was gone she recovered the core of her assurance.

Philip was a great consolation to her. He asserted that the war was monstrous, that it should never have been, and that men should refuse to consider it as anything but a colossal, disgraceful accident.

She, in her German soul, knew that it was no accident. It was inevitable, and even necessary. But Philip's attitude soothed her enormously, restored her to herself.

Alan never came back. In the spring of 1915 he was missing. She had never mourned for him. She had never really considered him dead. In a certain sense she had triumphed. The queen-bee had recovered her sway, as queen of the earth; the woman, the mother, the female with the ear of corn in her hand, as against the man with the sword.

Philip had gone through the war as a journalist, always throwing his weight on the side of humanity, and human truth and peace. He had been an inexpressible consolation. And in 1921 she had married him.

The thread of fate might be spun, it might even be measured out, but the hand of Lachesis had been stayed from cutting it through.

At first it was wonderfully pleasant and restful and voluptuous, especially for a woman of thirty-eight, to be married to Philip. Katherine felt he caressed her senses, and soothed her, and gave her what she wanted.

Then, gradually, a curious sense of degradation started in her spirit. She felt unsure, uncertain. It was almost like having a disease. Life became dull and unreal to her, as it had never been before. She did not even struggle and suffer. In the numbness of her flesh she could feel no reactions. Everything was turning into mud.

Then again, she would recover, and *enjoy* herself wonderfully. And after a while, the suffocating sense of nullity and degradation once more. Why, why, why did she feel degraded, in her secret soul? *Never*, of course, outwardly.

The memory of Alan came back into her. She still thought of him and his relentlessness with an arrested heart, but without the angry hostility she used to feel. A little awe of him, of his memory, stole back into her spirit. She resisted it. She was not used to feeling awe.

She realized, however, the difference between being married to a soldier, a ceaseless born fighter, a sword not to be sheathed, and this other man, this cunning civilian, this subtle equivocator, this adjuster of the scales of truth.

Philip was cleverer than she was. He set her up, the queen-bee, the mother, the woman, the female judgement, and he served her with subtle, cunning homage. He put the scales, the balance in her hand. But also, cunningly, he blindfolded her, and manipulated the scales when she was sightless.

Dimly she had realized all this. But only dimly, confusedly, because she was blindfolded. Philip had the subtle, fawning power that could keep her always blindfolded.

Sometimes she gasped and gasped from her oppressed lungs. And sometimes the bony, hard, masterful, but honest face of Alan would come back, and suddenly it would seem to her

that she was all right again, that the strange, voluptuous suffo-
cation, which left her soul in mud, was gone, and she could
breathe the air of the open heavens once more. Even fighting
air.

It came to her on the boat crossing the Channel. Suddenly
she seemed to feel Alan at her side again, as if Philip had never
existed. As if Philip had never meant anything more to her than
the shop-assistant measuring off her orders. And escaping, as it
were, by herself across the cold, wintry Channel, she suddenly
deluded herself into feeling as if Philip had never existed, only
Alan had ever been her husband. He was her husband still. And
she was going to meet him.

This gave her her blitheness in Paris, and made the Frenchmen so nice to her. For the Latins love to feel a woman is really
enveloped in the spell of some man. Beyond all race is the
problem of man and woman.

Katherine now sat dimly, vaguely excited and almost happy
in the railway carriage on the East railroad. It was like the old
days when she was going home to Germany. Or even more like
the old days when she was coming back to Alan. Because, in
the past, when he was her husband, feel as she might towards
him, she could never get over the sensation that the wheels of
the railway carriage had wings, when they were taking her back
to him. Even when she knew that he was going to be awful to
her, hard and relentless and destructive, still the motion went on
wings.

Whereas towards Philip she moved with a strange, disintegrating reluctance. She decided not to think of him.

As she looked unseeing out of the carriage window, suddenly, with a jolt, the wintry landscape realized itself in her
consciousness. The flat, grey, wintry landscape, ploughed fields
of greyish earth that looked as if they were compounded of the
clay of dead men. Pallid, stark, thin trees stood like wire beside
straight, abstract roads. A ruined farm between a few more
trees. And a dismal village filed past, with smashed houses like
rotten teeth between the straight rows of the village street.

With sudden horror she realized that she must be in the
Marne country, the ghastly Marne country, century after century digging the corpses of frustrated men into its soil. The

border country, where the Latin races and the Germanic neutralize one another into horrid ash.

Perhaps even the corpse of her own man among that grey clay.

It was too much for her. She sat ashy herself with horror, wanting to escape.

'If I had only known,' she said. 'If only I had known, I would have gone by Basle.'

The train drew up at Soissons; name ghastly to her. She simply tried to make herself unreceptive to everything. And mercifully luncheon was served. She went down to the restaurant car, and sat opposite to a little French officer in horizon-blue uniform, who suggested anything but war. He looked so naïve, rather childlike and nice, with the certain innocence that so many French people preserve under their so-called wickedness, that she felt really relieved. He bowed to her with an odd, shy little bow when she returned him his half-bottle of red wine, which had slowly jigged its way the length of the table, owing to the motion of the train. How nice he was! And how he would give himself to a woman, if she would only find real pleasure in the male that he was.

Nevertheless, she herself felt very remote from this business of male and female, and giving and taking.

After luncheon, in the heat of the train and the flush of her half-bottle of white wine, she went to sleep again, her feet grilling uncomfortably on the iron plate of the carriage floor. And as she slept, life, as she had known it, seemed all to turn artificial to her, the sunshine of the world an artificial light, with smoke above, like the light of torches, and things artificially growing, in a night that was lit up artificially with such intensity that it gave the illusion of day. It had been an illusion, her life-day, as a ballroom evening is an illusion. Her love and her emotions, her very panic of love, had been an illusion. She realized how love had become panic-stricken inside her, during the war.

And now even this panic of love was an illusion. She had run to Philip to be saved. And now, both her panic-love and Philip's salvation were an illusion.

What remained then? Even panic-stricken love, the intensest

thing, perhaps, she had ever felt, was only an illusion. What was left? The grey shadows of death?

When she looked out again it was growing dark, and they were at Nancy. She used to know this country as a girl. At half-past seven she was in Strasburg, where she must stay the night as there was no train over the Rhine till morning.

The porter, a blond, hefty fellow, addressed her at once in Alsatian German. He insisted on escorting her safely to her hotel – a German hotel – keeping guard over her like an appointed sentinel, very faithful and competent, so different from Frenchmen.

It was a cold, wintry night, but she wanted to go out after dinner to see the minster. She remembered it all so well, in that other life.

The wind blew icily in the street. The town seemed empty, as if its spirit had left it. The few squat, hefty foot-passengers were all talking the harsh Alsatian German. Shop-signs were in French, often with a little concession to German underneath. And the shops were full of goods, glutted with goods from the once-German factories of Mulhausen and other cities.

She crossed the night-dark river, where the wash-houses of the washerwomen were anchored along the stream, a few odd women still kneeling over the water's edge, in the dim electric light, rinsing their clothes in the grim, cold water. In the big square the icy wind was blowing, and the place seemed a desert. A city once more conquered.

After all she could not remember her way to the cathedral. She saw a French policeman in his blue cape and peaked cap, looking a lonely, vulnerable, silky specimen in this harsh Alsatian city. Crossing over to him she asked him in French where was the cathedral.

He pointed out to her, the first turning on the left. He did not seem hostile; nobody seemed really hostile. Only the great frozen weariness of winter in a conquered city, on a weary everlasting border line.

And the Frenchmen seemed far more weary, and also more sensitive than the crude Alsations.

She remembered the little street, the old, overhanging houses with black timbers and high gables. And like a great ghost, a reddish flush in its darkness, the uncanny cathedral breasting the oncomer, standing gigantic, looking down in darkness out of darkness, on the pigmy humanness of the city. It was built of reddish stone, that had a flush in the night, like dark flesh. And vast, an incomprehensibly tall, strange thing, it looked down out of the night. The great rose window, poised high, seemed like a breast of the vast Thing, and prisms and needles of stone shot up, as if it were plumage, dimly, half-visible in heaven.

There it was, in the upper darkness of the ponderous winter night, like a menace. She remembered, her spirit used in the past to soar aloft with it. But now, looming with a faint rust of blood out of the upper black heavens, the Thing stood suspended, looking down with vast, demonish menace, calm and implacable.

Mystery and dim, ancient fear came over the woman's soul. The cathedral looked so strange and demonish-heathen. And an ancient, indomitable blood seemed to stir in it. It stood there like some vast silent beast with teeth of stone, waiting, and wondering when to stoop against this pallid humanity.

And dimly she realized that behind all the ashy pallor and sulphur of our civilization, lurks the great blood-creature waiting, implacable and eternal, ready at last to crush our white brittleness and let the shadowy blood move erect once more, in a new implacable pride and strength. Even out of the lower heavens looms the great blood-dusky Thing, blotting out the Cross it was supposed to exalt.

The scroll of the night sky seemed to roll back, showing a huge, blood-dusky presence looming enormous, stooping, looking down, awaiting its moment.

As she turned to go away, to move away from the closed wings of the minster, she noticed a man standing on the pavement, in the direction of the post-office which functions obscurely in the Cathedral Square. Immediately, she knew that that man, standing dark and motionless, was Alan. He was alone, motionless, remote.

He did not move towards her. She hesitated, then went in his direction, as if going to the post-office. He stood perfectly motionless, and her heart died as she drew near. Then, as she passed, he turned suddenly, looking down on her.

It was he, though she could hardly see his face, it was so dark, with a dusky glow in the shadow.

'Alan!' she said.

He did not speak, but laid his hand detainingly on her arm, as he used in the early days, with strange silent authority. And turning her with a faint pressure on her arm, he went along with her, leisurely, through the main street of the city, under the arcade where the shops were still lighted up.

She glanced at his face; it seemed much more dusky, and duskily ruddy, than she had known him. He was a stranger: and yet it was he, no other. He said nothing at all. But that was also in keeping. His mouth was closed, his watchful eyes seemed changeless, and there was a shadow of silence around him, impenetrable, but not cold. Rather aloof and gentle, like the silence that surrounds a wild animal.

She knew that she was walking with his spirit. But that even did not trouble her. It seemed natural. And there came over her again the feeling she had forgotten, the restful, thoughtless pleasure of a woman who moves in the aura of the man to whom she belongs. As a young woman she had had this unremarkable, yet very precious feeling, when she was with her husband. It had been a full contentment; and perhaps the fullness of it had made her unconscious of it. Later, it seemed to her she had almost wilfully destroyed it, this soft flow of contentment which she, a woman, had from him as a man.

Now, afterwards, she realized it. And as she walked at his side through the conquered city, she realized that it was the one enduring thing a woman can have, the intangible soft flood of contentment that carries her along at the side of the man she is married to. It is her perfection and her highest attainment.

Now, in the afterwards, she knew it. Now the strife was gone. And dimly she wondered why, why, why she had ever fought against it. No matter what the man does or is, as a person, if a woman can move at his side in this dim, full flood of contentment, she has the highest of him, and her scratching efforts at getting more than this are her ignominious efforts at self-nullity.

Now, she knew it, and she submitted. Now that she was walking with a man who came from the halls of death, to her, for her relief. The strong, silent kindliness of him towards her, even now, was able to wipe out the ashy, nervous horror of the world from her body. She went at his side, still and released, like one newly unbound, walking in the dimness of her own contentment.

At the bridge-head he came to a standstill, and drew his hand from her arm. She knew he was going to leave her. But he looked at her from under his peaked cap, darkly but kindly, and he waved his hand with a slight, kindly gesture of farewell, and of promise, as if in farewell he promised never to leave her, never to let the kindliness go out in his heart, to let it stay here always.

She hurried over the bridge with tears running down her cheeks, and on to her hotel. Hastily she climbed to her room. And as she undressed, she avoided the sight of her own face in the mirror. She must not rupture the spell of his presence.

Now, in the afterwards she realized *how* careful she must be, not to break the mystery that enveloped her. Now that she knew he had come back to her from the dead, she was aware how precious and how fragile the coming was. He had come back with his heart dark and kind, wanting her even in the afterwards. And not in any sense must she go against him. The warm, powerful, silent ghost had come back to her. It was he. She must not even try to think about him definitely, not to realize him or to understand. Only in her own woman's soul could she silently ponder him, darkly, and know him present in her, without ever staring at him or trying to find him out. Once she tried to lay hands on him, to *have* him, to *realize* him, he would be gone for ever, and gone for ever this last precious flood of her woman's peace.

'Ah, no!' she said to herself. 'If he leaves his peace with me, I must ask no questions whatsoever.'

And she repented, silently, of the way she had questioned and demanded answers, in the past. What were the answers, when she had got them? Terrible ash in the mouth.

She now knew the supreme modern terror, of a world all ashy and nerve-dead. If a man could come back out of death to save her from this, she would not ask questions of him, but be humble, and beyond tears grateful.

In the morning, she went out into the icy wind, under the

grey sky, to see if he would be there again. Not that she *needed* him : his presence was still about her. But he might be waiting.

The town was stony and cold. The people looked pale, chilled through, and doomed in some way. Very far from her they were. She felt a sort of pity of them, but knew she could do nothing, nothing in time or eternity. And they looked at her, and looked quickly away again, as if they were uneasy in themselves.

The cathedral reared its great reddish-grey façade in the stark light; but it did not loom as in the night. The cathedral square was hard and cold. Inside, the church was cold and repellent, in spite of the glow of stained glass. And he was nowhere to be found.

So she hastened away to her hotel and to the station, to catch the 10.30 train into Germany.

It was a lonely, dismal train, with a few forlorn souls waiting to cross the Rhine. Her Alsatian porter looked after her with the same dogged care as before. She got into the first-class carriage that was going through to Prague – she was the only passenger travelling first. A real French porter, in blouse and moustache, and swagger, tried to say something a bit jeering to her, in his few words of German. But she only looked at him, and he subsided. He didn't really want to be rude. There was a certain hopelessness even about that.

The train crept slowly, disheartened, out of town. She saw the weird humped-up creature of the cathedral in the distance, pointing its one finger above the city. Why, oh, why, had the old Germanic races put it there, like that !

Slowly the country disintegrated into the Rhine flats and marshes, the canals, the willow trees, the overflow streams, the wet places frozen but not flooded. Weary the place all seemed. And old Father Rhine flowing in greenish volume, implacable, separating the races now weary of race struggle, but locked in the toils as in the coils of a great snake, unable to escape. Cold, full, green, and utterly disheartening the river came along under the wintry sky, passing beneath the bridge of iron.

There was a long wait in Kehl, where the German officials and the French observed a numb, dreary kind of neutrality. Passport and customs examination was soon over. But the train waited and waited, as if unable to get away from that point of pure negation, where the two races neutralized one another, and no polarity was felt, no life – no principle dominated.

Katherine Farquhar just sat still, in the suspended silence of her husband's return. She heeded neither French nor German, spoke one language or the other at need, hardly knowing. She waited, while the hot train steamed and hissed, arrested at the perfect neutral point of the new border line, just across the Rhine.

And at last a little sun came out, and the train silently drew away, nervously, from the neutrality.

In the great flat field of the Rhine plain, the shallow flood water was frozen, the furrows ran straight towards nowhere, the air seemed frozen, too, but the earth felt strong and barbaric, it seemed to vibrate, with its straight furrows, in a deep, savage undertone. There was the frozen, savage thrill in the air also, something wild and unsubdued, pre-Roman.

This part of the Rhine valley, even on the right bank in Germany, was occupied by the French; hence the curious vacancy, the suspense, as if no men lived there, but some spirit was watching, watching over the vast, empty, straight furrowed fields and the water meadows. Stillness, emptiness, suspense, and a sense of something still impending.

A long wait in the station of Appenweier, on the main line of the Right-bank railway. The station was empty. Katherine remembered its excited, thrilling bustle in pre-war days.

'Yes,' said the German guard to the station-master, 'what do they hurry us out of Strasburg for, if they are only going to keep us so long here?'

The heavy Badisch German! The sense of resentful impotence in the Germans! Katherine smiled to herself. She realized that here the train left the occupied territory.

At last they set off, northwards, free for the moment, in Germany. It was the land beyond the Rhine, Germany of the pine forests. The very earth seemed strong and unsubdued, bristling with a few reeds and bushes, like savage hair. There was the same silence, and waiting, and the old barbaric undertone of the white-skinned north, under the waning civilization. The audible overtone of our civilization seemed to be wearing thin, the old, low, pine-forest hum and roar of the ancient north seemed to be sounding through. At least, in Katherine's inner ear.

And there were the ponderous hills of the Black Forest, heaped and waiting sullenly, as if guarding the inner Germany. Black round hills, black with forest, save where white snow-patches of field had been cut out. Black and white, waiting there in the near distance, in sullen guard.

She knew the country so well. But not in this present mood, the emptiness, the sullenness, the heavy, recoiled waiting.

Steinbach! Then she was nearly there! She would have to change in Oos, for Baden-Baden, her destination. Probably Philip would be there to meet her, in Oos; he would have come down from Heidelberg.

Yes, there he was! And at once she thought he looked ill, yellowish. His figure hollow and defeated.

'Aren't you well?' she asked, as she stepped out of the train on to the empty station.

'I'm frightfully cold,' he said. 'I can't get warm.'

'And the train was so hot,' she said.

At last a porter came to carry her bags across to the little connecting train.

'How are you?' he said, looking at her with a certain pinched look in his face, and fear in his eyes.

'All right! It all feels very queer,' she said.

'I don't know how it is,' he said, 'but Germany freezes my inside, and does something to my chest.'

'We needn't stay long,' she said easily.

He was watching the bright look in her face. And she was thinking how queer and *chétif* he looked! Extraordinary! As she looked at him she felt for the first time, with curious clarity, that it was humiliating to be married to him, even in name. She was humiliated even by the fact that her name was Katherine Farquhar. Yet she used to think it a nice name!

'Just think of me married to that little man!' she thought to herself. 'Think of my having his name!'

It didn't fit. She thought of her own name: Katherine von Todtnau; or of her married name: Katherine Anstruther. The first seemed most fitting. But the second was her second nature. The third, Katherine Farquhar, wasn't her at all.

'Have you seen Marianne?' she asked.

'Oh, yes!'

He was very brief. What was the matter with him?

'You'll have to be careful, with your cold,' she said politely.

'I *am* careful!' he cried petulantly.

Marianne, her sister, was at the station, and in two minutes they were rattling away in German, and laughing and crying and exploding with laughter again, Philip quite ignored. In these days of frozen economy, there was no taxi. A porter would wheel up the luggage on a trolley, the new arrivals walked to their little hotel, through the half-deserted town.

'But the little one is quite nice!' said Marianne deprecatingly.

'Isn't he!' cried Katherine in the same tone.

And both sisters stood still and laughed in the middle of the street. 'The little one' was Philip.

'The other was more a man,' said Marianne. 'But I'm sure this one is easier. *The little one!* Yes, he *should* be easier,' and she laughed in her mocking way.

'The stand-up-mannikin!' said Katherine, referring to those little toy men weighted at the base with lead, that always stand up again.

Philip was very unhappy in this atmosphere. His strength was in his weakness, his appeal, his clinging dependence. He quite cunningly got his own way, almost every time : but always by seeming to give in. In every emergency he bowed as low as need be and let the storm pass over him. Then he rose again, the same as ever, sentimental, on the side of the angels, offering defiance to nobody. The defiant men had been killed off during the war. He had seen it and secretly smiled. When the lion is shot, the dog gets the spoil. So he had come in for Katherine, Alan's lioness. A live dog is better than a dead lion. And so the little semi-angelic journalist exulted in the triumph of his weakness.

But in Germany, in weird post-war Germany, he seemed snuffed out again. The air was so cold and vacant, all feeling seemed to have gone out of the country. Emotion, even sentiment, was numbed quite dead, as in a frost-bitten limb. And if the sentiment were numbed out of him, he was truly dead.

'I'm most frightfully glad you've come, Kathy,' he said. 'I could hardly have held out another day here, without you. I feel you're the only thing on earth that remains real.'

'You don't seem very real to me,' she said.

'I'm not real! I'm *not*! – not when I'm alone. But when I'm with you I'm the most real man alive. I know it!'

This was the sort of thing that had fetched her in the past, thrilled her through and through in her womanly conceit, even made her fall in love with the little creature who could so generously admit such pertinent truths. So different from the lordly Alan, who expected a woman to bow down to him!

Now, however, some of the coldness of numbed Germany seemed to have got into her breast too. She felt a cruel derision of the whimpering little beast who claimed reality only through a woman. She did not answer him, but looked out at the snow falling between her and the dark trees. Another world! When the snow left off, how bristling and ghostly the cold fir-trees looked, tall, conical creatures crowding darkly and half-whitened with snow! So tall, so wolfish!

Philip shivered and looked yellower. There was shortage of fuel, shortage of food, shortage of everything. He wanted Katherine to go to Paris with him. But she would stay at least two weeks near her people. The shortage she would put up with. She saw at evening the string of decent townsfolk waiting in the dark – the town was not half-lighted – to fill their hot-water bottles at the hot spring outside the Kurhaus, silent, spectral, unable to afford fire to heat their own water. And she felt quite cold about Philip's shivering. Let him shiver.

The snow was crisp and dry, she walked out in the forest, up the steep slopes. The world was curiously vacant, gone wild again. She realized how very quickly the world would go wild, if catastrophes overtook. mankind. Philip, yellow and hollow, would trudge stumbling and reeling beside her: ludicrous. He was a man who never would walk firm on his legs. Now he just flopped. She could feel Alan among the trees, the thrill and vibration of him. And sometimes she would glance with beating heart at a great round fir-trunk that stood so alive and potent, so physical, bristling all its vast drooping greenness above the snow. She could feel him, Alan, in the trees' potent presence. She wanted to go and press herself against the trunk. But Philip would sit down on the snow, saying:

'Look here, Kathy, I can't go any farther. I've simply got no strength left!'

She stood on the path, proud, contemptuous, but silent, looking away towards where the dull, reddish rocks cropped out. And there, among the rocks, she was sure, Alan was waiting for her. She felt fierce and overbearing. Yet she took the stumbling Philip home.

He was really ill. She put him to bed, and he stayed in bed. The doctor came. But Philip was in a state of panic, afraid of everything. Katherine would walk out by herself, into the forest. She was expecting Alan, and was tingling to meet him. Then Philip would lie in bed half-conscious, and when she came back he would say, his big eyes glowing:

'You must have been *very far*!' And on the last two words he would show his large front teeth in a kind of snarl.

'Not very far,' she said.

One day Alan came to her, from out of the dull reddish rocks in the forest. He was wearing a kilt that suited him so: but a khaki tunic. And he had no cap on. He came walking towards her, his knees throwing the kilt in the way she knew so well. He came triumphantly, rather splendid, and she waited trembling. He was always utterly silent. But he led her away with his arm round her, and she yielded in a complete yielding she had never known before. And among the rocks he made love to her, and took her in the silent passion of a husband, took a complete possession of her.

Afterwards she walked home in a muse, to find Philip seriously ill. She could see, he really might die. And she didn't care a bit. But she tended him, and stayed with him, and he seemed to be better.

The next day, however, she wanted to go out in the afternoon, she *must*! She could feel her husband waiting, and the call was imperative. She must go. But Philip became almost hysterical when she wanted to leave him.

'I assure you I shall die while you are out! I assure you I shall die if you leave me now!' He rolled his eyes wildly, and looked so queer, she felt it was true. So she stayed, sullen and full of resentment, her consciousness away among the rocks.

The afternoon grew colder and colder. Philip shivered in bed, under the great bolster.

'But it's a murderous cold! It's murdering me!' he said.

She did not mind it. She sat abstracted, remote from him, her spirit going out into the frozen evening. A very powerful flow seemed to envelop her in another reality. It was Alan calling to her, holding her. And the hold seemed to grow stronger every hour.

She slept in the same room as Philip. But she had decided not to go to bed. He was really very weak. She would sit up with him. Towards midnight he roused, and said faintly :

'Katherine, I can't bear it!' – and his eyes rolled up showing only the whites.

'What? What can't you bear?' she said, bending over him.

'I can't bear it! I can't bear it! Hold me in your arms. Hold me! Hold me!' he whispered in pure terror of death.

Curiously reluctant, she began to push her hands under his shoulders, to raise him. As she did so, the door opened, and Alan came in, bareheaded, and a frown on his face. Philip lifted feeble hands, and put them round Katherine's neck, moaning faintly. Silent, bareheaded. Alan came over to the bed and loosened the sick man's hands from his wife's neck, and put them down on the sick man's own breast.

Philip unfurled his lips and showed his big teeth in a ghastly grin of death. Katherine felt his body convulse in strange throes under her hands, then go inert. He was dead. And on his face was a sickly grin of a thief caught in the very act.

But Alan drew her away, drew her to the other bed, in the silent passion of a husband come back from a very long journey.

Jimmy and the Desperate Woman

'HE is very fine and strong somewhere, but he does need a level-headed woman to look after him.'

That was the *friendly* feminine verdict upon him. It flattered him, it pleased him, it galled him.

Having divorced a very charming and clever wife, who had held this opinion for ten years, and at last had got tired of the level-headed protective game, his gall was uppermost.

'I want to throw Jimmy out on the world, but I know the poor little man will go and fall on some woman's bosom. That's the worst of him. If he could only stand alone for ten minutes. But he can't. At the same time, there *is* something fine about him, something rare.'

This had been Clarissa's summing-up as she floated away in the arms of the rich young American. The rich young American got rather angry when Jimmy's name was mentioned. Clarissa was now *his* wife. But she did sometimes talk as if she were still married to Jimmy.

Not in Jimmy's estimation, however. That worm had turned. Gall was uppermost. Gall and wormwood. He knew exactly what Clarissa thought – and said – about him. And the 'something fine, something rare, something strong' which he was supposed to have 'about him' was utterly outbalanced, in his feelings at least, by the 'poor little man' nestled upon 'some woman's bosom', which he was supposed to *be*.

'I am *not*,' he said to himself, 'a poor little man nestled upon some woman's bosom. If I could only find the right sort of woman, she should nestle on mine.'

Jimmy was now thirty-five, and this point, to nestle or to be nestled, was the emotional crux and turning-point.

He imagined to himself some really *womanly* woman, to whom he should be *only* 'fine and strong', and not for one moment 'the poor little man'. Why not some simple uneducated girl, some Tess of the D'Urbervilles, some wistful Gretchen, some humble Ruth gleaning an aftermath? Why not? Surely the world was full of such!

The trouble was he never met them. He only met sophisticated women. He really never had a chance of meeting 'real' people. So few of us ever do. Only the people we *don't* meet are the 'real' people, the simple, genuine, direct, spontaneous, unspoilt souls. Ah, the simple, genuine, unspoilt people we *don't* meet! What a tragedy it is!

Because, of course, they must be there! Somewhere! Only we never come across them.

Jimmy was terribly handicapped by his position. It brought him into contact with so many people. Only never the right sort. Never the 'real' people : the simple, genuine, unspoilt, etc., etc.

He was editor of a high-class, rather highbrow, rather successful magazine, and his rather personal, very candid editorials brought him shoals, swarms, hosts of admiring acquaintances. Realize that he was handsome, and could be extraordinarily 'nice', when he liked, and was really very clever, in his own critical way, and you see how many chances he had of being adored and protected.

In the first place his good looks : the fine, clean lines of his face, like the face of the laughing faun in one of the faun's unlaughingly, moody moments. The long, clean lines of the cheeks, the strong chin and the slightly arched, full nose, the beautiful dark-grey eyes with long lashes, and the thick black brows. In his mocking moments, when he seemed most himself, it was a pure Pan face, with thick black eyebrows cocked up, and grey eyes with a sardonic goaty gleam, and nose and mouth curling with satire. A good-looking, smooth-skinned satyr. That was Jimmy at his best. In the opinion of his men friends.

In his own opinion, he was a sort of Martyred Saint Sebastian, at whom the wicked world shot arrow after arrow – Mater Dolorosa nothing to him – and he counted the drops of blood as they fell : when he could keep count. Sometimes – as for instance when Clarissa said she was really departing with a rich young American, and should she divorce Jimmy, or was Jimmy going to divorce her? – then the arrows assailed him like a flight of starlings flying straight at him, jabbing at him, and the drops of martyred blood simply spattered down, he couldn't keep count.

So, naturally, he divorced Clarissa.

In the opinion of his men friends, he was, or should be, a consistently grinning faun, satyr, or Pan-person. In his own opinion, he was a Martyred Saint Sebastian with the mind of a Plato. In the opinion of his woman friends, he was a fascinating little man with a profound understanding of life and the capacity really to understand a woman and to make a woman feel a queen; which of course was to make a woman feel her *real* self . . .

He might, naturally, have made rich and resounding marriages, especially after the divorce. He didn't. The reason was, secretly, his resolve never to make any woman feel a queen any more. It was the turn of the women to make him feel a king.

Some unspoilt, unsophisticated, wild-blooded woman, to whom he would be a sort of Solomon of wisdom, beauty, and wealth. She would need to be in reduced circumstances to appreciate his wealth, which amounted to the noble sum of three thousand pounds and a little week-ending cottage in Hampshire. And to be unsophisticated she would have to be a woman of the people. Absolutely.

At the same time, not just the 'obscure vulgar simplican'.

He received many letters, many, many, many, enclosing poems, stories, articles, or more personal unbosomings. He read them all : like a solemn rook pecking and scratching among the litter.

And one – not one letter, but one correspondent – might be *the* one – Mrs Emilia Pinnegar, who wrote from a mining village in Yorkshire. She was, of course, unhappily married.

Now Jimmy had always had a mysterious feeling about these dark and rather dreadful mining villages in the north. He himself had scarcely set foot north of Oxford. He felt that these miners up there must be the real stuff. And Pinnegar was a name, surely! And Emilia!

She wrote a poem, with a brief little note, that, if the editor of the *Commentator* thought the verses of no value, would he simply destroy them. Jimmy, as editor of the *Commentator*, thought the verses quite good and admired the brevity of the note. But he wasn't sure about printing the poem. He wrote back, Had Mrs Pinnegar nothing else to submit?

Then followed a correspondence. And at length, upon request, this from Mrs Pinnegar:

'You ask me about myself, but what shall I say? I am a woman of thirty-one, with one child, a girl of eight, and I am married to a man who lives in the same house with me, but goes to another woman. I try to write poetry, if it is poetry, because I have no other way of expressing myself at all, and even if it doesn't matter to anybody besides myself, I feel I must and will express myself, if only to save myself from developing cancer or some disease that women have. I was a school-teacher before I was married, and I got my certificates at Rotherham College. If I could, I would teach again, and live alone. But married women teachers can't get jobs any more, they aren't allowed –'

THE COAL-MINER

BY HIS WIFE

THE donkey-engine's beating noise.
And the rattle, rattle of the sorting screens
Come down on me like the beat of his heart,
And mean the same as his breathing means.

The burning big pit-hill with fumes
Fills the air like the presence of that fair-haired man.
And the burning fire burning deeper and deeper
Is his will insisting since time began.

As he breathes the chair goes up and down
In the pit-shaft; he lusts as the wheel-fans spin
The sucking air: he lives in the coal
Underground: and his soul is a strange engine.

That is the manner of man he is.
I married him and I should know.
The mother earth from bowels of coal
Brought him forth for the overhead woe.

This was the poem that the editor of the *Commentator* hesitated about. He reflected, also, that Mrs Pinnegar didn't sound like one of the nestling, unsophisticated rustic type. It was something else that still attracted him: something desperate in a woman, something tragic.

THE NEXT EVENT

IF at evening, when the twilight comes,
    You ask me what the day has been,
I shall not know. The distant drums
    Of some new-comer intervene

Between me and the day that's been.
    Some strange man leading long columns
Of unseen soldiers through the green
    Sad twilight of these smoky slums.

And as the darkness slowly numbs
    My senses, everything I've seen
Or heard the daylight through, becomes
    Rubbish behind an opaque screen.

Instead, the sound of muffled drums
    Inside myself: I have to lean
And listen as my strength succumbs,
    To hear what these oncomings mean.

Perhaps the Death-God striking his thumbs
    On the drums in a deadly rat-ta-ta-plan.
Or a strange man marching slow as he strums
    The tune of a new weird hope in Man.

What does it matter! The day that began
    In coal-dust is ending the same, in crumbs
Of darkness like coal. I live if I can;
    If I can't, then I welcome whatever comes.

This poem sounded so splendidly desperate, the editor of the *Commentator* decided to print it, and, moreover, to see the authoress. He wrote, Would she care to see him, if he happened to be in her neighbourhood? He was going to lecture in Sheffield. She replied, Certainly.

He gave his afternoon lecture, on *Men in Books and Men in Life*. Naturally, men in books came first. Then he caught a train to reach the mining village where the Pinnegars lived.

It was February, with gruesome patches of snow. It was dark when he arrived at Mill Valley, a sort of thick, turgid darkness full of menace, where men speaking in a weird accent went past like ghosts, dragging their heavy feet and emitting the weird scent of the coal-mine underworld. Weird and a bit gruesome it was.

He knew he had to walk uphill to the little market-place. As he went, he looked back and saw the black valleys with bunches of light, like camps of demons it seemed to him. And the demonish smell of sulphur and coal in the air, in the heavy, pregnant, clammy darkness.

They directed him to New London Lane, and down he went down another hill. His skin crept a little. The place felt uncanny and hostile, hard, as if iron and minerals breathed into the black air. Thank goodness he couldn't see much, or be seen. When he had to ask his way the people treated him in a 'heave-half-a-brick-at-him' fashion.

After much weary walking and asking, he entered a lane between trees, in the cold slushy mud of the unfrozen February. The mines, apparently, were on the outskirts of the town, in some mud-sunk country. He could see the red, sore fires of the burning pit-hill through the trees, and he smelt the sulphur. He felt like some modern Ulysses wandering in the realms of Hecate. How much more dismal and horrible, a modern Odyssey among mines and factories, than any Sirens, Scyllas or Charybdises.

So he mused to himself as he waded through icy black mud, in a black lane, under black trees that moaned an accompaniment to the sound of the coal-mine's occasional hissing and chuffing, under a black sky that quenched even the electric sparkle of the colliery. And the place seemed uninhabited like a cold black jungle.

At last he came in sight of a glimmer. Apparently, there were dwellings. Yes, a new little street, with one street-lamp, and the houses all apparently dark. He paused. Absolute desertion. Then three children.

They told him the house, and he stumbled up a dark passage. There was light on the little backyard. He knocked, in some trepidation. A rather tall woman, looking down at him with a 'Who are you?' look, from the step above.

'Mrs Pinnegar?'

'Oh, is it you, Mr Frith? Come in.'

He stumbled up the step into the glaring light of the kitchen. There stood Mrs Pinnegar, a tall woman with a face like a mask of passive anger, looking at him coldly. Immediately he felt his own shabbiness and smallness. In utter confusion, he stuck out his hand.

'I had an awful time getting here,' he said. 'I'm afraid I shall make a frightful mess of your house.' He looked down at his boots.

'That's all right,' she said. 'Have you had your tea?'

'No – but don't you bother about me.'

There was a little girl with fair hair in a fringe over her forehead, troubled blue eyes under the fringe, and two dolls. He felt easier.

'Is this your little girl?' he asked. 'She's awfully nice. What is her name?'

'Jane.'

'How are you, Jane?' he said. But the child only stared at him with the baffled, bewildered, pained eyes of a child who lives with hostile parents.

Mrs Pinnegar set his tea, bread and butter, jam, and buns. Then she sat opposite him. She was handsome, dark straight brows and grey eyes with yellow grains in them, and a way of looking straight at you as if she were used to holding her own. Her eyes were the nicest part of her. They had a certain kindliness, mingled, like the yellow grains among the grey, with a relentless, unyielding feminine will. Her nose and mouth were straight, like a Greek mask, and the expression was fixed. She gave him at once the impression of a woman who has made a mistake, who knows it, but who will not change : who cannot now change.

He felt very uneasy. Being a rather small, shambling man, she made him aware of his physical inconspicuousness. And she said not a word, only looked down on him, as he drank his tea, with that changeless look of a woman who is holding her own against Man and Fate. While, from the corner across the kitchen, the little girl with her fair hair and her dolls watched him also in absolute silence, from her hot blue eyes.

'This seems a pretty awful place,' he said to her.

'It is. It's absolutely awful,' the woman said.

'You ought to get away from it,' he said.

But she received this in dead silence.

It was exceedingly difficult to make any headway. He asked about Mr Pinnegar. She glanced at the clock.

'He comes up at nine,' she said.

'Is he down the mine?'

'Yes. He's on the afternoon shift.'

There was never a sound from the little girl.

'Doesn't Jane ever talk?' he asked.

'Not much,' said the mother, glancing round.

He talked a little about his lectures, about Sheffield, about London. But she was not really interested. She sat there rather distant, very laconic, looking at him with those curious unyielding eyes. She looked to him like a woman who has had her revenge, and is left stranded on the reefs where she wrecked her opponent. Still unrelenting, unregretting, unyielding, she seemed rather undecided as to what her revenge had been, and what it had all been about.

'You ought to get away from here,' he said to her.

'Where to?' she asked.

'Oh' – he made a vague gesture – 'anywhere, so long as it is *quite* away.'

She seemed to ponder this, under her portentous brow.

'I don't see what difference it would make,' she said. Then glancing round at her child : 'I don't see what difference anything would make, except getting out of the world altogether. But there's *her* to consider.' And she jerked her head in the direction of the child.

Jimmy felt definitely frightened. He wasn't used to this sort of grimness. At the same time he was excited. This handsome, laconic woman, with her soft brown hair and her unflinching eyes with their gold flecks, seemed to be challenging him to something. There was a touch of challenge in her remaining gold-flecked kindness. Somewhere, she had a heart. But what had happened to it? And v᾿ y?

What had gone wrong with her? In some way, she must have gone against herself.

'Why don't you come and live with me?' he said, like the little gambler he was.

The queer, conflicting smile was on his face. He had taken up her challenge, like a gambler. The very sense of a gamble, in which he could not lose desperately, excited him. At the same time, he was scared of her, and determined to get beyond his scare.

She sat and watched him, with the faintest touch of a grim smile on her handsome mouth.

'How do you mean, live with you?' she said.

'Oh – I mean what it usually means,' he said, with a little puff of self-conscious laughter.

'You're evidently not happy here. You're evidently in the wrong circumstances altogether. You're obviously *not* just an ordinary woman. Well, then, break away. When I say, Come and live with me, I mean just what I say. Come to London and live with me, as my wife, if you like, and then if we want to marry, when you get a divorce, why, we can do it.'

Jimmy made his speech more to himself than to the woman. That was how he was. He worked out all his things inside himself, as if it were all merely an interior problem of his own. And while he did so, he had an odd way of squinting his left eye and wagging his head loosely, like a man talking absolutely to himself, and turning his eyes inwards.

The woman watched him in a sort of wonder. This was something she was *not* used to. His extraordinary manner, and his extraordinary bald proposition, roused her from her own tense apathy.

'Well!' she said. 'That's got to be thought about. What about *her*?' – and again she jerked her head towards the round-eyed child in the corner. Jane sat with a completely expressionless face, her little red mouth fallen a little open. She seemed in a sort of trance : as if she understood like a grown-up person, but, as a child, sat in a trance, unconscious.

The mother wheeled round in her chair and stared at her child. The little girl stared back at her mother, with hot, troubled, almost guilty blue eyes. And neither said a word. Yet they seemed to exchange worlds of meaning.

'Why, of course,' said Jimmy, twisting his head again, 'she'd come, too.'

The woman gave a last look at her child, then turned to him, and started watching *him* with that slow, straight stare.

'It's not' – he began, stuttering – 'it's not anything *sudden* and unconsidered on my part. I've been considering it for quite a long time – ever since I had the first poem, and your letter.'

He spoke still with his eyes turned inwards, talking to himself. And the woman watched him unflinchingly.

'Before you ever saw me?' she asked, with a queer irony.

'Oh, of course. Of course before I ever saw you. Or else I never *should* have seen you. From the very first, I had a definite feeling –'

He made odd, sharp gestures, like a drunken man, and he spoke like a drunken man, his eyes turned inward, talking to himself. The woman was no more than a ghost moving inside his own consciousness, and he was addressing her there.

The actual woman sat outside looking on in a sort of wonder. This was really something new to her.

'And now you see me, do you want me, really, to come to London?'

She spoke in a dull tone of incredulity. The thing was just a little preposterous to her. But why not? It would have to be something a little preposterous, to get her out of the tomb she was in.

'Of course I do!' he cried, with another scoop of his head and scoop of his hand. '*Now* I do *actually* want you, now I actually see you.' He never looked at her. His eyes were still turned in. He was still talking to himself, in a sort of drunkenness with himself.

To her, it was something extraordinary. But it roused her from apathy.

He became aware of the hot blue eyes of the hot-cheeked little girl fixed upon him from the distant corner. And he gave a queer little giggle.

'Why, it's more than I could ever have hoped for,' he said, 'to have you and Jane to live with me! Why, it will mean *life* to me.' He spoke in an odd, strained voice, slightly delirious. And for the first time he looked up at the woman and, apparently, *straight* at her. But, even as he seemed to look straight at her, the curious cast was in his eye, and he was only looking at himself, inside himself, at the shadows inside his own consciousness.

'And when would you like me to come?' she asked, rather coldly.

'Why, as soon as possible. Come back with me tomorrow, if you will. I've got a little house in St John's Wood, *waiting* for you. Come with me tomorrow. That's the simplest.'

She watched him for some time, as he sat with ducked head. He looked like a man who is drunk – drunk with himself. He was going bald at the crown, his rather curly black hair was thin.

'I couldn't come tomorrow, I should need a few days,' she said.

She wanted to see his face again. It was as if she could not remember what his face was like, this strange man who had appeared out of nowhere, with such a strange proposition.

He lifted his face, his eyes still cast in that inturned, blind look. He looked now like a Mephistopheles who has gone blind. With his black brows cocked up, Mephistopheles, Mephistopheles blind and begging in the street.

'Why, of course, it's wonderful that it's happened like this for me,' he said, with odd pouting emphasis, pushing out his lips. 'I was finished, absolutely finished. I was finished while Clarissa was with me. But after she'd gone, I was *absolutely* finished. And I thought there was no chance for me in the world again. It seems to me perfectly marvellous that this has happened – that I've come across you –' he lifted his face sightlessly – 'and Jane – Jane – why she's *really* too good to be true.' He gave a slight hysterical laugh. 'She really is.'

The woman, and Jane, watched him with some embarrassment.

'I shall have to settle up here, with Mr Pinnegar,' she said, rather coldly musing. 'Do you want to see him?'

'Oh, I –' he said, with a deprecating gesture, 'I don't *care*. But if you think I'd better – why, certainly –'

'I do think you'd better,' she said.

'Very well, then, I *will*. I'll see him whenever you like.'

'He comes in soon after nine,' she said.

'All right, I'll see him then. Much better. But I suppose I'd better see about finding a place to sleep first. Better not leave it too late.'

'I'll come with you and ask for you.'

'Oh, you'd better not, really. If you tell me where to go –'

He had taken on a protective tone : he was protecting her against herself and against scandal. It was his manner, his rather Oxfordy manner, more than anything else, that went beyond her. She wasn't used to it.

Jimmy plunged out into the gulfing blackness of the Northern night, feeling how horrible it was, but pressing his hat on his brow in a sense of strong adventure. He was going through with it.

At the baker's shop, where she had suggested he should ask for a bed, they would have none of him. Absolutely they didn't like the looks of him. At the Pub, too, they shook their heads : didn't want to have anything to do with him. But, in a voice more expostulatingly Oxford than ever, he said :

'But look here – you can't ask a man to sleep under one of these hedges. Can't I see the landlady?'

He persuaded the landlady to promise to let him sleep on the big, soft settee in the parlour, where the fire was burning brightly. Then, saying he would be back about ten, he returned through mud and drizzle up New London Lane.

The child was in bed, a saucepan was boiling by the fire. Already the lines had softened a little in the woman's face.

She spread a cloth on the table. Jimmy sat in silence, feeling that she was hardly aware of his presence. She was absorbed, no doubt, in the coming of her husband. The stranger merely sat on the sofa, and waited. He felt himself wound up tight. And once he was really wound up, he could go through with anything.

They heard the nine o'clock whistle at the mine. The woman then took the saucepan from the fire and went into the scullery. Jimmy could smell the smell of potatoes being strained. He sat quite still. There was nothing for him to do or say. He was wearing his big black-rimmed spectacles, and his face, blank and expressionless in the suspense of waiting, looked like the death-mask of some sceptical philosopher, who could wait through the ages, and who could hardly distinguish life from death at any time.

Came the heavy-shod tread up the house entry, and the man entered, rather like a blast of wind. The fair moustache stuck out from the blackish, mottled face, and the fierce blue eyes rolled their whites in the coal-blackened sockets.

'This gentleman is Mr Frith,' said Emily Pinnegar.

Jimmy got up, with a bit of an Oxford wriggle, and held out his hand, saying : 'How do you do?'

His grey eyes, behind the spectacles, had an uncanny whitish gleam.

'My hand's not fit to shake hands,' said the miner. 'Take a seat.'

'Oh, nobody minds coal-dust,' said Jimmy, subsiding on to the sofa. 'It's clean dirt.'

'They say so,' said Pinnegar.

He was a man of medium height, thin, but energetic in build. Mrs Pinnegar was running hot water into a pail from the bright brass tap of the stove, which had a boiler to balance the oven. Pinnegar dropped heavily into a wooden armchair, and stooped to pull off his ponderous grey pit-boots. He smelled of the strange, stale underground. In silence he pulled on his slippers, then rose, taking his boots into the scullery. His wife followed with the pail of hot water. She returned and spread a coarse roller-towel on the steel fender. The man could be heard washing in the scullery, in the semi-dark. Nobody said anything. Mrs Pinnegar attended to her husband's dinner.

After a while, Pinnegar came running in, naked to the waist, and squatted plumb in front of the big red fire, on his heels. His head and face and the front part of his body were all wet. His back was grey and unwashed. He seized the towel from the fender and began to rub his face and head with a sort of brutal vigour, while his wife brought a bowl, and with a soapy flannel silently washed his back, right down to the loins, where the trousers were rolled back. The man was entirely oblivious of the stranger – this washing was part of the collier's ritual, and nobody existed for the moment. The woman, washing her husband's back, stooping there as he kneeled with knees wide apart, squatting on his heels on the rag hearthrug, had a peculiar look on her strong, handsome face, a look sinister and derisive. She was deriding something or somebody; but Jimmy could not make out whom or what.

It was a new experience for him to sit completely and brutally excluded, from a personal ritual. The collier vigorously rubbed his own fair short hair, till it all stood on end, then he stared into the red-hot fire, oblivious, while the red colour burned in his cheeks. Then again he rubbed his breast and his body with the rough towel, brutally, as if his body were some machine he was cleaning, while his wife, with a peculiar slow movement, dried his back with another towel.

She took away the towel and bowl. The man was dry. He still squatted with his hands on his knees, gazing abstractedly, blankly into the fire. That, too, seemed part of his daily ritual. The colour flushed in his cheeks, his fair moustache was rubbed on end. But his hot blue eyes stared hot and vague into the red coals, while the red glare of the coal fell on his breast and naked body.

He was a man of about thirty-five, in his prime, with a pure smooth skin and no fat on his body. His muscles were not large, but quick, alive with energy. And as he squatted bathing abstractedly in the glow of the fire, he seemed like some pure-moulded engine that sleeps between its motions, with incomprehensible eyes of dark iron-blue.

He looked round, always averting his face from the stranger on the sofa, shutting him out of consciousness. The wife took out a bundle from the dresser-cupboard, and handed it to the outstretched, work-scarred hand of the man on the hearth. Curious, that big, horny, work-battered clean hand, at the end of the suave, thin naked arm.

Pinnegar unrolled his shirt and undervest in front of the fire, warmed them for a moment in the glow, vaguely, sleepily, then pulled them over his head. And then at last he rose, with his shirt hanging over his trousers, and in the same abstract, sleepy way, shutting the world out of his consciousness, he went out again to the scullery, pausing at the same dresser-cupboard to take out his rolled-up day trousers.

Mrs Pinnegar took away the towels and set the dinner on the table – rich, oniony stew out of a hissing brown stew-jar, boiled potatoes, and a cup of tea. The man returned from the scullery, in his clean flannelette shirt and black trousers, his fair hair neatly brushed. He planked his wooden armchair beside the table, and sat heavily down, to eat.

Then he looked at Jimmy, as one wary, probably hostile man looks at another.

'You're a stranger in these parts, I gather?' he said. There was something slightly formal, even a bit pompous, in his speech.

'An absolute stranger,' replied Jimmy, with a slight aside grin.

The man dabbed some mustard on his plate, and glanced at his food to see if he would like it.

'Come from a distance, do you?' he asked, as he began to eat. As he ate, he seemed to become oblivious again of Jimmy, bent his head over his plate, and ate. But probably he was ruminating something all the time, with barbaric wariness.

'From London,' said Jimmy warily.

'London!' said Pinnegar, without looking from his plate.

Mrs Pinnegar came and sat, in ritualistic silence, in her tall-backed rocking-chair under the light.

'What brings you this way, then?' asked Pinnegar, stirring his tea.

'Oh!' Jimmy writhed a little on the sofa. 'I came to see Mrs Pinnegar.'

The miner took a hasty gulp of tea.

'You're acquainted then, are you?' he said, still without looking round. He sat with his side-face to Jimmy.

'Yes, we are *now*,' explained Jimmy. 'I didn't know Mrs Pinnegar till this evening. As a matter of fact, she sent me some poems for the *Commentator* – I'm the editor – and I thought they were very good, so I wrote and told her so. Then I felt I wanted to come and see her, and she was willing, so I came.'

The man reached out, cut himself a piece of bread, and swallowed a large mouthful.

'You thought her poetry was good?' he said, turning at last to Jimmy and looking straight at him, with a stare something like the child's, but aggressive. 'Are you going to put it in your magazine?'

'Yes, I think I am,' said Jimmy.

'I never read but one of her poems – something about a collier she knew all about, because she'd married him,' he said, in his peculiar harsh voice, that had a certain jeering clang in it, and a certain indomitableness.

Jimmy was silent. The other man's harsh fighting-voice made him shrink.

'I could never get on with the *Commentator* myself,' said Pinnegar, looking round for his pudding, pushing his meat-plate aside. 'Seems to me to go a long way round to get nowhere.'

'Well, probably it *does*,' said Jimmy, squirming a little. 'But so long as the *way* is interesting! I don't see that anything gets anywhere at present – certainly no periodical.'

'I don't know,' said Pinnegar. 'There's some facts in the *Liberator* – and there's some ideas in the *Janus*. I can't see the use, myself, of all these feelings folk say they have. They get you nowhere.'

'But,' said Jimmy, with a slight pouf of laughter, 'where do you *want* to get? It's all very well talking about getting somewhere, but where, where in the world today do you *want* to get? In general, I mean. If you want a better job in the mine – all right, go ahead and get it. But when you begin to talk about getting somewhere, in *life* – why, you've got to know what you're talking about.'

'I'm a man, aren't I?' said the miner, going very still and hard.

'But what do you *mean*, when you say you're a man?' snarled Jimmy, really exasperated. 'What do you mean? Yes, you *are* a man. But what about it?'

'Haven't I the right to say I won't be made use of?' said the collier, slow, harsh, and heavy.

'You've got a right to *say* it,' retorted Jimmy, with a pouf of laughter. 'But it doesn't *mean* anything. We're all made use of, from King George downwards. We have to be. When you eat your pudding you're making use of hundreds of people – including your wife.'

'I know it. I know it. It makes no difference, though. I'm not going to be made use of.'

Jimmy shrugged his shoulders.

'Oh, all right!' he said. 'That's just a phrase, like any other.'

The miner sat very still in his chair, his face going hard and remote. He was evidently thinking over something that was stuck like a barb in his consciousness, something he was trying to harden over, as the skin sometimes hardens over a steel splinter in the flesh.

'I'm nothing but made use of,' he said, now talking hard and final, to himself, and staring out into space. 'Down the pit, I'm made use of, and they give me a wage, such as it is. At the house, I'm made use of, and my wife sets the dinner on the table as if I was a customer in a shop.'

'But what do you *expect*?' cried Jimmy, writhing in his chair.

'Me? What do I expect? I expect nothing. But I tell you what –' he turned, and looked straight and hard into Jimmy's eyes – 'I'm not going to put up with anything either.'

Jimmy saw the hard finality in the other man's eyes, and squirmed away from it.

'If you *know* what you're not going to put up with –' he said.

'I don't want my wife writing poetry! And sending it to a parcel of men she's never seen. *I* don't want my wife sitting like Queen Boadicea, when I come home, and a face like a stone wall with holes in it. I don't know what's wrong with her. She doesn't know herself. But she does as she likes. Only, mark you, I do the same.'

'Of course!' cried Jimmy, though there was no of course about it.

'She's told you I've got another woman?'

'Yes.'

'And I'll tell you for why. If I give in to the coal face, and go down the mine every day to eight hours' slavery, more or less, somebody's got to give in to me.'

'Then,' said Jimmy, after a pause, 'if you mean you want your wife to submit to you – well, that's the problem. You have to marry the woman who *will* submit.'

It was amazing, this from Jimmy. He sat there and lectured the collier like a Puritan Father, completely forgetting the disintegrating flutter of Clarissa, in his own background.

'I want a wife who'll please me, who'll want to please me,' said the collier.

'Why should *you* be pleased, any more than anybody else?' asked the wife coldly.

'My child, my little girl wants to please me – if her mother would let her. But the women hang together. I tell you' – and here he turned to Jimmy, with a blaze in his dark blue eyes – 'I want a woman to please me, a woman who's anxious to please me. And if I can't find her in my own home, I'll find her out of it.'

'I hope she pleases you,' said the wife, rocking slightly.

'Well,' said the man, 'she does.'

'Then why don't you go and live with her altogether?' she said.

He turned and looked at her.

'Why don't I?' he said. 'Because I've got my home. I've got my house, I've got my wife, let her be what she may, as a woman to live with. And I've got my child. Why should I break it all up?'

'And what about me?' she asked, coldly and fiercely.

'You? You've got a home. You've got a child. You've got a man who works for you. You've got what you want. You do as you like –'

'Do I?' she asked, with intolerable sarcasm.

'Yes. Apart from the bit of work in the house, you do as you like. If you want to go, you can go. But while you live in my house, you must respect it. You bring no men here, you see.'

'Do *you* respect your home?' she said.

'Yes! I do! If I get another woman – who pleases me – I deprive you of nothing. All I ask of you is to do your duty as a housewife.'

'Down to washing your back!' she said, heavily sarcastic; and, Jimmy thought, a trifle vulgar.

'Down to washing my back, since it's got to be washed,' he said.

'What about the other woman? Let her do it.'

'This is my home.'

The wife gave a strange movement, like a mad woman.

Jimmy sat rather pale and frightened. Behind the collier's quietness he felt the concentration of almost cold anger and an unchanging will. In the man's lean face he could see the bones, the fixity of the male bones, and it was as if the human soul, or spirit, had gone into the living skull and skeleton, almost invulnerable.

Jimmy, for some strange reason, felt a wild anger against this bony and logical man. It was the hard-driven coldness, fixity, that he could not bear.

'Look here!' he cried, in a resonant Oxford voice, his eyes glaring and casting inwards behind his spectacles. 'You say Mrs Pinnegar is *free* – free to do as she pleases. In that case you have no objection if she comes with me right away from here.'

The collier looked at the pale, strange face of the editor in wonder. Jimmy kept his face slightly averted, and sightless, seeing nobody. There was a Mephistophelian tilt about the eyebrows, and a Martyred Sebastian straightness about the mouth.

'Does she *want* to?' asked Pinnegar, with devastating incredulity. The wife smiled faintly, grimly. She could see the vanity of her husband in his utter inability to believe that she could prefer the other man to him.

'That,' said Jimmy, 'you must ask her yourself. But it's what I came here for : to ask her to come and live with me, and bring the child.'

'You came without having seen her, to ask her that?' said the husband, in growing wonder.

'Yes,' said Jimmy, vehemently, nodding his head with drunken emphasis. 'Yes! Without ever having seen her!'

'You've caught a funny fish this time, with your poetry,' he said, turning with curious husband-familiarity to his wife. She hated this off-hand husband-familiarity.

'What sort of fish have *you* caught?' she retorted. 'And what did you catch *her* with?'

'Bird-lime!' he said, with a faint, quick grin.

Jimmy was sitting in suspense. They all three sat in suspense, for some time.

'And what are you saying to him?' said the collier at length.

Jimmy looked up, and the malevolent half-smile on his face made him look rather handsome again, a mixture of faun and Mephisto. He glanced curiously, invitingly, at the woman who was watching him from afar.

'I say yes!' she replied, in a cool voice.

The husband became very still, sitting erect in his wooden armchair and staring into space. It was as if he were fixedly watching something fly away from him, out of his own soul. But he was not going to yield at all, to any emotion.

He could not now believe that this woman should *want* to leave him. Yet she did.

'I'm sure it's all for the best,' said Jimmy, in his Puritan-Father voice. 'You don't mind, really' – he drawled uneasily – 'if she brings the child. I give you my word I'll do my very best for it.'

The collier looked at him as if he were very far away. Jimmy quailed under the look. He could see that the other man was relentlessly killing the emotion in himself, stripping himself, as it were, of his own flesh, stripping himself to the hard unemotional bone of the human male.

'I give her a blank cheque,' said Pinnegar, with numb lips. 'She does as she pleases.'

'So much for fatherly love, compared with selfishness,' she said.

He turned and looked at her with that curious power of remote anger. And immediately she became still, quenched.

'I give you a blank cheque, as far as I'm concerned,' he repeated abstractedly.

'It *is* blank indeed!' she said, with her first touch of bitterness.

Jimmy looked at the clock. It was growing late : he might be shut out of the public-house. He rose to go, saying he would return in the morning. He was leaving the next day, at noon, for London.

He plunged into the darkness and mud of that black, night-ridden country. There was a curious elation in his spirits, mingled with fear. But then he always needed an element of fear, really, to elate him. He thought with terror of those two human beings left in that house together. The frightening state of tension ! He himself could never bear an extreme tension. He always had to compromise, to become apologetic and pathetic. He would be able to manage Mrs Pinnegar that way. Emily ! He must get used to saying it. Emily ! The Emilia was absurd. He had never known an Emily.

He felt really scared, and really elated. He was doing something big. It was not that he was in *love* with the woman. But, my God, he wanted to take her away from that man. And he wanted the adventure of her. Absolutely the adventure of her. He felt really elated, really himself, really manly.

But in the morning he returned rather sheepishly to the collier's house. It was another dark, drizzling day, with black trees, black road, black hedges, blackish brick houses, and the smell and the sound of collieries under a skyless day. Like living in some weird underground.

Unwillingly he went up that passage-entry again, and knocked at the back door, glancing at the miserable little back garden with its cabbage-stalks and its ugly sanitary arrangements.

The child opened the door to him : with her fair hair, flushed cheeks, and hot, dark-blue eyes.

'Hello, Jane !' he said.

The mother stood tall and square, by the table, watching him with portentous eyes, as he entered. She was handsome, but her skin was not very good : as if the battle had been too much for her health. Jimmy glanced up at her smiling his slow, ingratiating smile, that always brought a glow of success into a woman's spirit. And as he saw her gold-flecked eyes searching in his eyes, without a bit of kindliness, he thought to himself : 'My God, however am I going to sleep with that woman !' His will was ready, however, and he would manage it somehow.

And when he glanced at the motionless, bony head and lean figure of the collier seated in the wooden armchair by the fire, he was more ready. He must triumph over that man.

'What train are you going by?' asked Mrs Pinnegar.

'By the twelve-thirty.' He looked up at her as he spoke, with the wide, shining, childlike, almost coy eyes that were his peculiar asset. She looked down at him in a sort of interested wonder. She seemed almost fascinated by his child-like, shining, inviting dark-grey eyes, with their long lashes : such an absolute change from that resentful unyielding that looked out always from the back of her husband's blue eyes. Her husband always seemed like a menace to her, in his thinness, his concentration, his eternal unyielding. And this man looked at one with the wide, shining, fascinating eyes of a young Persian kitten, something at once bold and shy and coy and strangely inviting. She fell at once under their spell.

'You'll have dinner before you go,' she said.

'No !' he cried in panic, unwilling indeed to eat before that other man. 'No, I ate a fabulous breakfast. I will get a sandwich when I change in Sheffield : *really* !'

She had to go out shopping. She said she would go out to the station with him when she got back. It was just after eleven.

'But look here,' he said, addressing also the thin abstracted man who sat unnoticing, with a newspaper, 'we've got to get this thing settled. I *want* Mrs Pinnegar to come and live with me, her and the child. And she's coming ! So don't you think, now, it would be better if she came right along with me today ! Just put a few things in a bag and come along. Why drag the thing out ?'

'I tell you,' replied the husband, 'she has a blank cheque from me to do as she likes.'

'All right, then ! Won't you do that? Won't you come along with me now?' said Jimmy, looking up at her exposedly, but casting his eyes a bit inwards. Throwing himself with deliberate impulsiveness on her mercy.

'I can't !' she said decisively. 'I can't come today.'

'But why not – really? Why not, while I'm here? You have that blank cheque, you can do as you please –'

'The blank cheque won't get me far,' she said rudely. 'I can't come today, anyhow.'

'When can you come, then?' he said, with that queer, petulant pleading. 'The sooner the better, surely.'

'I can come on Monday,' she said abruptly.

'Monday !' He gazed up at her in a kind of panic, through his spectacles. Then he set his teeth again, and nodded his head up and down. 'All right, then ! Today is Saturday. Then Monday !'

'If you'll excuse me,' she said, 'I've got to go out for a few things. I'll walk to the station with you when I get back.'

She bundled Jane into a little sky-blue coat and bonnet, put on a heavy black coat and black hat herself, and went out.

Jimmy sat very uneasily opposite the collier, who also wore spectacles to read. Pinnegar put down the newspaper and pulled the spectacles off his nose, saying something about a Labour Government.

'Yes,' said Jimmy. 'After all, best be logical. If you *are* democratic, the only logical thing is a Labour Government.

Though, personally, one Government is as good as another, to me.'

'Maybe so!' said the collier. 'But *something's* got to come to an end, sooner or later.'

'Oh, a great deal!' said Jimmy, and they lapsed into silence.

'Have you been married before?' asked Pinnegar, at length.

'Yes. My wife and I are divorced.'

'I suppose you want me to divorce *my* wife?' said the collier.

'Why – yes! – that would be best –'

'It's the same to me,' said Pinnegar; 'divorce or no divorce. I'll *live* with another woman, but I'll never *marry* another. Enough is as good as a feast. But if she wants a divorce, she can have it.'

'It would certainly be best,' said Jimmy.

There was a long pause. Jimmy wished the woman would come back.

'I look on you as an instrument,' said the miner. 'Something had to break. You are the instrument that breaks it.'

It was strange to sit in the room with this thin, remote, wilful man. Jimmy was a bit fascinated by him. But, at the same time, he hated him because he could not be in the same room with him without being under his spell. He felt himself dominated. And he hated it.

'My wife,' said Pinnegar, looking up at Jimmy with a peculiar, almost humorous, teasing grin, 'expects to see me go to the dogs when she leaves me. It is her last hope.'

Jimmy ducked his head and was silent, not knowing what to say. The other man sat still in his chair, like a sort of infinitely patient prisoner, looking away out of the window and waiting.

'She thinks,' he said again, 'that she has some wonderful future awaiting her somewhere, and you're going to open the door.'

And again the same amused grin was in his eyes.

And again Jimmy was fascinated by the man. And again he hated the spell of this fascination. For Jimmy wanted to be, in his own mind, the strongest man among men, but particularly among women. And this thin, peculiar man could dominate him. He knew it. The very silent unconsciousness of Pinnegar dominated the room, wherever he was.

Jimmy hated this.

At last Mrs Pinnegar came back, and Jimmy set off with her. He shook hands with the collier.

'Good-bye!' he said.

'Good-bye!' said Pinnegar, looking down at him with those amused blue eyes, which Jimmy knew he would never be able to get beyond.

And the walk to the station was almost a walk of conspiracy against the man left behind, between the man in spectacles and the tall woman. They arranged the details for Monday. Emily was to come by the nine o'clock train: Jimmy would meet her at Marylebone, and install her in his house in St John's Wood. Then, with the child, they would begin a new life. Pinnegar would divorce his wife, or she would divorce him: and then, another marriage.

Jimmy got a tremendous kick out of it all on the journey home. He felt he had really done something desperate and adventurous. But he was in too wild a flutter to analyse any results. Only, as he drew near London, a sinking feeling came over him. He was desperately tired after it all, almost too tired to keep up.

Nevertheless, he went after dinner and sprang it all on Severn.

'You damn fool!' said Severn, in consternation. 'What did you do it for?'

'Well,' said Jimmy, writhing. 'Because *I wanted* to.'

'Good God! The woman sounds like the head of Medusa. You're a hero of some stomach, I must say! Remember Clarissa?'

'Oh,' writhed Jimmy. 'But this is different.'

'Ay, her name's Emma, or something of that sort, isn't it?'

'Emily!' said Jimmy briefly.

'Well, you're a fool, anyway, so you may as well keep on acting in character. I've no doubt, by playing weeping-willow, you'll outlive all the female storms you ever prepare for yourself. I never yet did see a weeping-willow uprooted by a gale, so keep on hanging your harp on it, and you'll be all right. Here's luck! But for a man who was looking for a little Gretchen to adore him, you're a corker!'

Which was all that Severn had to say. But Jimmy went home

with his knees shaking. On Sunday morning he wrote an anxious letter. He didn't know how to begin it: *Dear Mrs Pinnegar* and *Dear Emily* seemed either too late in the day or too early. So he just plunged in, without dear anything.

'I want you to have this before you come. Perhaps we have been precipitate. I only beg you to decide *finally*, for yourself, before you come. Don't come, please, unless you are absolutely sure of yourself. If you are *in the least* unsure, wait a while, wait till you are quite certain, one way or the other.

'For myself, if you don't come I shall understand. But please send me a telegram. If you do come, I shall welcome both you and the child. Yours ever – J.F.'

He paid a man his return fare, and three pounds extra, to go on the Sunday and deliver this letter.

The man came back in the evening. He had delivered the letter. There was no answer.

Awful Sunday night: tense Monday morning!

A telegram: *Arrive Marylebone 12.50 with Jane. Yours ever. Emily.*

Jimmy set his teeth and went to the station. But when he felt her looking at him, and so met her eyes: and after that saw her coming slowly down the platform, holding the child by the hand, her slow cat's eyes smouldering under her straight brows, smouldering at him: he almost swooned. A sickly grin came over him as he held out his hand. Nevertheless he said:

'I'm *awfully* glad you came.'

And he sat in the taxi, a perverse but intense desire for her came over him, making him almost helpless. He could feel, so strongly, the presence of that other man about her, and this went to his head like neat spirits. That other man! In some subtle, inexplicable way, he was actually bodily present, the husband. The woman moved in his aura. She was hopelessly married to him.

And this went to Jimmy's head like neat whisky. Which of the two would fall before him with a greater fall – the woman, or the man, her husband?

The Last Laugh

THERE was a little snow on the ground, and the church clock had just struck midnight. Hampstead in the night of winter for once was looking pretty, with clean white earth and lamps for moon, and dark sky above the lamps.

A confused little sound of voices, a gleam of hidden yellow light. And then the garden door of a tall, dark Georgian house suddenly opened, and three people confusedly emerged. A girl in a dark blue coat and fur turban, very erect: a fellow with a little dispatch-case, slouching: a thin man with a red beard, bareheaded, peering out of the gateway down the hill that swung in a curve downwards towards London.

'Look at it! A new world!' cried the man in the beard, ironically, as he stood on the step and peered out.

'No, Lorenzo! It's only whitewash!' cried the young man in the overcoat. His voice was handsome, resonant, plangent, with a weary sardonic touch. As he turned back his face was dark in shadow.

The girl with the erect, alert head, like a bird, turned back to the two men.

'What was that?' she asked, in her quick, quiet voice.

'Lorenzo says it's a new world. I say it's only whitewash,' cried the man in the street.

She stood still and lifted her woolly, gloved finger. She was deaf and was taking it in.

Yes, she had got it. She gave a quick, chuckling laugh, glanced very quickly at the man in the bowler hat, then back at the man in the stucco gateway, who was grinning like a satyr and waving good-bye.

'Good-bye, Lorenzo!' came the resonant, weary cry of the man in the bowler hat.

'Good-bye!' came the sharp, night-bird call of the girl.

The green gate slammed, then the inner door. The two were alone in the street, save for the policeman at the corner. The road curved steeply downhill.

'You'd better mind how you *step*!' shouted the man in the

bowler hat, leaning near the erect, sharp girl, and slouching in his walk. She paused a moment to make sure what he had said.

'Don't mind me, I'm quite all right. Mind yourself!' she said quickly. At that very moment he gave a wild lurch on the slippery snow, but managed to save himself from falling. She watched him, on tiptoes of alertness. His bowler hat bounced away in the thin snow. They were under a lamp near the curve. As he ducked for his hat he showed a bald spot, just like a tonsure, among his dark, thin, rather curly hair. And when he looked up at her, with his thick black brows sardonically arched, and his rather hooked nose self-derisive, jamming his hat on again, he seemed like a satanic young priest. His face had beautiful lines, like a faun, and a doubtful martyred expression. A sort of faun on the Cross, with all the malice of the complication.

'Did you hurt yourself?' she asked, in her quick, cool, unemotional way.

'No!' he shouted derisively.

'Give me the machine, won't you?' she said, holding out her woolly hand. 'I believe I'm safer.'

'Do you *want* it?' he shouted.

'Yes, I'm sure I'm safer.'

He handed her the little brown dispatch-case, which was really a Marconi listening machine for her deafness. She marched erect as ever. He shoved his hands deep in his overcoat pockets and slouched along beside her, as if he wouldn't make his legs firm. The road curved down in front of them, clean and pale with snow under the lamps. A motor-car came churning up. A few dark figures slipped away into the dark recesses of the houses, like fishes among rocks above a seabed of white sand. On the left was a tuft of trees sloping upwards into the dark.

He kept looking around, pushing out his finely shaped chin and his hooked nose as if he were listening for something. He could still hear the motor-car climbing on to the Heath. Below was the yellow, foul-smelling glare of the Hampstead Tube station. On the right the trees.

The girl, with her alert pink-and-white face, looked at him sharply, inquisitively. She had an odd nymph-like inquisitiveness, sometimes like a bird, sometimes a squirrel, sometimes a rabbit: never quite like a woman. At last he stood still, as if he would go no farther. There was a curious, baffled grin on his smooth, cream-coloured face.

'James,' he said loudly to her, leaning towards her ear. 'Do you hear somebody *laughing*?'

'Laughing?' she retorted quickly. 'Who's laughing?'

'I don't know. *Somebody*!' he shouted, showing his teeth at her in a very odd way.

'No, I hear nobody,' she announced.

'But it's most *extraordinary*!' he cried, his voice slurring up and down. 'Put on your machine.'

'Put it on?' she retorted. 'What for?'

'To see if you can *hear* it,' he cried.

'Hear what?'

'The *laughing*. Somebody laughing. It's most *extraordinary*.'

She gave her odd little chuckle and handed him her machine. He held it while she opened the lid and attached the wires, putting the band over her head and the receivers at her ears, like a wireless operator. Crumbs of snow fell down the cold darkness. She switched on : little yellow lights in glass tubes shone in the machine. She was connected, she was listening. He stood with his head ducked, his hands shoved down in his overcoat pockets.

Suddenly he lifted his face and gave the weirdest, slightly neighing laugh, uncovering his strong, spaced teeth and arching his black brows, and watching her with queer, gleaming, goat-like eyes.

She seemed a little dismayed.

'There!' he said. 'Didn't you hear it?'

'I heard *you*,' she said, in a tone which conveyed that *that* was enough.

'But didn't you hear *it*?' he cried, unfurling his lips oddly again.

'No!' she said.

He looked at her vindictively, and stood again with ducked head. She remained erect, her fur hat in her hand, her fine bobbed hair banded with the machine-band and catching crumbs of snow, her odd, bright-eyed, deaf nymph's face lifted with blank listening.

'There!' he cried, suddenly perking up his gleaming face. 'You mean to tell me you can't –' He was looking at her almost diabolically. But something else was too strong for him. His face wreathed with a startling, peculiar smile, seeming to gleam, and suddenly the most extraordinary laugh came bursting out of him, like an animal laughing. It was a strange neighing sound, amazing in her ears. She was startled, and switched her machine quieter.

A large form loomed up: a tall, clean-shaven young policeman. 'A radio?' he asked laconically.

'No, it's my machine. I'm deaf!' said Miss James quickly and distinctly. She was not the daughter of a peer for nothing.

The man in the bowler hat lifted his face and glared at the fresh-faced young policeman with a peculiar white glare in his eyes.

'Look here!' he said distinctly. 'Did you hear someone laughing?'

'Laughing? I heard you, sir.'

'No, *not* me.' He gave an impatient jerk of his arm, and lifted his face again. His smooth, creamy face seemed to gleam, there were subtle curves of derisive triumph in all its lines. He was careful not to look directly at the young policeman. 'The most extraordinary laughter I ever heard,' he added, and the same touch of derisive exultation sounded in his tones.

The policeman looked down on him cogitatingly.

'It's perfectly all right,' said Miss James coolly. 'He's not drunk. He just hears something that we don't hear.'

'Drunk!' echoed the man in the bowler hat, in profoundly amused derision. 'If I were merely drunk –' And off he went again in the wild, neighing, animal laughter, while his averted face seemed to flash.

At the sound of the laughter something roused in the blood of the girl and of the policeman. They stood nearer to one another, so that their sleeves touched and they looked wonderingly across at the man in the bowler hat. He lifted his black brows at them.

'Do you mean to say you heard nothing?' he asked.

'Only you,' said Miss James.

'Only you, sir!' echoed the policeman.

'What was it like?' asked Miss James.

'Ask me to *describe* it!' retorted the young man, in extreme contempt. 'It's the most marvellous sound in the world.'

And truly he seemed wrapped up in a new mystery.

'Where does it come from?' asked Miss James, very practical.

'*Apparently,*' he answered in contempt, 'from over there.' And he pointed to the trees and bushes inside the railings over the road.

'Well, let's go and see!' she said. 'I can carry my machine and go on listening.'

The man seemed relieved to get rid of the burden. He shoved his hands in his pockets again and sloped off across the road. The policeman, a queer look flickering on his fresh young face, put his hand round the girl's arm carefully and subtly to help her. She did not lean at all on the support of the big hand, but she was interested, so she did not resent it. Having held herself all her life intensely aloof from physical contact, and never having let any man touch her, she now, with a certain nymph-like voluptuousness, allowed the large hand of the young police-man to support her as they followed the quick wolf-like figure of the other man across the road uphill. And she could feel the presence of the young policeman, through all the thickness of his dark-blue uniform, as something young and alert and bright.

When they came up to the man in the bowler hat, he was standing with his head ducked, his ears pricked, listening beside the iron rail inside which grew big black holly-trees tufted with snow, and old, ribbed, silent English elms.

The policeman and the girl stood waiting. She was peering into the bushes with the sharp eyes of a deaf nymph, deaf to the world's noises. The man in the bowler hat listened intensely. A lorry rolled downhill, making the earth tremble.

'There!' cried the girl, as the lorry rumbled darkly past. And she glanced round with flashing eyes at the policeman, her fresh soft face gleaming with startled life. She glanced straight into the puzzled, amused eyes of the young policeman. He was just enjoying himself.

'Don't you see?' she said, rather imperiously.

'What is it, Miss?' answered the policeman.

'I mustn't point,' she said. 'Look where I look.'

And she looked away with brilliant eyes, into the dark holly bushes. She must see something, for she smiled faintly, with subtle satisfaction, and she tossed her erect head in all the pride of vindication. The policeman looked at her instead of into the bushes. There was a certain brilliance of triumph and vindication in all the poise of her slim body.

'I always knew I should see him,' she said triumphantly to herself.

'Whom do you see?' shouted the man in the bowler hat.

'Don't you see him too?' she asked, turning round her soft, arch, nymph-like face anxiously. She was anxious for the little man to see.

'No, I see nothing. What do you see, James?' cried the man in the bowler hat, insisting.

'A man.'

'Where?'

'There. Among the holly bushes.'

'Is he there now?'

'No! He's gone.'

'What sort of a man?'

'I don't know.'

'What did he look like?'

'I can't tell you.'

But at that instant the man in the bowler hat turned suddenly, and the arch, triumphant look flew to his face.

'Why, he must be *there*!' he cried, pointing up the grove. 'Don't you hear him laughing? He must be behind those trees.'

And his voice, with curious delight, broke into a laugh again, as he stood and stamped his feet on the snow, and danced to his own laughter, ducking his head. Then he turned away and ran swiftly up the avenue lined with old trees.

He slowed down as a door at the end of a garden path, white with untouched snow, suddenly opened, and a woman in a long-fringed shawl stood in the light. She peered out into the night. Then she came down to the low garden gate. Crumbs of snow still fell. She had dark hair and a tall dark comb.

'Did you knock at my door?' she asked of the man in the bowler hat.

'I? No!'

'Somebody knocked at my door.'

'Did they? Are you sure? They can't have done. There are no footmarks in the snow.'

'Nor are there!' she said. 'But somebody knocked and called something.'

'That's very curious,' said the man. 'Were you expecting someone?'

'No. Not exactly expecting anyone. Except that one is always expecting Somebody, you know.' In the dimness of the snow-lit night he could see her making big, dark eyes at him.

'Was it someone laughing?' he said.

'No. It was no one laughing, exactly. Someone knocked, and I ran to open, hoping as one always hopes, you know –'

'What?'

'Oh – that something wonderful is going to happen.'

He was standing close to the low gate. She stood on the opposite side. Her hair was dark, her face seemed dusky, as she looked up at him with her dark, meaningful eyes.

'Did you wish someone would come?' he asked.

'Very much,' she replied, in her plangent Jewish voice. She must be a Jewess.

'No matter who?' he said, laughing.

'So long as it was a man I could like,' she said in a low, meaningful, falsely shy voice.

'Really!' he said. 'Perhaps after all it was I who knocked – without knowing.'

'I think it was,' she said. 'It must have been.'

'Shall I come in?' he asked, putting his hand on the little gate.

'Don't you think you'd better?' she replied.

He bent down, unlatching the gate. As he did so the woman in the black shawl turned, and, glancing over her shoulder, hurried back to the house, walking unevenly in the snow, on her high-heeled shoes. The man hurried after her, hastening like a hound to catch up.

Meanwhile the girl and the policeman had come up. The girl stood still when she saw the man in the bowler hat going up the garden walk after the woman in the black shawl with the fringe.

'Is he going in?' she asked quickly.

'Looks like it, doesn't it?' said the policeman.

'Does he know that woman?'

'I can't say. I should say he soon will,' replied the policeman.

'But who is she?'

'I couldn't say who she is.'

The two dark, confused figures entered the lighted doorway, then the door closed on them.

'He's gone,' said the girl outside on the snow. She hastily began to pull off the band of her telephone-receiver, and switched off her machine. The tubes of secret light disappeared, she packed up the little leather case. Then, pulling on her soft fur cap, she stood once more ready.

The slightly martial look which her long, dark-blue, military-seeming coat gave her was intensified, while the slightly anxious, bewildered look of her face had gone. She seemed to stretch herself, to stretch her limbs free. And the inert look had left her full soft cheeks. Her cheeks were alive with the glimmer of pride and a new dangerous surety.

She looked quickly at the tall young policeman. He was clean-shaven, fresh-faced, smiling oddly under his helmet, waiting in subtle patience a few yards away. She saw that he was a decent young man, one of the waiting sort.

The second of ancient fear was followed at once in her by a blithe, unaccustomed sense of power.

'Well!' she said. 'I should say it's no use waiting.' She spoke decisively.

'You don't have to wait for him, do you?' asked the policeman.

'Not at all. He's much better where he is.' She laughed an odd, brief laugh. Then glancing over her shoulder, she set off down the hill, carrying her little case. Her feet felt light, her legs felt long and strong. She glanced over her shoulder again. The young policeman was following her, and she laughed to herself. Her limbs felt so lithe and so strong, if she wished she could easily run faster than he. If she wished she could easily kill him, even with her hands.

So it seemed to her. But why kill him? He was a decent young fellow. She had in front of her eyes the dark face among the holly bushes, with the brilliant mocking eyes. Her breast felt full of power, and her legs felt long and strong and wild. She was surprised herself at the strong, bright, throbbing sensation beneath her breasts, a sensation of triumph and of rosy anger. Her hands felt keen on her wrists. She who had always declared she had not a muscle in her body! Even now, it was not muscle, it was a sort of flame.

Suddenly it began to snow heavily, with fierce frozen puffs of wind. The snow was small, in frozen grains, and hit sharp on her face. It seemed to whirl round her as if she herself were whirling in a cloud. But she did not mind. There was a flame in her, her limbs felt flamey and strong, amid the whirl.

And the whirling, snowy air seemed full of presences, full of strange unheard voices. She was used to the sensation of noises taking place which she could not hear. This sensation became very strong. She felt something was happening in the wild air.

The London air was no longer heavy and clammy, saturated with ghosts of the unwilling dead. A new, clean tempest swept down from the Pole, and there were noises.

Voices were calling. In spite of her deafness she could hear someone, several voices, calling and whistling, as if many people were hallooing through the air :

'He's come back! Aha! He's come back!'

There was a wild, whistling, jubilant sound of voices in the storm of snow. Then obscured lightning winked through the snow in the air.

'Is that thunder and lightning?' she asked of the young policeman, as she stood still, waiting for his form to emerge through the veil of whirling snow.

'Seems like it to me,' he said.

And at that very moment the lightning blinked again, and the dark, laughing face was near her face, it almost touched her cheek.

She started back, but a flame of delight went over her.

'There!' she said. 'Did you see that?'

'It lightened,' said the policeman.

She was looking at him almost angrily. But then the clean, fresh animal look of his skin, and the tame-animal look in his frightened eyes amused her, she laughed her low, triumphant laugh. He was obviously afraid, like a frightened dog that sees something uncanny.

The storm suddenly whistled louder, more violently, and, with a strange noise like castanets, she seemed to hear voices clapping and crying :

'He is here! He's come back!'

She nodded her head gravely.

The policeman and she moved on side by side. She lived alone in a little stucco house in a side street down the hill. There was a church and a grove of trees and then the little old row of houses. The wind blew fiercely, thick with snow. Now and again a taxi went by, with its lights showing weirdly. But the world seemed empty, uninhabited save by snow and voices.

As the girl and the policeman turned past the grove of trees near the church, a great whirl of wind and snow made them stand still, and in the wild confusion they heard a whirling of sharp, delighted voices, something like seagulls, crying:

'He's here! He's here!'

'Well, I'm jolly glad he's back,' said the girl calmly.

'What's that?' said the nervous policeman, hovering near the girl.

The wind let them move forward. As they passed along the railings it seemed to them the doors of the church were open, and the windows were out, and the snow and the voices were blowing in a wild career all through the church.

'How extraordinary that they left the church open!' said the girl.

The policeman stood still. He could not reply.

And as they stood they listened to the wind and the church full of whirling voices all calling confusedly.

'*Now* I hear the laughing,' she said suddenly.

It came from the church: a sound of low, subtle, endless laughter, a strange, naked sound.

'Now I hear it!' she said.

But the policeman did not speak. He stood cowed, with his tail between his legs, listening to the strange noises in the church.

The wind must have blown out one of the windows, for they could see the snow whirling in volleys through the black gap, and whirling inside the church like a dim light. There came a sudden crash, followed by a burst of chuckling, naked laughter. The snow seemed to make a queer light inside the building, like ghosts moving, big and tall.

There was more laughter, and a tearing sound. On the wind, pieces of paper, leaves of books, came whirling among the snow through the dark window. Then a white thing, soaring like a crazy bird, rose up on the wind as if it had wings, and lodged on a black tree outside, struggling. It was the altar-cloth.

There came a bit of gay, trilling music. The wind was running over the organ-pipes like pan-pipes, quickly up and down. Snatches of wild, gay, trilling music, and bursts of the naked low laughter.

'Really!' said the girl. 'This is most extraordinary. Do you hear the music and the people laughing?'

'Yes, I hear somebody on the organ!' said the policeman.

'And do you get the puff of warm wind? Smelling of spring. Almond blossom, that's what it is! A most marvellous scent of almond blossom. *Isn't* it an extraordinary thing!'

She went on triumphantly past the church, and came to the row of little old houses. She entered her own gate in the little railed entrance.

'Here I am!' she said finally. 'I'm home now. Thank you very much for coming with me.'

She looked at the young policeman. His whole body was white as a wall with snow, and in the vague light of the arc-lamp from the street his face was humble and frightened.

'Can I come in and warm myself a bit?' he asked humbly. She knew it was fear rather than cold that froze him. He was in mortal fear.

'Well!' she said. 'Stay down in the sitting-room if you like. But don't come upstairs, because I am alone in the house. You can make up the fire in the sitting-room, and you can go when you are warm.'

She left him on the big, low couch before the fire, his face bluish and blank with fear. He rolled his blue eyes after her as she left the room. But she went up to her bedroom, and fastened her door.

In the morning she was in her studio upstairs in her little house, looking at her own paintings and laughing to herself. Her canaries were talking and shrilly whistling in the sunshine that followed the storm. The cold snow outside was still clean, and the white glare in the air gave the effect of much stronger sunshine than actually existed.

She was looking at her own paintings, and chuckling to herself over their comicalness. Suddenly they struck her as absolutely absurd. She quite enjoyed looking at them, they seemed to her so grotesque. Especially her self-portrait, with its nice brown hair and its slightly opened rabbit-mouth and its baffled, uncertain rabbit eyes. She looked at the painted face and laughed in a long, rippling laugh, till the yellow canaries like faded daffodils almost went mad in an effort to sing louder. The girl's long, rippling laugh sounded through the house uncannily.

The housekeeper, a rather sad-faced young woman of a superior sort – nearly all people in England are of the superior sort, superiority being an English ailment – came in with an inquiring and rather disapproving look.

'Did you call, Miss James?' she asked loudly.

'No. No, I didn't call. Don't shout, I can hear quite well,' replied the girl.

The housekeeper looked at her again.

'You knew there was a young man in the sitting-room?' she said.

'No. Really!' cried the girl. 'What, the young policeman? I'd forgotten all about him. He came in in the storm to warm himself. Hasn't he gone?'

'No, Miss James.'

'How extraordinary of him! What time is it? Quarter to nine! Why didn't he go when he was warm? I must go and see him, I suppose.'

'He says he's lame,' said the housekeeper censoriously and loudly.

'Lame! That's extraordinary. He certainly wasn't last night. But don't shout. I can hear quite well.'

'Is Mr Marchbanks coming in to breakfast, Miss James?' said the housekeeper, more and more censorious.

'I couldn't say. But I'll come down as soon as mine is ready. I'll be down in a minute, anyhow, to see the policeman. Extraordinary that he is still here.'

She sat down before her window, in the sun, to think a while. She could see the snow outside, the bare, purplish trees. The air all seemed rare and different. Suddenly the world had become quite different: as if some skin or integument had broken, as if the old, mouldering London sky had crackled and rolled back, like an old skin, shrivelled, leaving an absolutely new blue heaven.

'It really is extraordinary!' she said to herself. 'I certainly saw that man's face. What a wonderful face it was! I shall never forget it. Such laughter! He laughs longest who laughs last. He certainly will have the last laugh. I like him for that : he will laugh last. Must be someone really extraordinary! How very nice to be the one to laugh last. He certainly will. What a wonderful being! I suppose I must call him a being. He's not a person exactly.

'But how wonderful of him to come back and alter all the world immediately! *Isn't* that extraordinary. I wonder if he'll have altered Marchbanks. Of course Marchbanks never *saw* him. But he heard him. Wouldn't that do as well, I wonder! – I *wonder*!'

She went off into a muse about Marchbanks. She and he were *such* friends. They had been friends like that for almost two years. Never lovers. Never that at all. But *friends*.

And after all, she had been in love with him : in her head. This seemed now so funny to her : that she had been, in her head, so much in love with him. After all, life was too absurd.

Because now she saw herself and him as such a funny pair. He was funnily taking life terribly seriously, especially his own life. And she so ridiculously *determined* to save him from himself. Oh, how absurd! *Determined* to save him from himself, and wildly in love with him in the effort. The determination to save him from himself.

Absurd! Absurd! Absurd! Since she had seen the man laughing among the holly-bushes – *such* extraordinary, wonderful laughter – she had seen her own ridiculousness. Really, what fantastic silliness, saving a man from himself! Saving anybody. What fantastic silliness! How much more amusing and lively to let a man go to perdition in his own way. Perdition was more amusing than salvation anyhow, and a much better place for most men to go to.

She had never been in love with any man, and only spuriously in love with Marchbanks. She saw it quite plainly now. After all, what nonsense it all was, this being-in-love business. Thank goodness she had never made the humiliating mistake.

No, the man among the holly-bushes had made her see it all so plainly : the ridiculousness of being in love, the *infra dig.* business of chasing a man or being chased by a man.

'Is love *really* so absurd and *infra dig.*?' she said aloud to herself.

'Why, of course!' came a deep, laughing voice.

She started round, but nobody was to be seen.

'I expect it's that man again!' she said to herself. 'It really *is* remarkable, you know. I consider it's a remarkable thing that I never really wanted a man, *any* man. And there I am over thirty. It *is* curious. Whether it's something wrong with me, or right with me, I can't say. I don't know till I've proved it. But I believe, if that man kept on laughing something would happen to me.'

She smelt the curious smell of almond blossom in the room, and heard the distant laugh again.

'I do wonder why Marchbanks went with that woman last night – that Jewish-looking woman. Whatever could he want of her? – or she him? So strange, as if they both had made up their minds to something! How extraordinarily puzzling life is! So messy, it all seems.

'Why does nobody ever laugh like that man? He *did* seem so wonderful. So scornful! And so proud! And so real! With those laughing, scornful, amazing eyes, just laughing and disappearing again. I can't imagine him chasing a Jewish-looking woman. Or chasing any woman, thank goodness. It's all *so* messy. My policeman would be messy if one would let him: like a dog. I do dislike dogs, really I do. And men do seem so doggy! – '

But even while she mused, she began to laugh again to herself with a long, low chuckle. How wonderful of that man to come and laugh like that and make the sky crack and shrivel like an old skin! Wasn't he wonderful! Wouldn't it be wonderful if he just touched her. Even touched her. She felt, if he touched her, she herself would emerge new and tender out of an old, hard skin. She was gazing abstractedly out of the window.

'There he comes, just now,' she said abruptly. But she meant Marchbanks, not the laughing man.

There he came, his hands still shoved down in his overcoat pockets, his head still rather furtively ducked, in the bowler hat, and his legs still rather shambling. He came hurrying across the road, not looking up, deep in thought, no doubt. Thinking profoundly, with agonies of agitation, no doubt about his last night's experience. It made her laugh.

She, watching from the window above, burst into a long laugh, and the canaries went off their heads again.

He was in the hall below. His resonant voice was calling, rather imperiously:

'James! Are you coming down?'

'No,' she called. 'You come up.'

He came up two at a time, as if his feet were a bit savage with the stairs for obstructing him.

In the doorway he stood staring at her with a vacant, sardonic look, his grey eyes moving with a queer light. And she looked back at him with a curious, rather haughty carelessness.

'Don't you want your breakfast?' she asked. It was his custom to come and take breakfast with her each morning.

'No,' he answered loudly. 'I went to a tea-shop.'

'Don't shout,' she said. 'I can hear you quite well.'

He looked at her with mockery and a touch of malice.

'I believe you always could,' he said, still loudly.

'Well, anyway, I can now, so you needn't shout,' she replied.

And again his grey eyes, with the queer, greyish phosphorescent gleam in them, lingered malignantly on her face.

'Don't look at me,' she said calmly. 'I know all about everything.'

He burst into a pouf of malicious laughter.

'Who taught you – the policeman?' he cried.

'Oh, by the way, he must be downstairs! No, he was only incidental. So, I suppose, was the woman in the shawl. Did you stay all night?'

'Not entirely. I came away before dawn. What did you do?'

'Don't shout. I came home long before dawn.' And she seemed to hear the long, low laughter.

'Why, what's the matter?' he said curiously. 'What have you been doing?'

'I don't quite know. Why? – are you going to call me to account?'

'Did you hear that laughing?'

'Oh, yes. And many more things. And saw things too.'

'Have you seen the paper?'

'No. Don't shout, I can hear.'

'There's been a great storm, blew out the windows and doors of the church outside here, and pretty well wrecked the place.'

'I saw it. A leaf of the church Bible blew right in my face: from the Book of Job –' She gave a low laugh.

'But what else did you see?' he cried loudly.

'I saw *him*.'

'Who?'

'Ah, that I can't say.'

'But what was he like?'

'That I can't tell you. I don't really know.'

'But you must know. Did your policeman see him too?'

'No, I don't suppose he did. My policeman!' And she went off into a long ripple of laughter. 'He is by no means mine. But I *must* go downstairs and see him.'

'It's certainly made you very strange,' Marchbanks said. 'You've got no *soul*, you know.'

'Oh, thank goodness for that!' she cried. 'My policeman has one, I'm sure. *My policeman*!' and she went off again into a long peal of laughter, the canaries pealing shrill accompaniment.

'What's the matter with you?' he said.

'Having no soul. I never had one really. It was always fobbed off on me. Soul was the only thing there was between you and me. Thank goodness it's gone. Haven't you lost yours? The one that seemed to worry you, like a decayed tooth?'

'But what are you *talking* about?' he cried.

'I don't know,' she said. 'It's all so extraordinary. But look here, I *must* go down and see my policeman. He's downstairs in the sitting-room. You'd better come with me.'

They went down together. The policeman, in his waistcoat and shirt-sleeves, was lying on the sofa, with a very long face.

'Look here!' said Miss James to him. 'Is it true you're lame?'

'It is true. That's why I'm here. I can't walk,' said the fair-haired young man as tears came to his eyes.

'But how did it happen? You weren't lame last night,' she said.

'I don't know how it happened – but when I woke up and tried to stand up, I couldn't do it.' The tears ran down his distressed face.

'How very extraordinary!' she said. 'What can we do about it?'

'Which foot is it?' asked Marchbanks. 'Let us have a look at it.'

'I don't like to,' said the poor devil.

'You'd better,' said Miss James.

He slowly pulled off his stocking, and showed his white left foot curiously clubbed, like the weird paw of some animal. When he looked at it himself, he sobbed.

And as he sobbed, the girl heard again the low, exulting laughter. But she paid no heed to it, gazing curiously at the weeping young policeman.

'Does it hurt?' she asked.

'It does if I try to walk on it,' wept the young man.

'I'll tell you what,' she said. 'We'll telephone for a doctor, and he can take you home in a taxi.'

The young fellow shamefacedly wiped his eyes.

'But have you no idea how it happened?' asked Marchbanks anxiously.

'I haven't myself,' said the young fellow.

At that moment the girl heard the low, eternal laugh right in her ear. She started, but could see nothing.

She started round again as Marchbanks gave a strange, yelping cry, like a shot animal. His white face was drawn, distorted in a curious grin, that was chiefly agony but partly wild recognition. He was staring with fixed eyes at something. And in the rolling agony of his eyes was the horrible grin of a man who realizes he has made a final, and this time fatal, fool of himself.

'Why,' he yelped in a high voice, 'I knew it was he!' And with a queer shuddering laugh he pitched forward on the carpet and lay writhing for a moment on the floor. Then he lay still, in a weird, distorted position, like a man struck by lightning.

Miss James stared with round, staring brown eyes.

'Is he dead?' she asked quickly.

The young policeman was trembling so that he could hardly speak. She could hear his teeth chattering.

'Seems like it,' he stammered.

There was a faint smell of almond blossom in the air.

In Love

'WELL, my dear!' said Henrietta. 'If I had such a worried look on my face, when I was going down to spend the week-end with the man I was engaged to – and going to be married to in a month – well! I should either try and change my face, or hide my feelings, or something.'

'You shut up!' said Hester curtly. 'Don't look at my face, if it doesn't please you.'

'Now, my dear Hester, don't go into one of your tempers! Just look in the mirror, and you'll see what I mean.'

'Who cares what you mean! You're not responsible for my face,' said Hester desperately, showing no intention of looking in the mirror, or of otherwise following her sister's kind advice.

Henrietta, being the younger sister, and mercifully unengaged, hummed a tune lightly. She was only twenty-one, and had not the faintest intention of jeopardizing her peace of mind by accepting any sort of fatal ring. Nevertheless, it *was* nice to see Hester 'getting off', as they say; for Hester was nearly twenty-five, which is serious.

The worst of it was, lately Hester had had her famous 'worried' look on her face, when it was a question of the faith-ful Joe: dark shadows under the eyes, drawn lines down the cheeks. And when Hester looked like that, Henrietta couldn't help feeling the most horrid jangled echo of worry and appre-hension in her own heart, and she hated it. She simply couldn't stand that sudden feeling of fear.

'What I mean to say,' she continued, 'is – that it's jolly un-fair to Joe, if you go down looking like that. Either put a better face on it, or –' But she checked herself. She was going to say 'don't go.' But really, she did hope that Hester would go through with this marriage. Such a weight off her, Henrietta's, mind.

'Oh, hang!' cried Hester. 'Shut up!' And her dark eyes flashed a spark of fury and misgiving at the young Henrietta.

Henrietta sat down on the bed, lifted her chin, and composed her face like a meditating angel. She really was intensely fond of Hester, and the worried look was such a terribly bad sign.

'Look here, Hester!' she said. 'Shall I come down to Markbury with you? *I* don't mind, if you'd like me to.'

'My dear girl,' cried Hester in desperation, 'what earthly use do you think that would be?'

'Well, I thought it might take the edge off the intimacy, if that's what worries you.'

Hester re-echoed with a hollow, mocking laugh.

'Don't be such a *child*, Henrietta, really!' she said.

And Hester set off alone, down to Wiltshire, where her Joe had just started a little farm, to get married on. After being in the artillery, he had got sick and tired of business : besides, Hester would never have gone into a little suburban villa. Every woman sees her home through a wedding ring. Hester had only taken a squint through her engagement ring, so far. But, Ye Gods! not Golders Green, not even Harrow!

So Joe had built a little brown wooden bungalow – largely with his own hands : and at the back was a small stream with two willows, old ones. At the sides were brown sheds, and chicken runs. There were pigs in a hog-proof wire fence, and two cows in a field, and a horse. Joe had thirty-odd acres, with only a youth to help him. But of course, there would be Hester.

It all looked very new and tidy. Joe was a worker. He, too, looked rather new and tidy, very healthy and pleased with himself. He didn't even see the 'worried look'. Or, if he did, he only said :

'You're looking a bit fagged, Hester. Going up to the City takes it out of you, more than you know. You'll be another girl down here.'

'Shan't I just!' cried Hester.

She did like it, too! – the lots of white and yellow hens, and the pigs so full of pep! And the yellow thin blades of willow leaves showering softly down at the back of her house, from the leaning old trees. She liked it awfully : especially the yellow leaves on the earth.

She told Joe she thought it was all lovely, topping, fine! And he was awfully pleased. Certainly *he* looked fit enough.

The mother of the helping youth gave them dinner at half-past twelve. The afternoon was all sunshine and little jobs to do, after she had dried the dishes for the mother of the youth.

'Not long now, Miss, before you'll be cooking at this range: and a good little range it is.'

'Not long now, no!' echoed Hester, in the hot little wooden kitchen, that was overheated from the range.

The woman departed. After tea, the youth also departed and Joe and Hester shut up the chickens and the pigs. It was nightfall. Hester went in and made the supper, feeling somehow a bit of a fool, and Joe made a fire in the living-room, he feeling rather important and luscious.

He and Hester would be alone in the bungalow, till the youth appeared next morning. Six months ago, Hester would have enjoyed it. They were so perfectly comfortable together, he and she. They had been friends, and his family and hers had been friends for years, donkey's years. He was a perfectly decent boy, and there would never have been anything messy to fear from him. Nor from herself. Ye Gods, no!

But now, alas, since she had promised to marry him, he had made the wretched mistake of falling 'in love' with her. He had never been that way before. And if she had known he would get this way now, she would have said decidedly : Let us remain friends, Joe, for this sort of thing is a come-down. Once he started cuddling and petting, she couldn't stand him. Yet she felt she ought to. She imagined she even ought to like it. Though where the *ought* came from, she could not see.

'I'm afraid, Hester,' he said sadly, 'you're not in love with me as I am with you.'

'Hang it all!' she cried. 'If I'm not, you ought to be jolly well thankful, that's all I've got to say.'

Which double-barrelled remark he heard, but did not register. He never liked looking anything in the very pin-point middle of the eye. He just left it, and left all her feelings comfortably in the dark. Comfortably for him, that is.

He was extremely competent at motor-cars and farming and all that sort of thing. And surely she, Hester, was as complicated as a motor-car! Surely she had as many subtle little valves and magnetos and accelerators and all the rest of it, to her make-up! If only he would try to handle *her* as carefully as he

handled his car! She needed starting, as badly as ever any auto-
mobile did. Even if a car had a self-starter, the man had to
give it the right twist. Hester felt she would need a lot of
cranking up, if ever she was to start off on the matrimonial
road with Joe. And he, the fool, just sat in a motionless car and
pretended he was making heaven knows how many miles an
hour.

This evening she felt really desperate. She had been quite all
right doing things with him, during the afternoon, about the
place. Then she liked being with him. But now that it was
evening and they were alone, the stupid little room, the cosy
fire, Joe, Joe's pipe, and Joe's smug sort of hypocritical face, all
was just too much for her.

'Come and sit here, dear,' said Joe persuasively, patting the
sofa at his side. And she, because she believed a *nice* girl would
have been only too delighted to go and sit 'there', went and
sat beside him. But she was boiling. What cheek! What
cheek of him even to have a sofa! She loathed the vulgarity of
sofas.

She endured his arm round her waist, and a certain pressure
of his biceps which she presumed was cuddling. He had carefully knocked his pipe out. But she thought how smug and silly
his face looked, all its natural frankness and straightforwardness
had gone. How ridiculous of him to stroke the back of her
neck! How idiotic he was, trying to be lovey-dovey! She wondered what sort of sweet nothings Lord Byron, for example,
had murmured to his various ladies. Surely not so blithering,
not so incompetent! And how monstrous of him, to kiss her
like that.

'I'd infinitely rather you'd play to me, Joe,' she snapped.

'You don't want me to play to you tonight, do you, dear?'
he said.

'Why not tonight? I'd love to hear some Tchaikowsky,
something to stir me up a bit.'

He rose obediently, and went to the piano. He played quite
well. She listened. And Tchaikowsky might have stirred her
up all right. The music itself, that is. If she hadn't been so
desperately aware that Joe's love-making, if you can call it such,
became more absolutely impossible after the sound of the music.

'That was fine!' she said. 'Now do me my favourite nocturne.'

While he concentrated on the fingering, she slipped out of the house.

Oh! she gasped a sigh of relief to be in the cool October air. The darkness was dim, in the west was a half moon freshly shining, and all the air was motionless, dimness lay like a haze on the earth.

Hester shook her hair, and strode away from the bungalow, which was a perfect little drum, re-echoing to her favourite nocturne. She simply rushed to get out of earshot.

Ah! the lovely night! She tossed her short hair again, and felt like Mazeppa's horse, about to dash away into the infinite. Though the infinite was only a field belonging to the next farm. But Hester felt herself seething in the soft moonlight. Oh! to rush away over the edge of the beyond! if the beyond, like Joe's breadknife, did have an edge to it. 'I know I'm an idiot,' she said to herself. But that didn't take away the wild surge of her limbs. Oh! If there were only some other solution, instead of Joe and his spooning. Yes, SPOONING! The word made her lose the last shred of her self-respect, but she said it aloud.

There was, however, a bunch of strange horses in this field, so she made her way cautiously back through Joe's fence. It was just like him, to have such a little place that you couldn't get away from the sound of his piano, without trespassing on somebody else's ground.

As she drew near the bungalow, however, the drumming of Joe's piano suddenly ceased. Oh, Heaven! she looked wildly round. An old willow leaned over the stream. She stretched, crouching, and with the quickness of a long cat, climbed up into the net of cool-bladed foliage.

She had scarcely shuffled and settled into a tolerable position, when he came round the corner of the house and into the moonlight, looking for her. How dare he look for her! She kept as still as a bat among the leaves, watching him as he sauntered with erect, tiresomely manly figure and lifted head, staring around in the darkness. He looked for once very ineffectual, insignificant and at a loss. Where was his supposed male magic? Why was he so slow and unequal to the situation?

There! He was calling softly and self-consciously: 'Hester! Hester! Where have you put yourself?'

He was angry really. Hester kept still in her tree, trying not to fidget. She had not the faintest intention of answering him. He might as well have been on another planet. He sauntered vaguely and unhappily out of sight.

Then she had a qualm. 'Really, my girl, it's a bit thick, the way you treat him! Poor old Joe!'

Immediately something began to hum inside her: 'I hear those tender voices calling Poor Old Joe!'

Nevertheless, she didn't want to go indoors to spend the evening *tête à tête* – my word! – with him.

'Of course it's absurd to think I could possibly fall in love like that. I would rather fall into one of his pig-troughs. It's so frightfully common. As a matter of fact, it's just a proof that he doesn't love me.'

This thought went through her like a bullet. 'The very fact of his being in love with me proves that he doesn't love me. No man that loved a woman could be in love with her like that. It's so insulting to her.'

She immediately began to cry. And fumbling in her sleeve for her hanky, she nearly fell out of the tree. Which brought her to her senses.

In the obscure distance she saw him returning to the house, and she felt bitter. 'Why did he start all this mess? I never wanted to marry anybody, and I certainly never bargained for anybody falling in love with me. Now I'm miserable, and I feel abnormal. Because the majority of girls must like this in-love business, or men wouldn't do it. And the majority must be normal. So *I'm* abnormal, and I'm up a tree. I loathe myself. As for Joe, he's spoilt all there was between us, and he expects me to marry him on the strength of it. It's perfectly sickening! What a mess life is. How I loathe messes!'

She immediately shed a few more tears, in the course of which she heard the door of the bungalow shut with something of a bang. He had gone indoors, and he was going to be right-eously offended. A new misgiving came over her.

The willow tree was uncomfortable. The air was cold and damp. If she caught another chill she'd probably snuffle all winter long. She saw the lamplight coming warm from the window of the bungalow, and she said 'Damn!' which meant, in her case, that she was feeling bad.

She slid down out of the tree, and scratched her arm and probably damaged one of her nicest pair of stockings. 'Oh, hang!' she said with emphasis, preparing to go into the bungalow and have it out with poor old Joe. 'I will *not* call him Poor Old Joe!'

At that moment she heard a motor-car slow down in the lane, and there came a low, cautious toot from a hooter. Headlights shone at a standstill near Joe's new iron gate.

'The cheek of it! The unbearable cheek of it! There's that young Henrietta come down on me!'

She flew along Joe's cinder-drive like a maenad.

'Hello, Hester!' came Henrietta's young voice, coolly floating from the obscurity of the car. 'How's everything?'

'What cheek!' cried Hester. 'What amazing cheek!' She leaned on Joe's iron gate, and panted.

'How's everything?' repeated Henrietta's voice blandly.

'What do you mean by it?' demanded Hester, still panting.

'Now, my girl, don't go off at a tangent! We weren't coming in unless you came out. You needn't think we want to put our noses in your affairs. We're going down to camp on Bonamy. Isn't the weather too divine!'

Bonamy was Joe's pal, also an old artillery man, who had set up a 'farm' about a mile farther along the land. Joe was by no means a Robinson Crusoe in his bungalow.

'Who are you, anyway?' demanded Hester.

'Same old birds,' said Donald, from the driver's seat. Donald was Joe's brother. Henrietta was sitting in front, next to him.

'Same as ever,' said Teddy, poking his head out of the car. Teddy was a second cousin.

'Well,' said Hester, sort of climbing down. 'I suppose you may as well come in, now you *are* here. Have you eaten?'

'Eaten, yes,' said Donald. 'But we aren't coming in this trip, Hester, don't you fret.'

'Why not?' flashed Hester, up in arms.

' 'Fraid of brother Joe,' said Donald.

'Besides, Hester,' said Henrietta anxiously, 'you know you don't want us.'

'Henrietta, don't be a fool!' flashed Hester.

'*Well*, Hester – !' remonstrated the pained Henrietta.

'Come on in, and no more nonsense!' said Hester.

'Not this trip, Hester,' said Donald.

'No, sir!' said Teddy.

'But what idiots you all are! Why not?' cried Hester.

' 'Fraid of our elder brother,' said Donald.

'All right,' said Hester. 'Then I'll come along with you.'

She hastily opened the gate.

'Shall I just have a peep? I'm pining to see the house,' said Henrietta, climbing with a long leg over the door of the car.

The night was now dark, the moon had sunk. The two girls crunched in silence along the cinder track to the house.

'You'd say, if you'd rather I didn't come in – or if Joe'd rather,' said Henrietta anxiously. She was very much disturbed in her young mind, and hoped for a clue. Hester walked on without answering. Henrietta laid her hand on her sister's arm. Hester shook it off, saying :

'My dear Henrietta, do be normal!'

And she rushed up the three steps to the door, which she flung open, displaying the lamplit living-room, Joe in an arm-chair by the low fire, his back to the door. He did not turn round.

'Here's Henrietta!' cried Hester, in a tone which meant: '*How's that?*'

He got up and faced round, his brown eyes in his stiff face very angry.

'How did *you* get here?' he asked rudely.

'Came in a car,' said young Henrietta, from her Age of Innocence.

'With Donald and Teddy – they're there just outside the gate,' said Hester. The old gang!

'Coming in?' asked Joe, with greater anger in his voice.

'I suppose you'll go out and invite them,' said Hester.

Joe said nothing, just stood like a block.

'I expect you'll think it's awful of me to come intruding,' said Henrietta meekly. 'We're just going on to Bonamy's.' She gazed innocently round the room. 'But it's an adorable little place, awfully good taste in a cottagey sort of way. I like it awfully. Can I warm my hands?'

Joe moved from in front of the fire. He was in his slippers. Henrietta dangled her long red hands, red from the night air, before the grate.

'I'll rush right away again,' she said.

'Oh-h,' drawled Hester curiously. 'Don't do that!'

'Yes, I must. Donald and Teddy are waiting.'

The door stood wide open, the headlights of the car could be seen in the lane.

'Oh-h!' Again that curious drawl from Hester. 'I'll tell them you're staying the night with me. I can do with a bit of company.'

Joe looked at her.

'What's the game?' he said.

'No game at all! Only now Tatty's come, she may as well stay.'

'Tatty' was the rather infrequent abbreviation of 'Henrietta'.

'Oh, but Hester!' said Henrietta. 'I'm going on to Bonamy's with Donald and Teddy.'

'Not if I want you to stay here!' said Hester.

Henrietta looked all surprised, resigned helplessness.

'What's the game?' repeated Joe. 'Had you fixed up to come down here tonight?'

'No, Joe, really!' said Henrietta, with earnest innocence. 'I hadn't the faintest idea of such a thing, till Donald suggested it, at four o'clock this afternoon. Only the weather was too perfectly divine, we had to go out somewhere, so we thought we'd descend on Bonamy. I hope *he* won't be frightfully put out, as well.'

'And if we had arranged it, it wouldn't have been a crime,' struck in Hester. 'And anyway, now you're here you might as well all camp here.'

'Oh, no, Hester! I know Donald will never come inside the gate. He was angry with me for making him stop, and it was I who tooted. It wasn't him, it was me. The curiosity of Eve, I suppose. Anyhow I've put my foot in it, as usual. So now I'd better clear out as fast as I can. Good night!'

She gathered her coat round her with one arm and moved vaguely to the door.

'In that case, I'll come along with you,' said Hester.

'But, Hester!' cried Henrietta. And she looked inquiringly at Joe.

'I know as little as you do,' he said, 'what's going on.'

His face was wooden and angry, Henrietta could make nothing of him.

'Hester!' cried Henrietta. 'Do be sensible! What's gone wrong! Why don't you at least *explain*, and give everybody a chance! Talk about being normal! – you're always flinging it at *me*!'

There was a dramatic silence.

'What's happened?' Henrietta insisted, her eyes very bright and distressed, her manner showing that she was determined to be sensible.

'Nothing, of course!' mocked Hester.

'Do *you* know, Joe?' said Henrietta, like another Portia, turning very sympathetically to the man.

For a moment Joe thought how much nicer Henrietta was than her sister.

'I only know she asked me to play the piano, and then she dodged out of the house. Since then, her steering gear's been out of order.'

'Ha-ha-ha!' laughed Hester falsely and melodramatically. 'I like that. I like my dodging out of the house! I went out for a breath of fresh air. I should like to know whose steering gear is out of order, talking about my dodging out of the house!'

'You dodged out of the house,' said Joe.

'Oh, did I? And why should I, pray?'

'I suppose you have your own reasons.'

'I have too. And very good reasons.'

There was a moment of stupefied amazement . . . Joe and Hester had known each other so well, for such a long time. And now look at them!

'But why did you, Hester?' asked Henrietta, in her most breathless naïve fashion.

'Why did I what?'

There was a low toot from the motor-car in the lane.

'They're calling me! Good-bye!' cried Henrietta, wrapping her coat round her and turning decisively to the door.

'If you go, my girl, I'm coming with you,' said Hester.

'But why?' cried Henrietta in amazement. The horn tooted again. She opened the door, and called into the night:

'Half a minute!' Then she closed the door again, softly, and turned once more in her amazement to Hester.

'But why, Hester?'

Hester's eyes almost squinted with exasperation. She could hardly bear even to glance at the wooden and angry Joe.

'Why?'

'Why?' came the soft reiteration of Henrietta's question. All the attention focused on Hester, but Hester was a sealed book.

'Why?'

'She doesn't know herself,' said Joe, seeing a loophole.

Out rang Hester's crazy and melodramatic laugh.

'Oh, doesn't she!' Her face flew into sudden strange fury. 'Well, if you want to know, I absolutely *can't stand* your making love to me, if that's what you call the business.'

Henrietta let go the door handle, and sank weakly into a chair.

The worst had come to the worst. Joe's face became purple, then slowly paled to yellow.

'Then,' said Henrietta in a hollow voice, 'you can't marry him.'

'I couldn't possibly marry him if he kept on being *in love* with me.' She spoke the two words with almost snarling emphasis.

'And you couldn't possibly marry him if he *wasn't*,' said the guardian angel, Henrietta.

'Why not?' cried Hester. 'I could stand him all right till he started being in love with me. Now, he's simply out of the question.'

There was a pause, out of which came Henrietta's:

'After all, Hester, a man's *supposed* to be in love with the woman he wants to marry.'

'Then he'd better keep it to himself, that's all I've got to say.'

There was a pause. Joe, silent as ever, looked more wooden and sheepishly angry.

'But, Hester! Hasn't a man *got* to be in love with you? –'

'Not with me! You've not had it to put up with, my girl.' Henrietta sighed helplessly.

'Then you can't marry him, that's obvious. What an awful pity!'

A pause.

'Nothing can be so perfectly humiliating as a man making love to you,' said Hester. '*I loathe* it.'

'Perhaps it's because it's the wrong man,' said Henrietta sadly, with a glance at the wooden and sheepish Joe.

'I don't believe I could stand that sort of thing, with *any* man. Henrietta, do you know what it is, being stroked and cuddled? It's too perfectly awful and ridiculous.'

'Yes!' said Henrietta, musing sadly. 'As if one were a perfectly priceless meat pie, and the dog licked it tenderly before he gobbled it up. It *is* rather sickening, I agree.'

'And what's so awful, a perfectly decent man will go and get that way. Nothing is so awful as a man who has fallen in love,' said Hester.

'I know what you mean, Hester. So doggy!' said Henrietta sadly.

The motor horn tooted exasperatedly. Henrietta rose like a Portia who has been a failure. She opened the door, and suddenly yelled fiercely into the night:

'Go on without me. I'll walk. Don't wait.'

'How long will you be?' came a voice.

'I don't know. If I want to come, I'll walk,' she yelled.

'Come back for you in an hour.'

'Right,' she shrieked, and slammed the door in their distant faces. Then she sat down dejectedly, in the silence. She was going to stand by Hester. That *fool*, Joe, standing there like a mutton-head!

They heard the car start, and retreat down the lane.

'Men are awful!' said Henrietta dejectedly.

'Anyhow, you're mistaken,' said Joe with sudden venom, to Hester. 'I'm not in love with you, Miss Clever.'

The two women looked at him as if he were Lazarus risen.

'And I never was in love with you, that way,' he added, his brown eyes burning with a strange fire of self-conscious shame and anger, and naked passion.

'Well, what a liar you must be then. That's all I can say!' replied Hester coldly.

'Do you mean,' said young Henrietta acidly, 'that you put it all on?'

'I thought she expected it of me,' he said, with a nasty little smile that simply paralysed the two young women. If he had turned into a boa-constrictor, they would not have been more amazed. That sneering little smile! Their good-natured Joe!

'I thought it was expected of me,' he repeated, jeering.

Hester was horrified.

'Oh, but how beastly of you to do it!' cried Henrietta to him.

'And what a lie!' cried Hester. 'He liked it.'

'Do you think he did, Hester?' said Henrietta.

'I liked it in a way,' he said impudently. 'But I shouldn't have liked it, if I thought she didn't.'

Hester flung out her arms.

'Henrietta,' she cried, 'why can't we kill him?'

'I wish we could,' said Henrietta.

'What are you to do, when you know a girl's rather strict, and you like her for it – and you're not going to be married for a month – and – and you – and you've got to get over the interval somehow – and what else does Rudolf Valentino do for you? – you like *him* –'

'He's dead, poor dear. But I loathed him, *really*,' said Hester.

'You didn't seem to,' said he.

'Well, anyhow, you aren't Rudolf Valentino, and I loathe *you* in the role.'

'You won't get a chance again. I loathe *you* altogether.'

'And I'm extremely relieved to hear it, my boy.'

There was a lengthy pause, after which Henrietta said with decision :

'Well, that's that! Will you come along to Bonamy's with me, Hester, or shall I stay here with you?'

'*I* don't care, my girl,' said Hester with bravado.

'Neither do I care what you do,' said he. 'But I call it pretty rotten of you, not to tell me right out, at first.'

'I thought it was real with you then, and I didn't want to hurt you,' said Hester.

'You look as if you didn't want to hurt me,' he said.

'Oh, *now*,' she said, 'since it was all pretence, it doesn't matter.'

'I should say it doesn't,' he retorted.

There was a silence. The clock, which was intended to be their family clock, ticked rather hastily.

'Anyway,' he said, 'I consider you've let me down.'

'I like that!' she cried, 'considering what you've played off on me!'

He looked her straight in the eye. They knew each other so well.

Why had he tried that silly love-making game on her? It was a betrayal of their simple intimacy. He saw it plainly, and repented.

And she saw the honest, patient love for her in his eyes, and the queer, quiet, central desire. It was the first time she had seen it, that quiet, patient, central desire of a young man who has suffered during his youth, and seeks now almost with the slowness of age. A hot flush went over her heart. She felt herself responding to him.

'What have you decided, Hester?' said Henrietta.

'I'll stay with Joe, after all,' said Hester.

'Very well,' said Henrietta. 'And I'll go along to Bonamy's.' She opened the door quietly, and was gone.

Joe and Hester looked at one another from a distance.

'I'm sorry, Hester,' said he.

'You know, Joe,' she said, 'I don't mind what you do, if you love me *really*.'

Glad Ghosts

I KNEW Carlotta Fell in the early days before the war. Then she was escaping into art, and was just 'Fell'. That was at our famous but uninspired school of art, the Thwaite, where I myself was diligently murdering my talent. At the Thwaite they always gave Carlotta the Still-life prizes. She accepted them calmly, as one of our conquerors, but the rest of the students felt vicious about it. They called it buttering the laurels, because Carlotta was Hon., and her father a well-known peer.

She was by way of being a beauty, too. Her family was not rich, yet she had come into five hundred a year of her own, when she was eighteen; and that to us, was an enormity. Then she appeared in the fashionable papers, affecting to be wistful, with pearls, slanting her eyes. Then she went and did another of her beastly still-lifes, a cactus-in-a-pot.

At the Thwaite, being snobs, we were proud of her too. She showed off a bit, it is true, playing bird of paradise among the pigeons. At the same time, she *was* thrilled to be with us, and out of her own set. Her wistfulness and yearning 'for something else' was absolutely genuine. Yet she was not going to hobnob with us either, at least not indiscriminately.

She was ambitious, in a vague way. She wanted to coruscate, somehow or other. She had a family of clever and 'distinguished' uncles, who had flattered her. What then?

Her cactuses-in-a-pot were admirable. But even she didn't expect them to start a revolution. Perhaps she would rather glow in the wide if dirty skies of life, than in the somewhat remote and unsatisfactory ether of Art.

She and I were 'friends' in a bare, stark, but real sense. I was poor, but I didn't really care. She didn't really care either. Whereas I did care about some passionate vision which, I could feel, lay embedded in the half-dead body of this life. The quick body within the dead. I could *feel* it. And I wanted to get at it, if only for myself.

She didn't know what I was after. Yet she could feel that I was It, and, being an aristocrat of the Kingdom of It, as well as the realm of Great Britain, she was loyal – loyal to me because of It, the quick body which I imagined within the dead.

Still, we never had much to do with one another. I had no money. She never wanted to introduce me to her own people. I didn't want it either. Sometimes we had lunch together, sometimes we went to a theatre, or we drove in the country, in some car that belonged to neither of us. We never flirted or talked love. I don't think she wanted it, any more than I did. She wanted to marry into her own surroundings, and I knew she was of too frail a paste to face my future.

Now I come to think of it, she was always a bit sad when we were together. Perhaps she looked over seas she would never cross. She belonged finally, fatally, to her own class. Yet I think she hated them. When she was in a group of people who talked 'smart', titles and *beau monde* and all that, her rather short nose would turn up, her wide mouth press into discontent, and a languor of bored irritation come even over her broad shoulders. Bored irritation, and a loathing of climbers, a loathing of the ladder altogether. She hated her own class : yet it was also sacrosanct to her. She disliked, even to me, mentioning the title of her friends. Yet the very hurried resentment with which she said, when I asked her, Who is it? –

'Lady Nithsdale, Lord Staines – old friends of my mother,' proved that the coronet was wedged into her brow, like a ring of iron grown into a tree.

She had another kind of reverence for a true artist : perhaps more genuine, perhaps not; anyhow, more free and easy.

She and I had a curious understanding in common : an inkling, perhaps, of the unborn body of life hidden within the body of this half-death which we call life; and hence a tacit hostility to the commonplace world, its inert laws. We were rather like two soldiers on a secret mission in an enemy country. Life, and people, was an enemy country to us both. But she would never declare herself.

She always came to me to find out what I thought, particularly in a moral issue. Profoundly, fretfully discontented with the conventional moral standards, she didn't know how to take a stand of her own. So she came to me. She had to try to get her own feelings straightened out. In that she showed her old

British fibre. I told her what, as a young man, I thought : and usually she was resentful. She did so want to be conventional. She would even act quite perversely, in her determination to be conventional. But she always had to come back to me, to ask me again. She depended on me morally. Even when she disagreed with me, it soothed her, and restored her to know my point of view. Yet she disagreed with me.

We had then a curious abstract intimacy, that went very deep, yet showed no obvious contact. Perhaps I was the only person in the world with whom she felt, in her uneasy self, at home, at peace. And to me, she was always of my own *intrinsic* sort, of my own species. Most people are just another species to me. They might as well be turkeys.

But she would always *act* according to the conventions of her class, even perversely. And I knew it.

So, just before the war she married Lord Lathkill. She was twenty-one. I did not see her till war was declared; then she asked me to lunch with her and her husband, in town. He was an officer in a Guards regiment, and happened to be in uniform, looking very handsome and well-set-up, as if he expected to find the best of life served up to him for ever. He was very dark, with dark eyes and fine black hair, and a very beautiful, diffident voice, almost womanish in its slow, delicate inflections. He seemed pleased and flattered at having Carlotta for a wife.

To me he was beautifully attentive, almost deferential, because I was poor, and of the other world, those poor devils of outsiders. I laughed at him a little, and laughed at Carlotta, who was a bit irritated by the gentle delicacy with which he treated me.

She was elated too. I remember her saying :

'We need war, don't you think? Don't you think men need the fight, to keep life chivalrous and put martial glamour into it?'

And I remember saying, 'I think we need some sort of fight; but my sort isn't the war sort.' It was August, we could take it lightly.

'What's your sort?' she asked quickly.

'I don't know : single-handed, anyhow,' I said, with a grin.

Lord Lathkill made me feel like a lonely sansculotte, he was so completely unostentatious, so very willing to pay all the attention to me, and yet so subtly complacent, so unquestionably sure of his position. Whereas I was a not very sound earthenware pitcher which had already gone many times to the well.

He was not conceited, not half as *conceited* as I was. He was willing to leave me all the front of the stage, even with Carlotta. He felt so sure of some things, like a tortoise in a glittering, polished tortoiseshell that mirrors eternity. Yet he was not quite easy with me.

'You are Derbyshire?' I said to him, looking into his face. 'So am I! I was born in Derbyshire.'

He asked me with a gentle, uneasy sort of politeness, where? But he was a bit taken aback. And his dark eyes, brooding over me, had a sort of fear in them. At the centre they were hollow with a certain misgiving. He was so sure of *circumstances*, and not by any means sure of the man in the middle of the circumstances. Himself! Himself! That was already a ghost.

I felt that he saw in me something crude but real, and saw himself as something in its own way perfect, but quite unreal. Even his love for Carlotta, and his marriage, was a circumstance that was inwardly unreal to him. One could tell by the curious way in which he waited, before he spoke. And by the hollow look, almost a touch of madness, in his dark eyes, and in his soft, melancholy voice.

I could understand that she was fascinated by him. But God help him if ever circumstances went against him!

She had to see me again, a week later, to talk about him. So she asked me to the opera. She had a box, and we were alone, and the notorious Lady Perth was two boxes away. But this was one of Carlotta's conventional perverse little acts, with her husband in France. She only wanted to talk to me about him.

So she sat in the front of her box, leaning a little to the audience and talking sideways to me. Anyone would have known at once there was a *liaison* between us, how *dangereuse* they would never have guessed. For there, in the full view of the world – her world at least, not mine – she was talking sideways to me, saying in a hurried, yet stony voice :

'What do you think of Luke?'

She looked up at me heavily, with her sea-coloured eyes, waiting for my answer.

'He's tremendously charming,' I said, above the theatreful of faces.

'Yes, he's that!' she replied, in the flat, plangent voice she had when she was serious, like metal ringing flat, with a strange far-reaching vibration. 'Do you think he'll be happy?'

'*Be* happy!' I ejaculated. 'When, *be* happy?'

'With me,' she said, giving a sudden little snirt of laughter, like a schoolgirl, and looking up at me shyly, mischievously, anxiously.

'If you make him,' I said, still casual.

'How can I make him?'

She said it with flat plangent earnestness. She was always like that, pushing me deeper in than I wanted to go.

'Be happy yourself, I suppose : and quite sure about it. And then *tell* him you're happy, and tell him he is, too, and he'll be it.'

'Must I do all that?' she said rapidly. 'Not otherwise?'

I knew I was frowning at her, and she was watching my frown.

'Probably not,' I said roughly. 'He'll never make up his mind about it himself.'

'How did you know?' she asked, as if it had been a mystery.

'I didn't. It only seems to me like that.'

'Seems to you like that,' she re-echoed, in that sad, clean monotone of finality, always like metal. I appreciate it in her, that she does not murmur or whisper. But I wished she left me alone, in that beastly theatre.

She was wearing emeralds, on her snow-white skin, and leaning forward gazing fixedly down into the auditorium, as a crystal-gazer into a crystal. Heaven knows if she saw all those little facets of faces and plastrons. As for me, I knew that, like a sansculotte, I should never be king till breeches were off.

'I had terrible work to make him marry me,' she said, in her swift, clear low tones.

'Why?'

'He was frightfully in love with me. He *is*! But he thinks he's unlucky ...'

'Unlucky, how? In cards or in love?' I mocked.

'In both,' she said briefly, with sudden cold resentment at my flippancy. There was over her eyes a glaze of fear. 'It's in their family.'

'What did you say to him?' I asked, rather laboured, feeling the dead weight.

'I promised to have luck for two,' she said. 'And war was declared a fortnight later.'

'Ah, well!' I said. 'That's the world's luck, not yours.'

'Quite!' she said.

There was a pause.

'Is his family supposed to be unlucky?' I asked.

'The Worths? Terribly! They really are!'

It was interval, and the box door had opened. Carlotta always had her eye, a good half of it at least, on the external happenings. She rose, like a reigning beauty – which she wasn't, and never became – to speak to Lady Perth, and, out of spite, did not introduce me.

Carlotta and Lord Lathkill came, perhaps a year later, to visit us when we were in a cottage in Derbyshire, and he was home on leave. She was going to have a child, and was slow, and seemed depressed. He was vague, charming, talking about the country and the history of the lead mines. But the two of them seemed vague, as if they never got anywhere.

The last time I saw them was when the war was over, and I was leaving England. They were alone at dinner, save for me. He was still haggard, with a wound in the throat. But he said he would soon be well. His slow, beautiful voice was a bit husky now. And his velvety eyes were hardened, haggard, but there was weariness, emptiness in the hardness.

I was poorer than ever, and felt a little weary myself. Carlotta was struggling with his silent emptiness. Since the war, the melancholy fixity of his eyes was more noticeable, the fear at the centre was almost monomania. She was wilting and losing her beauty.

There were twins in the house. After dinner, we went straight up to look at them, to the night nursery. They were two boys, with their father's fine dark hair, both of them.

He had put out his cigar, and leaned over the cots, gazing in silence. The nurse, dark-faced and faithful, drew back. Carlotta glanced at her children; but more helplessly, she gazed at him.

'Bonny children! Bonny boys, aren't they, nurse?' I said softly.

'Yes, sir!' she said quickly. 'They are!'

'Ever think I'd have twins, roistering twins?' said Carlotta, looking at me.

'I never did,' said I.

'Ask Luke whether it's bad luck or bad management,' she said, with that schoolgirl's snirt of laughter, looking up apprehensively at her husband.

'Oh, I,' he said, turning suddenly and speaking loud, in his wounded voice. 'I call it amazing good luck, myself! Don't know what other people think about it.' Yet he had the fine, wincing fear in his body, of an injured dog.

After that, for years I did not see her again. I heard she had a baby girl. Then a catastrophe happened: both the twins were killed in a motor-car accident in America, motoring with their aunt.

I learned the news late, and did not write to Carlotta. What could I say?

A few months later, crowning disaster, the baby girl died of some sudden illness. The Lathkill ill-luck seemed to be working surely.

Poor Carlotta! I had no further news of her, only I heard that she and Lord Lathkill were both living in seclusion, with his mother, at the place in Derbyshire.

When circumstances brought me to England, I debated within myself whether I should write or not to Carlotta. At last I sent a note to the London address.

I had a reply from the country: 'So glad you are within reach again! When will you come and see us?'

I was not very keen on going to Riddings. After all, it was Lord Lathkill's place, and Lady Lathkill, his mother, was old and of the old school. And I always something of a sansculotte, who will only be king when breeches are off.

'Come to town,' I wrote, 'and let us have lunch together.'

She came. She looked older, and pain had drawn horizontal lines across her face.

'You're not a bit different,' she said to me.

'And you're only a little bit,' I said.

'Am I!' she replied, in a deadened, melancholic voice. 'Perhaps! I suppose while we live we've got to live. What do you think?'

'Yes, I think it. To be the living dead, that's awful.'

'Quite!' she said, with terrible finality.

'How is Lord Lathkill?' I asked.

'Oh,' she said. 'It's finished him, as far as living is concerned. But he's very willing for *me* to live.'

'And you, are you willing?' I said.

She looked up into my eyes, strangely.

'I'm not sure,' she said. 'I need help. What do you think about it?'

'Oh, God, live if you can!'

'Even take help?' she said with her strange involved simplicity, 'Ah, certainly.'

'Would you recommend it?'

'Why, yes! You are a young thing –' I began.

'Won't you come down to Riddings?' she said quickly.

'And Lord Lathkill – and his mother?' I asked.

'They want you.'

'Do you want me to come?'

'I want you to, yes! Will you?'

'Why, yes, if you want me.'

'When, then?'

'When you wish.'

'Do you mean it?'

'Why, of course.'

'You're not afraid of the Lathkill ill-luck?'

'I!' I exclaimed in amazement; such amazement, that she gave her schoolgirl snirt of laughter.

'Very well, then,' she said. 'Monday? Does that suit you?'

We made arrangements, and I saw her off at the station.

I knew Riddings, Lord Lathkill's place, from the outside. It was an old Derbyshire stone house, at the end of the village of Middleton : a house with three sharp gables, set back not very

far from the high-road, but with a gloomy moor for a park
behind.

Monday was a dark day over the Derbyshire hills. The green
hills were dark, dark green, the stone fences seemed almost
black. Even the little railway station, deep in the green, cleft
hollow, was of stone, and dark and cold, and seemed in the
underworld.

Lord Lathkill was at the station. He was wearing spectacles,
and his brown eyes stared strangely. His black hair fell lank
over his forehead.

'I'm so awfully glad you've come,' he said. 'It is cheering
Carlotta up immensely.'

Me, as a man myself, he hardly seemed to notice. I was something which arrived, and was expected. Otherwise he had an
odd, unnatural briskness of manner.

'I hope I shan't disturb your mother, Lady Lathkill,' I said
as he tucked me up in the car.

'On the contrary,' he sang, in his slow voice, 'she is looking
forward to your coming as much as we both are. Oh, no, don't
look on Mother as too old-fashioned, she's not so at all. She's
tremendously up to date in art and literature and that kind of
thing. She has her leaning towards the uncanny – spiritualism,
and that kind of thing – nowadays, but Carlotta and I think
that if it gives her an interest, all well and good.'

He tucked me up most carefully in the rugs, and the servant
put a footwarmer at my feet.

'Derbyshire, you know, is a cold county,' continued Lord
Lathkill, 'especially among the hills.'

'It's a very dark county,' I said.

'Yes, I suppose it is, to one coming from the tropics. We, of
course, don't notice it; we rather like it.'

He seemed curiously smaller, shrunken, and his rather long
cheeks were sallow. His manner, however, was much more
cheerful, almost communicative. But he talked, as it were, to
the faceless air, not really to me. I wasn't really there at all. He
was talking to himself. And when once he looked at me, his
brown eyes had a hollow look, like gaps with nothing in them
except a haggard, hollow fear. He was gazing through the
windows of nothingness, to see if I were really there.

It was dark when we got to Riddings. The house had no door in the front, and only two windows upstairs were lit. It did not seem very hospitable. We entered at the side, and a very silent manservant took my things.

We went upstairs in silence, in the dead-seeming house. Carlotta had heard us, and was at the top of the stairs. She was already dressed; her long white arms were bare; she had something glittering on a dull green dress.

'I was so afraid you wouldn't come,' she said, in a dulled voice, as she gave me her hand. She seemed as if she would begin to cry. But of course she wouldn't. The corridor, dark-panelled and with blue carpet on the floor, receded dimly, with a certain dreary gloom. A servant was diminishing in the distance, with my bags, silently. There was a curious, unpleasant sense of the fixity of the materials of the house, the obscene triumph of dead Matter. Yet the place was warm, central-heated.

Carlotta pulled herself together, and said, dulled:

'Would you care to speak to my mother-in-law before you go to your room? She would like it.'

We entered a small drawing-room, abruptly. I saw the water-colours on the walls and a white-haired lady in black bending round to look at the door as she rose, cautiously.

'This is Mr Morier, Mother-in-law,' said Carlotta, in her dull, rather quick way, 'on his way to his room.'

The dowager Lady Lathkill came a few steps forward leaning from heavy hips, and gave me her hand. Her crest of hair was snow white, and she had curious blue eyes, fixed, with a tiny dot of a pupil, peering from her pink, soft-skinned face of an old well-preserved woman. She wore a lace fichu. The upper part of her body was moderately slim, leaning forward slightly from her heavy black-silk hips.

She murmured something to me, staring at me fixedly for a long time, but as a bird does, with shrewd, cold, far-distant sight. As a hawk, perhaps, looks shrewdly far down, in his search. Then, muttering, she presented to me the other two people in the room: a tall, short-faced, swarthy young woman with the hint of a black moustache; and a plump man in a dinner-jacket, rather bald and ruddy, with a little grey moustache, but yellow under the eyes. He was Colonel Hale.

They all seemed awkward, as if I had interrupted them at a seance. I didn't know what to say: they were utter strangers to me.

'Better come and choose your room, then,' said Carlotta, and I bowed dumbly, following her out of the room. The old Lady Lathkill still stood planted on her heavy hips, looking half round after us with her ferret's blue eyes. She had hardly any eyebrows, but they were arched high up on her pink, soft forehead, under the crest of icily white hair. She had never emerged for a second from the remote place where she unyieldingly kept herself.

Carlotto, Lord Lathkill and I tramped in silence down the corridor and round a bend. We could none of us get a word out. As he suddenly, rather violently flung open a door at the end of the wing, he said, turning round to me with a resentful, hangdog air:

'We did you the honour of offering you our ghost room. It doesn't look much, but it's our equivalent for a royal apartment.'

It was a good-sized room with faded, red-painted panelling showing remains of gilt, and the usual big, old mahogany furniture, and a big pinky-faded carpet with big, whitish, faded roses. A bright fire was burning in the stone fireplace.

'Why?' said I, looking at the stretches of the faded, once handsome carpet.

'Why what?' said Lord Lathkill. 'Why did we offer you this room?'

'Yes! No! Why is it your equivalent for a royal apartment?'

'Oh, because our ghost is as rare as sovereignty in her visits, and twice as welcome. Her gifts are infinitely more worth having.'

'What sort of gifts?'

'The family fortune. She invariably restores the family fortune. That's why we put you here, to tempt her.'

'What temptation should I be? – especially to restoring your family fortunes. I didn't think they needed it, anyhow.'

'Well!' he hesitated. 'Not exactly in money: we can manage modestly that way; but in everything else but money –'

There was a pause. I was thinking of Carlotta's 'luck for two.' Poor Carlotta! She looked worn now. Especially her chin looked worn, showing the edge of the jaw. She had sat herself down in a chair by the fire, and put her feet on the stone fender, and was leaning forward, screening her face with her hand, still careful of her complexion. I could see her broad, white shoulders, showing the shoulder-blades, as she leaned forward, beneath her dress. But it was as if some bitterness had soaked all the life out of her, and she was only weary, or inert, drained of her feelings. It grieved me, and the thought passed through my mind that a man should take her in his arms and cherish her body, and start her flame again. If she would let him, which was doubtful.

Her courage was fallen, in her body; only her spirit fought on. She would have to restore the body of her life, and only a living body could do it.

'What *about* your ghost?' I said to him. 'Is she really ghastly?'

'Not at all!' he said. 'She's supposed to be lovely. But I have no experience, and I don't know anybody who has. We hoped you'd come, though, and tempt her. Mother had a message about you, you know.'

'No, I didn't know.'

'Oh, yes! When you were still in Africa. The medium said: "There is a man in Africa. I can only see M, a double M. He is thinking of your family. It would be good if he entered your family." Mother was awfully puzzled, but Carlotta said "Mark Morier" at once.'

'That's not why I asked you down,' said Carlotta quickly, looking round, shading her eyes with her hand as she looked at me.

I laughed, saying nothing.

'But, of course,' continued Lord Lathkill, ' you *needn't* have this room. We have another one ready as well. Would you like to see it?'

'How does your ghost manifest herself?' I said, parrying.

'Well, I hardly know. She seems to be a very grateful *presence*, and that's about all I do know. She was apparently quite *persona grata* to everyone she visited. *Gratissima*, apparently!'

'*Benissimo!*' said I.

A servant appeared in the doorway, murmuring something I could not hear. Everybody in the house, except Carlotta and Lord Lathkill, seemed to murmur under their breath.

'What's she say?' I asked.

'If you will stay in this room? I told her you might like a room on the front. And if you'll take a bath?' said Carlotta.

'Yes!' said I. And Carlotta repeated to the maidservant.

'And for heaven's sake speak to me loudly,' said I to that elderly correct female in her starched collar, in the doorway.

'Very good, sir!' she piped up. 'And shall I make the bath hot, or medium?'

'Hot!' said I, like a cannon-shot.

'Very good, sir!' she piped up again, and her elderly eyes twinkled as she turned and disappeared.

Carlotta laughed, and I sighed.

We were six at table. The pink Colonel with the yellow creases under his blue eyes sat opposite me, like an old boy with a liver. Next to him sat Lady Lathkill, watching from her distance. Her pink, soft old face, naked-seeming, with its pin-point blue eyes, was a real modern witch-face.

Next me, on my left, was the dark young woman, whose slim, swarthy arms had an indiscernible down on them. She had a blackish neck, and her expressionless yellow-brown eyes said nothing, under level black brows. She was inaccessible. I made some remarks, without result. Then I said:

'I didn't hear your name when Lady Lathkill introduced me to you.'

Her yellow-brown eyes stared into mine for some moments before she said:

'Mrs Hale!' Then she glanced across the table. 'Colonel Hale is my husband.'

My face must have signalled my surprise. She stared into my eyes very curiously, with a significance I could not grasp, a long, hard stare. I looked at the bald, pink head of the Colonel bent over his soup, and I returned to my own soup.

'Did you have a good time in London?' said Carlotta.

'No,' said I. 'It was dismal.'

'Not a good word to say for it?'

'Not one.'

'No nice people?'

'Not my sort of nice.'

'What's your sort of nice?' she asked, with a little laugh.

The other people were stone. It was like talking into a chasm.

'Ah! If I knew myself, I'd look for them! But not sentimental, with a lot of soppy emotions on top, and nasty ones underneath.'

'Who are you thinking of?' Carlotta looked up at me as the man brought the fish. She had a crushed sort of roguishness. The other diners were images.

'I? Nobody. Just everybody. No, I think I was thinking of the Obelisk Memorial Service.'

'Did you go to it?'

'No, but I fell into it.'

'Wasn't it moving?'

'Rhubarb, senna, that kind of moving!'

She gave a little laugh, looking up into my face, from the fish.

'What was wrong with it?'

I noticed that the Colonel and Lady Lathkill each had a little dish of rice, no fish, and that they were served second – oh, humility!–and that neither took the white wine. No, they had no wine glasses. The remoteness gathered about them, like the snows on Everest. The dowager peered across at me occasionally, like a white ermine out of the snow, and she had that cold air about her, of being good, and containing a secret of goodness : remotely, ponderously, fixedly knowing better. And I, with my chatter, was one of those fabulous fleas that are said to hop upon glaciers.

'Wrong with it? *It* was wrong, all wrong. In the rain, a soppy crowd, with soppy bare heads, soppy emotions, soppy chrysanthemums and prickly laurustinus! A steam of wet mob-emotions! Ah, no, it shouldn't be allowed.'

Carlotta's face had fallen. She again could feel death in her bowels, the kind of death the war signifies.

'Wouldn't you have us honour the dead?' came Lady Lathkill's secretive voice across at me, as if a white ermine had barked.

'Honour the dead!' My mind opened in amazement. 'Do you think they'd be honoured?'

I put the question in all sincerity.

'They would understand the *intention* was to honour them,' came her reply.

I felt astounded.

'If I were dead, would I be honoured if a great, steamy wet crowd came after me with soppy chrysanthemums and prickly laurustinus? Ugh! I'd run to the nethermost ends of Hades. Lord, how I'd run from them!'

The manservant gave us roast mutton, and Lady Lathkill and the Colonel chestnuts in sauce. Then he poured the burgundy. It was good wine. The pseudo-conversation was interrupted.

Lady Lathkill ate in silence, like an ermine in the snow, feeding on his prey. Sometimes she looked round the table, her blue eyes peering fixedly, completely uncommunicative. She was very watchful to see that we were all properly attended to; 'The currant jelly for Mr Morier,' she would murmur, as if it were her table. Lord Lathkill, next her, ate in complete absence. Sometimes she murmured to him, and he murmured back, but I never could hear what they said. The Colonel swallowed the chestnuts in dejection, as if all were weary duty to him now. I put it down to his liver.

It was an awful dinner-party. I never could hear a word anybody said, except Carlotta. They all let their words die in their throats, as if the larynx were the coffin of sound.

Carlotta tried to keep her end up, the cheerful hostess sort of thing. But Lady Lathkill somehow, in silence and apparent humility, had stolen the authority that goes with the hostess, and she hung on to it grimly, like a white ermine sucking a rabbit. Carlotta kept glancing miserably at me, to see what I thought. I didn't think anything. I just felt frozen within the tomb. And I drank the good, good warm burgundy.

'Mr Morier's glass!' murmured Lady Lathkill, and her blue eyes with their black pin-points rested on mine a moment.

'Awfully nice to drink good burgundy!' said I pleasantly.

She bowed her head slightly, and murmured something inaudible.

'I beg your pardon?'

'Very glad you like it!' she repeated, with distaste at having to say it again, out loud.

'Yes, I do. It's good.'

Mrs Hale, who sat tall and erect and alert, like a black she-fox, never making a sound, looked round at me to see what sort of specimen I was. She was just a bit intrigued.

'Yes, thanks,' came a musical murmur from Lord Lathkill. 'I think I *will* take some more.'

The man, who had hesitated, filled his glass.

'I'm awfully sorry I can't drink wine,' said Carlotta, absently. 'It has the wrong effect on me.'

'I should say it has the wrong effect on everybody,' said the Colonel, with an uneasy attempt to be there. 'But some people like the effect, and some don't.'

I looked at him in wonder. Why was he chipping in? He looked as if he'd liked the effect well enough, in his day.

'Oh, no!' retorted Carlotta coldly. 'The effect on different people is quite different.'

She closed with finality, and a further frost fell on the table.

'Quite so,' began the Colonel, trying, since he'd gone off the deep end, to keep afloat.

But Carlotta turned abruptly to me.

'Why is it, do you think, that the effect is so different on different people?'

'And on different occasions,' said I, grinning through my burgundy. 'Do you know what they say? They say that alcohol, if it has an effect on your psyche, takes you back to old states of consciousness, and old reactions. But some people it doesn't stimulate at all, there is only a nervous reaction of repulsion.'

'There's certainly a nervous reaction of repulsion in me,' said Carlotta.

'As there is in all higher natures,' murmured Lady Lathkill.

'Dogs hate whisky,' said I.

'That's quite right,' said the Colonel. 'Scared of it!'

'I've often thought,' said I, 'about those old states of consciousness. It's supposed to be an awful retrogression, reverting back to them. Myself, my desire to go onwards takes me back a little.'

'Where to?' said Carlotta.

'Oh, I don't know! To where you feel a bit warm, and like smashing the glasses, don't you know?

   J'avons bien bu et nous boirons!
   Cassons les verres, nous les payerons!
    Compagnons! Voyez-vous bien!
    Voyez-vous bien!
    Voyez! voyez! voyez-vous bien
    Que les d'moiselles sont belles
    Où nous allons!'

I had the effrontery to sing this verse of an old soldiers' song
while Lady Lathkill was finishing her celery and nut salad.
I sang it quite nicely, in a natty, well-balanced little voice,
smiling all over my face meanwhile. The servant, as he went
round for Lady Lathkill's plate, furtively fetched a look at me.
Look! thought I. *You chicken that's come untrussed!*

The partridges had gone, we had swallowed the flan, and
were at dessert. They had accepted my song in complete silence.
Even Carlotta! My flan had gone down in one gulp, like an
oyster.

'You're quite right!' said Lord Lathkill, amid the squashing
of walnuts. 'I mean the state of mind of a Viking, shall we say,
or of a Catiline conspirator, might be frightfully good for us, if
we could recapture it.'

'A Viking!' said I, stupified. And Carlotta gave a wild snirt
of laughter.

'Why not a Viking?' he asked in all innocence.

'A Viking!' I repeated, and swallowed my port. Then I
looked round at my black-browed neighbour.

'Why do you never say anything?' I asked.

'What should I say?' she replied, frightened at the thought.

I was finished. I gazed into my port as if expecting the ultimate
revelation.

Lady Lathkill rustled her finger-tips in the finger-bowl, and
laid down her napkin decisively. The Colonel, old buck, rose at
once to draw back her chair. *Place aux hommes!* I bowed to my
neighbour, Mrs Hale, a most disconcerting bow, and she made
a circuit to get by me.

'You won't be awfully long?' said Carlotta, looking at me
with her slow, hazel-green eyes, between mischief and wistfulness and utter depression.

Lady Lathkill steered heavily past me as if I didn't exist,
perching rather forward, with her crest of white hair, from her
big hips. She seemed abstracted, concentrated on something, as
she went.

I closed the door, and turned to the men.

> 'Dans la première auberge
> *J'eus b'en bu!'*

sang I in a little voice.

'Quite right,' said Lord Lathkill. 'You're quite right.'

And we sent the port round.

'This house,' I said, 'needs a sort of spring cleaning.'

'You're quite right,' said Lord Lathkill.

'There's a bit of a dead smell!' said I. 'We need Bacchus, and Eros, to sweeten it up, to freshen it.'

'You think Bacchus and Eros?' said Lord Lathkill, with complete seriousness; as if one might have telephoned for them.

'In the best sense,' said I. As if we were going to get them from Fortnum and Mason's, at least.

'What exactly is the best sense?' asked Lord Lathkill.

'Ah! The flame of life! There's a dead smell here.'

The Colonel fingered his glass with thick, inert fingers, uneasily.

'Do you think so?' he said looking up at me heavily.

'Don't you?'

He gazed at me with blank, glazed blue eyes, that had deathly yellow stains underneath. Something was wrong with him, some sort of breakdown. He should have been a fat, healthy, jolly old boy. Not very old either : probably not quite sixty. But with this collapse on him, he seemed, somehow, to smell.

'You know,' he said, staring at me with a sort of gruesome challenge, then looking down at his wine, 'there's more things than we're aware of, happening to us!' He looked up at me again, shutting his full lips under his little grey moustache, and gazing with a glazed defiance.

'Quite!' said I.

He continued to gaze at me with glazed, gruesome defiance.

'Ha!' He made a sudden movement, and seemed to break up, collapse and become brokenly natural. 'There, you've said it. I married my wife when I was a kid of twenty.'

'Mrs Hale?' I exclaimed.

'Not this one' – he jerked his head towards the door – 'my first wife.' There was a pause; he looked at me with shamed eyes, then turned his wine-glass round and his head dropped. Staring at his twisting glass, he continued : 'I married her when I was twenty, and she was twenty-eight. You might say, she married me. Well, there it was! We had three children – I've got three married daughters – and we got on all right. I suppose she mothered me, in a way. And I never thought a thing. I was content enough, wasn't tied to her apron strings, and she never asked questions. She was always fond of me, and I took it for granted. I took it for granted. Even when she died – I was away in Salonika – I took it for granted, if you understand me. It was part of the rest of things – war – life – death. I knew I should feel lonely when I got back. Well, then I got buried – shell dropped, and the dug-out caved in – and that queered me. They sent me home. And the minute I saw the Lizard light – it was evening when we got up out of the Bay – I realized that Lucy had been waiting for me. I could feel her there, at my side, more plainly than I feel you now. And do you know, at that moment I woke up to her, and she made an awful impression on me. She seemed, if you get me, tremendously powerful, important; everything else dwindled away. There was the Lizard light blinking a long way off, and that meant home. And all the rest was my wife, Lucy : as if her skirts filled all the darkness. In a way, I was frightened; but that was because I couldn't quite get myself into line. I felt : *Good God! I never knew her!* And she was this tremendous thing! I felt like a child, and as weak as a kitten. And, believe me or not, from that day to this she's never left me. I know quite well she can hear what I'm saying. But she'll let me tell you. I knew that at dinner-time.'

'But what made you marry again?' I said.

'She made me!' He went a trifle yellow on his cheek-bones. 'I could feel her telling me, *"Marry! Marry!"* Lady Lathkill had messages from her too; she was her great friend in life. I didn't think of marrying. But Lady Lathkill had the same message, that I must marry. Then a medium described the girl in detail : my present wife. I knew her at once, friend of my daughters. After that the messages became more insistent, waking me three and four times in the night. Lady Lathkill urged me to propose, and I did it, and was accepted. My present wife was just twenty-eight, the age Lucy had been –'

'How long ago did you marry the present Mrs Hale?'

'A little over a year ago. Well I thought I had done what was required of me. But directly after the wedding, such a state of terror came over me – perfectly unreasonable – I became almost unconscious. My present wife asked me if I was ill, and I said

I was. We got to Paris. I felt I was dying. But I said I was going out to see a doctor, and I found myself kneeling in a church. Then I found peace – and Lucy. She had her arms round me, and I was like a child at peace. I must have knelt there for a couple of hours, in Lucy's arms. I *never* felt like that when she was alive : why, I couldn't stand that sort of thing ! It's all come on after – after – And now, I daren't offend Lucy's spirit. If I do, I suffer tortures till I've made peace again, till she folds me in her arms. Then I can live. But she won't let me go near the present Mrs Hale. I – I – I daren't go near her.'

He looked up at me with fear, and shame, and shameful secrecy, and a sort of gloating showing in his unmanned blue eyes. He had been talking as if in his sleep.

'Why did your dead wife urge you to marry again?' I said.

'I don't know,' he replied. 'I don't know. She was older than I was, and all the cleverness was on her side. She was a very clever woman, and I was never much in the intellectual line, myself. I just took it for granted she liked me. She never showed jealousy, but I think now, perhaps she was jealous all the time, and kept it under. I don't know. I think she never felt quite straight about having married me. It seems like that. As if she had something on her mind. Do you know, while she was alive, I never gave it a thought. And now I'm aware of nothing else but her. It's as if her spirit wanted to live in my body, or at any rate – I don't know –'

His blue eyes were glazed, almost fishy, with fear and gloating shame. He had a short nose, and full, self-indulgent lips, and a once-comely chin. Eternally a careless boy of thirteen. But now, care had got him in decay.

'And what does your present wife say?' I asked.

He poured himself some more wine.

'Why,' he replied, 'except for her, I shouldn't mind so much. She says nothing. Lady Lathkill has explained everything to her, and she agrees that – that – a spirit from the other side is more important than mere pleasure – you know what I mean. Lady Lathkill says that this is a preparation for my next incarnation, when I am going to serve Woman, and help Her to take Her place.'

He looked up again, trying to be proud in his shame.

'Well, what a damned curious story!' exclaimed Lord Lathkill. 'Mother's idea for herself – she had it in a message too – is that she is coming on earth the next time to save the animals from the cruelty of man. That's why she hates meat at table, or anything that has to be killed.'

'And does Lady Lathkill encourage you in this business with your dead wife?' said I.

'Yes. She helps me. When I get as you might say at cross purposes with Lucy – with Lucy's spirit, that is – Lady Lathkill helps to put it right between us. Then I'm all right, when I know I'm loved.'

He looked at me stealthily, cunningly.

'Then you're all wrong,' said I, 'surely.'

'And do you mean to say,' put in Lord Lathkill, 'that you don't live with the present Mrs Hale at all? Do you mean to say you never *have* lived with her?'

'I've got a higher claim on me,' said the unhappy Colonel.

'My God!' said Lord Lathkill.

I looked in amazement: the sort of chap who picks up a woman and has a good time with her for a week, then goes home as nice as pie, and now look at him! It was obvious that he had a terror of his black-browed new wife, as well as of Lucy's spirit. A devil and a deep sea with vengeance!

'A damned curious story!' mused Lord Lathkill. 'I'm not so sure I like it. Something's wrong somewhere. We shall have to go upstairs.'

'Wrong!' said I. 'Why, Colonel, don't you turn round and quarrel with the spirit of your first wife, fatally and finally, and get rid of her?'

The Colonel looked at me, still diminished and afraid, but perking up a bit, as we rose from table.

'How would you go about it?' he said.

'I'd just face her, wherever she seemed to be, and say : *"Lucy, go to Blazes!"* '

Lord Lathkill burst into a loud laugh, then was suddenly silent as the door noiselessly opened, and the dowager's white hair and pointed uncanny eyes peered in, then entered.

'I think I left my papers in here, Luke,' she murmured.

'Yes, mother. There they are. We're just coming up.'

'Take your time.'

He held the door, and ducking forward she went out again, clutching some papers. The Colonel had blenched yellow on his cheek-bones.

We went upstairs to the small drawing-room.

'You were a long time,' said Carlotta, looking in all our faces. 'Hope the coffee's not cold. We'll have fresh if it is.'

She poured out, and Mrs Hale carried the cups. The dark young woman thrust out her straight, dusky arm, offering me sugar, and gazing at me with her unchanging, yellow-brown eyes. I looked back at her, and being clairvoyant in this house, was conscious of the curves of her erect body, the sparse black hairs there would be on her strong-skinned dusky thighs. She was a woman of thirty, and she had had a great dread lest she should never marry. Now she was as if mesmerized.

'What do you do usually in the evenings?' I said.

She turned to me as if startled, as she nearly always did when addressed.

'We do nothing,' she replied. 'Talk; and sometimes Lady Lathkill reads.'

'What does she read?'

'About spiritualism.'

'Sounds pretty dull.'

She looked at me again, but she did not answer. It was difficult to get anything out of her. She put up no fight, only remained in the same swarthy, passive, negative resistance. For a moment I wondered that no men made love to her : it was obvious they didn't. But then, modern young men are accustomed to be attracted, flattered, impressed : they expect an effort to please. And Mrs Hale made none : didn't know how. Which for me was her mystery. She was passive, static, locked up in a resistant passivity that had fire beneath it.

Lord Lathkill came and sat by us. The Colonel's confession had had an effect on him.

'I'm afraid,' he said to Mrs Hale, 'you have a thin time here.'

'Why?' she asked.

'Oh, there is so little to amuse you. Do you like to dance?'

'Yes,' she said.

'Well, then,' he said, 'let us go downstairs and dance to the

Victrola. There are four of us. You'll come, of course?' he said
to me.

Then he turned to his mother.

'Mother, we shall go down to the morning-room and dance.
Will you come too? Will you, Colonel?'

The dowager gazed at her son.

'I will come and look on,' she said.

'And I will play the pianola, if you like,' volunteered the
Colonel.

We went down, and pushed aside the chintz chairs and the
rugs. Lady Lathkill sat in a chair, the Colonel worked away at
the pianola. I danced with Carlotta, Lord Lathkill with Mrs
Hale.

A quiet soothing came over me, dancing with Carlotta. She
was very still and remote, and she hardly looked at me. Yet the
touch of her was wonderful, like a flower that yields itself to
the morning. Her warm, silken shoulder was soft and grateful
under my hand, as if it knew me with that second knowledge
which is part of one's childhood, and which so rarely blossoms
again in manhood and womanhood. It was as if we had known
each other perfectly, as children, and now, as man and woman,
met in the full, further sympathy. Perhaps, in modern people,
only after long suffering and defeat, can the naked intuition
break free between woman and man.

She, I knew, let the strain and the tension of all her life
depart from her then, leaving her nakedly still, within my
arm. And I only wanted to be with her, to have her in my
touch.

Yet after the second dance she looked at me, and suggested
that she should dance with her husband. So I found myself with
the strong, passive shoulder of Mrs Hale under my hand, and
her inert hand in mine, as I looked down at her dusky, dirty-
looking neck – she wisely avoided powder. The duskiness of her
mesmerized body made me see the faint dark sheen of her
thighs, with intermittent black hairs. It was as if they shone
through the silk of her mauve dress, like the limbs of a half-
wild animal, that is locked up in its own helpless dumb winter,
a prisoner.

She knew, with the heavy intuition of her sort, that I

glimpsed her crude among the bushes, and felt her attraction. But she kept looking away over my shoulder, with her yellow eyes, towards Lord Lathkill.

Myself or him, it was a question of which got there first. But she preferred him. Only for some things she would rather it were me.

Luke had changed curiously. His body seemed to have come alive, in the dark cloth of his evening suit; his eyes had a devil-may-care light in them, his long cheeks a touch of scarlet, and his black hair fell loose over his forehead. He had again some of that Guardsman's sense of well-being and claim to the best in life, which I had noticed the first time I saw him. But now it was a little more florid, defiant, with a touch of madness.

He looked down at Carlotta with uncanny kindness and affection. Yet he was glad to hand her over to me. He, too, was afraid of her : as if with her his bad luck had worked. Whereas, in a throb of crude brutality, he felt it would not work with the dark young woman. So, he handed Carlotta over to me with relief, as if, with me, she would be safe from the doom of his bad luck. And he, with the other woman, would be safe from it too. For the other woman was outside the circle.

I was glad to have Carlotta again : to have that inexpressible delicate and complete quiet of the two of us, resting my heart in a balance now at last physical as well as spiritual. Till now, it had always been a fragmentary thing. Now, for this hour at least, it was whole, a soft, complete, physical flow, and a unison deeper even than childhood.

As she danced she shivered slightly, and I seemed to smell frost in the air. The Colonel, too, was not keeping the rhythm.

'Has it turned colder?' I said.

'I wonder !' she answered, looking up at me with a slow beseeching. Why, and for what was she beseeching me? I pressed my hand a little closer, and her small breasts seemed to speak to me. The Colonel recovered the rhythm again.

But at the end of the dance she shivered again, and it seemed to me I too was chilled.

'Has it suddenly turned colder?' I said, going to the radiator. It was quite hot.

'It seems to me it has,' said Lord Lathkill, in a queer voice.

The Colonel was sitting abjectly on the music stool, as if broken.

'Shall we have another? Shall we try a tango?' said Lord Lathkill. 'As much of it as we can manage?'

'I – I –' the Colonel began, turning round on the seat, his face yellow. 'I'm not sure –'

Carlotta shivered. The frost seemed to touch my vitals. Mrs Hale stood stiff, like a pillar of brown rock-salt, staring at her husband.

'We had better leave off,' murmured Lady Lathkill, rising.

Then she did an extraordinary thing. She lifted her face, staring to the other side, and said suddenly, in a clear, cruel sort of voice :

'Are you here, Lucy?'

She was speaking across to the spirits. Deep inside me leaped a jump of laughter. I wanted to howl with laughter. Then instantly, I went inert again. The chill gloom seemed to deepen suddenly in the room, everybody was overcome. On the piano-seat the Colonel sat yellow and huddled, with a terrible hang-dog look of guilt on his face. There was a silence, in which the cold seemed to creak. Then came again the peculiar bell-like ringing of Lady Lathkill's voice :

'Are you here? What do you wish us to do?'

A dead and ghastly silence, in which we all remained trans-fixed. Then from somewhere came two slow thuds, and a sound of drapery moving. The Colonel, with mad fear in his eyes, looked round at the uncurtained windows, and crouched on his seat.

'We must leave this room,' said Lady Lathkill.

'I'll tell you what, Mother,' said Lord Lathkill curiously; 'you and the Colonel go up, and we'll just turn on the Victrola.'

That was almost uncanny of him. For myself, the cold effluence of these people had paralysed me. Now I began to rally. I felt that Lord Lathkill was sane, it was these other people who were mad.

Again from somewhere indefinite came two slow thuds.

'We must leave this room,' repeated Lady Lathkill in mon-otony.

'All right, Mother. You go. I'll just turn on the Victrola.'

And Lord Lathkill strode across the room. In another moment the monstrous barking howl of the opening of a jazz tune, an event far more extraordinary than thuds, poured from the unmoving bit of furniture called a Victrola.

Lady Lathkill silently departed. The Colonel got to his feet.

'I wouldn't go if I were you, Colonel,' said I. 'Why not dance? I'll look on this time.'

I felt as if I were resisting a rushing, cold dark current.

Lord Lathkill was already dancing with Mrs Hale, skating delicately along, with a certain smile of obstinacy, secrecy, and excitement kindled on his face. Carlotta went up quietly to the Colonel, and put her hand on his broad shoulder. He let himself be moved into the dance, but he had no heart in it.

There came a heavy crash, out of the distance. The Colonel stopped as if shot : in another moment he would go down on his knees. And his face was terrible. It was obvious he really felt another presence, other than ours, blotting us out. The room seemed dree and cold. It was heavy work, bearing up.

The Colonel's lips were moving, but no sound came forth. Then, absolutely oblivious of us, he went out of the room.

The Victrola had run down. Lord Lathkill went to wind it up again, saying :

'I suppose mother knocked over a piece of furniture.'

But we were all of us depressed, in abject depression.

'Isn't it awful !' Carlotta said to me, looking up beseechingly.

'Abominable !' said I.

'What do you think there is in it?'

'God knows. The only thing is to stop it, as one does hysteria. It's on a par with hysteria.'

'Quite,' she said.

Lord Lathkill was dancing, and smiling very curiously down into his partner's face. The Victrola was at its loudest.

Carlotta and I looked at one another, with hardly the heart to start again. The house felt hollow and gruesome. One wanted to get out, to get away from the cold, uncanny blight which filled the air.

'Oh, I say, keep the ball rolling,' called Lord Lathkill.

'Come,' I said to Carlotta.

Even then she hung back a little. If she had not suffered, and lost so much, she would have gone upstairs at once to struggle in the silent wrestling of wills with her mother-in-law. Even now, *that* particular fight drew her, almost the strongest. But I took her hand.

'Come,' I said. 'Let us dance it down. We'll roll the ball the opposite way.'

She danced with me, but she was absent, unwilling. The empty gloom of the house, the sense of cold, and of deadening opposition, pressed us down. I was looking back over my life, and thinking how the cold weight of an unliving spirit was slowly crushing all warmth and vitality out of everything. Even Carlotta herself had gone numb again, cold and resistant even to me. The thing seemed to happen wholesale in her.

'One has to choose to live,' I said, dancing on.

But I was powerless. With a woman, when her spirit goes inert in opposition, a man can do nothing. I felt my life flow sinking in my body.

'This house is awfully depressing,' I said to her, as we mechanically danced. 'Why don't you *do* something? Why don't you get out of this tangle? Why don't you break it?'

'How?' she said.

I looked down at her, wondering why she was suddenly hostile.

'You needn't fight,' I said. 'You needn't fight it. Don't get tangled up in it. Just side-step, on to another ground.'

She made a pause of impatience before she replied :

'I don't see where I am to side-step to, precisely.'

'You do,' said I. 'A little while ago, you were warm and unfolded and good. Now you are shut up and prickly, in the cold. You needn't be. Why not stay warm?'

'It's nothing I do,' she said coldly.

'It is. Stay warm to me. I am here. Why clutch in a tug-of-war with Lady Lathkill?'

'Do I clutch in a tug-of-war with my mother-in-law?'

'You know you do.'

She looked up at me, with a faint little shadow of guilt and beseeching, but with a *moue* of cold obstinacy dominant.

'Let's have done,' said I.

And in cold silence we sat side by side on the lounge.

The other two danced on. They at any rate were in unison. One could see from the swing of their limbs. Mrs Hale's yellow-brown eyes looked at me every time she came round.

'Why does she look at me?' I said.

'I can't imagine,' said Carlotta, with a cold grimace.

'I'd better go upstairs and see what's happening,' she said, suddenly rising and disappearing in a breath.

Why should she go? Why should she rush off to the battle of wills with her mother-in-law? In such a battle, while one has any life to lose, one can only lose it. There is nothing positively to be done, but to withdraw out of the hateful tension.

The music ran down. Lord Lathkill stopped the Victrola.

'Carlotta gone?' he said.

'Apparently.'

'Why didn't you stop her?'

'Wild horses wouldn't stop her.'

He lifted his hand with a mocking gesture of helplessness.

'The lady loves her will,' he said. 'Would you like to dance?'

I looked at Mrs Hale.

'No,' I said. 'I won't butt in. I'll play the pianola. The Victrola's a brute.'

I hardly noticed the passage of time. Whether the others danced or not, I played, and was unconscious of almost everything. In the midst of one rattling piece, Lord Lathkill touched my arm.

'Listen to Carlotta. She says closing time,' he said, in his old musical voice, but with the sardonic ring of war in it now.

Carlotta stood with her arms dangling, looking like a penitent schoolgirl.

'The Colonel has gone to bed. He hasn't been able to manage a reconciliation with Lucy,' she said. 'My mother-in-law thinks we ought to let him try to sleep.'

Carlotta's slow eyes rested on mine, questioning, penitent – or so I imagined – and somewhat sphinx-like.

'Why, of course,' said Lord Lathkill. 'I wish him all the sleep in the world.'

Mrs Hale said never a word.

'Is Mother retiring too?' asked Luke.

'I think so.'

'Ah! then supposing we up and look at the supper-tray.'

We found Lady Lathkill mixing herself some nightcap brew over a spirit-lamp: something milky and excessively harmless. She stood at the sideboard stirring her potations, and hardly noticed us. When she had finished she sat down with her steaming cup.

'Colonel Hale all right, Mother?' said Luke, looking across at her.

The dowager, under her uplift of white hair, stared back at her son. There was an eye-battle for some moments, during which he maintained his arch, debonair ease, just a bit crazy.

'No,' said Lady Lathkill, 'he is in great trouble.'

'Ah!' replied her son. 'Awful pity we can't do anything for him. But if flesh and blood can't help him, I'm afraid I'm a dud. Suppose he didn't mind our dancing? Frightfully good for *us*! We've been forgetting that we're flesh and blood, Mother.'

He took another whisky and soda, and gave me one. And in a paralysing silence Lady Lathkill sipped her hot brew, Luke and I sipped our whiskies, the young woman ate a little sandwich. We all preserved an extraordinary aplomb, and an obstinate silence.

It was Lady Lathkill who broke it. She seemed to be sinking downwards, crouching into herself like a skulking animal.

'I suppose,' she said, 'we shall all go to bed?'

'You go, Mother. We'll come along in a moment.'

She went, and for some time we four sat silent. The room seemed to become pleasanter, the air was more grateful.

'Look here,' said Lord Lathkill at last. 'What do you think of this ghost business?'

'I?' said I. 'I don't like the atmosphere it produces. There may be ghosts, and spirits, and all that. The dead must be somewhere; there's no such place as nowhere. But they don't affect me particularly. Do they you?'

'Well,' he said, 'no, not directly. Indirectly I suppose it does.'

'I think it makes a horribly depressing atmosphere, spiritualism,' said I. 'I want to kick.'

'Exactly! And ought one?' he asked in his terribly sane-seeming way.

This made me laugh. I knew what he was up to.

'I don't know what you mean by *ought*,' said I. 'If I really want to kick, if I know I can't stand a thing, I kick. Who's going to authorize me, if my own genuine feeling doesn't?'

'Quite,' he said, staring at me like an owl, with a fixed, meditative stare.

'Do you know,' he said, 'I suddenly thought at dinner-time, what corpses we all were, sitting eating our dinners. I thought it when I saw you look at these little Jerusalem artichoke things in a white sauce. Suddenly it struck me, you were alive and twinkling, and we were all bodily dead. Bodily dead, if you understand. Quite alive in other directions, but bodily dead. And whether we ate vegetarian or meat made no difference. We were bodily dead.'

'Ah, with a slap in the face,' said I, 'we come to life! You or I or anybody.'

'I *do* understand poor Lucy,' said Luke. 'Don't you? She forgot to be flesh and blood while she was alive, and now she can't forgive herself, nor the Colonel. That must be pretty rough, you know, not to realize it till you're dead, and you haven't, so to speak, anything left to go on. I mean, it's awfully important to be flesh and blood.'

He looked so solemnly at us, we three broke simultaneously into a uneasy laugh.

'Oh, but I *do* mean it,' he said. 'I've only realized how very extraordinary it is to be a man of flesh and blood, alive. It seems so ordinary, in comparison, to be dead, and merely spirit. That seems so commonplace. But fancy having a living face, and arms, and thighs. Oh, my God, I'm glad I've realized in time!'

He caught Mrs Hale's hand, and pressed her dusky arm against his body.

'Oh, but if one had died without realizing it!' he cried. 'Think how ghastly for Jesus, when he was risen and wasn't touchable! How very awful, to have to say *Noli me tangere!* Ah, touch me, touch me *alive!*'

He pressed Mrs Hale's hand convulsively against his breast. The tears had already slowly gathered in Carlotta's eyes and were dropping on to her hands in her lap.

'Don't cry, Carlotta,' he said. 'Really, don't. We haven't

killed one another. We're too decent, after all. We've almost become two spirits side by side. We've almost become two ghosts to one another, wrestling. Oh, but I want you to get back your body, even if I can't give it you. I want my flesh and blood, Carlotta, and I want you to have yours. We've suffered so much the other way. And the children, it is as well they are dead. They were born of our will and our disembodiment. Oh, I feel like the Bible. Clothe me with flesh again, and wrap my bones with sinew, and let the fountain of blood cover me. My spirit is like a naked nerve on the air.'

Carlotta had ceased to weep. She sat with her head dropped, as if asleep. The rise and fall of her small, slack breasts was still heavy, but they were lifting on a heaving sea of rest. It was as if a slow, restful dawn were rising in her body, while she slept. So slack, so broken she sat, it occurred to me that in this crucifixion business the crucified does not put himself alone on the cross. The woman is nailed even more inexorably up, and crucified in the body even more cruelly.

It is a monstrous thought. But the deed is even more monstrous. Oh, Jesus, didn't you know that you couldn't be crucified alone? – that the two thieves crucified along with you were the two women, your wife and your mother! You called them two thieves. But what would they call you, who had their women's bodies on the cross? The abominable trinity on Calvary!

I felt an infinite tenderness for my dear Carlotta. She could not yet be touched. But my soul streamed to her like warm blood. So she sat slack and drooped, as if broken. But she was not broken. It was only the great release.

Luke sat with the hand of the dark young woman pressed against his breast. His face was warm and fresh, but he, too, breathed heavily, and stared unseeing. Mrs Hale sat at his side erect and mute. But she loved him, with erect, black-faced, remote power.

'Morier!' said Luke to me. 'If you can help Carlotta, you will, won't you? I can't do any more for her now. We are in mortal fear of each other.'

'As much as she'll let me,' said I, looking at her drooping figure, that was built on such a strong frame.

The fire rustled on the hearth as we sat in complete silence. How long it lasted I cannot say. Yet we were none of us startled when the door opened.

It was the Colonel, in a handsome brocade dressing-gown, looking worried.

Luke still held the dark young woman's hand clasped against his thigh. Mrs Hale did not move.

'I thought you fellows might help me,' said the Colonel, in a worried voice, as he closed the door.

'What is wrong, Colonel?' said Luke.

The Colonel looked at him, looked at the clasped hands of Luke and the dark young woman, looked at me, looked at Carlotta, without changing his expression of anxiety, fear, and misery. He didn't care about us.

'I can't sleep,' he said. 'It's gone wrong again. My head feels as if there was a cold vacuum in it, and my heart beats, and something screws up inside me. I know it's Lucy. She hates me again. I can't stand it.'

He looked at us with eyes half glazed, obsessed. His face seemed as if the flesh were breaking under the skin, decomposing.

'Perhaps, poor thing,' said Luke, whose madness seemed really sane this night, 'perhaps you hate *her*.'

Luke's strange concentration instantly made us feel a tension, as of hate, in the Colonel's body.

'I?' The Colonel looked up sharply, like a culprit. 'I! I wouldn't say that, if I were you.'

'Perhaps that's what's the matter,' said Luke, with mad, beautiful calm. 'Why can't you feel kindly towards her, poor thing! She must have been done out of a lot while she lived.'

It was as if he had one foot in life and one in death, and knew both sides. To us it was like madness.

'I – I!' stammered the Colonel; and his face was a study. Expression after expression moved across it : of fear, repudiation, dismay, anger, repulsion, bewilderment, guilt. 'I was good to her.'

'Ah, yes,' said Luke. 'Perhaps *you* were good to her. But was your body good to poor Lucy's body, poor dead thing!'

He seemed to be better acquainted with the ghost than with us.

The Colonel gazed blankly at Luke, and his eyes went up and down, up and down, up and down, up and down.

'My body!' he said blankly.

And he looked down amazedly at his little round stomach, under the silk gown, and his stout knee, in its blue-and-white pyjama.

'My body!' he repeated blankly.

'Yes,' said Luke. 'Don't you see, you may have been awfully good to her. But her poor woman's body, were you ever good to that?'

'She had everything she wanted. She had three of my children,' said the Colonel dazedly.

'Ah yes, that may easily be. But your body of a man, was it ever good to her body of a woman? That's the point. If you understand the marriage service : with my body I thee worship. That's the point. No getting away from it.'

The queerest of all accusing angels did Lord Lathkill make, as he sat there with the hand of the other man's wife clasped against his thigh. His face was fresh and naïve, and the dark eyes were bright with a clairvoyant candour, that was like madness, and perhaps was supreme sanity.

The Colonel was thinking back, and over his face a slow understanding was coming.

'It may be,' he said. 'It may be. Perhaps, that way, I despised her. It may be, it may be.'

'I know,' said Luke. 'As if she weren't worth noticing, what you did to her. Haven't I done it myself? And don't I know now, it's a horrible thing to do, to oneself as much as to her? Her poor ghost, that ached, and never had a real body! It's not so easy to worship with the body. Ah, if the Church taught us that sacrament : *with my body I thee worship!* that would easily make up for any honouring and obeying the woman might do. But that's why she haunts you. You ignored and disliked her body, and she was only a living ghost. Now she wails in the afterworld, like a still-wincing nerve.'

The Colonel hung his head, slowly pondering. Pondering with all his body. His young wife watched the sunken, bald head in a kind of stupor. His day seemed so far from her day. Carlotta had lifted her face; she was beautiful again, with the tender before-dawn freshness of a new understanding.

She was watching Luke, and it was obvious he was another man to her. The man she knew, the Luke who was her husband, was gone, and this other strange, uncanny creature had taken his place. She was filled with wonder. Could one so change, as to become another creature entirely? Ah, if it were so! If she herself, as she knew herself, could cease to be! If that woman who was married to Luke, married to him in an intimacy of misfortune that was like a horror, could only cease to be, and let a new, delicately-wild Carlotta take her place!

'It may be,' said the Colonel, lifting his head. 'It may be.' There seemed to come a relief over his soul, as he realized. 'I didn't worship her with my body. I think maybe I worshipped other women that way; but maybe I never did. But I thought I was good to her. And I thought she didn't want it.'

'It's no good thinking. We all want it,' asserted Luke. 'And before we die, we know it. I say, before we die. It may be after. But everybody wants it, let them say and do what they will. Don't you agree, Morier?'

I was startled when he spoke to me. I had been thinking of Carlotta: how she was looking like a girl again, as she used to look at the Thwaite, when she painted cactuses-in-a-pot. Only now, a certain rigidity of the will had left her, so that she looked even younger than when I first knew her, having now a virginal, flower-like *stillness* which she had not had then. I had always believed that people could be born again : if they would only let themselves.

'I'm sure they do,' I said to Luke.

But I was thinking, if people were born again, the old circumstances would not fit the new body.

'What about yourself, Luke?' said Carlotta abruptly.

'I!' he exclaimed, and the scarlet showed in his cheek. 'I! I'm not fit to be spoken about. I've been moaning like the ghost of disembodiment myself, ever since I became a man.'

The Colonel said never a word. He hardly listened. He was pondering, pondering. In his way, he, too, was a brave man.

'I have an idea what you mean,' he said. 'There's no deny-
ing it, I didn't like her body. And now, I suppose, it's too late.'

He looked up bleakly : in a way, willing to be condemned,
since he knew vaguely that something was wrong. Anything
better than the blind torture.

'Oh, I don't know,' said Luke. 'Why don't you, even now,
love her a little with your real heart? Poor disembodied thing!
Why don't you take her to your warm heart, even now, and
comfort her inside there? Why don't you be kind to her poor
ghost, bodily?'

The Colonel did not answer. He was gazing fixedly at Luke.
Then he turned, and dropped his head, alone in a deep silence.
Then, deliberately, but not lifting his head, he pulled open his
dressing-gown at the breast, unbuttoned the top of his pyjama
jacket, and sat perfectly still, his breast showing white and very
pure, so much younger and purer than his averted face. He
breathed with difficulty, his white breast rising irregularly. But
in the deep isolation where he was, slowly a gentleness of compassion came over him, moulding his elderly features with
strange freshness, and softening his blue eye with a look it had
never had before. Something of the tremulous gentleness of a
young bridegroom had come upon him, in spite of his baldness,
his silvery little moustache, the weary marks of his face.

The passionate, compassionate soul stirred in him and was
pure, his youth flowered over his face and eyes.

We sat very still, moved also in the spirit of compassion.
There seemed a presence in the air, almost a smell of blossom,
as if time had opened and gave off the perfume of spring. The
Colonel gazed in silence into space, his smooth white chest, with
the few dark hairs, open and rising and sinking with life.

Meanwhile his dark-faced young wife watched as if from
afar. The youngness that was on him was not for her.

I knew that Lady Lathkill would come. I could feel her far
off in her room, stirring and sending forth her rays. Swiftly I
steeled myself to be in readiness. When the door opened, I rose
and walked across the room.

She entered with characteristic noiselessness, peering in round
the door, with her crest of white hair, before she ventured
bodily in. The Colonel looked at her swiftly, and swiftly covered

his breast, holding his hand at his bosom, clutching the silk of his robe.

'I was afraid,' she murmured, 'that Colonel Hale might be in trouble.'

'No,' said I. 'We are all sitting very peacefully. There is no trouble.'

Lord Lathkill also rose.

'No trouble at all, I assure you, Mother!' he said.

Lady Lathkill glanced at us both, then turned heavily to the Colonel.

'She is unhappy tonight?' she asked.

The Colonel winced.

'No,' he said hurriedly. 'No, I don't think so.' He looked up at her with shy, wincing eyes.

'Tell me what I can do,' she said in a very low tone, bending towards him.

'Our ghost is walking tonight, Mother,' said Lord Lathkill. 'Haven't you felt the air of spring, and smelt the plum-blossom? Don't you feel us all young? Our ghost is walking, to bring Lucy home. The Colonel's breast is quite extraordinary, white as plum-blossom, Mother, younger-looking than mine, and he's already taken Lucy into his bosom, in his breast, where he breathes like the wind among trees. The Colonel's breast is white and extraordinarily beautiful, Mother, I don't wonder poor Lucy yearned for it, to go home into it at last. It's like going into an orchard of plum-blossom, for a ghost.'

His mother looked round at him, then back at the Colonel, who was still clutching his hand over his chest, as if protecting something.

'You see, I didn't understand where I'd been wrong,' he said, looking up at her imploringly. 'I never realized that it was my body which had not been good to her.'

Lady Lathkill curved sideways to watch him. But her power was gone. His face had come smooth with the tender glow of compassionate life, that flowers again. She could not get at him.

'It's no good, Mother. You know our ghost is walking. She's supposed to be absolutely like a crocus, if you know what I mean : harbinger of spring in the earth. So it says in my great-grandfather's diary : for she rises with silence like a crocus at the feet, and violets in the hollows of the heart come out. For she is of the feet and the hands, the thighs and breast, the face and the all-concealing belly, and her name is silent, but her odour is of spring, and her contact is the all-in-all.' He was quoting from his great-grandfather's diary, which only the sons of the family read. And as he quoted he rose curiously on his toes, and spread his fingers, bringing his hands together till the finger-tips touched. His father had done that before him, when he was deeply moved.

Lady Lathkill sat down heavily in the chair next the Colonel. 'How do you feel?' she asked him, in a secretive mutter.

He looked round at her, with the large blue eyes of candour. 'I never knew what was wrong,' he said, a little nervously. 'She only wanted to be looked after a bit, not to be a homeless, houseless ghost. It's all right! She's all right here.' He pressed his clutched hand on his breast. 'It's all right; it's all right. She'll be all right now.'

He rose, a little fantastic in his brocade gown, but once more manly, candid and sober.

'With your permission,' he said, 'I will retire.' – He made a little bow. – 'I am glad you helped me. I didn't know – didn't know.'

But the change in him, and his secret wondering were so strong on him, he went out of the room scarcely being aware of us.

Lord Lathkill threw up his arms, and stretched, quivering.

'Oh, pardon, pardon,' he said, seeming, as he stretched, quivering, to grow bigger and almost splendid, sending out rays of fire to the dark young woman. 'Oh, Mother, thank you for my limbs and my body! Oh, Mother, thank you for my knees and my shoulders at this moment! Oh, Mother, thank you that my body is straight and alive! Oh, Mother, torrents of spring, torrents of spring, whoever said that?'

'Don't you forget yourself, my boy?' said his mother.

'Oh no, dear no! Oh, Mother dear, a man has to be in love in his thighs, the way you ride a horse. Why don't we stay in love that way all our lives? Why do we turn into corpses with consciousness? Oh, Mother of my body, thank you for my body, you strange woman with white hair! I don't know much about you, but my body comes from you, so thank you, my dear. I shall think of you tonight!'

'Hadn't we better go?' she said, beginning to tremble.

'Why, yes,' he said, turning and looking strangely at the dark young woman. 'Yes, let us go; let us go!'

Carlotta gazed at him, then, with strange, heavy, searching look, at me. I smiled to her, and she looked away. The dark young woman looked over her shoulder as she went out. Lady Lathkill hurried past her son, with head ducked. But still he laid his hand on her shoulder, and she stopped dead.

'Good night, Mother; Mother of my face and my thighs. Thank you for the night to come, dear Mother of my body.'

She glanced up at him rapidly, nervously, then hurried away. He stared after her, then switched off the light.

'Funny old Mother!' he said. 'I never realized before that she was the mother of my shoulders and my hips, as well as my brain. Mother of my thighs!'

He switched off some of the lights as we went, accompanying me to my room.

'You know,' he said, 'I can understand that the Colonel is happy, now the forlorn ghost of Lucy is comforted in his heart. After all, he married her! And she must be content at last: he has a beautiful chest, don't you think? Together they will sleep well. And then he will begin to live the life of living again. How friendly the house feels tonight! But, after all, it is my old home. And the smell of plum-blossom – don't you notice it? It is our ghost, in silence like a crocus. There, your fire has died down! But it's a nice room! I hope our ghost will come to you. I think she will. Don't speak to her. It makes her go away. She, too, is a ghost of silence. We talk far too much. But now I am going to be silent, too, and a ghost of silence. Good night!'

He closed the door softly and was gone. And softly, in silence, I took off my things. I was thinking of Carlotta, and a little sadly, perhaps, because of the power of circumstance over us. This night I could have worshipped her with my body, and she, perhaps, was stripped in the body to be worshipped. But it was not for me, at this hour, to fight against circumstances.

I had fought too much, even against the most imposing circumstances, to use any more violence for love. Desire is a sacred thing, and should not be violated.

'Hush!' I said to myself. 'I will sleep, and the ghost of my silence can go forth, in the subtle body of desire, to meet that which is coming to meet it. Let my ghost go forth, and let me not interfere. There are many intangible meetings, and unknown fulfilments of desire.'

So I went softly to sleep, as I wished to, without interfering with the warm, crocus-like ghost of my body.

And I must have gone far, far down the intricate galleries of sleep, to the very heart of the world. For I know I passed on beyond the strata of images and words, beyond the iron veins of memory, and even the jewels of rest, to sink in the final dark like a fish, dumb, soundless, and imageless, yet alive and swimming.

And at the very core of the deep night the ghost came to me, at the heart of the ocean of oblivion, which is also the heart of life. Beyond hearing, or even knowledge of contact, I met her and knew her. How I know it I don't know. Yet I know it with eyeless, wingless knowledge.

For man in the body is formed through countless ages, and at the centre is the speck, or spark, upon which all his formation has taken place. It is even not himself, deep beyond his many depths. Deep from him calls to deep. And according as deep answers deep, man glistens and surpasses himself.

Beyond all the pearly mufflings of consciousness, of age upon age of consciousness, deep calls yet to deep, and sometimes is answered. It is calling and answering, new-awakened God calling within the deep of man, and new God calling answer from the other deep. And sometimes the other deep is a woman, as it was with me, when my ghost came.

Women were not unknown to me. But never before had woman come, in the depths of night, to answer my deep with her deep. At the ghost came, came as a ghost of silence, still in the depth of sleep.

I know she came. I know she came even as a woman, to my man. But the knowledge is darkly naked as the event. I only know, it was so. In the deep of sleep a call was called from the deeps of me, and answered in the deeps, by a woman among women. Breasts or thighs or face, I remember not a touch, no, nor a movement of my own. It is all complete in the profundity of darkness. Yet I know it was so.

I awoke towards dawn, from far, far away. I was vaguely conscious of drawing nearer and nearer, as the sun must have been drawing towards the horizon, from the complete beyond. Till at last the faint pallor of mental consciousness coloured my waking.

And then I was aware of a pervading scent, as of plum-blossom, and a sense of extraordinary silkiness – though where, and in what contact, I could not say. It was as the first blemish of dawn.

And even with so slight a conscious registering, *it* seemed to disappear. Like a whale that has sounded to the bottomless seas. That knowledge of *it*, which was the mating of the ghost and me, disappeared from me, in its rich weight of certainty, as the scent of the plum-blossom moved down the lanes of my consciousness, and my limbs stirred in a silkiness for which I have no comparison.

As I became aware, I also became uncertain. I wanted to be certain of *it*, to have definite evidence. And as I sought for evidence, it disappeared, my perfect knowledge was gone. I no longer knew in full.

Now as the daylight slowly amassed, in the windows from which I had put back the shutters, I sought in myself for evidence, and in the room.

But I shall never know. I shall never know if it was a ghost, some sweet spirit from the innermost of the ever-deepening cosmos; or a woman, a very woman, as the silkiness of my limbs seems to attest; or a dream, a hallucination! I shall never know. Because I went away from Riddings in the morning, on account of the sudden illness of Lady Lathkill.

'You will come again,' Luke said to me. 'And in any case, you will never really go away from us.'

'Good-bye,' she said to me. 'At last it was perfect!'

She seemed so beautiful, when I left her, as if it were the ghost again, and I was far down the deeps of consciousness.

The following autumn, when I was overseas once more, I had a letter from Lord Lathkill. He wrote very rarely.

'Carlotta has a son,' he said, 'and I an heir. He has yellow hair, like a little crocus, and one of the young plum-trees in the orchard has come out of all season into blossom. To me he is flesh and blood of our ghost itself. Even mother doesn't look over the wall, to the other side, any more. It's all this side for her now.

'So our family refuses to die out, by the grace of our ghost. We are calling him Gabriel.

'Dorothy Hale also is a mother, three days before Carlotta. She has a black lamb of a daughter, called Gabrielle. By the bleat of the little thing, I know its father. Our own is a blue-eyed one, with the dangerous repose of a pugilist. I have no fears of our family misfortune for him, ghost-begotten and ready-fisted.

'The Colonel is very well, quiet and self-possessed. He is farming in Wiltshire, raising pigs: It is a passion with him, the *crême de la crême* of swine. I admit, he has golden sows as elegant as a young Diane de Poictiers, and young hogs like Perseus in the first red-gold flush of youth. He looks me in the eye, and I look him back, and we understand. He is quiet, and proud now, and very hale and hearty, raising swine *ad maiorem gloriam Dei*. A good sport!

'I am in love with this house and its inmates, including the plum-blossom-scented one, she who visited you, in all the peace. I cannot understand why you wander in uneasy and distant parts of the earth. For me, when I am at home, I am there. I have peace upon my bones, and if the world is going to come to a violent and untimely end, as prophets aver, I feel the house of Lathkill will survive, built upon our ghost. So come back, and you'll find we shall not have gone away ...'

None of That

I met Luis Colmenares in Venice, not having seen him for years. He is a Mexican exile living on the scanty remains of what was once wealth, and eking out a poor and lonely existence by being a painter. But his art is only a sedative to him. He wanders about like a lost soul, mostly in Paris or in Italy, where he can live cheaply. He is rather short, rather fat, pale, with black eyes which are always looking the other way, and a spirit the same, always averted.

'Do you know who is in Venice?' he said to me. 'Cuesta! He is in the Hôtel Romano. I saw him bathing yesterday on the Lido.'

There was a world of gloomy mockery in this last sentence.

'Do you mean Cuesta, the bull-fighter?' I asked.

'Yes. Don't you know, he retired? Do you remember? An American woman left him a lot of money. Did you ever see him?'

'Once,' said I.

'Was it before the revolution? Do you remember, he retired and bought a *hacienda* very cheap from one of Madero's generals, up in Chihuahua? It was after the Carranzista, and I was already in Europe.'

'How does he look now?' I said.

'Enormously fat, like a yellow, round, small whale in the sea. You saw him? You know he was rather short and rather fat always. I think his mother was a Mixtec Indian woman. Did you ever know him?'

'No,' said I. 'Did you?'

'Yes. I knew him in the old days, when I was rich, and thought I should be rich for ever.'

He was silent, and I was afraid he had shut up for good. It was unusual for him to be even as communicative as he had been. But it was evident that having seen Cuesta, the toreador whose fame once rang through Spain and through Latin America, had moved him deeply. He was in a ferment, and could not quite contain himself.

'But he wasn't interesting, was he?' I said. 'Wasn't he just a – a bull-fighter – a brute?'

Colmenares looked at me out of his own blackness. He didn't want to talk. Yet he had to.

'He was a brute, yes,' he admitted grudgingly. 'But not just a brute. Have you seen him when he was at his best? Where did you see him? I never liked him in Spain, he was too vain. But in Mexico he was very good. Have you seen him play with the bull, and play with death? He was marvellous. Do you remember him, what he looked like?'

'Not very well,' said I.

'Short, and broad, and rather fat, with rather a yellow colour, and a pressed-in nose. But his eyes, they were marvellous, also rather small, and yellow, and when he looked at you, so strange and cool, you felt your inside melting. Do you know that feeling? He looked into the last little place of you, where you keep your courage. Do you understand? And so you felt yourself melting. Do you know what I mean?'

'More or less, perhaps,' said I.

Colmenares' black eyes were fixed on my face, dilated and gleaming, but not really seeing me at all. He was seeing the past. Yet a curious force streamed out of his face; one understood him by the telepathy of passion, inverted passion.

'And in the bull-ring, he was marvellous. He would stand with his back to the bull, and pretend to be adjusting his stocking, while the bull came charging on him. And with a little glance over his shoulder, he would make a small movement, and the bull had passed him without getting him. Then he would smile a little, and walk after it. It is marvellous that he was not killed hundreds of times, but I saw him bathing on the Lido today, like a fat, small whale. It is extraordinary! But I did not see his eyes . . .'

A queer look of abstracted passion was on Colmenares' fat, pale, clean-shaven face. Perhaps the toreador had cast a spell over him, as over so many people in the old and the new world.

'It is strange that I have never seen eyes anywhere else like his. Did I tell you, they were yellow, and not like human eyes at all? They didn't look at you. I don't think they ever looked at any-body. He only looked at the little bit inside your body where you keep your courage. I don't think he could see people, any more than an animal can : I mean see them personally, as I see you and you see me. He was an animal, a marvellous animal. I have often thought, if human beings had not developed minds and speech, they would have become marvellous animals like Cuesta, with those marvellous eyes, much more marvellous than a lion's or a tiger's. Have you noticed a lion or a tiger never sees you personally? It never really looks at you. But also it is afraid to look at the last little bit of you, where your courage lives inside you. But Cuesta was not afraid. He looked straight at it, and it melted.'

'And what was he like, in ordinary life?' said I.

'He did not talk, was very silent. He was not clever at all. He was not even clever enough to be a general. And he could be very brutal and disgusting. But usually he was quiet. But he was always *something*. If you were in the room with him, you always noticed him more than anybody, more than women or men, even very clever people. He was stupid, but he made you physically aware of him; like a cat in the room. I tell you, that little bit of you where you keep your courage was enchanted by him; he put over you an enchantment.'

'Did he do it on purpose?'

'Well! It is hard to say. But he knew he could do it. To some people, perhaps, he could not do it. But he never saw such people. He only saw people who were in his enchantment. And of course, in the bull-ring, he mesmerized everybody. He could draw the natural magnetism of everybody to him – everybody. And then he was marvellous, he played with death as if it were a kitten, so quick, quick as a star, and calm as a flower, and all the time, laughing at death. It is marvellous he was never killed. But he retired very young. – And then suddenly it was he who killed the bull, with one hand, one stroke. He was very strong. And the bull sank down at his feet, heavy with death. The people went mad! And he just glanced at them, with his yellow eyes, in a cool, beautiful contempt, as if he were an animal that wrapped the skin of death round him. Ah, he was wonderful! And today I saw him bathing on the Lido, in an American bathing-suit, with a woman. His bathing-suit was just a little more yellow than he is. – I have held the towel when he was being rubbed down and massaged, often. He had the body of an Indian, very smooth, with hardly any hair, and creamy-yellow. I always thought it had something childish about it, so soft. But also, it had the same mystery as his eyes, as if you could never touch it, as if, when you touched it, still it was not he. When he had no clothes on, he was naked. But it seemed he would have many, many more nakednesses before you really came to *him*. – Do you understand me at all? Or does it seem to you foolish?'

'It interests me,' I said. 'And women, of course, fell for him by the thousand?'

'By the million! And they were mad because of him. Women went mad, once they felt : im. It was not like Rudolf Valentino, sentimental. It was madness, like cats in the night which howl, no longer knowing whether they are on earth or in hell or in paradise. So were the women. He could have had forty beautiful women every night, and different ones each night, from the beginning of the year to the end.'

'But he didn't, naturally?'

'Oh, no! At first, I think, he took many women. But later, when I knew him, he took none of those that besieged him. He had two Mexican women whom he lived with, humble women, Indians. And all the others he spat at, and spoke of them with terrible, obscene language. I think he would have liked to whip them, or kill them, for pursuing him.'

'Only he must enchant them when he was in the bull-ring,' said I.

'Yes. But that was like sharpening his knife on them.'

'And when he retired – he had plenty of money – how did he amuse himself?'

'He was rich, he had a big *hacienda*, and many people like slaves to work for him. He raised cattle. I think he was very proud to be *hacendado* and *patrón* of so many people, with a little army of his own. I think he was proud, living like a king. – I had not heard of him for years. Now, suddenly, he is in Venice with a Frenchwoman, a Frenchwoman who talks bad Spanish –'

'How old is he?'

'How old? He is about fifty, or a little less.'

'So young! And will you speak to him?'

'I don't know. I can't make up my mind. If I speak to him, he will think I want money.'

There was a certain note of hatred now in Colmenares' voice.

'Well, why shouldn't he give you money? He is still rich, I suppose?'

'Rich, yes! He must always be rich. He has got American money. An American woman left him half a million dollars. Did you never hear of it?'

'No. Then why shouldn't he give you money? I suppose you often gave him some, in the past?'

'Oh, that – that is *quite* the past. He will never give me anything – or a hundred francs, something like that! Because he is mean. Did you never hear of the American woman who left him half a million dollars, and committed suicide?'

'No. When was it?'

'It was a long time ago – about 1914, or 1913. I had already lost all my money. Her name was Ethel Cane. Did you never hear of her?'

'I don't think I did,' I said, feeling it remiss not to have heard of the lady.

'Ah! You should have known her. She was extraordinary. I had known her in Paris, even before I came back to Mexico and knew Cuesta well. She was almost as extraordinary as Cuesta: one of those American women, born rich, but what we should call provincial. She didn't come from New York or Boston, but somewhere else. Omaha or something. She was blonde, with thick, straight, blonde hair, and she was one of the very first to wear it short, like a Florentine page-boy. Her skin was white, and her eyes very blue, and she was not thin. At first, there seemed something childish about her – do you know that look, rather round cheeks and clear eyes, so false-innocent? Her eyes especially were warm and naïve and false-innocent, but full of light. Only sometimes they were bloodshot. Oh, she was extraordinary! It was only when I knew her better I noticed how her blonde eyebrows gathered together above her nose, in a diabolic manner. She was much too much a personality to be a lady, and she had all that terrible American energy! Ah! energy! She was a dynamo. In Paris she was married to a dapper little pink-faced American who got yellow at the gills, bilious, running after her when she would not have him. He painted pictures and wanted to be modern. She knew all the people, and had all sorts come to her, as if she kept a human menagerie. And she bought old furniture and brocades; she would go mad if she saw someone get a piece of velvet brocade with the misty bloom of years on it, that she coveted. She coveted such things, with lust, and would go into a strange sensual trance, looking at some old worm-eaten chair. And she would go mad if someone else got it, and not she: that nasty old wormy chair of the quattrocento! Things! She was mad about "things". – But it was only for a time. She always got tired, especially of her own enthusiasms.

'That was when I knew her in Paris. Then I think she divorced that husband, and, when the revolutions in Mexico became quieter, she came to Mexico. I think she was fascinated by the idea of Carranza. If ever she heard of a man who seemed to have a dramatic sort of power in him, she must know that man. It was like her lust for brocade and old chairs and a perfect aesthetic setting. Now it was to know the most dangerous man, especially if he looked like a prophet or a reformer. She was a socialist also, at this time. She no longer was in love with chairs.

'She found' me again in Mexico: she knew thousands of people, and whenever one of them might be useful to her, she remembered him. So she remembered me, and it was nothing to her that I was now poor. I know she thought of me as "that little Luis Something", but she had a certain use for me, and found, perhaps, a certain little flavour in me. At least she asked me often to dinner, or to drive with her. She was curious, quite reckless and a daredevil, yet shy and awkward out of her own *milieu*. It was only in intimacy that she was unscrupulous and dauntless as a devil incarnate. In public, and in strange places, she was very uneasy, like one who has a bad conscience towards society, and is afraid of it. And for that reason she could never go out without a man to stand between her and all the others.

'While she was in Mexico, I was that man. She soon discovered that I was satisfactory. I would perform all the duties of a husband without demanding any of the rights. Which was what she wanted. I think she was looking round for a remarkable and epoch-making husband. But, of course, it would have to be a husband who would be a fitting instrument for her remarkable and epoch-making energy and character. She was extraordinary, but she could only work through individuals, through others. By herself she could accomplish nothing. She lay on a sofa and mused and schemed, with the energy boiling inside her. Only when she had a group, or a few real individuals, or just one man, then she could start something, and make them all dance in a tragi-comedy, like marionettes.

'But in Mexico, men do not care for women who will make them dance like puppets. In Mexico, women must run in the dust like the Indian women, with meek little heads. American women are not very popular. Their energy, and their power to make other people do things, are not in request. The men would rather go to the devil in their own way, than be sent there by the women, with a little basket in which to bring home the goods.

'So Ethel found not a cold shoulder, but a number of square, fat backs turned to her. They didn't want her. The revolutionaries would not take any notice of her at all. They wanted no woman interfering. General Isidor Garabay danced with her, and expected her immediately to become his mistress. But, as she said, she was having *none of that*. She had a terrible way of saying "I'm having none of that!" – like hitting a mirror with a hammer. And as nobody wanted to get into trouble over her, they were having none of her.

'At first, of course, when the generals saw her white shoulders and blonde hair and innocent face, they thought at once : "Here is a *type* for us!" They were not deceived by her innocent look. But they were deceived by what looked like her helplessness. The blood would come swelling into her neck and face, her eyes would go hot, her whole figure would swell with repellent energy, and she would say something very American and very crushing, in French, or in American. None of *that*! Stop *that*!

'She, too, had a lot of power. She could send out of her body a repelling energy, to compel people to submit to her will. Men in Europe or the United States nearly always crumpled up before her. But in Mexico she had come to the wrong shop. The men

were a law to themselves. While she was winning and rather
lovely, with her blue eyes so full of light and her white skin
glistening with energetic health, they expected her to become
at once their mistress. And when they saw, very quickly, that
she was having *none of that*, they turned on their heels and
showed her their fat backs. Because she was clever, and remarkable, and had wonderful energy and a wonderful power for
making people dance while she pulled the strings, they didn't
care a bit. They, too, wanted *none of that*. They would, perhaps,
have carried her off and shared her as a mistress, except for the
fear of trouble with the American Government.

'So, soon, she began to be bored, and to think of returning to
New York. She said that Mexico was a place without a soul and
without a culture, and it had not even brain enough to be
mechanically efficient. It was a city and a land of naughty little
boys doing obscene little things, and one day it would learn its
lesson. I told her that history is the account of a lesson which
nobody ever learns, and she told me the world certainly *had*
progressed. Only not in Mexico, she supposed. I asked her why
she had come, then, to Mexico. And she said she had thought
there was something doing, and she would like to be in it. But
she found it was only naughty and mostly cowardly little boys
letting off guns and doing mediocre obscenities, so she would
leave them to it. I told her I supposed it was life. And she replied
that since it was not good enough for her, it was not life to
her.

'She said all she wanted was to live the life of the imagination
and get it acted on. At the time, I thought this ridiculous. I thought
she was just trying to find somebody to fall in love with. Later,
I saw she was right. She had an imaginary picture of herself as
an extraordinary and potent woman who would make a stupendous change in the history of man. Like Catherine of Russia,
only cosmopolitan, not merely Russian. And it is true, she *was*
an extraordinary woman, with tremendous power of will, and
truly amazing energy, even for an American woman. She was
like a locomotive-engine stoked up inside and bursting with
steam, which it has to let off by rolling a lot of trucks about.
But I did not see how this was to cause a change in the tide of
mortal affairs. It was only a part of the hubbub of traffic. She

sent the trucks bouncing against one another with a clash of buffers, and sometimes she derailed some unfortunate item of the rolling-stock. But I did not see how this was to change the history of mankind. She seemed to have arrived just a little late, as some heroes, and heroines also, today, always do.

'I wondered always, why she did not take a lover. She was a woman between thirty and forty, very healthy and full of this extraordinary energy. She saw many men, and was always drawing them out, always on the *qui vive* to start them rolling down some incline. She attracted men, in a certain way. Yet she had no lover.

'I wondered even with regard to myself. We were friends, and a great deal together. Certainly I was under her spell. I came running as soon as I thought she wanted me. I did the things she suggested I should do. Even among my own acquaintances, when I found everybody laughing at me and disliking me for being at the service of an American woman, and I tried to rebel against her, and put her in her place, as the Mexicans say – which means, to them, in bed with no clothes on – still, the moment I saw her, with a look and a word she won me round. She was very clever. She flattered me, of course. She made me feel intelligent. She drew me out. There was her cleverness. She made *me* clever. I told her all about Mexico : all my life : all my ideas of history, philosophy. I sounded awfully clever and original, to myself. And she listened with such attention, which I thought was deep interest in what I was saying. But she was waiting for something she could fasten on, so that she could "start something". That was her constant craving, to "start something". But, of course, I thought she was interested in *me*.

'She would lie on a large couch that was covered with old sarapes – she began to buy them as soon as she came to Mexico – herself wrapped in a wonderful black shawl that glittered all over with brilliant birds and flowers in vivid colour, a very fine specimen of the embroidered shawls our Mexican ladies used to wear at a bull-fight or in an open-air *fiesta* : and there, with her white arms glistening through the long fringe of the shawl, the old Italian jewellery rising on her white, dauntless breast, and her short, thick, blonde hair falling like yellow metal, she would draw me out, draw me out. I never talked so much in my life before or since. Always talk! And I believe I talked very well, really, really very clever. But nothing besides talk! Sometimes I stayed till after midnight. And sometimes she would snort with impatience or boredom, rather like a horse, flinging back her head and shaking that heavy blonde hair. And I think some part of her wanted me to make love to her.

'But I didn't. I couldn't. I was there, under her influence, in her power. She could draw me out in talk, marvellously. I'm sure I was very clever indeed. But any other part of me was stiff, petrified. I couldn't even touch her. I couldn't even take her hand in mine. It was a physical impossibility. When I was away from her, I could think of her and of her white, healthy body with a voluptuous shiver. I could even run to her apartment, intending to kiss her, and make her my mistress that very night. But the moment I was in her presence, it left me. I could not touch her. I was averse from touching her. Physically, for some reason, I hated her.

'And I felt within myself, it was because she was repelling me and because she was always hating men, hating all active maleness in a man. She only wanted passive maleness, and then this "talk", this life of the imagination, as she called it. Inside herself she seethed, and she thought it was because she wanted to be made love to, very much made love to. But it wasn't so. She seethed against all men, with repulsion. She was cruel to the body of a man. But she excited his mind, his spirit. She loved to do that. She loved to have a man hanging round, like a servant. She loved to stimulate him, especially his mind. And she, too, when the man was not there, she thought she wanted him to be her lover. But when he was there, and he wanted to gather for himself that mysterious fruit of her body, she revolted against him with a fearful hate. A man must be *absolutely* her servant, and only that. That was what she meant by the life of the imagination.

'And I was her servant. Everybody jeered at me. But I said to myself, I would make her my mistress. I almost set my teeth to do it. That was when I was away from her. When I came to her, I could not even touch her. When I tried to make myself touch her, something inside me began to shudder. It was impossible. – And I knew it was because, with her inner body, she was repelling me, always really repelling me.

'Yet she wanted me too. She was lonely : lonesome, she said. She was lonesome, and she would have liked to get me making love to her external self. She would even, I think, have become my mistress, and allowed me to take her sometimes for a little, miserable, humiliating moment, then quickly have got rid of me again. But I couldn't do it. Her inner body *never* wanted me. And I couldn't just be her prostitute. Because immediately she would have despised me, and insulted me if I had persisted in trying to get some satisfaction of her. I knew it. She had already had two husbands, and she was a woman who always ached to tell *all*, everything. She had told me too much. I had seen one of her American husbands. I did not choose to see myself in a similar light : or plight.

'No, she wanted to live the life of the imagination. She said, the imagination could master everything; so long, of course, as one was not shot in the head, or had an eye put out. Talking of the Mexican atrocities, and of the famous case of raped nuns, she said it was all nonsense that a woman was broken because she had been raped. She could rise above it. The imagination could rise above *anything*, that was not real organic damage. If one lived the life of the imagination, one could rise above any experience that ever happened to one. One could even commit murder, and rise above that. – By using the imagination, and by using cunning, a woman can justify herself in anything, even the meanest and most bad things. A woman uses her imagination on her own behalf, and she becomes more innocent to herself than an innocent child, no matter what bad things she has done.'

'Men do that, too,' I interrupted. 'It's the modern dodge. That's why everybody today is innocent. To the imagination all things are pure, if you did them yourself.'

Colmenares looked at me with quick, black eyes, to see if I were mocking him. He did not care about me and my interruptions. He was utterly absorbed in his recollections of that woman, who had made him so clever, and who had made him her servant, and from whom he had never had any satisfaction.

'And then what?' I asked him. 'Then did she try her hand on Cuesta?'

'Ah!' said Colmenares, rousing, and glancing at me suspiciously again. 'Yes! That was what she did. And I was jealous. Though I couldn't bring myself to touch her, yet I was excruciated with jealousy, because she was interested in someone else. She was interested in someone besides myself, and my vanity suffered tortures of jealousy. Why was I such a fool? Why, even now, could I kill that fat, yellow pig Cuesta? A man is always a fool.'

'How did she meet the bull-fighter?' I asked. 'Did you introduce him to her?'

'She went once to the bull-fight, because everyone was talking about Cuesta. She did not care for such things as the bull-ring; she preferred the modern theatre, Duse and Reinhardt, and "things of the imagination". But now she was going back to New York, and she had never seen a bull-fight, so she must see one. I got seats in the shade – high up, you know – and went with her.

'At first she was very disgusted, and very contemptuous, and a little frightened, you know, because a Mexican crowd in a bull-ring is not very charming. She was afraid of people. But she sat stubborn and sulky, like a sulky child, saying : Can't they do anything more subtle than this, to get a thrill? It's on such a low level!

'But when Cuesta at last began to play with a bull, she began to get excited. He was in pink and silver, very gorgeous, and looking very ridiculous, as usual. Till he began to play; and then there really was something marvellous in him, you know, so quick and so light and so playful – do you know? When he was playing with a bull and playing with death in the ring, he was the most playful thing I have ever seen : more playful than kittens or leopard cubs, and you know how they play; do you? Oh, marvellous! more gay and light than if they had lots of wings all over them, all wings of playing! Well, he was like that, playing with death in the ring, as if he had all kinds of gay little wings to spin him with the quickest, tiniest, most beautiful little movements, quite unexpected, like a soft leopard cub. And then at the end, when he killed the bull and the blood squirted past him, ugh! it was as if all his body laughed, and still the same soft, surprised laughter like a young thing, but more cruel than anything you can imagine. He fascinated me, but I always hated him. I would have liked to stick him as he stuck the bulls.

'I could see that Ethel was trying not to be caught by his spell. He had the most curious charm, quick and unexpected like play, you know, like leopard kittens, or slow sometimes, like tiny little bears. And yet the perfect cruelty. It was the joy in cruelty! She hated the blood and messiness and dead animals. Ethel hated all that. It was not the life of the imagination. She was very pale, and very silent. She leaned forward and hardly moved, looking white and obstinate and subdued. And Cuesta had killed three bulls before she made any sign of any sort. I did not speak to her. The fourth bull was a beauty, full of life, curling and prancing like a narcissus-flower in January. He was a very special bull, brought from Spain, and not so stupid as the others. He pawed the ground and blew the breath on the ground, lowering his head. And Cuesta opened his arms to him with a little smile, but endearing, lovingly endearing, as a man might open his arms to a little maiden he really loves, but, really, for her to come to his body, his warm open body, to come softly. So he held his arms out to the bull, with love. And that was what fascinated the women. They screamed and they fainted, longing to go into the arms of Cuesta, against his soft, round body, that was more yearning than a fico. But the bull, of course, rushed past him, and only got two darts sticking in his shoulder. That was the love.

'Then Ethel shouted, *Bravo! Bravo!* and I saw that she, too, had gone mad. Even Cuesta heard her, and he stopped a moment and looked at her. He saw her leaning forward, with her short, thick hair hanging like yellow metal, and her face dead-white, and her eyes glaring to his, like a challenge. They looked at one another, for a second, and he gave a little bow, then turned away. But he was changed. He didn't play so unconsciously any more : he seemed to be thinking of something, and forgetting himself. I was afraid he would be killed; but so afraid! He seemed absent-minded, and taking risks too great. When the bull came after him over the gangway barrier, he even put his hand on its head as he vaulted back, and one horn caught his sleeve and tore it just a little. Then he seemed to be absent-mindedly looking at the tear, while the bull was almost touching him again. And the bull was mad. Cuesta was a dead man it seemed, for sure; yet he seemed to wake up and *waked* himself just out of reach. It was like an awful dream, and it seemed to last for hours. I think it must have been a long time, before the bull was killed. He killed him at last, as a man takes his mistress at last because he is almost tired of playing with her. But he liked to kill his own bull.

'Ethel was looking like death, with beads of perspiration on her face. And she called to him: "That's enough! That's enough now! *Ya es bastante! Basta!*" He looked at her, and heard what she said. They were both alike there, they heard and saw in a flash. And he lifted his face, with the rather squashed nose and the yellow eyes, and he looked at her, and though he was so far away, he seemed quite near. And he was smiling like a small boy. But I could see he was looking at the little place in her body, where she kept her courage. And she was trying to catch his look on her imagination, not on her naked inside body. And they both found it difficult. When he tried to look at her, she set her imagination in front of him, like a mirror they put in front of a wild dog. And when she tried to catch him in her imagination, he seemed to melt away, and was gone. So neither really had caught the other.

'But he played with two more bulls, and killed them, without ever looking at her. And she went away when the people were applauding him, and did not look at him. Neither did she speak to me of him. Neither did she go to any more bull-fights.

'It was Cuesta who spoke to me of her, when I met him at Clavel's house. He said to me, in his very coarse Spanish: And what about your American skirt? – I told him, there was nothing to say about her. She was leaving for New York. So he told me to ask her if she would like to come and say good-bye to Cuesta, before she went. I said to him: But why should I mention your name to her? She has never mentioned yours to me. He made an obscene joke to me.

'And it must have been because I was thinking of him that she said that evening: Do you know Cuesta? – I told her I did, and she asked me what I thought of him. I told her I thought he was marvellous beast, but he wasn't really a man. "But he is a beast with imagination," she said to me. "Couldn't one get a response out of him?" I told her I didn't know, but I didn't want to try. I would leave Cuesta to the bull-ring. I would never dream of trying my imagination on him. She said, always ready with an answer : "But wasn't there a marvellous *thing* in him, something quite exceptional?" I said, maybe! But so has a rattlesnake a marvellous thing in him : two things, one in his mouth, one in his tail. But I didn't want to try to get response out of a rattlesnake. She wasn't satisfied, though. She was tortured. I said to her : "Anyhow, you are leaving on Thursday." "No, I've put it off," she said. "Till when?" "Indefinite," she said.

'I could tell she was tormented. She had been tormented ever since she had been to the bull-fight, because she couldn't get past Cuesta. She couldn't get past him, as the Americans say. He seemed like a fat, squat, yellow-eyed demon just smiling at her, and dancing ahead of her. "Why don't you bring him here?" she said at last, though she didn't want to say it. – "But why? What is the good of bringing him here? Would you bring a criminal here, or a yellow scorpion?" – "I would if I wanted to find out about it." – "But what is there to find out about Cuesta? He is just a sort of beast. He is less than a man." – "Maybe he's a *schwarze Bestie*," she said, "and I'm a *blonde Bestie*. Anyway, bring him."

'I always did what she wanted me to, though I never wanted to myself. So it was now. I went to a place where I knew Cuesta would be, and he asked me : "How is the blonde skirt? Has she gone yet?" – I said, "No. Would you like to see her?" – He looked at me with his yellow eyes, and that pleasant look which was really hate undreaming. "Did she tell you to ask me?" he said. "No," I said. "We were talking of you, and she said, bring the fabulous animal along and let us see what he really is." – "He is the animal for her meat, this one," he said, in his vulgar way. Then he pretended he wouldn't come. But I knew he would. So I said I would call for him.

'We were going in the evening, after tea, and he was dressed to kill, in a light French suit. We went in his car. But he didn't take flowers or anything. Ethel was nervous and awkward, offering us cocktails and cigarettes, and speaking French, though Cuesta didn't understand any French at all. There was another old American woman there, for chaperon.

'Cuesta just sat on a chair, with his knees apart and his hands between his thighs, like an Indian. Only his hair, which was done up in his little pigtail, and taken back from his forehead, made him look like a woman, or a Chinaman; and his flat nose and little yellow eyes made him look like a Chinese idol, maybe a god or a demon, as you please. He just sat and said nothing, and had that look on his face which wasn't a smile, and wasn't a grimace, it was nothing. But to me it meant rhapsodic hate.

'She asked him in French if he liked his profession, and how long he had been doing it, and if he got a great kick out of it, and was he a pure-blood Indian? – all that kind of thing. I translated to him as short as possible, Ethel flushing with embarrassment. He replied just as short, to me, in his coarse, flat sort of voice, as if he knew it was mere pretence. But he looked at her, straight into her face, with that strange, far-off sort of stare, yet very vivid, taking no notice of her, yet staring right into her : as if all that she was putting forward to him was merely window-dressing, and he was just looking way in, to the marshes and the jungle in her, where she didn't even look herself. It made one feel as if there was a mountain behind her, Popocatepetl, that he was staring at, expecting a mountain-lion to spring down off a tree on the slopes of the mountain, or a snake to lean down from a bough. But the mountain was all she stood for, and the mountain-lion or the snake was her own animal self, that he was watching for, like a hunter.

'We didn't stay long, but when we left she asked him to come in whenever he liked. He wasn't really the person to have calling on one : and he knew it, as she did. But he thanked her, and hoped he would one day be able to receive her at her – meaning his – humble house in the Guadalupe Road, where everything was her own. She said : "Why, sure, I'll come one day. I should love to." Which he understood, and bowed himself out like some quick but lurking animal; quick as a scorpion, with silence of venom the same.

'After that he would call fairly often, at about five o'clock, but never alone, always with some other man. And he never said anything, always responded to her questions in the same short way, and always looked at her when he was speaking to the other man. He never once *spoke* to her – always spoke to his interpreter, in his flat, coarse Spanish. And he always looked at *her* when he was speaking to someone else.

'She tried every possible manner in which to touch his imagination : but never with any success. She tried the Indians, the Aztecs, the history of Mexico, politics, Don Porfirio, the bull-ring, love, women, Europe, America – and all in vain. All she got out of him was *Verdad!* He was utterly uninterested. He actually *had* no mental imagination. Talk was just a noise to him. The only spark she roused was when she talked of money. Then the queer half-smile deepened on his face, and he asked his interpreter if the Señora was very rich. To which Ethel replied she didn't really know what he meant by rich : he must be rich himself. At which, he asked the interpreter friend if she had more than a million American dollars. To which she replied that perhaps she had – but she wasn't sure. And he looked at her so strangely, even more like a yellow scorpion about to sting.

'I asked him later, what made him put such a crude question? Did he think of offering to marry her? – "Marry a —?" he replied, using an obscene expression. But I didn't know even then what he really intended. Yet I saw he had her on his mind.

'Ethel was gradually getting into a state of tension. It was as if something tortured her. She seemed like a woman who would go insane. I asked her : "Why, whatever's wrong with you?" "I'll tell you, Luis," she said, "but don't you say anything to anybody, mind. It's Cuesta! I don't know whether I want him or not." – "You don't know whether he wants *you* or not," said I. – "I can handle that," she said, "if I know about myself : if I know my own mind. But I don't. My mind says he's a nada-nada, a dumb-bell, no brain, no imagination, no anything. But my body says he's marvellous, and he's got something I haven't got, and he's stronger than I am, and he's more an angel or a devil than a man, and I'm too merely human to get him – and all that, till I feel I shall just go crazy, and take an overdose of drugs. What am I to *do* with my body, I tell you? What am I to *do* with it? I've got to master it. I've got to be *more* than that man. I've got to get all round him, and past him, I've *got* to."

– "Then just take the train to New York tonight, and forget him," I said. – "I can't! That's side-tracking. I *won't* side-track my body. I've got to get the best of it. I've got to." – "Well," I said, "you're a point or two beyond me. If it's a question of getting all round Cuesta, and getting past him, why, take the train, and you'll forget him in a fortnight. Don't fool yourself you're in love with the fellow." – "I'm afraid he's stronger than I am," she cried out. – "And what then? He's stronger than I am, but that doesn't prevent me sleeping. A jaguar even is stronger than I am, and an anaconda could swallow me whole. I tell you, it's all in a day's march. There's a kind of animal called Cuesta. Well, what of it?"

'She looked at me, and I could tell I made no impression on her. She despised me. She sort of wanted to go off the deep end about something. I said to her : "God's love, Ethel, cut out the Cuesta caprice! It's not even good acting." But I might just as well have mewed, for all the notice she took of me.

'It was as if some dormant Popocatepetl inside her had begun to erupt. She didn't love the fellow. Yet she was in a blind kill-me-quick sort of state, neither here nor there, nor hot nor cold, nor desirous nor undesirous, but just simply *insane*. In a certain kind of way, she seemed to want him. And in a very definite kind of way, she seemed *not* to want him. She was in a kind of hysterics, lost her feet altogether. I tried might and main to get her away to the United States. She'd have come sane enough, once she was there. But I thought she'd kill me, when she found I'd been trying to interfere. Oh, she was not quite in her mind, that's sure.

' "If my body is stronger than my imagination, I shall kill myself," she said. – "Ethel," I said, "people who talk of killing themselves always call a doctor if they cut their finger. What's the quarrel between your body and your imagination? Aren't they the same thing?" – "No!" she said. "If the imagination has the body under control, you can do anything, it doesn't matter what you do, physically. If my body was under the control of my imagination, I could take Cuesta for my lover, and it would be an imaginative act. But if my body acted without my imagination, I – I'd kill myself." – "But what do you mean by your body acting without your imagination?" I said. "You are not a child. You've been married twice. You know what it means. You even have two children. You must have had at least several lovers. If Cuesta is to be another of your lovers, I think it is deplorable, but I think it only shows you are very much like all the other women who fall in love with him. If you've fallen in love with him, your imagination has nothing to do but to accept the fact and put as many roses on the ass's head as you like." - She looked at me very solemnly, and seemed to think about it. Then she said : 'But my imagination has not fallen in love with him. He wouldn't meet me imaginatively. He's a brute. And once I start, where's it going to end? I'm afraid my body has fallen - not fallen in love with him, but fallen *for* him. It's abject! And if I can't get my body on its feet again, and either forget him or else get him to make it an imaginative act with me - I - I shall kill myself." - "All right," said I. "I don't know what you are talking about, imaginative acts and unimaginative acts. The act is always the same." - "It isn't!" she cried, furious with me. "It is either imaginative or else it's *impossible* - to me." Well, I just spread my hands. What could I say, or do? I simply hated her way of putting it. Imaginative act! Why, I would hate performing an imaginative act with a woman. Damn it, the act is either real, or let it alone. But now I knew why I had never even touched her, or kissed her, not once : because I couldn't stand that imaginative sort of bullying from her. It is death to a man.

'I said to Cuesta : "Why do you go to Ethel? Why don't you stay away, and make her go back to the United States? Are you in love with her?" - He was obscene, as usual. "Am I in love with a cuttle-fish, that is all arms and eyes, and no legs or tail! That blonde is a cuttlefish. She is an octopus, all arms and eyes and beak, and a lump of jelly." - "Then why don't you leave her alone ?" "Even cuttlefish is good when it's cooked in sauce," he said. "You had much better leave her alone," I said. - "Leave her alone yourself, my esteemed Señor," he said to me. And I knew I had better go no further.

'She said to him one evening, when only I was there - and she said it in Spanish, direct to him : "Why do you never come alone to see me? Why do you always come with another person? Are you afraid?" He looked at her, and his eyes never changed. But he said, in his usual flat, meaningless voice: "It is because I cannot speak, except Spanish." – "But we could understand one another," she said, giving one of her little violent snorts of impatience and embarrassed rage. "Who knows!" he replied, imperturbably.

'Afterwards, he said to me: "What does she want? She hates a man as she hates a red-hot iron. A white devil, as sacred as the communion wafer!" – "Then why don't you leave her alone?" I said. – "She is so rich," he smiled. "She has all the world in her thousand arms. She is as rich as God. The Archangels are poor beside her, she is so rich and so white-skinned and white-souled." – "Then all the more, why don't you leave her alone?" – But he did not answer me.

'He went alone, however, to see her. But always in the early evening. And he never stayed more than half-an-hour. His car, well known everywhere, waited outside: till he came out in his French-grey suit and glistening brown shoes, his hat rather on the back of his head.

'What they said to one another, I don't know. But she became always more distraught and absorbed, as if she were brooding over a single idea. I said to her: "Why take it so seriously? Dozens of women have slept with Cuesta, and think no more of it. Why take him seriously?" – "I don't," she said. "I take myself seriously, that's the point." – "Let it be the point. Go on taking yourself seriously, and leave him out of the question altogether."

'But she was tired of my playing the wise uncle, and I was tired of her taking herself seriously. She took herself so seriously, it seemed to me she would deserve what she got, playing the fool with Cuesta. Of course she did not love him at all. She only wanted to see if she could make an impression on him, make him yield to her will. But all the impression she made on him was to make him call her a squid and an octopus and other nice things. And I could see their "love" did not go forward at all.

' "Have you made love to her?" I asked him. – "I have not touched the zopilote," he said. "I hate her bare white neck."

"But still he went to see her: always, for a very brief call, before sundown. She asked him to come to dinner, with me. He said he could never come to dinner, nor after dinner, as he was always engaged from eight o'clock in the evening onwards. She looked at him as much as to tell him she knew it was a lie and a subterfuge, but he never turned a hair. He was, she put it, utterly unimaginative : an impervious animal.

' "You, however, come one day to your poor house in the Guadalupe Road," he said – meaning his house. He had said it, suggestively, several times.

' "But you are always engaged in the evening," she said.

' "Come, then, at night – come at eleven, when I am free," he said, with supreme animal impudence, looking into her eyes.

' "Do you receive calls so late?" she said, flushing with anger and embarrassment and obstinacy.

' "At times," he said. "When it is very special."

'A few days later, when I called to see her as usual, I was told she was ill, and could see no one. The next day, she was still not to be seen. She had had a dangerous nervous collapse. The third day, a friend rang me up to say, Ethel was dead.

'The thing was hushed up. But it was known she had poisoned herself. She left a note to me, in which she merely said : "It is as I told you. Good-bye. But my testament holds good."

'In her will, she had left half her fortune to Cuesta. The will had been made some ten days before her death – and it was allowed to stand. He took the money –'

Colmenares' voice tailed off into silence.

'Her body had got the better of her imagination, after all,' I said.

'It was worse than that,' he said.

'How?'

He was a long time before he answered. Then he said :

'She actually went to Cuesta's house that night, way down there beyond the Volador market. She went by appointment. And there in his bedroom he handed her over to half a dozen of his bull-ring gang, with orders not to bruise her. – Yet at the inquest there were a few deep, strange bruises, and the doctors made reports. Then apparently the visit to Cuesta's house came to light, but no details were ever told. Then there was another revolution, and in the hubbub this affair was dropped. It was too shady, anyhow. Ethel had certainly encouraged Cuesta at her apartment.'

'But how do you know he handed her over like that?'

'One of the men told me himself. He was shot afterwards.'

A Modern Lover

THE road was heavy with mud. It was labour to move along it. The old, wide way, forsaken and grown over with grass, used not to be so bad. The farm traffic from Coney Grey must have cut it up. The young man crossed carefully again to the strip of grass on the other side.

It was a dreary, out-of-doors track, saved only by low fragments of fence and occasional bushes from the desolation of the large spaces of arable and of grassland on either side, where only the unopposed wind and the great clouds mattered, where even the little grasses bent to one another indifferent of any traveller. The abandoned road used to seem clean and firm. Cyril Mersham stopped to look round and to bring back old winters to the scene, over the ribbed red land and the purple wood. The surface of the field seemed suddenly to lift and break. Something had startled the peewits, and the fallow flickered over with pink gleams of birds white-breasting the sunset. Then the plovers turned, and were gone in the dusk behind.

Darkness was issuing out of the earth, and clinging to the trunks of the elms which rose like weird statues, lessening down the wayside. Mersham laboured forwards, the earth sucking and smacking at his feet. In front the Coney Grey farm was piled in shadow on the road. He came near to it, and saw the turnips heaped in a fabulous heap up the side of the barn, a buttress that rose almost to the eaves, and stretched out towards the cart-ruts in the road. Also, the pale breasts of the turnips got the sunset, and they were innumerable orange glimmers piled in the dusk. The two labourers who were pulping at the foot of the mound stood shadow-like to watch as he passed, breathing the sharp scent of turnips.

It was all very wonderful and glamorous here, in the old places that had seemed so ordinary. Three-quarters of the scarlet sun was settling among the branches of the elm in front, right ahead where he would come soon. But when he arrived at the brow where the hill swooped downwards, where the broad road ended suddenly, the sun had vanished from the space before him, and the evening star was white where the night surged up against the retreating, rose-coloured billow of day. Mersham passed through the stile and sat upon the remnant of the thorn-tree on the brink of the valley. All the wide space before him was full of a mist of rose, nearly to his feet. The large ponds were hidden, the farms, the fields, the far-off coal-mine, under the rosy outpouring of twilight. Between him and the spaces of Leicestershire and the hills of Derbyshire, between him and all the South Country which he had fled, was the splendid rose-red strand of sunset, and the white star keeping guard.

Here, on the lee-shore of day, was only the purple showing of the woods and the great hedge below him; and the roof of the farm below him, with a film of smoke rising up. Unreal, like a dream which wastes a sleep with unrest, was the South and its hurrying to and fro. Here, on the farther shore of the sunset, with the flushed tide at his feet, and the large star flashing with strange laughter, did he himself naked walk with lifted arms into the quiet flood of life.

What was it he wanted, sought in the slowly lapsing tide of days? Two years he had been in the large city in the south. There always his soul had moved among the faces that swayed on the thousand currents in that node of tides, hovering and wheeling and flying low over the faces of the multitude like a sea-gull over the waters, stooping now and again, and taking a fragment of life – a look, a contour, a movement – to feed upon. Of many people, his friends, he had asked that they would kindle again the smouldering embers of their experience; he had blown the low fires gently with his breath, and had leaned his face towards their glow, and had breathed in the words that rose like fumes from the revived embers, till he was sick with the strong drug of sufferings and ecstasies and sensations, and the dreams that ensued. But most folk had choked out the fires of their fiercer experience with rubble of sentimentality and stupid fear, and rarely could he feel the hot destruction of Life fighting out its way.

Surely, surely somebody could give him enough of the philtre of life to stop the craving which tortured him hither and thither, enough to satisfy for a while, to intoxicate him till he could laugh the crystalline laughter of the star, and bathe in the retreating flood of twilight like a naked boy in the surf, clasping the waves and beating them and answering their wild clawings with laughter sometimes, and sometimes gasps of pain.

He rose and stretched himself. The mist was lying in the valley like a flock of folded sheep; Orion had strode into the sky, and the Twins were playing towards the West. He shivered, stumbled down the path, and crossed the orchard, passing among the dark trees as if among people he knew.

2

He came into the yard. It was exceedingly, painfully muddy. He felt a disgust of his own feet, which were cold, and numbed, and heavy.

The window of the house was uncurtained, and shone like a yellow moon, with only a large leaf or two of ivy, and a cord of honeysuckle hanging across it. There seemed a throng of figures moving about the fire. Another light gleamed mysteriously among the out-buildings. He heard a voice in the cowshed, and the impatient movement of a cow, and the rhythm of milk in the bucket.

He hesitated in the darkness of the porch; then he entered without knocking. A girl was opposite him, coming out of the dairy doorway with a loaf of bread. She started, and they stood a moment looking at each other across the room. They advanced to each other; he took her hand, plunged overhead, as it were, for a moment in her great brown eyes. Then he let her go, and looked aside, saying some words of greeting. He had not kissed her; he realized that when he heard her voice :

'When did you come?'

She was bent over the table, cutting bread-and-butter. What was it in her bowed, submissive pose, in the dark, small head with its black hair twining and hiding her face, that made him wince and shrink and close over his soul that had been open like a foolhardy flower to the night? Perhaps it was her very submission, which trammelled him, throwing the responsibility of her wholly on him, making him shrink from the burden of her.

Her brothers were home from the pit. They were two well-built lads of twenty and twenty-one. The coal-dust over their faces was like a mask, making them inscrutable, hiding any glow of greeting, making them strangers. He could only see their eyes wake with a sudden smile, which sank almost immediately, and they turned aside. The mother was kneeling at a big brown stew-jar in front of the open oven. She did not rise, but gave him her hand, saying: 'Cyril! How are you?' Her large dark eyes wavered and left him. She continued with the spoon in the jar.

His disappointment rose as water suddenly heaves up the side of a ship. A sense of dreariness revived, a feeling, too, of the cold wet mud that he had struggled through.

These were the people who, a few months before, would look up in one fine broad glow of welcome whenever he entered the door, even if he came daily. Three years before, their lives would draw together into one flame, and whole evenings long would flare with magnificent mirth, and with play. They had known each other's lightest and deepest feelings. Now, when he came back to them after a long absence, they withdrew, turned aside. He sat down on the sofa under the window, deeply chagrined. His heart closed tight like a fir-cone, which had been open and full of naked seeds when he came to them.

They asked him questions of the South. They were starved for news, they said, in that God-forsaken hole.

'It is such a treat to hear a bit of news from outside,' said the mother.

News! He smiled, and talked, plucking for them the leaves from off his tree: leaves of easy speech. He smiled, rather bitterly, as he slowly reeled off his news, almost mechanically. Yet he knew – and that was the irony of it – that they did not want his 'records'; they wanted the timorous buds of his hopes, and the unknown fruits of his experiences, full of the taste of tears and what sunshine of gladness had gone to their ripening. But they asked for his 'news', and, because of some subtle perversity, he gave them what they begged, not what they wanted, not what he desired most sincerely to give them.

Gradually he exhausted his store of talk, that he had thought was limitless. Muriel moved about all the time, laying the table and listening, only looking now and again across the barren garden of his talk into his windows. But he hardened his heart and turned his head from her. The boys had stripped to their waists, and had knelt on the hearth-rug and washed themselves in a large tin bowl, the mother sponging and drying their backs. Now they stood wiping themselves, the firelight bright and rosy on their fine torsos, their heavy arms swelling and sinking with life. They seemed to cherish the firelight on their bodies. Benjamin, the younger, leaned his breast to the warmth, and threw back his head, showing his teeth in a voluptuous little smile. Mersham watched them, as he had watched the peewits and the sunset.

Then they sat down to their dinners, and the room was dim with the steam of food. Presently the father and the eldest brother were in from the cow-sheds, and all assembled at table. The conversation went haltingly; a little badinage on Mersham's part, a few questions on politics from the father. Then there grew an acute, fine feeling of discord. Mersham, particularly sensitive, reacted. He became extremely attentive to the others at table, and to his own manner of eating. He used English that was exquisitely accurate, pronounced with the Southern accent, very different from the heavily-sounded speech of the home folk. His nicety contrasted the more with their rough, country habit. They became shy and awkward, fumbling for something to say. The boys ate their dinners hastily, shovelling up the mass as a man shovels gravel. The eldest son clambered roughly with a great hand at the plate of bread-and-butter. Mersham tried to shut his eyes. He kept up all the time a brilliant tea-talk that they failed to appreciate in that atmosphere. It was evident to him; without forming the idea, he felt how irrevocably he was removing them from him, though he had loved them. The irony of the situation appealed to him, and added brightness and subtlety to his wit. Muriel, who had studied him so thoroughly, confusedly understood. She hung her head over her plate, and ate little. Now and again she would look up at him, toying all the time with her knife – though it was a family for ugly hands – and would address him some barren question. He always answered the question, but he invariably disregarded her look of earnestness, lapped in his unbreakable armour of light irony. He acknowledged, however, her power in the flicker of irritation that accompanied his reply. She quickly hid her face again.

They did not linger at tea, as in the old days. The men rose, with an 'Ah, well!' and went about their farm-work. One of the lads lay sprawling for sleep on the sofa; the other lighted a cigarette and sat with his arms on his knees, blinking into the fire. Neither of them ever wore a coat in the house, and their shirt-sleeves and their thick bare necks irritated the stranger still further by accentuating his strangeness. The men came tramping in and out to the boiler. The kitchen was full of bustle, of the carrying of steaming water, and of draughts. It seemed like a place out of doors. Mersham shrank up in his corner, and pretended to read the *Daily News*. He was ignored, like an owl sitting in the stalls of cattle.

'Go in the parlour, Cyril. Why don't you? It's comfortable there.'

Muriel turned to him with this reproach, this remonstrance, almost chiding him. She was keenly aware of his discomfort, and of his painful discord with his surroundings. He rose without a word and obeyed her.

3

The parlour was a long, low room with red colourings. A bunch of mistletoe hung from the beam, and thickly-berried holly was over the pictures – over the little gilt-blazed water-colours that he hated so much because he had done them in his teens, and nothing is so hateful as the self one has left. He dropped in the tapestried chair called the Countess, and thought of the changes which this room had seen in him. There, by that hearth, they had threshed the harvest of their youth's experience, gradually burning the chaff of sentimentality and false romance that covered the real grain of life. How infinitely far away, now, seemed *Jane Eyre* and George Eliot. These had marked the beginning. He smiled as he traced the graph on-wards, plotting the points with Carlyle and Ruskin, Schopen-hauer and Darwin and Huxley, Omar Khayyam, the Russians, Ibsen and Balzac; then Guy de Maupassant and *Madame Bovary*. They had parted in the midst of *Madame Bovary*. Since then had come only Nietzsche and William James. They had not done so badly, he thought, during those years which now he was apt to despise a little, because of their dreadful strenuousness, and because of their later deadly, unrelieved seriousness. He wanted her to come in and talk about the old times. He crossed to the other side of the fire and lay in the big horsehair chair, which pricked the back of his head. He looked about, and stuffed behind him the limp green cushions that were always sweating down.

It was a week after Christmas. He guessed they had kept up the holly and mistletoe for him. The two photographs of himself still occupied the post of honour on the mantelpiece; but between them was a stranger. He wondered who the fellow could be; good-looking he seemed to be; but a bit of a clown beside the radiant, subtle photos of himself. He smiled broadly at his own arrogance. Then he remembered that Muriel and her people were leaving the farm come Lady-day. Immediately, in valediction, he began to call up the old days, when they had romped and played so boisterously, dances, and wild charades, and all mad games. He was just telling himself that those were the days, the days of unconscious, ecstatic fun, and he was smiling at himself over his information, when she entered.

She came in, hesitating. Seeing him sprawling in his old abandonment, she closed the door softly. For a moment or two she sat, her elbows on her knees, her chin in her hands, sucking her little finger, and withdrawing it from her lips with a little pop, looking all the while in the fire. She was waiting for him, knowing all the time he would not begin. She was trying to feel him, as it were. She wanted to assure herself of him after so many months. She dared not look at him directly. Like all brooding, constitutionally earnest souls, she gave herself away unwisely, and was defenceless when she found herself pushed back, rejected so often with contempt.

'Why didn't you tell me you were coming?' she asked at last.

'I wanted to have exactly one of the old tea-times, and evenings.'

'Ay!' she answered with hopeless bitterness. She was a dreadful pessimist. People had handled her so brutally, and had cheaply thrown away her most sacred intimacies.

He laughed, and looked at her kindly.

'Ah, well, if I'd thought about it I should have known this was what to expect. It's my own fault.'

'Nay,' she answered, still bitterly; 'it's not your fault. It's ours. You bring us to a certain point, and when you go away, we lose it all again, and receive you like creatures who have never known you.'

'Never mind,' he said easily. 'If it is so, it is! How are you?'

She turned and looked full at him. She was very handsome; heavily moulded, coloured richly. He looked back smiling into her big, brown, serious eyes.

'Oh, I'm very well,' she answered, with puzzled irony. 'How are you?'

'Me? You tell me. What do you think of me?'

'What do I think?' She laughed a little nervous laugh and shook her head. 'I don't know. Why – you look well – and very much of a gentleman.'

'Ah – and you are sorry?'

'No – No, I am not! No! Only you're different, you see.'

'Ah, the pity! I shall never be as nice as I was at twenty-one, shall I?' He glanced at his photo on the mantelpiece, and smiled, gently chaffing her.

'Well – you're different – it isn't that you're not so nice, but different. I always think you're like that, really.'

She, too, glanced at the photo, which had been called the portrait of an intellectual prig, but which was really that of a sensitive, alert, exquisite boy. The subject of the portrait lay smiling at her. Then he turned voluptuously, like a cat spread out in the chair.

'And this is the last of it all –!'

She looked up at him, startled and pitiful.

'Of this phase, I mean,' he continued, indicating with his eyes the room, the surroundings. 'Of Crossleigh Bank, I mean, and this part of our lives.'

'Ay!' she said, bowing her head, and putting into the exclamation all her depth of sadness and regret. He laughed.

'Aren't you glad?' he asked.

She looked up, startled, a little shocked.

'Good-bye's a fine word,' he explained. 'It means you're going to have a change, and a change is what you, of all people, want.'

Her expression altered as she listened.

'It's true,' she said. 'I do.'

'So you ought to say to yourself, "What a treat! I'm going to say good-bye directly to the most painful phase of my life." You make up your mind it shall be the most painful, by refusing to be hurt so much in the future. There you are! "Men at most times are masters of their fates", etcetera.'

She pondered his method of reasoning, and turned to him with a little laughter that was full of pleading and yearning.

'Well,' he said, lying, amiably smiling, 'isn't that so? – and aren't you glad?'

'Yes!' she nodded. 'I am – very glad.'

He twinkled playfully at her, and asked, in a soft voice :

'Then what do you want?'

'Yes!' she replied, a little breathlessly. 'What do I?' She looked at him with a rash challenge that pricked him.

'Nay,' he said, evading her, 'do you even ask me that?'

She veiled her eyes, and said, meekly in excuse :

'It's a long time since I asked you anything, isn't it?'

'Ay! I never thought of it. Whom have you asked in the interim?'

'Whom have I asked?' – she arched her brows and laughed a monosyllable of scorn.

'No one, of course !' he said, smiling. 'The world asks questions of you, you ask questions of me, and I go to some oracle in the dark, don't I?'

She laughed with him.

'No!' he said, suddenly serious. 'Supposing you must answer me a big question – something I can never find out by myself?'

He lay out indolently in the chair and began smiling again. She turned to look with intensity at him, her hair's fine foliage all loose round her face, her dark eyes haunted with doubt, her finger at her lips. A slight perplexity flickered over his eyes.

'At any rate,' he said, 'you have something to give me.'

She continued to look at him with dark, absorbing eyes. He

probed her with his regard. Then he seemed to withdraw, and his pupils dilated with thought.

'You see,' he said, 'life's no good but to live – and you can't live your life by yourself. You must have a flint and a steel, both, to make the spark fly. Supposing you be my flint, my white flint, to spurt out red fire for me?'

'But how do you mean?' she asked breathlessly.

'You see,' he continued, thinking aloud as usual : 'thought – that's not life. It's like washing and combing and carding and weaving the fleece that the year of life has produced. Now I think – we've carded and woven to the end of our bundle – nearly. We've got to begin again – you and me – living together, see? Not speculating and poetizing together – see?'

She did not cease to gaze absorbedly at him.

'Yes?' she whispered, urging him on.

'You see – I've come back to you – to you –' He waited for her.

'But,' she said huskily, 'I don't understand.'

He looked at her with aggressive frankness, putting aside all her confusions.

'Fibber !' he said gently.

'But –' she turned in her chair from him – 'but not clearly.'

He frowned slightly :

'Nay, you should be able by now to use the algebra of speech. Must I count up on your fingers for you what I mean, unit by unit, in bald arithmetic?'

'No – no !' she cried, justifying herself; 'but how can I understand – the change in you? You used to say – you couldn't. – Quite opposite.'

He lifted his head as if taking in her meaning.

'Ah, yes, I have changed. I forget. I suppose I must have changed in myself. I'm older – I'm twenty-six. I used to shrink from the thought of having to kiss you, didn't I?' He smiled very brightly, and added, in a soft voice. 'Well – I don't now.'

She flushed darkly and hid her face from him.

'Not,' he continued, with slow, brutal candour – 'not that I know any more than I did then – what love is – as you know it – but – I think you're beautiful – and we know each other so well – as we know nobody else, don't we? And so we ...'

His voice died away, and they sat in a tense silence, listening to the noise outside, for the dog was barking loudly. They heard a voice speaking and quieting him. Cyril Mersham listened. He heard the clatter of the barn door latch, and a slurring ring of a bicycle-bell brushing the wall.

'Who is it?' he asked, unsuspecting.

She looked at him, and confessed with her eyes, guiltily, beseeching. He understood immediately.

'Good Lord! – Him?' He looked at the photo on the mantelpiece. She nodded with her usual despair, her finger between her lips again. Mersham took some moments to adjust himself to the new situation.

'Well – so *he's* in my place! Why didn't you tell me?'

'How could I? – he's not. Besides – you never would have a place.' She hid her face.

'No,' he drawled, thinking deeply. 'I wouldn't. It's my fault, altogether.' Then he smiled, and said whimsically, 'But I thought you kept an old pair of my gloves in the chair beside you.'

'So I did, so I did!' she justified herself again with extreme bitterness, 'till you asked me for them. You told me to – to take another man – and I did as you told me – as usual.'

'Did I tell you? – did I tell you? I suppose I must. I suppose I am a fool. And do you like him?'

She laughed aloud, with scorn and bitterness.

'He's very good – and he's very fond of me.'

'Naturally!' said Mersham, smiling and becoming ironical. 'And how firmly is he fixed?'

4

She was mortified, and would not answer him. The question for him now was how much did this intruder count. He looked, and saw she wore no ring – but perhaps she had taken it off for his coming. He began diligently to calculate what attitude he might take. He had looked for many women to wake his love, but he had been always disappointed. So he had kept himself virtuous, and waited. Now he would wait no longer. No woman and he could ever understand each other so well as he and Muriel whom he had fiercely educated into womanhood along with his own struggling towards a manhood of independent outlook. They had breathed the same air of thought, they had been beaten with the same storms of doubt and disillusionment, they had expanded together in days of pure poetry. They had grown so; spiritually, or rather psychically, as he preferred to say, they were married; and now he found himself thinking of the way she moved about the house.

The outer door had opened and a man had entered the kitchen, greeting the family cordially, and without any formality. He had the throaty, penetrating voice of a tenor singer, and it came distinctly over the vibrating rumble of the men's talking. He spoke good, easy English. The boys asked him about the 'iron-men' and the electric haulage, and he answered them with rough technicalities, so Mersham concluded he was a working electrician in the mine. They continued to talk casually for some time, though there was a false note of secondary interest in it all. Then Benjamin came forward and broke the check, saying, with a dash of braggart taunting :

'Muriel's in th' parlour, Tom, if you want her.'

'Oh, is she? I saw a light in; I thought she might be.' He affected indifference, as if he were kept thus at every visit. Then he added, with a touch of impatience, and of the proprietor's interest : 'What is she doing?'

'She's talking. Cyril Mersham's come from London.'

'What ! – is *he* here?'

Mersham sat listening, smiling. Muriel saw his eyelids lift. She had run up her flag of challenge taut, but continually she slackened towards him with tenderness. Now her flag flew out bravely. She rose, and went to the door.

'Hello !' she said, greeting the stranger with a little song of welcome in one word, such as girls use when they become aware of the presence of their sweetheart.

'You've got a visitor, I hear,' he answered.

'Yes. Come along, come in !'

She spoke softly, with much gentle caressing.

He was a handsome man, well set-up, rather shorter than Mersham. The latter rose indolently, and held out his hand, smiling curiously into the beautiful, generous blue eyes of the other.

'Cyril – Mr Vickers.'

Tom Vickers crushed Mersham's hand, and answered his steady, smiling regard with a warm expansion of feeling, then bent his head, slightly confused.

'Sit here, will you?' said Mersham, languidly indicating the armchair.

'No, no, thanks, I won't. I shall do here, thanks.' Tom Vickers took a chair and placed it in front of the fire. He was confusedly charmed with Mersham's natural frankness and courtesy.

'If I'm not intruding,' he added, as he sat down.

'No, of course not!' said Muriel, in her wonderfully soft, fond tones – the indulgent tone of a woman who will sacrifice anything to love.

'Couldn't!' added Mersham lazily. 'We're always a public meeting, Muriel and I. Aren't we, Miel? We're discussing affinities, that ancient topic. You'll do for an audience. We agree so beastly well, we two. We always did. It's her fault. Does she treat you so badly?'

The other was rather bewildered. Out of it all he dimly gathered that he was suggested as the present lover of Muriel, while Mersham referred to himself as the one discarded. So he smiled, reassured.

'How – badly?' he asked .

'Agreeing with you on every point?'

'No, I can't say she does that,' said Vickers, smiling, and looking with little warm glances at her.

'Why, we never disagree, you know!' she remonstrated, in the same deep indulgent tone.

'I see,' Mersham said languidly, and yet keeping his wits keenly to the point. 'You agree with everything she says. Lord, how interesting!'

Muriel arched eyelids with a fine flare of intelligence across at him, and laughed.

'Something like that,' answered the other man, also indulgently, as became a healthy male towards one who lay limply in a chair and said clever nothings in a lazy drawl. Mersham noted the fine limbs, the solid, large thighs, and the thick wrists. He was classifying his rival among the men of hand-some, healthy animalism, and good intelligence, who are chil-

dren in simplicity, who can add two and two, but never xy and
yx. His contours, his movements, his repose were, strictly, lov-
able. 'But,' said Mersham to himself, 'if I were blind, or sor-
rowful, or very tired, I should not want him. He is one of the
men, as George Moore says, whom his wife would hate after a
few years for the very way he walked across the floor. I can
imagine him with a family of children, a fine father. But unless
he had a domestic wife –'

Muriel had begun to make talk to him.

'Did you cycle?' she asked, in that irritating private tone so
common to lovers, a tone that makes a third person an im-
pertinence.

'Yes – I was rather late,' he replied, in the same caressing
manner. The sense did not matter, the caress was everything.

'Didn't you find it very muddy?'

'Well, I did – but not any worse than yesterday.'

Mersham sprawled his length in the chair, his eyelids almost
shut, his fine white hands hanging over the arms of the chair
like dead-white stoats from a bough. He was wondering how
long Muriel would endure to indulge her sweetheart thus. Soon
she began to talk second-hand to Mersham. They were speaking
of Tom's landlady.

'You don't care for her, do you?' she asked, laughing in-
sinuatingly, since the shadow of his dislike for other women
heightened the radiance of his affection for her.

'Well, I can't say that I love her.'

'How is it you always fall out with your landladies after six
months? You must be a wretch to live with.'

'Nay, I don't know that I am. But they're all alike; they're
jam and cakes at first, but after a bit they're dry bread.'

He spoke with solemnity, as if he uttered a universal truth.
Mersham's eyelids flickered now and again. Muriel turned to
him :

'Mr Vickers doesn't like lodgings,' she said.

Mersham understood that Vickers therefore wanted to marry
her; he also understood that as the pretendant tired of his landladies, so his wife and he would probably weary one another.
He looked this intelligence at Muriel, and drawled :

'Doesn't he? Lodgings are ideal. A good lodger can always

boss the show, and have his own way. It's the time of his life.'

'I don't think!' laughed Vickers.

'It's true,' drawled Mersham torpidly, giving his words the effect of droll irony. 'You're evidently not a good lodger. You only need to sympathize with a landlady – against her husband generally – and she'll move heaven and earth for you.'

'Ah!' laughed Muriel, glancing at Mersham. 'Tom doesn't believe in sympathizing with women – especially married women.'

'I don't!' said Tom emphatically, '– it's dangerous.'

'You leave it to the husband,' said Mersham.

'I do that! I don't want 'em coming to me with their troubles. I should never know the end.'

'Wise of you. Poor woman! So you'll broach your barrel of sympathy for your wife, eh, and for nobody else?'

'That's it. Isn't that right?'

'Oh, quite. Your wife will be a privileged person. Sort of home-brewed beer to drink *ad infinitum*? Quite all right, that!'

'There's nothing better,' said Tom, laughing.

'Except a change,' said Mersham. 'Now, I'm like a cup of tea to a woman.'

Muriel laughed aloud at this preposterous cynicism, and knitted her brows to bid him cease playing ball with bombs.

'A fresh cup each time. Women never weary of tea. Muriel, I can see you having a rich time. Sort of long after-supper drowse with a good husband.'

'Very delightful!' said Muriel sarcastically.

'If she's got a good husband, what more can she want?' asked Tom, keeping the tone of banter, but really serious and somewhat resentful.

'A lodger – to make things interesting.'

'Why,' said Muriel, intervening, 'do women like you so?'

Mersham looked up at her, quietly, smiling into her eyes. She was really perplexed. She wanted to know what he put in the pan to make the balance go down so heavily on his side. He had, as usual, to answer her seriously and truthfully, so he said:

'Because I can make them believe that black is green or purple – which it is, in reality.' Then, smiling broadly as she wakened again with admiration for him, he added: 'But you're trying to make me conceited, Miel – to stain my virgin modesty.'

Muriel glanced up at him with softness and understanding, and laughed low. Tom gave a guffaw at the notion of Mersham's virgin modesty. Muriel's brow wrinkled with irritation, and she turned from her sweetheart to look in the fire.

5

Mersham, all unconsciously, had now developed the situation to the climax he desired. He was sure that Vickers would not count seriously in Muriel's movement towards himself. So he turned away, uninterested.

The talk drifted for some time, after which he suddenly bethought himself:

'I say, Mr Vickers, will you sing for us? You do sing, don't you?'

'Well – nothing to speak of,' replied the other modestly, wondering at Mersham's sudden change of interest. He looked at Muriel.

'Very well,' she answered him, indulging him now like a child. 'But –' she turned to Mersham – 'but do you, really?'

'Yes, of course. Play some of the old songs. Do you play any better?'

She began *Honour and Arms*.

'No, not that!' cried Mersham. 'Something quiet – *Sois triste et sois belle*.' He smiled gently at her, suggestively. 'Try *Du bist wie eine Blume*, or *Pur dicesti*.'

Vickers sang well, though without much imagination. But the songs they sang were the old songs that Mersham had taught Muriel years before, and she played with one of his memories in her heart. At the end of the first song, she turned and found him looking at her, and they met again in the poetry of the past.

'Daffodils,' he said softly, his eyes full of memories.

She dilated, quivered with emotion, in response. They had sat on the rim of the hill, where the wild daffodils stood up to the sky, and there he had taught her, singing line by line, *Du bist wie eine Blume*. He had no voice, but a very accurate ear.

The evening wore on to ten o'clock. The lads came through the room on their way to bed. The house was asleep save the father, who sat alone in the kitchen, reading *The Octopus*. They went in to supper.

Mersham had roused himself and was talking well. Muriel stimulated him, always, and turned him to talk of art and philosophy – abstract things that she loved, of which only he had ever spoken to her, of which only he could speak, she believed, with such beauty. He used quaint turns of speech, contradicted himself waywardly, then said something sad and whimsical, all in a wistful, irresponsible manner so that even the men leaned indulgent and deferential to him.

'Life,' he said, and he was always urging this on Muriel in one form or another, 'life is beautiful, so long as it is consuming you. When it is rushing through you, destroying you, life is glorious. It is best to roar away, like a fire with a great draught, white-hot to the last bit. It's when you burn a slow fire and save fuel that life's not worth having.'

'You believe in a short life and a merry,' said the father.

'Needn't be either short or merry. Grief is part of the fire of life – and suffering – they're the root of the flame of joy, as they say. No! With life, we're like the man who was so anxious to provide for his old age that he died at thirty from inanition.'

'That's what we're not likely to do,' laughed Tom.

'Oh, I don't know. You live most intensely in human contact – and that's what we shrink from, poor timid creatures, from giving our soul to somebody to touch; for they, bungling fools, will generally paw it with dirty hands.'

Muriel looked at him with dark eyes of grateful understanding. She herself had been much pawed, brutally, by her brothers. But, then, she had been foolish in offering herself.

'And,' concluded Mersham, 'you are washed with the whitest fire of life – when you take a woman you love – and understand.'

Perhaps Mersham did not know what he was doing. Yet his whole talk lifted Muriel as in a net, like a sea-maiden out of the waters, and placed her in his arms, to breathe his thin, rare atmosphere. She looked at him, and was certain of his pure earnestness, and believed implicitly he could not do wrong.

Vickers believed otherwise. He would have expressed his opinion, whatever it might be, in an : 'Oh, ay, he's got plenty to say, and he'll keep on saying it – but, hang it all . . . !'

For Vickers was an old-fashioned, inarticulate lover; such as has been found the brief joy and the unending disappointment of a woman's life. At last he found he must go, as Mersham would not precede him. Muriel did not kiss him good-bye, nor did she offer to go out with him to his bicycle. He was angry at this, but more angry with the girl than with the man. He felt that she was fooling about, 'showing off' before the stranger. Mersham was a stranger to him, and so, in his idea, to Muriel. Both young men went out of the house together, and down the rough brick track to the barn. Mersham made whimsical little jokes : 'I wish my feet weren't so fastidious. They dither when they go in a soft spot like a girl who's touched a toad. Hark at that poor old wretch – she sounds as if she'd got whooping-cough.'

'A cow is not coughing when she makes that row,' said Vickers.

'Pretending, is she? – to get some Owbridge's? Don't blame her. I guess she's got chilblains, at any rate. Do cows have chilblains, poor devils?'

Vickers laughed and felt he must take this man into his protection. 'Mind,' he said, as they entered the barn, which was very dark. 'Mind your forehead against this beam.' He put one hand on the beam and stretched out the other to feel for Mersham. 'Thanks,' said the latter gratefully. He knew the position of the beam to an inch, however dark the barn, but he allowed Vickers to guide him past it. He rather enjoyed being taken into Tom's protection.

Vickers carefully struck a match, bowing over the ruddy core of light and illuminating himself like some beautiful lantern in the midst of the high darkness of the barn. For some moments he bent over his bicycle-lamp, trimming and adjusting the wick, and his face, gathering all the light on its ruddy beauty, seemed luminous and wonderful. Mersham could see the down on his cheeks above the razor-line, and the full lips in shadow beneath the moustache, and the brush of the eyebrows between the light.

'After all,' said Mersham, 'he's very beautiful; she's a fool to give him up.'

Tom shut the lamp with a snap, and carefully crushed the match under his foot. Then he took the pump from the bicycle, and crouched on his heels in the dimness, inflating the tyre. The swift, unerring, untiring stroke of the pump, the light balance and the fine elastic adjustment of the man's body to his movements pleased Mersham.

'She could have,' he was saying to himself, 'some glorious hours with this man – yet she'd rather have me, because I can make her sad and set her wondering.'

But to the man he was saying :

'You know, love isn't the twin-soul business. With you, for instance, women are like apples on a tree. You can have one that you can reach. Those that look best are overhead, but it's no good bothering with them. So you stretch up, perhaps you pull down a bough and just get your fingers round a good one. Then it swings back and you feel wild and you say your heart's broken. But there are plenty of apples as good for you no higher than your chest.'

Vickers smiled, and thought there was something in it – generally; but for himself, it was nothing.

They went out of the barn to the yard gate. He watched the young man swing over his saddle and vanish, calling 'good night'.

'*Sic transit*', he murmured – meaning Tom Vickers, and beautiful lustihood that is unconscious like a blossom.

Mersham went slowly in the house. Muriel was clearing away the supper things, and laying the table again for the men's breakfasts. But she was waiting for him as clearly as if she had stood watching in the doorway. She looked up at him, and instinctively he lifted his face towards her as if to kiss her. They smiled, and she went on with her work.

The father rose, stretching his burly form, and yawning. Mersham put on his overcoat.

'You will come a little way with me?' he said. She answered him with her eyes. The father stood, large and silent, on the hearthrug. His sleepy, mazed disapproval had no more effect than a little breeze which might blow against them. She smiled brightly at her lover, like a child, as she pinned on her hat.

It was very dark outside in the starlight. He groaned heavily, and swore with extravagance as he went ankle-deep in mud.

'See, you should follow me. Come here,' she commanded, delighted to have him in charge.

'Give me your hand,' he said, and they went hand-in-hand over the rough places. The fields were open, and the night went up to the magnificent stars. The wood was very dark, and wet; they leaned forward and stepped stealthily, and gripped each other's hands fast with a delightful sense of adventure. When they stood and looked up a moment, they did not know how the stars were scattered among the tree-tops till he found the three jewels of Orion right in front.

There was a strangeness everywhere, as if all things had ventured out alive to play in the night, as they do in fairy-tales; the trees, the many stars, the dark spaces, and the mysterious waters below uniting in some magnificent game.

They emerged from the wood on to the bare hillside. She came down from the wood-fence into his arms, and he kissed her, and they laughed low together. Then they went on across the wild meadows where there was no path.

'Why don't you like him?' he asked playfully.

'Need you ask?' she said, simply.

'Yes. Because he's heaps nicer than I am.'

She laughed a full laugh of amusement.

'He is! Look! He's like summer, brown and full of warmth. Think how splendid and fierce he'd be –'

'Why do you talk about him?' she said.

'Because I want you to know what you're losing – and you won't till you see him in my terms. He is very desirable – I should choose him in preference to me – for myself.'

'Should you?' she laughed. 'But,' she added with soft certainty, 'you don't understand.'

'No – I don't. I suppose it's love; your sort, which is beyond me. I shall never be blindly in love, shall I?'

'I begin to think you never will,' she answered, not very sadly. 'You won't be blindly anything.'

'The voice of love!' he laughed; and then, 'No, if you pull

your flowers to pieces, and find how they pollinate, and where are the ovaries, you don't go in blind ecstasies over them. But they mean more to you; they are intimate, like friends of your heart, not like wonderful, dazing fairies.'

'Ay!' she assented, musing over it with the gladness of understanding him. 'And then?'

Softly, almost without words, she urged him to the point.

'Well,' he said, 'you think I'm a wonderful, magical person, don't you? – and I'm not – I'm not as good, in the long run, as your Tom, who thinks you are a wonderful, magical person.'

She laughed and clung to him as they walked. He continued, very carefully and gently : 'Now, I don't imagine for a moment that you are princessy or angelic or wonderful. You often make me thundering mad because you're an ass . . .'

She laughed low with shame and humiliation.

'Nevertheless – I come from the south to you – because – well, with you I can be just as I feel, conceited or idiotic, without being afraid to be myself . . .' He broke off suddenly : 'I don't think I've tried to make myself out to you – any bigger or better than I am?' he asked her wistfully.

'No,' she answered, in beautiful, deep assurance. 'No! That's where it is. You have always been so honest. You are more honest than anybody ever –' She did not finish, being deeply moved. He was silent for some time, then he continued, as if he must see the question to the end with her :

'But, you know – I do like you not to wear corsets. I like to see you move inside your dress.'

She laughed, half shame, half pleasure.

'I wondered if you'd notice,' she said.

'I did – directly.' There was a space of silence, after which he resumed : 'You see – we would marry tomorow – but I can't keep myself. I am in debt –'

She came close to him, and took his arm.

'– And what's the good of letting the years go, and the beauty of one's youth –?'

'No,' she admitted, very slowly and softly, shaking her head.

'So – well! – you understand, don't you? And if you're willing – you'll come to me, won't you? – just naturally, as you used to come and go to church with me? – and it won't be – it won't be me coaxing you – reluctant? Will it?'

They had halted in front of a stile which they would have to climb. She turned to him in silence, and put up her face to him. He took her in his arms, and kissed her, and felt the night-mist with which his moustache was drenched, and he bent his head and rubbed his face on her shoulder, and then pressed his lips on her neck. For a while they stood in silence, clasped together. Then he heard her voice, muffled in his shoulder, saying :

'But – but, you know – it's much harder for the woman – it means something so different for a woman.'

'One can be wise,' he answered, slowly and gently. 'One need not blunder into calamities.'

She was silent for a time. Then she spoke again.

'Yes, but – if it should be – you see – I couldn't bear it.'

He let her go, and they drew apart, and the embrace no longer choked them from speaking. He recognized the woman defensive, playing the coward against her own inclinations, and even against her knowledge.

'If – if!' he exclaimed sharply, so that she shrank with a little fear. 'There need be no ifs – need there?'

'I don't know,' she replied, reproachfully, very quietly.

'If I say so –' he said, angry with her mistrust. Then he climbed the stile, and she followed.

'But you *do* know,' he exclaimed. 'I have given you books –'

'Yes – but –'

'But what?' He was getting really angry.

'It's so different for a woman – you don't know.'

He did not answer this. They stumbled together over the mole-hills, under the oak trees.

'And look – how we should have to be – creeping together in the dark –'

This stung him; at once, it was as if the glamour went out of life. It was as if she had tipped over the fine vessel that held the wine of his desire, and had emptied him of all his vitality. He had played a difficult, deeply-moving part all night, and now the lights suddenly switched out, and there was left only weariness. He was silent, tired, very tired, bodily and spiritually.

They walked across the wide, dark meadow with sunken heads. Suddenly she caught his arm.

'Don't be cold with me !' she cried.

He bent and kissed in acknowledgement the lips she offered him for love.

'No,' he said drearily; 'no, it is not coldness – only – I have lost hold – for tonight.' He spoke with difficulty. It was hard to find a word to say. They stood together, apart, under the old thorn-tree for some minutes, neither speaking. Then he climbed the fence, and stood on the highway above the meadow.

At parting also he had not kissed her. He stood a moment and looked at her. The water in a little brook under the hedge was running, chuckling with extraordinary loudness : away on Nethermere they heard the sad, haunting cry of the wild-fowl from the North. The stars still twinkled intensely. He was too spent to think of anything to say; she was too overcome with grief and fear and a little resentment. He looked down at the pale blotch of her face upturned from the low meadow beyond the fence. The thorn boughs tangled above her, drooping behind her like the roof of a hut. Beyond was the great width of the darkness. He felt unable to gather his energy to say anything vital.

'Good-bye,' he said. 'I'm going back – on Saturday. But – you'll write to me. Good-bye.'

He turned to go. He saw her white uplifted face vanish, and her dark form bend under the boughs of the tree, and go out into the great darkness. She did not say good-bye.

Strike-Pay

STRIKE-MONEY is paid in the Primitive Methodist Chapel.
The crier was round quite early on Wednesday morning to say
that paying would begin at ten o'clock.

The Primitive Methodist Chapel is a big barn of a place, built,
designed, and paid for by the colliers themselves. But it threat-
ened to fall down from its first form, so that a professional
architect had to be hired at last to pull the place together.

It stands in the Square. Forty years ago, when Bryan and
Wentworth opened their pits, they put up the 'squares' of miners'
dwellings. They are two great quadrangles of houses, enclosing
a barren stretch of ground, littered with broken pots and rub-
bish, which forms a square, a great, sloping, lumpy playground
for the children, a drying-ground for many women's washing.

Wednesday is still wash-day with some women. As the men
clustered round the Chapel, they heard the thud-thud-thud of
many pouches, women pounding away at the wash-tub with a
wooden pestle. In the Square the white clothes were waving in
the wind from a maze of clothes-lines, and here and there
women were pegging out, calling to the miners, or to the children who dodged under the flapping sheets.

Ben Townsend, the Union agent, has a bad way of paying.
He takes the men in order of his round, and calls them by
name. A big, oratorical man with a grey beard, he sat at the
table in the Primitive schoolroom, calling name after name. The
room was crowded with colliers, and a great group pushed up
outside. There was much confusion. Ben dodged from the Scar-
gill Street list, to the Queen Street. For this Queen Street men
were not prepared. They were not to the fore.

'Joseph Grooby – Joseph Grooby! Now, Joe, where are you?'

'Hold on a bit, Sorry!' cried Joe from outside. 'I'm shovin'
up.'

There was a great noise from the men.

'I'm takin' Queen Street. All you Queen Street men should
be ready. Here you are, Joe,' said the Union agent loudly.

'Five children!' said Joe, counting the money suspiciously.

'That's right, I think,' came the mouthing voice. 'Fifteen shillings, is it not?'

'A bob a kid,' said the collier.

'Thomas Sedgwick – how are you, Tom? Missis better?'

'Ay, 'er's shapin' nicely. Tha'rt hard at work today, Ben.' This was sarcasm on the idleness of a man wo had given up the pit to become a Union agent.

'Yes. I rose at four to fetch the money.'

'Dunna hurt thysen,' was the retort, and the men laughed.

'No – John Merfin!'

But the colliers, tired with waiting, excited by the strike spirit, began to rag. Merfin was young and dandiacal. He was choir-master at the Wesleyan Chapel.

'Does your collar cut, John?' asked a sarcastic voice out of the crowd.

'Hymn Number Nine.

> "Diddle-diddle dumpling, my son John
> Went to bed with his best suit on," '

came the solemn announcement.

Mr Merfin, his white cuffs down to his knuckles, picked up his half-sovereign, and walked away loftily.

'Sam Coutts!' cried the paymaster.

'Now, lad, reckon it up,' shouted the voice of the crowd, delighted.

Mr Coutts was a straight-backed ne'er-do-well. He looked at his twelve shillings sheepishly.

'Another two bob – he had twins a-Monday night – get thy money, Sam, tha's earned it – tha's addled it, Sam; dunna go be-out it. Let him ha' the two bob for 'is twins, mister,' came the clamour from the men around.

Sam Coutts stood grinning awkwardly.

'You should ha' given us notice, Sam,' said the paymaster suavely. 'We can make it all right for you next week –'

'Nay, nay, nay,' shouted a voice. 'Pay on delivery – the goods is there right enough.'

'Get thy money, Sam, tha's addled it,' became the universal cry, and the Union agent had to hand over another florin, to prevent a disturbance. Sam Coutts grinned with satisfaction.

'Good shot, Sam,' the men exclaimed.

'Ephraim Wharmby,' shouted the payman.

A lad came forward.

'Gi' him sixpence for what's on t'road,' said a sly voice.

'Nay, nay,' replied Ben Townsend; 'pay on delivery.'

There was a roar of laughter. The miners were in high spirits.

In the town they stood about in gangs, talking and laughing. Many sat on their heels in the market-place. In and out of the public-houses they went, and on every bar the half-sovereigns clicked.

'Comin' ter Nottingham wi' us, Ephraim?' said Sam Coutts, to the slender, pale young fellow of about twenty-two.

'I'm non walkin' that far of a gleamy day like this.'

'He has na got the strength,' said somebody, and a laugh went up.

'How's that?' asked another pertinent voice.

'He's a married man, mind yer,' said Chris Smitheringale, 'an' it ta'es a bit o' keepin' up.'

The youth was teased in this manner for some time.

'Come on ter Nottingham wi's; tha'll be safe for a bit,' said Coutts.

A gang set off, although it was only eleven o'clock. It was a nine-miles walk. The road was crowded with colliers travelling on foot to see the match between Notts and Aston Villa. In Ephraim's gang were Sam Coutts, with his fine shoulders and his extra florin, Chris Smitheringale, fat and smiling, and John Wharmby, a remarkable man, tall, erect as a soldier, black-haired and proud; he could play any musical instrument, he declared.

'I can play owt from a comb up'ards. If there's music to be got outer a thing, I back I'll get it. No matter what shape or form of instrument you set before me, it doesn't signify if I niver clapped eyes on it before, I's warrant I'll have a tune out of it in five minutes.'

He beguiled the first two miles so. It was true, he had caused a sensation by introducing the mandoline into the townlet, filling the hearts of his fellow-colliers with pride as he sat on the platform in evening dress, a fine soldierly man, bowing his black head, and scratching the mewing mandoline with hands that had only to grasp the 'instrument' to crush it entirely.

Chris stood a can round at the White Bull at Gilt Brook. John Wharmby took his turn at Kimberley top.

'We wunna drink again,' they decided, 'till we're at Cinder Hill. We'll non stop i' Nuttall.'

They swung along the high-road under the budding trees. In Nuttall Churchyard the crocuses blazed with yellow at the brim of the balanced, black yews. White and purple crocuses clipt up over the graves, as if the churchyard were bursting out in tiny tongues of flames.

'Sithee,' said Ephraim, who was an ostler down pit, 'sithee, here comes the Colonel. Sithee at his 'osses how they pick their toes up, the beauties!'

The colonel drove past the men, who took no notice of him.

'Hast heard, Sorry,' said Sam, 'as they're com'n out i' Germany, by the thousand, an' begun riotin'?'

'An' comin' out i' France simbitar,' cried Chris.

The men all gave a chuckle.

'Sorry,' shouted John Wharmby, much elated, 'we oughtna ter go back under a twenty per zent rise.'

'We should get it,' said Chris.

'An' easy! They can do nowt bi-out us, we'n on'y ter stop out long enough.'

'I'm willin',' said Sam, and there was a laugh. The colliers looked at one another. A thrill went through them as if an electric current passed.

'We'n on'y ter stick out, an' we s'll see who's gaffer.'

'Us!' cried Sam. 'Why, what can they do again' us, if we come out all over th' world?'

'Nowt!' said John Wharmby. 'Th' mesters is bobbin' about like corks on a cassivoy a'ready.' There was a large natural reservoir, like a lake, near Bestwood, and this supplied the simile.

Again there passed through the men that wave of elation, quickening their pulses. They chuckled in their throats. Beyond all consciousness was this sense of battle and triumph in the hearts of the working-men at this juncture.

It was suddenly suggested at Nuttall that they should go over the fields to Bulwell, and into Nottingham that way. They went single file across the fallow, past the wood, and over the railway, where now no trains were running. Two fields away was a troop of pit ponies. Of all colours, but chiefly of red or brown, they clustered thick in the field, scarcely moving, and the two lines of trodden earth patches showed where fodder was placed down the field.

'Theer's the pit 'osses,' said Sam. 'Let's run 'em.'

'It's like a circus turned out. See them skewbawd uns – seven skewbawd,' said Ephraim.

The ponies were inert, unused to freedom. Occasionally one walked round. But there they stood, two thick lines of ruddy brown and piebald and white, across the trampled field. It was a beautiful day, mild, pale blue, a 'growing day', as the men said, when there was the silence of swelling sap everywhere.

'Let's ha'e a ride,' said Ephraim.

The younger men went up to the horses.

'Come on – co-oop Taffy – co-oop Ginger.'

The horses tossed away. But having got over the excitement of being above-ground, the animals were feeling dazed and rather dreary. They missed the warmth and the life of the pit. They looked as if life were a blank to them.

Ephraim and Sam caught a couple of steeds, on whose backs they went careering round, driving the rest of the sluggish herd from end to end of the field. The horses were good specimens, on the whole, and in fine condition. But they were out of their element.

Performing too clever a feat, Ephraim went rolling from his mount. He was soon up again, chasing his horse. Again he was thrown. Then the men proceeded on their way.

They were drawing near to miserable Bulwell, when Ephraim, remembering his turn was coming to stand drinks, felt in his pocket for his beloved half-sovereigns, his strike-pay. It was not there. Through all his pockets he went, his heart sinking like lead.

'Sam,' he said. 'I believe I'n lost that ha'ef a sovereign.'

'Tha's got it somewheer about thee,' said Chris.

They made him take off his coat and waistcoat. Chris examined the coat, Sam the waistcoat, whilst Ephraim searched his trousers.

'Well,' said Chris, 'I'n foraged this coat, an' it's non theer.'

'An' I'll back my life as th' on'y bit a metal on this wa'scoat is the buttons,' said Sam.

'An't it's non in my breeches,' said Ephraim. He took off his boots and his stockings. The half-sovereign was not here. He had not another coin in his possession.

'Well,' said Chris, 'we mun go back an' look for it.'

Back they went, four serious-hearted colliers, and searched the field, but in vain.

'Well,' said Chris, 'we s'll ha'e ter share wi' thee, that's a'.'

'I'm willin',' said John Wharmby.

'An' me,' said Sam.

'Two bob each,' said Chris.

Ephraim, who was in the depths of despair, shamefully accepted their six shillings.

In Bulwell they called in a small public-house, which had one long room with a brick floor, scrubbed benches and scrubbed tables. The central space was open. The place was full of colliers, who were drinking. There was a great deal of drinking during the strike, but not a vast amount drunk. Two men were playing skittles, and the rest were betting. The seconds sat on either side the skittle-board, holding caps of money, sixpences and coppers, the wagers of the 'backers'.

Sam, Chris, and John Wharmby immediately put money on the man who had their favour. In the end Sam declared himself willing to play against the victor. He was the Bestwood champion. Chris and John Wharmby backed him heavily, and even Ephraim the Unhappy ventured sixpence.

In the end, Sam had won half a crown, with which he promptly stood drinks and bread-and-cheese for his comrades. At half-past one they set off again.

It was a good match between Notts and Villa – no goals at half-time, two-none for Notts at the finish. The colliers were hugely delighted, especially as Flint, the forward for Notts, who was an Underwood man well known to the four comrades, did some handsome work, putting the two goals through.

Ephraim determined to go home as soon the the match was over. He knew John Wharmby would be playing the piano at the Punch Bowl, and Sam, who had a good tenor voice, singing, while Chris cut in with witticisms, until evening. So he bade them farewell, as he must get home. They, finding him somewhat of a damper on their spirits, let him go.

He was the sadder for having witnessed an accident near the football ground. A navvy, working at some drainage, carting an iron tip-tub of mud and emptying it, had got with his horse on to the deep deposit of ooze which was crusted over. The crust had broken, the man had gone under the horse, and it was some time before the people had realized he had vanished. When they found his feet sticking out, and hauled him forth, he was dead, stifled dead in the mud. The horse was at length hauled out, after having his neck nearly pulled from the socket.

Ephraim went home vaguely impressed with a sense of death, and loss, and strife. Death was loss greater than his own, the strike was a battle greater than that he would presently have to fight.

He arrived home at seven o'clock, just when it had fallen dark. He lived in Queen Street with his young wife, to whom he had been married two months, and with his mother-in-law, a widow of sixty-four. Maud was the last child remaining unmarried, the last of eleven.

Ephraim went up the entry. The light was burning in the kitchen. His mother-in-law was a big, erect woman, with wrinkled, loose face, and cold blue eyes. His wife was also large, with very vigorous fair hair, frizzy like unravelled rope. She had a quiet way of stepping, a certain cat-like stealth, in spite of her large build. She was five months pregnant.

'Might we ask wheer you've been to?' inquired Mrs Marriott, very erect, very dangerous. She was only polite when she was very angry.

'I'n bin ter th' match.'

'Oh indeed!' said the mother-in-law. 'And why couldn't we be told as you thought of jaunting off?'

'I didna know mysen,' he answered, sticking to his broad Derbyshire.

'I suppose it popped into your mind, an' so you darted off,' said the mother-in-law dangerously.

'I didn't. It wor Chris Smitheringale who exed me.'

'An' did you take much invitin'?'

'I didna want ter goo.'

'But wasn't there enough man beside your jacket to say no?'

He did not answer. Down at the bottom he hated her. But he was, to use his own words, all messed up with having lost his strike-pay and with knowing the man was dead. So he was more helpless before his mother-in-law, whom he feared. His wife neither looked at him nor spoke, but kept her head bowed. He knew she was with her mother.

'Our Maud's been waitin' for some money, to get a few things,' said the mother-in-law.

In silence, he put five-and-sixpence on the table.

'Take that up, Maud,' said the mother.

Maud did so.

'You'll want it for us board, shan't you?' she asked, furtively, of her mother.

'Might I ask if there's nothing you want to buy yourself, first?'

'No, there's nothink I want,' answered the daughter.

Mrs Marriott took the silver and counted it.

'And do you,' said the mother-in-law, towering upon the shrinking son, but speaking slowly and statelily, 'do you think I'm going to keep you and your wife for five-and-sixpence a week?'

'It's a' I've got,' he answered, sulkily.

'You've had a good jaunt, my sirs, if it's cost four-and-six-pence. You've started your game early, haven't you?'

He did not answer.

'It's a nice thing! Here's our Maud an' me been sitting since eleven o'clock this morning! Dinner waiting and cleared away, tea waiting and washed up; then in he comes crawling with five-and-sixpence. Five-and-sixpence for a man an' wife's board for a week, if you please!'

Still he did not say anything.

'You must think something of yourself, Ephraim Wharmby!' said his mother-in-law. 'You must think something of yourself. You suppose, do you, *I'm* going to keep you an' your wife, while you make a holiday, off on the nines to Nottingham, drink an' women.'

'I've neither had drink nor women, as you know right well,' he said.

'I'm glad we know summat about you. For you're that close, anybody'd think we was foreigners to you. You're a pretty little jockey, aren't you? Oh, it's a gala time for you, the strike is. That's all men strike for, indeed. They enjoy themselves, they do that. Ripping and racing and drinking, from morn till night, my sirs!'

'Is there ony tea for me?' he asked, in a temper.

'Hark at him! Hark-ye! Should I ask you whose house you think you're in? Kindly order me about, do. Oh, it makes him big, the strike does. See him land home after being out on the spree for hours, and give his orders, my sirs! Oh, strike sets the men up, it does. Nothing have they to do but guzzle and gallivant to Nottingham. Their wives'll keep them, oh yes. So long as they get something to eat at home, what more do they want! What more *should* they want, prithee? Nothing! Let the women and children starve and scrape, but fill the man's belly, and let him have his fling. My sirs, indeed, I think so! Let tradesmen go – what do they matter! Let rent go. Let children get what they can catch. Only the man will see *he's* all right. But not here, though!'

'Are you goin' ter gi'e me ony bloody tea?'

His mother-in-law started up.

'If tha dares ter swear at me, I'll lay thee flat.'

'Are yer – goin' ter – gi'e me – any blasted, ròtten, còssed, blòody tèa?' he bawled, in a fury, accenting every other word deliberately.

'Maud!' said the mother-in-law, cold and stately, 'if you gi'e him any tea after that, you're a trollops.' Whereupon she sailed out to her other daughter's.

Maud quietly got the tea ready.

'Shall y'ave your dinner warmed up?' she asked.

'Ay.'

She attended to him. Not that she was really meek. But – he was *her* man, not her mother's.